Praise for *The Language of Secrets*

'Khan delivers an action-packed police procedural complemented by strong characters with believable motives' – ***Associated Press***

'Exceptionally fine… A heartfelt novel for lovers of crime fiction and anyone interested in the complexities of living as a Muslim in the West today' – ***Library Journal*** (starred review)

'Sophisticated… The characters are well-drawn and pleasingly varied: Khattak is a compelling protagonist, a cerebral, reserved Muslim comfortable with his faith but not ruled by it, and the buoyant, hockey-loving Getty is an endearing foil. The cell members are afforded fully dimensional personalities and varied passions, ideals, and justifications for their actions; everyone has their reasons, Khan understands, and her nuanced exploration of those reasons elevates her second novel above the general run of detective fiction. A smart, measured, immersive dive into a poorly understood, terrifyingly relevant subculture of violent extremism' – ***Kirkus Reviews***

Praise for *The Unquiet Dead*

'Khan has brought every ounce of her intellect and professional experience in working with Muslim refugees to this affecting debut. Her use of certain mystery conventions echoes the masters… Yet for all of the echoes of the greats, Khan is a refreshing original… a debut to remember and one that even those who eschew the genre will devour in one breathtaking sitting' – ***LA Times***

'Gripping… An intelligent plot and graceful writing make *The Unquiet Dead* an outstanding debut that is not easily forgotten' – ***Associated Press***

'Beautiful and powerful' – ***Publishers Weekly*** (starred review)

'Compelling and hauntingly powerful… anyone looking for an intensely memorable mystery should put this book at the top of their list' – ***Library Journal*** (starred review)

'Khan's stunning debut is a poignant, elegantly written mystery laced with complex characters' – ***Kirkus Reviews***

'Heartbreaking… [a story] that needs to be told' – ***Booklist***

'An engrossing story that allows the author to sift through the emotional rubble of real-world tragedy. In the end, it isn't just gripping. It's devastating' – **Steve Hockensmith, Edgar-nominated author of *Holmes on the Range***

THE LANGUAGE
OF
SECRETS

An Esa Khattak and Rachel Getty Mystery

AUSMA ZEHANAT KHAN

NO EXIT PRESS

First published in the UK in 2017
by No Exit Press,
an imprint of Oldcastle Books Ltd,
PO Box 394,
Harpenden, Herts,
AL5 1XJ
noexit.co.uk

ISBN

978-0-85730-144-4 (print)
978-0-85730-145-1 (epub)

2 4 6 8 10 9 7 5 3 1

Typeset in 10.9pt Minion Pro
by Avocet Typeset, Somerton, Somerset, TA11 6RT
Printed and bound in Great Britain by Clays Ltd, Elcograf S.p.A.

For my husband, Nader Hashemi,
scholar, activist, defender of human rights.

We have watched the world grow dark around us –
you remain the light.

1

I came between a man and his thoughts,
like a breeze thrown over
the face of the moon.

THE SNATCH OF POETRY CAUGHT at Mohsin's thoughts, making a mockery of the thousands of burnt-out stars flung wide against the banner of the sky. Penniless stars, spending their dying light in hopes of winning accolades from poets who thought of nothing save the rumpus of love, except as a point of comparison.

The blue night of Cuba, stars in her hair –
Her eyes like stars, starry-eyed, in fact –
Bright star, glowing star, lost star, falling star, the countless
congregation, the silver-washed dusk, the pinpricks of night –

Mohsin found the celestial images ridiculous.

Especially when his personal light had gone unheralded – how cavalier of the poets not to have spoken of Mohsin's wife.

Sitara, he thought. *This wasn't how I expected to die.*

Blood leaked from his stomach onto the snow, joined by a second flow from his right leg, a deep red oozing that made him wonder how long it would take for the stars to fade, and whether anyone would come in response to his calls.

But why would any of the others come now? Wouldn't coming to Mohsin's rescue endanger everything the others had worked toward, everything they had planned for – everything they were still planning now? To call the police or summon an ambulance, to do everything in their power to save his life, when they had retreated to the woods for secrecy and darkness – no, the others would make a calculation, the same one they had made many times before.

What was one life measured against the impact of the Nakba?

What was one forty-year-old *shaheed*, when they were prepared to sacrifice innocents to their cause?

The night was purple, the stars a blurry reminder of the difference between Mohsin and the others. The light against the darkness, and other such clichés.

Mohsin had been pretending all this time. Shaking things up to see how they fell out.

He'd yielded to one leash, then another, jerked this way and that, nobody aware of what he was really up to.

What had Mohsin been doing with these people, these jihadists in the woods, scrambling around under cover of darkness, pretending to hunt one another like snipers?

The real question was: what wasn't he doing?

Even Sitara didn't know the answer to that.

He'd tried to be careful, using details from his life to build a fragile trust that would widen his network of contacts. He'd thought he'd been successful. People had trusted him, relied upon him, accepted his decision-making. They'd traveled to the backcountry of Algonquin at his suggestion. The winter camp had been Mohsin's idea. Or maybe Hassan had steered him in this direction, hunter rather than prey.

Don't encourage them to do anything they wouldn't choose to do on their own.

It was the mantra against entrapment, learned by rote at many after-hours meetings at hole-in-the-wall kebab shops, where the *doogh* was salty and the *koobideh* sublime.

He clarified his thoughts, the December chill scraping against his face. Not for the first time, he wished he'd opted for a fuller beard, with the signature of a mustache above it. But Sitara hadn't wanted him to keep a beard at all.

He thought of his wife with regret, of the growing distance between them in the weeks before the camp. She had wanted to come with him. How badly she had wanted to come. And if he'd really been planning a camping trip, he would have welcomed her presence beside him.

But not this, not now. Now he could be grateful that she was far away and safe.

He'd spent the summers of his childhood canoeing through lake country. From Smoke Lake to Big Porcupine. From Rock Lake to the Two Rivers. Or farther west, where the sunsets at Galeairy soaked up the requisite redness of Group of Seven maples.

So he'd known the terrain. And he'd thought he could outmaneuver Hassan in his plans for the jihadist training camp. He knew the routes out of the park and over the water. Hassan Ashkouri didn't.

Not the first thing he'd been wrong about, but probably the last.

And no one had warned him, not even Grace.

It was funny in a way, dying out here in this far-flung part of the forest, with the pines crackling under the weight of snow. The members of the camp had wanted to discuss remote detonation devices; they'd asked him to ferry weapons across the American border. Instead, Mohsin had rattled on about the geology of the park, the eskers and moraines of the Canadian Shield's bedrock. The boys had tossed around words like 'tundra' in response, and Mohsin had smiled into his beard, privately laughing at them all.

Jokers. Hustlers. Idiots. Fools.

But Mohsin was the biggest fool of all.

He hadn't changed anything. The training would continue.

While he met his death on a drumlin at the edge of a meltwater channel. A glaciofluvial landform, the glacier long extinct. He rolled the words over his tongue.

The stars were going out.

The stars shut down the night and my hopes.

He couldn't walk, couldn't move, the blood dribbling from his body at its steady pace, gluey against his hand.

I have dipped my fingers in martyr's blood. He said it to the sovereign sky, speaking to an audience of leaves.

Poetry – winding you up with its archive of questions, its vainglorious phrases.

And Mohsin loved a good, dirty limerick as much as any couplet of Faiz Ahmad Faiz, the greatest contemporary poet of his homeland. A poet he knew well, a poet he understood.

His breathing began to slow.

It would have been better, maybe, to recite the *kalima* as preparation for his meeting with his Creator, whether it took place in the southern or northern regions of the afterlife. Either was certainly possible. But Mohsin had always been something of a renegade, choosing to stand by himself, undefended.

Are you a stone wall, bleak and undefended?

He wasn't. He missed his friend, Esa Khattak.

And thought it sad that Esa didn't know that Mohsin still thought of him as a friend. Everything Mohsin had done up to this point – hadn't it been to reconnect with Esa, to prove they were more alike than his friend had come to believe? To win back Esa's regard?

Maybe there was a way.

He fumbled through his inside pockets for his Swiss Army Knife. A little at a time, he moved his hand against the rough bark of the tree his body had come to rest against.

This wasn't for Sitara.

There were other concerns apart from love.

And he couldn't offer the same love again.

2

ESA KHATTAK WAS GRATEFUL FOR Martine Killiam's call. She was a superintendent with the Royal Canadian Mounted Police, and she had asked for a consultation in his capacity as head of the Community Policing Section, a request that was both courteous and unmistakably firm.

He was relieved to be getting her call, given the outcome of his last case. The hounds of the press were at bay for now, but the rumors of a pending inquiry were gaining traction. The conclusion of the investigation into Christopher Drayton's death had sparked a national outcry, leading the Minister of Justice to issue a personal reprimand.

You've bungled this, Khattak. And you've taken Tom Paley down with you.

Khattak knocked on Martine Killiam's door.

Tom Paley, the chief war crimes historian at the Department of Justice, had been a friend. When he'd passed away from a heart attack last month, his case file on Christopher Drayton had vanished.

And now the press was calling for Khattak's head, accusing him of delay, denial, and too close an association with the Bosnian community. No one was happy with the outcome.

Esa thought of Tom, often. Of the care he'd taken to ensure that the truth about Drayton's death would come to light. Tom couldn't have foreseen that Esa would be left alone to face the glare of the national spotlight. And it occurred to Esa to wonder if Superintendent Killiam had been assigned the task of calling him to account.

At his knock, the superintendent rose from her desk to greet him. Her smile was tempered by the reticence of her manner as she shook Khattak's hand. A woman in her late fifties with a strong, square face, Killiam had spent her life in the RCMP, forging a respectable path for herself through narcotics and organized crime. The second half of her career had focused on human resources, with a portfolio that encompassed thousands of employees. With Killiam's appointment to the role of human resources officer, there had been a change in the wind for women who joined the Force. She'd originated a mentorship program that paired senior female officers with promising new candidates, alongside wider latitude and opportunities for promotion. But Killiam's most telling achievement was her strictly enforced zero-tolerance policy on sexual harassment.

Khattak respected Killiam's methodical approach to police work. It lacked imagination perhaps, but it could not be faulted on thoroughness. Behind the rimless glasses Killiam wore, he sensed she was making a similar evaluation of his background. And his current troubles with the Department of Justice.

'I asked you here because a man has been murdered in highly sensitive circumstances. I need your help as a liaison with INSET.'

Khattak glanced past the glass doors of Killiam's office to a space beset with human traffic. A small team was shifting through a thoroughfare of computer terminals and whiteboards, listening to a technical consultant explain a new operating system. A second group was gathered around the coffee machine. A few heads had nodded at Khattak in recognition as he passed. He'd raised a gloved hand in response.

Martine Killiam had asked him to meet at the Toronto base of operations for INSET, the Integrated National Security Enforcement Team. Khattak had once served as core personnel with INSET, before he'd been asked to head up CPS. Many of the men and women in the room were former colleagues.

'You're working something big,' he said. 'Is it terrorist activity? Cross-border?'

He'd noted the presence of officers from the Canada Border Services Agency.

'Sit down, won't you? What you see out there – we're at the tail end of an operation that's been running for two years. We simply didn't foresee this turn of events.'

'The murdered man was part of your operation? Is that where you need my assistance?'

If Killiam was asking for Khattak's help despite what had happened with the Drayton investigation, the INSET operation would have to be at a critical point.

'I need you to investigate the murder. The victim's father is well-known, both in the national media and in your community. He plans to use his platform to obtain justice for his son. If we don't stop him, we'll lose everything we've achieved to this point.' She rubbed her forehead, easing the deeply etched line between her brows. 'It's much worse than you can imagine. To be frank, you're the only person I could think of who stands the slightest chance of shutting him down.'

'Who is he? Who are you talking about? What happened to his son?'

'His son infiltrated a terrorist group that runs a training camp in the woods. He was found at Algonquin Park. He'd been shot twice, and left to bleed to death.'

She surprised Khattak by reaching across the desk to take his hand.

'Esa,' she said. 'I'm sorry. The man they killed is Mohsin Dar.'

He shrank away from the words, recoiled from her touch, flattening his hands against her desk.

'No,' he said. 'No, it's not Mohsin.'

Her face crinkled with a sympathy he couldn't bear.

He made his own face a blank in response.

There was supposed to be time to work things out with Mohsin, to meet at the mosque again, to embrace like long-lost brothers, to admit they missed each other.

Instead of Mo pointing the finger when Esa had been recruited to INSET.

You're making a mistake, brother. You can't come back from this.

Think what it means for the community.

You think about it. Every mosque in the city will shut its doors to you. You'll become a pariah, a resident spy. Is that what you want? To be the house Arab? To see your face in the papers as the inside man?

It's not what you're making it out to be.

You don't spy on those you call your own, brother. You work with them, for them.

They'd had many similar conversations during the volatile period after the September 11 attacks.

With the obstinacy of a younger man still uneasy with his Pashtun roots, Esa had answered, *You should be careful who you claim as your own.*

The ummah, *man, the* ummah. *We belong to it. You don't remember the paper?*

This had been Mohsin's favorite refrain. He believed in the Islamic nation, a supranational community whose faith transcended language, sect, ethnicity, and borders, tied together by a spiritual commonality.

For a brief time, Esa and Mohsin had been contributors to the newspaper at their university. Khattak's inclination had been for poetry, Mohsin's a highly emotional form of reportage. He'd taken the global Muslim community as his subject.

An article Mohsin had written to honor Afghan warriors in the aftermath of the Soviet withdrawal praised the simplicity of mujahideen worship, evoking the image of a solitary figure praying at the summit of a mountain fastness.

This was the weapon that won the war.

So Mohsin had believed.

The article had revealed a gaping ignorance of global politics. Of the future prospects of an illiterate society flush with weapons and drugs and rife with the divisions the Soviet occupation had suppressed, Mohsin had had little to say.

Khattak had found no fault with Mohsin's critique of the Russian invasion, but he'd wondered at his friend's refusal to see beyond that singular moment in history. Afghanistan's tribal past, its uncertain future, with decades of war still to come. The oft-named graveyard of empires, with many of its dead yet to be counted.

Mohsin's view of the world had been naive: friends versus enemies, *ummah* versus outsiders, the pain of the now measured against the sweet reward of the afterlife, though he'd never flung the word 'infidel' as an accusation. When he looked for common ground, he usually found it. But as with other members of their community, Mohsin's grievances had multiplied with time.

Khattak's eyes searched Killiam's face.

'He was an agent of the RCMP? When did that happen?'

And what did it mean that Mohsin had made such a choice when he'd broken with Esa for doing the same?

Killiam cleared her throat. 'Mohsin came to us through the Canadian Security Intelligence Service. We developed him as an agent. I'm not at liberty to say for how long.'

'But this camp you mentioned in the woods – that was your operation?'

Martine regarded him gravely.

'The operation is not over, Esa. It's moving to the tactical stage soon.' She passed him a folder across the desk. 'We've penetrated two cells that are working together on a bomb plot. They've designated four targets.' She counted them off on her fingers. 'Union Station, the CN Tower, Queen's Park, the SkyDome.

They're calling their attack the "New Year Nakba."'

Khattak's head came up from his perusal of the file.

'Nakba' was a word freighted with history.

It was the Arabic word for 'catastrophe'.

A catastrophe taken to heart by an undivided Muslim world –
a match to light a tinderbox.

Yawm an-Nakba, the Day of Catastrophe, commemorated
the day after Israel's Independence Day. It linked the founding
of the state of Israel to the loss of the Palestinian homeland,
when 700,000 Palestinians had fled or been expelled during the
1948 war. Settlement construction, home demolitions, and state-
sanctioned violence in the West Bank were only superseded by
the desperate human rights crisis in Gaza. They kept the memory
of Palestinian suffering fresh in the minds of the *ummah*.

The men behind the Nakba plot would have chosen the name
for its symbolic value as a Lydian stone of defeat.

The mighty against the weak.

The occupier against the indigenous.

The colonizer against the lost and defenseless.

But was Palestine still a touchstone after so many years? After
Afghanistan, Syria, Lebanon, Iraq?

Khattak closed the file with a snap. He couldn't bring himself
to look at the photographs of Mohsin. Just as he couldn't bring
himself to imagine that any of this was real.

'Is this serious, Superintendent? Are you telling me that
Canadians are training at a camp in Algonquin, with the
intention of carrying out a terrorist attack?' He pushed the folder
back across the desk. 'How are they coordinating it? Where are
they getting the weapons? Is there any operational legitimacy to
this?'

Killiam's eyes narrowed at Khattak's implication.

'We've put two years into this investigation, so you can trust
that it's not a hoax. These people may be amateurs, but they have
know-how and materials, and they've coordinated a plan. We've

been detailed and thorough. It's just as well that you don't know how thorough.'

The words gave Khattak pause. Killiam was hinting at the broad net cast by the Anti-Terrorism Act, known at its controversial inception as Bill C-36. It wasn't a subject he intended to debate with her. His reservations at the time of the introduction of the legislation had been noted in his personnel file. And he'd participated in debates about the recent, far more serious encroachment on civil liberties – the hammering home of Bill C-51, the new legislation with its unchecked surveillance powers and lack of civilian oversight.

He feared what they were becoming.

Killiam knew all this.

'And the takedown?' he asked.

Killiam's eyes narrowed. 'Sometime between Christmas and New Year's Day. That will be my call. What I need to know is whether you can handle Andy Dar, Mohsin's father.'

Khattak spread his hands helplessly.

'Do they have the bombs?' he asked.

'If Mohsin hadn't warned us in time, they'd have had everything they need to detonate four fertilizer bombs on location. We'll be taking over the delivery, switching out the fertilizer with inert material. We're in the setup phase of that operation now.'

Khattak didn't ask for details about the plan. Martine Killiam was Officer in Charge of a critical national security operation. She wasn't about to tell him anything that didn't directly relate to Mohsin Dar's murder. But he did worry that the takedown had yet to occur.

'You said you've run this operation for two years now. You don't have to answer, but by that I presume you mean surveillance. Do your intercepts indicate premeditation? Had the group in the woods planned to kill Mohsin at the camp?'

'There's no evidence that anyone in the group had uncovered Mohsin's agenda.'

'What about the second cell you mentioned? Is it possible they know their communications are being monitored?'

'It's quite clear that they don't.'

'So the tactical strike is on schedule.'

'Yes.'

'Then isn't it possible that Mohsin was murdered for reasons unrelated to his work as an RCMP agent?'

Killiam gave him a quick nod. 'That's exactly the line I want you to pursue with Mohsin's father. No one is to know anything about Mohsin's work with us. Not his father, not his wife. You're to treat this as a routine homicide investigation. You'll work your way through a list of suspects without tipping either your hand or mine.'

'Do you know who these suspects are?'

'There were seven people at Algonquin with Mohsin. Two of them are women who may or may not have been involved in the activities of the cell. They may be hangers-on or partners; we can't be certain. It would help if you tackle them first. Ask questions, dig around, but stay away from the camp itself. Don't do anything that would compromise the operation.'

'I can't work undercover,' he pointed out. 'Not after the press coverage I've received.'

Martine Killiam shrugged. If she had bowed before the weight of ridicule directed at women when she was coming up in the Force, she'd still be deferring to men with half her abilities and none of her insight. She had very little patience for self-doubt. But given what she was asking of Esa, she seemed prepared to unbend a little.

She pushed the buff-colored folder back at Khattak. 'You won't be undercover. You'll be there in your very well-known capacity as head of CPS, "transparently and fully representing the rights of minority communities."'

She quoted the CPS mandate back at Khattak with a scorn he knew was not directed at his work, but at the political maneuvering behind it. She was well aware of the risks inherent in Khattak's position. He would always be accused of failing some constituency or mandate – either the minority communities he'd been tasked to represent or the law he was meant to uphold. Only in rare cases would these objectives run together.

'I don't know that my history with Mohsin will make any difference to his father.'

The words sounded strange on his tongue, as if he was distancing himself from his friend. Their lives had brushed up against each other without touching anything that truly mattered, at the end.

'I won't apologize for saying this, Esa. Use whatever you can with Andy Dar. Make a religious appeal, make a personal appeal – try anything that might work. You know his radio program. We can't have him using it to raise questions about the camp. His grandstanding could scuttle the entire operation. You have to be seen as committed to solving Mohsin's murder.'

With a sense of genuine sadness, Khattak replied, 'I am committed.'

Killiam looked at him for a moment, but she left the comment alone.

'If you find you're not getting anywhere on the public front, send Rachel Getty in. You've been wise enough to keep her under wraps, but I've heard your partner is quite talented.'

Khattak smiled. 'More than talented,' he said. 'She's been a tremendous asset to CPS, and to me.'

He watched Martine Killiam take note of this on a writing pad at her elbow.

'Then you've done well to protect her from the spotlight, which in turn serves my operation now. Get her in if you can, but no one – and I can't emphasize this enough – breathes a word about Nakba.'

Khattak frowned. 'Is there any chance the attack could succeed?'

She avoided a direct answer.

'I'll leave the Outreach Coordinator to brief you on the details. You'll work with her, and report to the Special Assistant, as I believe you've done in the past. Anything you find out, you convey to me through him.'

But Khattak didn't know anyone with that rank in the RCMP.

'Inspector Ciprian Coale was promoted two years ago,' she told Khattak. 'And you already know the Outreach Coordinator.'

Khattak turned around in his chair. Two people were waiting outside Killiam's office, one with a nasty smile playing about his mouth. As their eyes met, Ciprian Coale sketched a salute, the gesture just short of offensive. A dark-haired woman in a navy-blue suit raised her hand to knock at Killiam's door.

It was Laine Stoicheva, Khattak's former partner.

3

RACHEL GETTY WAS GRIPPED BY a glorious sense of freedom. She was in the basement of her parents' house in Etobicoke, Ontario, on the west side of the Greater Toronto Area, or the GTA. Her dark brown hair was cinched high in a ponytail at the top of her head. She squinted with furious concentration over the task of tending to her black leather hockey skates. She was a throwback in that way. The newer composite materials allowed for less moisture inside the boot, and less cracking, but Rachel's skate boots fit her like a sleek second skin. They knew which way she would pivot on the ice even before she did, and were steadfast and sturdy around the ankles, much like Rachel herself.

She was sharpening the blades of her skates with a manual sharpener, taking a quiet pride in the task. The diamond-coated tusk smoothed out the rough spot on the skate with the bad edge, an imperfection fittingly labeled a trauma, and one that had cost her a goal in the previous night's game. A broad grin crossed Rachel's face, making her brown eyes spark with glints of gold. A missed opportunity here and there didn't matter. She'd still been selected as a forward for the all-star game that would take place just after New Year's.

And that was her Christmas present right there. She ran her fingers over both toe caps for one last check. Everything looked good, felt right. She wrapped the skates in a purple terrycloth towel – a superstitious practice that carried over from her first days in house league.

Keep your skates dry. Always protect the blades.

Advice that had served Rachel Getty well throughout her hockey career. That and the lessons in bluster and forechecking that Don Getty, her equally blusterous father, had taught her. Good lessons at the right time, when Don Getty was sober, but it didn't mean she would miss him now. She probably wouldn't miss him at all. Her boxes were packed and neatly labeled; the U-Haul van she had rented was parked on the curb outside her father's house. Her skates were the last thing on her list. Perhaps because they were the first things in her heart.

Twenty-eight years in Don Getty's house and now Sergeant Rachel Getty was striking out on her own. She trudged upstairs, cradling her skates as tenderly as a newborn. Don Getty was out at the pub, sparing her the necessity of a final goodbye. Rachel's mother waited dry-eyed on the porch, bundled into a white down jacket that had seen better days. The color made Lillian's pale skin seem ever paler, her lipstick the faintest remark on her lips. Lillian kneaded her unprotected hands together as Rachel loaded her skates into the van.

'You should go inside, Mum. It's too cold to be out here without a scarf and gloves.'

Lillian Getty shrugged, the thin cloud of her hair bobbing with the movement.

Everything about her mother was inconclusive, Rachel thought. Like an unfinished painting where the painter had daubed the outline in a hurry, forgetting to furnish the details. Blurry and smudged. Just as life had smudged out Lillian Getty.

Rachel felt the customary pang of sorrow for her mother, but this time it was unaccompanied by that pervasive feeling of guilt. There had been years of guilt, long slow months of worry and anguish, a constant state of turbulent existence for Rachel, who had floated along on the sea of her mother's emotions without once thinking to fight the tide.

Rachel slammed the door of the U-Haul.

Those days were in the past. She had found her peace, found

her way forward, despite the difficulties facing her team at work, including her boss, Esa Khattak, a man she had come to value and respect. Even the tension at work didn't diminish the sunlight that felt as if it were flooding from Rachel's veins to her heart.

She had just bought her first home, a brand-new condominium off Bloor West Village, not close enough to the popular neighborhood to be out of her financial grasp, though its maintenance fees were considerable. Rachel had been saving her money since her first day in the police force. The promotion to Community Policing had included a sizable salary bump. And without her younger brother Zachary in her life for so many years, she'd had nothing to spend her money on.

Moving day had been a long time coming.

The condo was small, but it was finished with discriminating taste and a decided eye for luxury. To Rachel, who had spent every winter of her life in cold and colder places, surrounded by dreariness, the new condominium was a breath of perpetual springtime. Nothing could dim her spirits today.

Her packing finished, she came to stand before her mother, forcing herself to meet Lillian Getty's eyes.

'You'll be okay, Mum. You won't even notice that I'm gone.'

Which was a kinder way of saying Lillian wouldn't miss her at all.

Unlike Zach, who'd been mourned from the first moment to the last.

Or so Rachel had thought, unaware of the secret Lillian had kept until Rachel had discovered it for herself.

She touched a tentative hand to Lillian's down-clad shoulder. A touch without contact, either given or received.

'Can I do anything for you before I go?'

She was eager to leave, afraid that Lillian would ask her to stay. In the last few weeks, Rachel had put her anxiety over her decision to move out to good use. Repainting and weatherproofing the front porch, the stairs. Organizing and dropping off years of hoarded materials to various local charities: old clothes, old books, bits and pieces of broken-down furniture. She had replaced the ceiling mounts in the house with contemporary light fixtures, insulated the windows against the coming winter, and resealed her parents' cracked driveway.

It was Rachel's way of absolving herself for the unspoken sin of moving on with her life. For being excited about her job. For having made friends and allegiances that gave her a sense of worth. And for having found her brother.

Lillian answered her daughter after a lengthy silence, as if she had been picking over the words to use, wanting to set each one in the right place, like the shells of small creatures gathered on family trips to the lake, lined up with care on the sill of the kitchen window. Shells Rachel had left untouched during her exhaustive purge of her parents' house, along with Lillian's records and magazines. And the gramophone with the missing needle.

'You've done more than enough, Rachel.' She dragged the words out, her hands fastened together in a grip that left her knuckles white. It wasn't the reproof Rachel took it for at first, because Lillian went on to add, 'More than I thought you would do. More than either of us could expect.'

Lillian took a deep breath, and Rachel sensed that her mother had chosen this final moment of interaction with her daughter to bring up that terrible betrayal – the secret of Zachary's whereabouts. Rachel didn't want to hear it. Not now, at this moment of unlooked-for happiness.

'You have a right to expect things of me, Mum,' she said quietly. 'Because I will come back. I will come back to see you.'

Lillian Getty nodded, letting Rachel prise her stiff hands apart and smooth them out. The winter chill bit at them both, the sound of the streetcar at the corner an intrusion into the moment.

'Think about coming to the all-star game,' Rachel offered. 'I might make MVP this year.'

Lillian dropped her eyes. Rachel knew her mother wouldn't

come. She hadn't come in years. But Lillian surprised her. She reached out and brushed her lips against Rachel's cheek, her thin lips dry and cold.

'Look for me there,' she said. 'Be happy, Rachel.'

Rachel hugged her once, quickly. As she turned to go, she said gruffly over her shoulder, 'The gramophone, Mum. In case you wanted to use it, I replaced the needle.'

4

MARTINE KILLIAM YIELDED HER PRIVATE office to the man and woman who waited to brief Khattak on Mohsin Dar's murder. Now Ciprian Coale sat behind Killiam's desk, ramrod-straight, and without the calm measure of welcome that Martine had offered in exchange for Khattak's help. Laine Stoicheva sat in the chair angled off to Khattak's right. Neither of them looked at the other.

Khattak focused his attention on Coale. He knew Coale would want to establish the parameters of the homicide investigation, while making it clear that he remained the man in charge, the man Killiam trusted to keep all the parts moving and perfectly oiled.

Two years ago Khattak and Coale had been colleagues of equal rank and equal status, though seconded to INSET from different law enforcement agencies. Coale was used to the military-like hierarchy and protocols of the RCMP. His elevation in rank had been long sought. He'd made no secret of the fact that he thought his credentials and experience were superior to Esa's. When Khattak's promotion to head of CPS had been announced, Coale had considered it a snub – one maneuvered by Khattak in secret.

If Coale was coordinating the RCMP operation with CPS, it would be because he was bearing a professional grudge.

A sharp-featured, imperious man in his late forties, Coale dressed the part of a senior RCMP officer, with the added bonus of a privately moneyed background. He'd attended the best schools, was known to golf at the most exclusive clubs, and was owed favors by everyone of note in the upper tiers of federal policing. He wore a Burberry suit in crisp black, a gray scarf arranged at his throat, presenting a carefully crafted image of sophistication that matched his austere, not-quite-good looks. Khattak couldn't help but notice that the platinum Bulgari pen Coale was tapping against Killiam's desk matched the heavy watch on the wrist that peeked out from snowy cuffs.

The nasty smile was still on Coale's mouth.

'You're back,' he said to Khattak, with no small measure of satisfaction.

'At the superintendent's request.' If Coale felt the need to establish his dominance, it was best that it be brought out into the open at once. 'Congratulations, Ciprian,' he said.

The other man's smile vanished. His nod was brusque. He did not congratulate Khattak on his CPS mandate in turn.

Khattak had never been able to tell if Coale was genuinely prejudiced against him, or if he'd spent too much time in the antiterrorism milieu. They'd worked numerous investigations together, and always Coale had found a moment to remind Khattak of the background he shared with many of those who were under INSET surveillance. Coale had referred to it as Khattak's 'special insight'. His tone now implied the inevitability of Khattak's return, given the nature of INSET's work.

'You're not here to do anything, Khattak – let me make that clear right now. Your only task is to babysit Andy Dar and keep him out of the spotlight. If you can handle that for the next two weeks, we'll have no further use for you.'

Khattak ignored the insult.

'That's not what I understood from the superintendent, Ciprian. I understand Mohsin Dar's murder has come under your jurisdiction only for national security reasons. Is Andy Dar aware of this?'

'If he was, there wouldn't be any need for a Community Policing presence, would there? I thought you were sharper than that.'

Khattak had just provided Coale with the perfect opportunity to raise the debacle at the Department of Justice. But Coale's use of it was restrained, perhaps because he saw the hint of danger in Khattak's face. 'You're already under the microscope. If you do anything to blow up my operation, finding yourself without a peg to hang your kufi on will be the least of your worries.'

Early in his career, Khattak had made the mistake of using the on-site chaplaincy office for personal prayer. Despite the fact that the chapel was nondenominational, unpleasant rumors had surfaced, slowing Khattak's progress to promotion. He knew his background had been thoroughly vetted before he'd joined INSET; what he hadn't understood as well was the impact it would have on his colleagues' perception of his loyalties.

Comments about Mecca were so well-worn by this point that Khattak had ceased to notice them. His seniority helped. And the CPS promotion had allowed him to change his environment altogether – although he had known, just as Ciprian Coale did, that surveillance of the Canadian Muslim community would remain a cornerstone of his work.

None of these thoughts appeared on Khattak's face. His eyes followed the tap-tapping of Coale's pen against the desk.

'It seems to me your operation is time-sensitive,' Khattak said. 'So hadn't you better brief me on the cell you've been surveilling?' He shifted in his chair to face Laine Stoicheva. If unpleasant things had to be dealt with, it was best to face them head-on. 'Why is Laine here? Surely, you're not expecting us to work together.'

His partnership with Laine Stoicheva had ended in acrimony. Laine's sexual harassment claim against Khattak had taken months to resolve. Though decisively exonerated, Khattak remained the subject of innuendo. This bothered him less than the fact that Laine's actions had divided him from his lifelong friend, Nathan Clare. She was a poisonous colleague, and everyone knew it. After the reprimand in Laine's personnel file, she'd been shuffled around the RCMP. Over time, she'd rebuilt her profile. Outreach Coordinator was a plum posting. He wondered how she'd gotten it.

Then he saw the possessive look that came into Coale's eyes as he watched Laine, and thought perhaps he knew. Laine didn't turn. She continued to face Ciprian Coale, a ploy Khattak recognized from the past because too many men had complimented Laine on the purity of her profile. She was dressed with restraint in a stark navy suit, her glossy hair pinned back, with no jewelry and little makeup.

She didn't need it. Laine Stoicheva was the most classically beautiful woman Khattak had ever seen. But still he found her presence abhorrent, a fact Ciprian Coale must have known.

'Laine's been on-site at Masjid un-Nur. As you can imagine, they don't take her very seriously there.'

Another crack at Khattak, this one aimed at the second-class status of women in the mosque. A rebuttal was pointless. Coale wasn't interested in shadings of the truth.

'She's here to brief you on what she knows, but you won't be working with her. You'll be reporting to me.'

A wave of cold anger washed over Khattak. His participation in Coale's investigation had been sought out by INSET, not the other way around. Neither he nor Community Policing had been imposed upon the operation. Coale's insults were needless, but perhaps they were intended to warn him away from the case. Or perhaps Coale was driven by a more subversive agenda. The rivalry had always been one-sided, unheeded by Khattak. Clearly, his inattention had rankled Coale. Shutting Khattak down at INSET would be the first step to convincing their more highly placed superiors that CPS was a miscalculation, superfluous to current law enforcement needs.

Khattak folded his hands on his lap, refusing to be drawn.

'I take it that Masjid un-Nur is the gathering place for the cell you have under surveillance.'

Laine angled her face toward him, and in the dim winter light that floated through the windows, he saw that she was not as young as he remembered. Lines had begun to settle in the angular folds of her neck. The corners of her mouth drooped a little. Her dark eyes were bleary.

The drinking had taken its toll.

But her voice when she spoke had lost none of its allure.

'Nur is a recent establishment, not as well-known or attended as any of the larger mosques at either end of the GTA. It's small, privately funded, located to the north of the city. Not quite Markham, not quite Scarborough. It's part of old Unionville.'

'There's already a sizable mosque in that area,' Khattak noted. In his capacity as head of CPS, he'd visited the Middlefield mosque often. It was a beautiful, spacious structure, its painted white arches paired with mirror-green windows that summoned the light, along with the faithful.

'Yes, we know. We believe that Middlefield has become too small to support the size of the congregation in the area. Nur could have been built to accommodate overflow. Or it could well be that the climate at Middlefield was inhospitable to the ideology of this particular cell.'

Khattak sensed discomfort behind her words, yet for the first time in recent memory, Laine was speaking to male colleagues without falling back upon a repertoire of mannerisms. Her white hand didn't dash to her hair, nor did she smooth it down over the front of her jacket. Her jet-black eyes didn't flash up at him, then away.

It was a straight, bare-boned conversation, much like the one he'd just had with Martine Killiam. And Khattak didn't trust it. Whatever Laine was doing now was just one more attempt at getting him to lower his guard.

'What do the wiretaps tell you?'

Coale scowled at the question. He hadn't known that Killiam would be quite so frank about the operation.

'Our surveillance began after Nur was established. We have no intercepts that speak to the founding of the mosque.' Laine cleared her throat. They had been speaking for less than ten minutes, yet she sounded depleted of energy. 'Mohsin came to us. He said he'd been hearing things on the basketball courts in his neighborhood from young men who were attending prayers at the mosque. He didn't think that Nur sounded like a healthy place to be.'

'Meaning what exactly?'

'There was a lot of negative talk, he said. More than just the usual summary of grievances: Palestine, Afghanistan, the invasion of Iraq. All of that, yes, but much more. There was concerted talk about the need for action – the need for a dramatic, decisive response.' Laine sounded like she was quoting someone. 'To end the humiliation of Muslims worldwide.'

Khattak showed no reaction to the tossed-off phrase 'summary of grievances'.

'So you infiltrated the mosque?'

'We sent Mohsin in, yes. We asked him to find out if it was anything more than talk. It turned out that it was. They've been planning the Nakba for more than two years.'

'Was Mohsin on your payroll?'

'Yes.' Laine's voice tightened. She knew what the question was aimed at. 'That doesn't mean he wasn't reliable. He wasn't doing it for the money.'

That would depend, Khattak thought, on what the compensation had been. In any case, there were the intercepts. A two-year operation would mean there were thousands of them.

'Why, then?'

'Mo used to have a saying. "Let's live together, brother. Let's just live." In that big, booming voice of his, smiling that huge smile. He thought the members of the cell were crazy. He also thought they were dangerous. And he was right.'

A nostalgic look came into Laine's eyes. Khattak was familiar with it. It was directed at convincing him that Mohsin Dar was a person she had cared for, rather than used. That she had valued Mohsin, and now regretted his death. Khattak didn't believe it.

Coale cut in. 'He'd won the confidence of a core group within a larger group, so much so that his reputation carried over to the second cell.'

'How many people are we talking about altogether?'

'Nearly two dozen. A lot of what you'd expect. Young kids, disaffected. But most without even that excuse.'

'Who, specifically, are you looking at? No, wait.' Khattak held up a hand in disavowal before Coale could shoot him down. 'Who should I be looking at?'

Coale's pen snapped against the desk with sudden force.

'You'll be talking to Andy Dar. Nothing more, nothing less.'

'If I'm not seen to be investigating the scene, or at a minimum interviewing those who were with Dar's son the night that he died, Dar won't stay quiet for more than a day.'

Laine intervened, sending Coale a look of entreaty.

'He's right, Ciprian. He has to be seen to be doing something.'

Justice must not only be done, it must be seen to be done.

Yet even Martine Killiam had hinted at the greater value ascribed to the façade of Khattak's investigation than to the actual truth it might uncover. He felt a pang of sorrow for Mohsin Dar, of no further use, discarded in death.

Coale interrupted his thoughts, his glance moving between Laine and Khattak, a brooding speculation in it.

'Laine has been withdrawn from the mosque. You won't be working with her at the scene, if that's what you're thinking.'

'It should be evident by now that I have no wish to do so.'

Laine turned her face away at the words. She pushed her hands against the edge of her seat, the long fingers clasping each other. Her unvarnished nails were clipped short, another departure from her normal feminine elegance.

Without looking at Khattak, she said, 'Tell him about Hassan Ashkouri. And the other members of the cell.'

A pleased glint came into Coale's eyes.

'Ashkouri is the ideologue, the ringleader. He's of Iraqi background with Canadian citizenship, though he came here late enough to have had experience of the war, something he uses to considerable effect. He's a frequent speaker at Nur mosque.'

'What credentials does he have?'

'Do these people need credentials? A few lines in Arabic are usually enough to win over a congregation. That and a bit of messianic charisma, and you have the makings of real trouble.'

When Khattak didn't respond to this, he went on, 'Ashkouri was preparing to become an Islamic scholar. The war in Iraq curtailed his plans. He's an engineer by training, financially quite successful.'

'So he's not the imam.'

'No. Nur's imam is a humble enough fellow, unworldly, inexperienced, too grateful to bite the hand that feeds him. He'll say and do whatever the mosque committee tells him to say.'

'Is he a member of the cell?'

This time Laine answered. 'No. In fact, the cell has made certain that the imam knows nothing about their private meetings. They have a word for them.' She withdrew her phone from within her blazer pocket and flicked through a series of screens. It was a delaying tactic. She would know the word by heart by now. 'They're called halaqas. The halaqas are a smoke screen for the organizers of the attack. When they meet, it's to advance some aspect of the plot.'

Khattak couldn't agree. It didn't make sense. A halaqa was a study circle, devoted to exploring and understanding theology. If a regular session was being held at the mosque, many of the mosque's congregants would expect to attend it. How could Hassan Ashkouri expect to maintain the secrecy of his plot?

He doubted that either Coale or Laine would be able to answer his question. And then he remembered what Martine Killiam had told him.

'The superintendent said there were seven people at the training camp, along with Mohsin Dar. Ashkouri must have been there. But there were two women also, is that correct?'

Laine nodded in quick response.

'Were these women at the halaqas?'

'Yes. Why?'

Khattak frowned in thought. 'Because halaqas in a mosque setting are typically segregated events. And they're open to the general public. The superintendent said that you haven't been able to determine if the women are members of the cell or not. That raises several questions: how did Ashkouri restrict attendance at these halaqas? Why wouldn't the imam be part of a discussion on theology? And if the purpose of these halaqas was to advance the terrorist plot as you say, wouldn't the presence of the women indicate membership in the cell?'

Coale snorted. 'Do you think we're amateurs, Khattak? Or that we've been waiting for you to deliver the truth to us from on high? I've said as much from the beginning.'

Laine rushed in to answer. 'The intercepts have never confirmed it. And neither did Mohsin, though he was part of the halaqas.'

'Then what did Mohsin tell you?'

'That Hassan Ashkouri was an operator. He convinced the imam to let him run a series of private sessions, not all of which were meetings of the cell. Some had another cover – poetry, Middle East history, Ashkouri's personal interests. He encouraged the attendance of women at the sessions. Given his generous donations to the mosque, the imam saw no need to object.'

'I see.' But Khattak didn't. The setup was unusual, burdened with unnecessary risk. And it didn't answer the question of how the two cells were communicating. He found his interest in the national security investigation stimulated by the questions mounting up in his mind. Were he still a member of INSET, he'd

34

have access to some, if not all, of the answers.

'Do members of both cells attend these halaqas?' And then, to get around Coale's insistence on blocking any information that could help him better understand Mohsin's murder, he added, 'Will they be among the suspects I'm to profile?'

An indirect way of getting at the same thing, while paying lip service to Coale.

'They haven't yet. So you won't have any contact with them.'

Coale sat back in his chair. It was Laine who added, as if apologizing for Coale, 'We don't know how the two cells are communicating. It's not by phone or private meetings, or we'd have surveillance to back that up. Whatever we've learned from Mohsin has come strictly from within Hassan Ashkouri's group. But Ashkouri didn't confide in Mo beyond a certain point.'

'That's not your problem, Khattak,' Coale interjected. 'You're to interview the people who were with Dar at the camp, but you're not to ask what reason they had for going up there, or what purpose the camp served.'

'What purpose did it serve?'

Khattak found himself looking to Laine for the answer. She stood, sending her chair to the ground in her hurry. When he rose to right it, her cold hand brushed his. She withdrew it at once, as if stung by the contact.

'I'll bring you what I have on the people at the camp. The men were there for commando training – the use of weapons, surveillance tactics, personal combat. The women...' She shook her head, putting a finger to her lips, a gesture Khattak recognized of old. 'One is just a girl. The other is a convert to Islam. Mo insisted they were not implicated.' A quick frown marred the smooth skin of her brow. 'Naturally, we had to wonder.'

'What about the weapon used to kill Mohsin? Has it been recovered?'

'No. We know it was a nine-millimeter Herstal, but that's all we know.'

There was an odd hesitation in her voice.

'Were there any other weapons at the camp?'

'They had bolt-action hunting rifles, but we only know that from surveillance photos taken prior to the training camp. There were no traces of ammunition at the scene.'

The camp had been a dry run then.

'And that's none of your business, Khattak. Keep it to yourself. You can go, Laine.'

Laine made for the door, brushing by Esa as she did so. Drawing away, he held the door until she had passed. When he turned back to look at Coale, he found the other man on his feet, his eyes on Laine.

It was time to quit fencing, to stop pretending that Khattak had any intention of abiding by Coale's absurd restrictions. And Laine's revelations had provided Esa with the opportunity to make his own position clear.

'I'll do as you say in terms of questioning those who were present at the camp. But we both know that whatever information I'm able to acquire will be limited. I've been authorized to send my partner in. It would be useful to have her join these halaqas.'

Coale's eyes narrowed. He knew that Khattak had just pulled rank on him. And whether or not he saw the value of Khattak's suggestion, he didn't like the suggestion at all. But neither did he seem as discomposed as Khattak had expected. There was a sense of triumph about Coale, a secret gloating as he fussed with the tails of his Hermès scarf.

'She won't be the only one you know at the halaqas, Khattak.'

It was Khattak's turn to take a step back, to ponder Coale's implicit threat.

'There's a lot you don't know about Hassan Ashkouri,' Coale continued. 'But I expected you'd have a better handle on your own household.' He smiled at Khattak's uncharacteristic hesitation. 'Your sister. I believe her name is Rukshanda. Ashkouri calls her Ruksh.' The smile faded, leaving behind a calculated menace.

'She's been under surveillance for some time now. I thought you might have known.'

He dragged the words out, waiting for Khattak's reply.

A tightness in his face at the unwanted knowledge, Khattak swallowed the heated response on his tongue. This was Coale's game, baiting Khattak into anger and indiscretion; there was nothing new in it. Hiding his impatience, Khattak said, 'Just tell me whatever it is you have to tell me.'

'Your sister,' Coale repeated, savoring the words. 'I thought you might know. She's engaged to be married to Ashkouri.'

5

ON HIS WAY OUT OF the INSET offices, Khattak paused to have a word with Gavin Chan, a former colleague. Chan had been a junior member of the team two years ago, especially gifted in telecommunications. If anyone would know about the intercepts, it would be Gavin Chan.

Chan walked him to the elevator, a compact individual with a head of spiky hair and a ferocious sense of attention to duty.

'You can't tell me anything, I know. But if you're part of the operation, you'll have heard about my sister. I need to know if she's in immediate danger. Is there any way I could have a look at transcripts of the intercepts?'

Chan stared at the wall, dropping his voice.

'It won't help you. There's thousands of them; you won't have enough time.' He stretched his arms behind his back with an impressive display of flexibility. 'I think I need a coffee. You wouldn't believe the things that cross my desk.' He wandered away to the stairs, tipping his head at a side door as he passed. 'Be careful,' he mouthed.

Khattak understood at once. Two agents walked off the elevator, nodding as they recognized him. He waited for the passage to clear, then pressed the button to send the elevator back to the ground floor. He crossed to the door Chan had indicated and slipped inside.

Chan preferred to work in a closed cubicle with the pleasant scent of a vanilla candle.

His computer was encrypted, connected to a series of monitors, all of which were dark. To one side of his desk was a copier, a printer, and a security-coded shredder. The desk was a study in organized chaos, dozens of file folders stacked in an order that made sense only to Chan. Placed on top of these was a time-coded memorandum.

The memo from Martine Killiam was addressed to Ciprian Coale, disclosing the name of the agents who were responsible for delivery of the fertilizer to a man named Rahman Aziz.

Khattak frowned. He took it as a personal affront when members of a terrorist cell ascribed the names of God to themselves. Rahman meant the 'Most Compassionate,' Aziz the 'Most Honorable'.

Neither was a fitting choice for a would-be bomb-maker.

He scanned the rest of the memo. The delivery date of the materials was unspecified, a fact that set him on edge. He knew the INSET team was highly competent. It didn't stop him from worrying that Hassan Ashkouri had discovered a way of moving ahead with his plans.

He heard voices in the corridor outside. The ping of the elevator, a whoosh of doors. Footsteps came closer, then the voices moved away.

He sorted quickly through the folders, scanning dates, times, locations for anything connected to Ruksh. Gavin had been right. It was too much raw data, and he had no means of prioritizing the information he sought. But one folder at the bottom of the pile caught his attention. It was a dossier on Ashkouri.

Amid the papers and photographs was a biography appended to Ashkouri's immigration file. A senior construction engineer, Ashkouri had been accepted as a skilled worker into Canada, where he'd rapidly found employment before branching off to form his own consultancy. At his thriving engineering firm, he'd hired three of the congregants at the mosque. Rahman Aziz's name was also on the list as one of Ashkouri's employees.

There was no information about Ashkouri's abandoned course

of studies as an Islamic scholar, where he had planned to study, or whether he'd been denied entry or exit visas that would have allowed him to follow his chosen course.

The Ashkouri family was from Baqouba, northeast of Baghdad. They had moved to Baghdad to flee the fighting between American and Iraqi forces. In 2013, they had returned to Baqouba to face additional tragedy with the bombing of the al-Sariya mosque.

Khattak felt the shock of memory. The attack on Sunni worshippers had followed the bombing of Shia neighborhoods and sites of worship, in a cycle of sectarian violence that had spread throughout the country.

His fingers held up a document. Ashkouri's parents and brothers had been killed in the al-Sariya attack. He had never been married, he had no children. Immediately after the attack, his immigration to Canada had been approved.

But there was nothing that connected Ashkouri to Ruksh. Frustrated, he tried Gavin's desk drawer, convinced that his ex-colleague had walked him to the elevator for a reason.

On the top of a pile was a blue folder similar to the one Martine Killiam had given Khattak. He flicked it open.

It was the same collection of photographs that were in the file in his possession.

Members of the training camp were cross-referenced with congregants at the mosque.

He was about to close the folder when he noticed a discrepancy.

He paged through the numbered photographs again.

Buried at the back were two additional photographs.

One was of himself. The other was a photograph of his sister.

Paper-clipped to the back of the folder was a typed list of names associated with the numbered photos. And beside the names a provisional status: Cell 1, Cell 2.

The space beside Khattak's name was blank.

But under his name was his sister's.

Rukshanda Khattak: Cell 1.

He closed the door to Gavin Chan's cubicle, heading for the stairs.

Laine Stoicheva was at the elevator as he turned.

She looked from Esa to Gavin's door, her eyebrows drawn together. The elevator doors opened and Gavin stepped out, holding a cup of coffee.

There was no time for Esa to warn him.

None of the three moved.

Then Laine stepped into the elevator, turning her face away.

The doors closed on anything Khattak might have said.

6

IF IT HAD BEEN COLD the day before, it was nothing compared with the experience of loading boxes onto a dolly and trundling them into the building that housed Rachel's new condominium. Her hands were red and rough with cold, while her body was sweating beneath her down jacket. She'd given up attempting to protect her face from the mid-December windchill. Her long Maple Leafs scarf caught under her feet, tripping her up as she struggled to yank the wheels of the dolly through the snow. The sidewalks were clear but the ramp to the service elevator wasn't.

She had no intention of complaining, though. It was the first day of her new life and 'disgruntled neighbor' wasn't the impression she wanted to make on the cheery young couples who inhabited the building. Thankfully, it was her last trip up the ramp. She'd cheated by using her police ID. No one would tag or tow the van she had left in the loading zone, so she could take a few minutes to unwrap herself from the cold, then drink her first cup of coffee in her brand-new kitchen.

Appraising her new kingdom, Rachel took a moment to absorb it all.

She was free, she was alone, she was blessed, and she was happy. Happier than she could ever remember being. She caught sight of her face in the mirror that hung over the console. Her chapped lips and puffy cheeks were red. An ember had caught her dull brown eyes and set them alight. Her face was set in an expression of lively good humor. Even the ponytail that had been trapped under her blue-and-white toque seemed bouncier than usual.

It was a great day to be Rachel Getty of Community Policing, Toronto. She gave herself a jaunty salute in the mirror just as the intercom buzzed.

'Hello?' she asked, pressing the button. Maybe the van was attracting more notice than she'd expected.

'May I come up, Rachel?'

It was Khattak, her boss. She cast a frantic look around her condo, seeing it with new eyes. Despite the two bedrooms, wasn't it terribly small and cramped? Didn't the boxes that were scattered everywhere diminish both its size and its charm? Why hadn't she dumped them all in her bedroom, instead of taking the trouble to ensure that each clearly labeled box had been placed in the room that its contents were destined for?

She buzzed Khattak in, scrambling to close her bedroom door and to clear the boxes from the comfortable leather couches she had bought for the living room. In the catalogue she had purchased them from, they'd been described as 'distressed'. She shook her head. She'd been aiming for the rustic elegance of Pottery Barn without wanting to spend quite that much money. Now she wondered if instead of good taste, her condo reflected a kind of slovenliness and corner-cutting.

Khattak knocked on the door.

She answered it with a reckless gaiety that made Khattak consider her closely before yielding his expensive overcoat and gloves to her. The understated elegance of his manner of dress was something she could only hope to emulate.

But when she thought about it, she knew she was happy to see him, and happy to have him in her new home, regardless of his opinion of it. And why should she assume his opinion would be negative?

For some time now, Khattak had been trying to expand their relationship from partners in policing to a genuine friendship.

He had asked to meet her family and invited her to meet his, requests Rachel had denied by means of trumped-up excuses. Now, in her own home, a place she could be proud of, and without the constant fug of the Getty family drama hanging over her head, she felt she could begin to reciprocate Esa Khattak's overtures.

'Have a seat, sir. It's freezing outside. I'll bring us some coffee.'

You could never second-guess the Canadian winter. You could have a cold snap one week and balmy temperatures the next. You could have snow up to your armpits from Halloween onward, or you could get it all in a relentless blast from January to early May. Once, in a gesture that had elicited ridicule from the rest of the country, the mayor of Toronto had called in the army to dig out the city.

The snow-removal system was one of the best in the world. It had to be. The city alone had two hundred salt trucks and six hundred snowplows waiting on standby. From the look of things, this wasn't going to be one of those winters mitigated by global warming. Instead, they'd been told to expect heavy snowfall now, massive flooding in parts of the country later.

Khattak took his coffee black; it was tea that he drank milky and sweet, a fact that Rachel was proud she remembered. He thanked her with a nod, engrossed in Rachel's new surroundings. Rachel had unpacked a few boxes in the living room, scattering her knick-knacks against the backdrop of leather couches and creamy white walls. She had also introduced touches of pale blue, with a narrow Indian runner on the floor and small pieces of Caithness glass that reflected the blue-gray of Highland lakes. On the small table beside Khattak was a picture of Rachel with her brother, Zachary, both dressed in Maple Leafs jerseys. The young Zachary was beaming up at his older sister, his skinny arms slung around her neck from behind. Rachel was beaming too, revealing the gap where one of her front teeth had been knocked out in a game.

'Your home is lovely, Rachel,' Khattak said, studying the photograph. 'It suits you.'

Rachel's face lit up with pleasure.

'Thank you, sir. When I've had a chance to settle in, I'll give you a proper tour. We didn't have anything else on for today, did we? Did I leave too early?'

Her schedule at CPS was flexible. When they were working a case, she worked for days on end without a break. At other times she was able to get away early. Not quite as secretive about her personal life as she had been in the past, she had told Khattak about her move, and about her upcoming all-star game.

'Nothing like that. And I'm sorry to encroach upon your personal time. But I needed to give you this.'

He handed Rachel an unsealed envelope taken from his inside jacket pocket. He had placed a much thicker folder on the table between them.

Rachel read the letter and then looked up at Khattak, puzzled. It was confirmation of a security clearance. *Her* security clearance.

'Why do I need this, sir?'

The letter was a pretext, she realized. Khattak could have given it to her tomorrow at the office. There was something premonitory about his manner, like a finger shoved into a leaky dike, or a hand held up to ward off a falling sky.

He told her about Mohsin Dar, passed the folder to her, showed her several photographs.

Rachel read through the file, taking her time, not quite able to believe what she was seeing.

'This isn't a joke? Or a farce of some kind? Someone reenacting the Toronto 18 on a grander scale? Weren't those boys just idiots in the woods?'

Some years ago, a similar plot had been attempted by a group of Muslim men scattered throughout the GTA. Their home base had been a mosque in Meadowvale.

'It came down to eleven convictions in the end. Two of them were life sentences. Hardly a joke.'

Rachel looked up from the file. 'They're treading the same ground, except it's Algonquin instead of Washago – and yes, they've expanded the number of targets: Queen's Park wasn't part of it before. Are they nuts? Do they have any idea what the traffic is like with the construction? How are they planning to get down there?' Another thought occurred to her. 'Is there a connection between the two plots? Between the past and the present?'

Or for that matter between the past, the present, and the recent attack upon Parliament Hill, seat of the federal government?

As she asked her questions, Rachel noticed that some of the tension seemed to be seeping from Khattak. He was more at ease, sitting back on the sofa. This was a system and a routine that he was familiar with, a comfortable back-and-forth that was not so comfortable as to have lost its edge.

'I wouldn't know. We're not meant to know. We're meant to give the appearance of investigating Dar's death.'

'Which means we're really investigating it,' Rachel cut in.

'Of course.' He looked surprised that she'd felt the need to say it. 'What's the point of going in at all, if we don't care that an innocent man is dead? A man who chose a dangerous means of serving his country?'

Rachel ducked the question. Like most Canadians, she found overt displays of patriotism embarrassing, unless it came in the form of rooting for Team Canada. She took her vacation days during the World Hockey Championships, and demonstrated her national pride by painting a maple leaf on her face. This was something else, it was deeper. Rachel, who was an agnostic about everything except crime, found herself uncomfortable.

'Going in?'

She knew it was the right question when Khattak's hands relaxed on his knees.

'My task is to recite the Community Policing mantra at the

46

mosque; you'll appear a day or so ahead of me with a cover story. You won't be Rachel Getty, police officer. And we won't know each other.'

Rachel eyed him, suspicious. 'Then who will I be?'

'A new recruit. Not to the active cell,' he corrected, when he saw her reaction. 'To the Masjid un-Nur. You're there because you live in the area and you're thinking about a conversion to Islam.'

'I don't live in the area,' Rachel said, panicking.

Khattak was patient in response. 'That's why it's a cover. And you'll talk to these people.' He nodded at the file. 'About Mohsin and the mosque, nothing more. But somehow or other, you've got to get yourself invited to one of Hassan Ashkouri's halaqas.'

'Without tipping him off? What if I blow the whole thing? Isn't that just what we need with everything that's happened at Justice? They'll crucify you, sir.'

A clumsy choice of words to direct at a practicing Muslim. She realized as much as soon as the words left her mouth.

Khattak didn't notice. He reached across the table for the folder, gathered up the photographs to place them inside.

'You don't have to do this, Rachel; of course I can't compel you. It's just – I owe Mohsin Dar something more than what he'll get from our colleagues at INSET.'

'You don't trust them?'

'I trust they have the right priorities. I understand that Mohsin can't be one of them.'

Rachel watched the heaviness settle back upon Khattak's shoulders, much like the light edging from the room, leaving the shadow of loss behind. Khattak was upset, and it wasn't just over the death of Mohsin Dar, a man he had known. Or the terrorist plot, as much as it had jolted her, as fantastic as it seemed.

She switched on the lamp beside her brother's photograph.

Things had changed; they were better. She was seeing Zach again, though much more infrequently than she wanted, and always on his terms. He wasn't ready to trust her with everything – his address, his friends, the girl he'd been dating for the past two years. They talked, but never about their parents, and Rachel was careful not to push him too hard.

But when she'd bought the condo, she'd made sure it had an extra bedroom, in case Zach ever felt like he needed a home – or needed her. She hadn't said it, but Zach had known. And for a fleeting moment, she'd glimpsed the young Zach again, the unmitigated faith in his eyes. Then he'd ducked his head and it was gone.

Always be as happy, Zach, she had thought, gazing at her brother's face in the photograph. She'd forgotten to wish the same for herself.

She'd backed Khattak all the way in the aftermath of what had happened with Drayton. She wouldn't do less now. Not when Ciprian Coale had left him isolated.

She thought of Khattak's friend, Nathan Clare, the famous writer. She had met him during the Drayton investigation. He was someone Khattak could talk to – and then from Nathan, her thoughts made a lightning connection.

'Who did you speak to at INSET, sir? Who briefed you?'

'We won't be working with her, Rachel. And if you do see her at the Nur mosque, you're not to engage with her. Keep your cover intact.'

He meant Laine Stoicheva, his terrifying ex-colleague.

Not so much a relic of the past as an unexploded ordnance. Still waiting to go off.

No wonder Khattak was wearied by the day. First Drayton, now this. And to have known the murdered man…

With an effort, Rachel kept her face from showing her sympathy.

'You said I'm to go in first, right away. Why is that, sir?'

'I'll be dealing with Andy Dar.' He made a dismissive gesture with his left hand, but Rachel caught the flare of hope in his eyes.

'And I've some things I need to manage at home.'

Rachel ordered pizza. It was her way of saying yes. And of getting Khattak to prepare her. She'd learned a great deal at CPS, from Khattak and the Muslim communities they'd worked with, but there were still a million things she could get wrong, a million ways she could land them both in further trouble.

'Do I need a headscarf, sir?'

Khattak gave her the glimmer of a smile.

The folder between them, they talked late into the night.

7

KHATTAK MET ANDY DAR AT his home in Rosedale, an old and affluent neighborhood situated between three ravines. Its charm lay in the abundance of roses that grew at the edges of the Jarvis estate, the historic homestead that had given rise to the neighborhood more than a century ago.

The silent weight of snow gave a sameness to the landscape, bearing down upon the spruce and pine trees, snaking over the branches of elms. Khattak drove south from the railway tracks that formed the neighborhood's northern boundary, navigating the slick roads with care, until he found Dar's house across from the old stone church. The windows of a beautifully crafted brick house fronted the small triangle of Whitney Park.

Khattak parked in the driveway and rang the doorbell.

The heavy bronze door was opened by a woman in her thirties wearing a loosely bound headscarf. Her face was bare of makeup, except for smudges of eyeliner that had leaked over the edges of her lower lids, darkening the circles beneath her tired eyes. She ignored the identification he presented, both her arms full of bulging file folders. When Khattak offered to take them from her, she seemed surprised at the attention.

'I'm Alia,' she said. 'My father-in-law is in the study.'

So this was Alia Dar, Mohsin Dar's wife – Mohsin Dar's widow now. As he followed her through the house, he took note of the fact that she was wearing slacks and a baggy tunic, instead of *shalwar kameez*, traditional Pakistani clothing. Her headscarf was worn casually, the way a woman of the subcontinent would wear it, with the long tail of her dark braid escaping from the bottom.

Khattak felt the automatic respect for a hijab-wearing woman that most men of his background and generation did, moderated by the analytical training of a police officer. A headscarf didn't make him stop thinking, or evaluating or wondering. It was simply something he was comfortable with, just as he was comfortable with its absence. His wife had not worn one, except at the mosque and religious gatherings, and he had always respected her choice.

A wry smile twisted Khattak's mouth. As with his sisters, his views on the matter had not been consulted, nor had there been any expectation that they would be, a lesson he had learned from his mild-mannered father. He wondered if the same had been true of Mohsin Dar.

He knew Andy Dar was an outspoken advocate of assimilation. A vociferous critic of practices he considered outmoded, Dar had sundered his ties with the city's Muslim communities years ago, reinventing himself in ever more disturbing incarnations, most recently that of broadcast journalist, a go-to source for scathing commentary on Islam.

Alia Dar knocked on the French doors that led the way into Andy Dar's study. The knock was hesitant, deferential, at odds with the expression on her face, a fleeting glimpse of her true feelings for her father-in-law, who waved them in.

Alia motioned Khattak to a chair, setting the heavy stack of folders down. Khattak waited. Dar was on the phone, giving Khattak time to study the photographs that cluttered the walls, a comprehensive list of dignitaries on personal terms with Dar. There was no photo of Nathan Clare, the writer and public intellectual, Khattak's closest friend.

The politics of Clare and Dar had never been aligned, even when Dar had been a welcome spokesperson in Toronto's Muslim communities. There was still a touch of charlatanism that hung about the man, along with the sense of relentless self-promotion. Perhaps reading Khattak's reluctance to engage with Andy Dar, Clare had kept his distance from Dar, a choice extenuated by time.

Andy Dar ended his call. The handshake he offered Khattak was brusque to the point of offense, and characteristic of his manner. He faced Khattak with a smirk, ignoring rank and every other indication of Esa Khattak's success.

'Well? What have you got for me, Khattak?' He noticed his daughter-in-law, sorting through the folders on his desk, moving between the desk and a set of black filing cabinets. 'What are you still doing here? Go and bring us some tea. Unless Khattak wants coffee.'

Khattak looked at Andy Dar steadily. However unpleasant Dar's attitude toward Khattak, his manner of speaking to his daughter-in-law was much more offensive.

He declined the offer of tea with a circumspect glance at Alia.

'I expect Mrs. Dar would like to stay and hear about her husband.'

Andy Dar ignored him. Flipping through his letters, he spoke with the modified British accent prevalent among his generation of well-educated South Asians.

'What is it you have to report to me?'

'I wanted to let you know that I've taken over the investigation. I'll be doing everything in my power to bring the person who killed your son to justice.'

Dar let out a short, sharp bark. 'What power do you have? None at all. What you're best known for is incompetence and inaction. You are letting yourself be used, Khattak. I warned you that this would happen. A Muslim inspector, to head up a *faltu* unit, and you fell for it.' His voice became a sneer. 'You wanted it, I'm sure. A little plume in your cap, a sign of acceptance that even white skin doesn't buy you. A chance to pass, to play at being *angrez*. Were it not for the fact of your rather difficult Pashtun name.'

Khattak considered this. The Urdu word *faltu* meant 'worthless', or 'extra'. It was borrowed from Portuguese, brought by the Portuguese colonization of Goa, India. As was *angrez*, a word that meant 'Englishman,' a loanword derived from 'inglés'.

Khattak marveled at the irony of Dar's choice of language, an irony that Dar little suspected, cultures bleeding into each other, leaving graceful, irretrievable traces of themselves.

'You're not being fair, Baba.' Alia's voice from the corner of the room was plain and unaccented. Like Khattak, she was Canadian-born. She brushed at the curls on her forehead, pulling her headscarf forward. 'Mohsin knew Inspector Khattak. He would have been glad to know that someone he respected was working on his behalf.'

'Did he mention me to you recently?'

Both Khattak's voice and glance at Alia were gentle. He considered the contrast between Andy Dar and his daughter-in-law, etched more sharply by Dar's not-unexpected invective. There was much in Dar's outburst to consider, not least its contradictions. It was Adnan Dar who had spent his life in pursuit of acceptance, and 'Andy' Dar who had chosen the straightforward path of assimilation. Except that assimilation was never quite as straightforward as an immigrant expected or hoped for. The accent, the dark skin, the unfamiliar ways – the distinctive and oft-feared religious practices. Much of this, Andy Dar had discarded. What he could not discard was his sense of being uprooted from himself, in search of a new mooring place. No matter how loudly he disparaged his personal heritage, he wasn't able to divorce himself from it – either in his own eyes, or in the eyes of others.

Khattak with his difficult name and Alia with her headscarf were both more comfortable and familiar with themselves than Andy Dar could hope to be, shouting blindly into the void.

Alia came away from the filing cabinet, leaning one hip against the desk.

'You don't visit the Nur mosque, I think. The mosque in old Unionville.'

'I haven't yet. Did Mohsin spend time there?'

Alia appeared uneasy. She reached for the mail that Andy Dar had been shuffling in his hands, and set it upon the desk. Khattak sensed that as with everything else, responsibility for Dar's mail would ultimately fall to her.

'A lot of time. He met – new people there. He was always at the mosque.'

'Wasting his time with idiots,' Andy Dar cut in. His voice was filled with outrage. And beneath the outrage, the pain that waited to encroach at his first quiet moment. 'And one of those fanatics killed him. They took him to the woods and murdered him, God knows why.' He darted an angry glance at Khattak. 'If you are not wholly incompetent yourself, perhaps you stand a chance of finding out what happened to my son.' He checked the time on his cell phone. 'But I will make sure of it myself by asking for answers on my program.'

And now Khattak felt the urgency of what Martine Killiam had shared with him, the need to curtail Dar before his behavior destroyed months of meticulous groundwork. The exigent need to find Dar another outlet for his pain, since Dar could not be thwarted, and had to be managed.

'I wonder if there's a way to make your intervention more effective.'

The innocence of Esa's suggestion masked a calculation.

'I don't see your broadcast as a onetime opportunity,' he continued. 'Your program could play a critical role, if it's handled with discretion.'

Dar glared at Khattak, his arms crossed in front of him.

'Suppose tonight you were to announce Mohsin's death on your program without mentioning the manner of his death. You could suggest that those who knew Mohsin attend a memorial for your son at a local mosque. In fact, the Nur mosque would be best.'

Khattak said this as if he had just thought of it. 'That would give me the excuse I need to conduct interviews at the mosque, narrowing down the list of suspects, and speeding my way to an arrest. Once we made the arrest, you could announce it on your broadcast.'

It was a ploy that depended on Andy Dar's obsession with his ratings.

'You should be up at Algonquin, investigating.' Dar was beginning to lose steam. 'Not here, and not at the mosque.'

'The scene has been thoroughly documented.' Khattak allowed a note of genuine compassion to enter his voice. 'Do you believe that Mohsin's killer is still at Algonquin Park?' And when Dar didn't speak, unwilling to make concessions, Khattak continued, 'I would be grateful for your help with this, sir. Mohsin's killer won't be expecting us to work together. I'd like to prove him wrong, wouldn't you?'

'He was my son,' Dar said, rallying a little. 'No one wants justice more than I do.'

Khattak thought of the pain that haunted Alia's eyes. He bowed his head and said, 'I'm sure that's true, sir.'

Alia walked out of the room.

'I will broadcast the news of the memorial on my program.' Dar frowned at the French doors Alia had closed behind her. 'I'll need time to sort out arrangements at the mosque.'

That was exactly what Khattak had counted on.

'And the announcement of the arrest will air first on my program, is that clear?'

'Very clear. Thank you.'

Khattak's hand was on the door. His thoughts had followed Alia from the room.

'One more thing, Khattak.'

Khattak turned back to face him. It shocked him to see that Dar's deep-set eyes were wet, though his voice was steady enough.

'He was my only child, my boy. If your efforts to find his killer do not succeed, I will use my program to take you down.'

Alia Dar was waiting for him on the front steps, a heavy bag of salt in her arms. Khattak took it from her, scattering the salt on the steps, spreading several more handfuls over the driveway.

He put the bag away inside the garage, the cold nipping at his bare face. Alia seemed oblivious to it. Her coat was unbuttoned, her hands free of gloves.

'I'd like to speak with you about Mohsin.'

Alia glanced at the windows to the den, where Andy Dar's silhouette appeared.

'We could take a walk,' she said. 'Chorley Park's not far from here. There are some nice trails. Unless you think it's too cold?'

'Don't you feel the cold?'

Alia Dar shrugged, her face blank.

Khattak suppressed a pang of pity.

'Get your gloves,' he said gently. 'And button up your coat. Then I'll walk with you.'

When she was dressed more sensibly for the weather, he let her lead the way to Chorley Park. The main pathway through the park had been shoveled, a bombast of white on either side of the cobbled walk. They trudged past sheltered butternut trees until Khattak called a halt at a small enclosure. A bench was set before a scenic outlook of shimmering trees that disappeared at the edge of the horizon against a crumbling erasure of sky.

He took a seat at the opposite end of the bench from Alia.

'You said Mohsin spoke of me.'

What Khattak wanted to know was whether Mohsin had wanted to speak to a contact at CPS, a contact he trusted, particularly if Mohsin had felt himself constrained in the role of a police agent under surveillance.

'He admired you. I know you haven't spoken much recently, but Mohsin followed your career. He called it "a spectacular ascent".' She raised her gloved hands to her mouth and blew on her fingers. 'And he didn't mean it as an insult, as Baba would have. He believed you would do some good. He said no one but you could take on such a role and succeed.'

Khattak felt a stab of regret. He hadn't spoken to Mohsin in years. He should have reached out, should have made Mohsin understand his decision, his choices. They had been friends in those promising years of youth, when everything seemed possible, destiny a series of choices, nothing set in stone, the years stretching ahead to a generous horizon.

They had plumbed the shape of the future through the silhouette of their dreams. They had never been as far apart as either man had later believed.

And then he realized.

Publicly, Mohsin had shunned Esa for taking up the appointment to head CPS. Yet he'd told Alia that he applauded Khattak's choice.

'I wish he had come to see me at CPS.'

'The mosque took up most of his time.'

'What about his regular work?'

'You know Mohsin. He was always a dabbler. A little bit of this, a little bit of that. Lately, he'd taken up work as a computer consultant. It was work he said he could do anywhere.'

The dabbling had included skills that had made Mohsin Dar invaluable to INSET. He was a former army cadet with a firearms license and extensive military and martial arts training. He had acquired the possession and acquisition license in order to work as an armored car security guard. The leap to computers was something Khattak would need to discuss with Ciprian Coale. Unless Alia could give him access to Mohsin's work space.

'Where did he do his work? At his father's house?'

'Mostly at home, sometimes at Nur.' She hesitated. 'When the police came to tell me of Mohsin's death, they searched the house and took away his computer.' She seemed to be weighing a dilemma – whether to trust Esa or not.

'I'll help you in any way I can,' he said.

She reached into her pocket for a set of keys. After a moment, she gave them to Khattak.

'I didn't give the police the keys to Mohsin's storage locker. I'm the only one who knows about it; it's registered under my name.'

Khattak felt a leap of excitement.

Here was something he could use, something INSET might have missed.

'Have you been to the locker?' he asked. 'Do you know what Mohsin keeps there?'

Alia shook her head. 'It would have made him angry. And he already had reasons to be angry with me. He was pushing me away. He didn't want me anywhere near Nur.'

'Why was that?'

'He said he was doing *dawah*, extending the invitation to Islam. He said that converts might be put off by my presence, because gender politics were hard to explain to newcomers.'

'And what did you say to that?'

She gave him a level glance.

'I'm not stupid. The converts were women, and Mohsin was the big man on campus. His personality attracted a lot of people. I think it went to his head, the way he was able to dazzle the people at Nur. I didn't want my husband spending time with other women. So I pressed him about going to Algonquin with him. He found his own way to stop me.'

She crossed the path to the fir tree. Standing under its heavy branches, she braced herself against the trunk and shook it. Snow floated down onto her head and shoulders like dandruff. A pair of kinglets singing above her head faltered into silence.

'I'm trying to feel something,' she said, before Khattak could ask. 'It's been a long time since I've felt anything.'

He didn't think she was referring just to Mohsin's death. What had this somber, capable woman suspected her husband of? Why that margin of pain in her eyes?

'How did he stop you from going to the camp?'

There was a long silence before she answered him. Covered in snow, she let the branches of the fir support her weight, buoying her up against the currents of wind.

'He said he would only take me if I began to wear the niqab.' Tears slid down her face, catching on the snowflakes. 'I'm a fifth-grade schoolteacher, I can't wear a veil across my face. Of course, I said no.' She came to sit on the bench again, this time closer to Khattak. 'He'd never tried to coerce me in matters of religion before. Yes, he talked wildly sometimes when he was younger. He said he would go for jihad in Chechnya or Afghanistan. But the imams at Jame Masjid always talked him out of these plans. This time, he told me I could quit my job because he was earning plenty of money. That was when I knew.'

'I'm not sure I understand.'

But her words were taking Khattak down a familiar road, through conversations with members of the mosque, through regrets and choices made, through countless lost opportunities. Times he should have spoken up, questions he should have asked, challenging others to an ethical reading of scripture in lieu of the tropes of dogma.

It had seemed like a burden that someone else should carry, yet he realized it belonged to him, just as it belonged to each of his coreligionists, this personal quest for an ethical life – and it couldn't be put down by choice, not without abandoning the field to the hardened and hidebound, whose rigid conservatism and eschewal of modernity contained within it the seeds of jihadist ideology. The one so dangerously close to the other, with the danger entirely unheeded.

Whatever the RCMP's picture of Mohsin was, it was dismally incomplete. They had been able to use him, but they had missed the depth of his commitment to the *ummah*. How that commitment had played itself out was something Khattak still needed to explore.

'Mohsin was in over his head. He'd fallen for someone, but it wasn't one of the women.'

'Then who?'

But he knew what Alia Dar was going to say before she said it.

'He was under the spell of Hassan Ashkouri.'

The man engaged to Khattak's younger sister.

8

THE LOCKER WAS IN A self-storage warehouse in North York, halfway between Mohsin's home in the West End and the Nur mosque in the north. Its setting in an industrial park far from the highway indicated that Mohsin had had need of secrecy – whether the secrecy was designed for his RCMP handlers or for members of Ashkouri's cell, Khattak couldn't say. What was evident was that Mohsin Dar must have trusted his wife enough to let her know of the locker's existence.

Khattak checked his watch, feeling the winter chill settle into his bones. He was waiting for Rachel to help him go through the locker. He hadn't called Coale, a deliberate choice. If he mentioned the storage locker, Coale would block his attempts to investigate. Time enough to tell Coale after the initial search.

Rachel pulled into the parking lot of the warehouse with a cheerful blast of her horn.

She was carrying a tray of Tim Hortons' coffees in one hand and polishing off a maple donut with the other. Stuffed between the coffee cups was a bag that Khattak suspected held another donut. Rachel was always hungry, though he had no idea where she put away the food.

He was glad she was here now – a part of the investigation where she could openly partner with him, away from prying eyes.

They walked over to the storage unit together, Khattak holding the tray while Rachel dug out her camera. The first of the three keys Alia had given Khattak unlocked the main door of one section of the warehouse. Khattak read out numbers until they came to the locker marked '114'.

'What is it, sir?' Rachel asked when he paused by the locker number.

'Mohsin had a taste for symbolism; it must be why he chose this locker. There are one hundred and fourteen chapters in the Qur'an.'

Setting down the cardboard tray, Khattak tried each of the two remaining keys. The second one turned in the lock. He rolled up the orange door of the locker.

And then it occurred to him, too late, to check for security cameras. What if Ashkouri or someone from his camp was watching the locker? Or Ciprian Coale?

He scanned possible locations for a camera. Nothing seemed out of place, and there was no laptop or desktop computer inside the locker, a possible precaution Mohsin had taken, preventing access through a webcam.

The locker housed an office chair, a desk, and a vintage manual typewriter.

A small lamp on the desk was plugged into the unit's electric socket by means of an extension cord. Behind the desk were metal bookshelves crammed with technical manuals, the rows numbered 1 to 20.

Khattak examined the desk without touching anything, listening to the click of Rachel's camera. They were wearing gloves, careful not to disturb the scene any more than necessary.

Khattak flicked on the lamp, flooding the desk with a halo of light.

There was a sheet of paper in the typewriter.

Two short sentences had been typed in faded ink.

We are men in the sun. We will show you the proof of it.

'Is that a threat of some kind, sir? A warning about the bomb plot?'

'I don't think so, Rachel.'

Khattak looked at her for long minutes, his mind following several tracks at once. Rachel waited without speaking. She retrieved her cooling coffee and sipped it, puzzling over the sheet of paper in the typewriter. Absentmindedly, she ate the second donut, this one a chocolate dip.

When she'd finished her coffee, she asked, 'Why not?'

Khattak studied Alia's keys, taking note of the desk's locked drawers. He touched the keys of the typewriter with his gloved hands, a finger pressed to the letter 'M'.

'Because I think it's a message for me.'

Rachel watched him try Alia Dar's keys in the drawers, unaccountably nervous. She couldn't shake the feeling that someone knew of their presence at the locker. She glanced around, but the passageway was empty. She moved closer to Khattak, peering over his shoulder.

There was a stack of unused paper in the top drawer. The second held a plain envelope that contained a single item: a penciled-in list of math problems, with many of the equations crossed out and begun again. There were small notations beside the penciled ratios.

ANFO.

ANNM.

Rachel's heart thumped with excitement. She crumpled up the Tim Hortons' bag.

'I know what this is, sir.'

Khattak nodded.

ANFO, or AN/FO, was something they both knew well.

Ammonium nitrate mixed with fuel oil.

The key component in a fertilizer bomb.

Khattak drank his coffee, reading the list of calculations.

If ANFO was ammonium nitrate/fuel oil, ANNM was its more

sophisticated variant, with nitromethane as the fuel ingredient. The explosive properties of ammonium nitrate were realized by adding fuel in a precisely measured ratio. A detonator that generated sufficient energy completed the necessary components of the bomb.

Mohsin – or one of his partners – had scrawled six words at the end of the list, words that filled Khattak with worry.

It's time to switch it up.

Switch what up? The date of the strike, or the bomb-making ingredients?

Rachel asked the question at the forefront of both their minds.

'Just whose side was Mohsin Dar on?'

Khattak looked around the storage locker.

'This can't be everything,' he said. 'There has to be something else.'

He examined one of the metal bookshelves, Rachel took the other, checking each of the numbered binders carefully. Everything confirmed what Alia Dar had described – Mohsin's interest in computer programming, his dabbling.

'This is like another language,' Rachel said, paging through the manuals. 'Besides, if there was anything here, INSET probably already has it.'

Khattak shook his head. The typewritten message meant something; so did the number of the locker. He looked at the rows of binders, taking out the fourteenth binder in the first row again: 1–14. He read each page closely, in case Mohsin had left a coded message.

'I thought the number might mean something,' he said, passing the binder to Rachel. She checked it as well. The page numbered 114 was a set of instructions on programming in Java that continued from the preceding pages.

She shoved the binder back into place, and as she did so she heard a small click. With a frown, she retrieved the binder, this time setting it down on the desk with a thud. The click sounded again. Moving the typewriter aside, she opened the binder and laid it flat on the desk. Then she tilted it up and checked the metal spine. There was a tiny gap between the metal spine and the plastic cover of the binder. She shook it and heard a slipping sound.

'There's something there, sir, you were right. But I can't quite reach it with my fingers.'

She passed the binder back to him, and this time Esa tried. By a combination of shaking the spine and sliding his fingers through the tiny opening, he was just able to touch the outline of a plastic square.

He tipped the binder upside down, and the square slid into his fingers.

He held it up in the dim light of the storage locker.

It was the memory card from a digital camera.

Rachel stared at it, thrilled. It wasn't the most sophisticated hiding place, but it had taken Khattak's insight into Mohsin to find it.

'My laptop's in the car.'

When she'd brought it to the locker and booted it up, the screen saver flared to life. It was a photograph of Zachary taken with friends in the Austrian Alps. He was making a peace sign, not quite able to disguise his sense of awe at his surroundings. Rachel cleared the screen before Khattak could say anything. She slid the memory card into her laptop's SD slot and clicked to open the files on the card. The files were password-protected.

They tried a few different options. Mohsin's name, Alia's name, the two names together, Mohsin's name and birth date. Finally, Khattak typed in Mohsin's initials, followed by the number of the locker: MD114.

A dozen photographs sprang up on Rachel's screen.

Each one showed a dwelling destroyed by a bomb attack, the

street and neighborhood in ruins: mangled vehicles, gaping brick walls, craters in the tarmac, blood running into gutters.

'What is this?' Rachel asked. '*Where* is this?'

Khattak pointed to the last photograph. Rachel pulled it up on her screen.

It was a photograph taken at Baghdad International Airport. Two men were hugging each other in an emotional greeting or farewell. The man whose face was to the camera was elderly, tears streaming down his face into a grizzled beard.

The other man's back was to the camera.

'That may be Hassan Ashkouri.'

When they had replaced the binder without finding anything more, Khattak called Coale to tell him of the discovery. Coale dismissed it in a few succinct phrases.

'We know about it, it doesn't matter. Leave the scene as it is.'

What Coale didn't share was whether Ashkouri or other members of his cell knew about the locker or its contents, or who the message in the typewriter may have been directed at. Khattak sounded a note of caution about the interception of the fertilizer.

'Maybe Ashkouri is onto you. You should let the superintendent know.'

'Of course I missed that, Khattak.' Coale's tone was derisive. 'Now stay the hell away from my operation, because I won't tell you again.'

He shut off the call without giving Esa a chance to respond.

In the background, Rachel cleared her throat.

'You told him about the photographs but you didn't tell him you think the message is for you.'

'Coale doesn't want to know.'

Rachel looked at him hopefully. 'But I do, sir.'

The storage locker was colder than the parking lot outside. They walked back to their cars, Rachel sliding into Khattak's BMW with a flutter of anxiety. She didn't like the effect that the call to Coale had had on Khattak – she hadn't seen him speak so carefully before, each word measured, holding his opinions in check, not meeting her eyes as he spoke.

'So what do you know that I don't?' she asked without preamble. 'What can you tell me about the photographs?'

'The typewritten message is more important. It tells us why the photographs matter.'

Khattak searched for a name on his phone, then passed the results over to Rachel. He waited until she had read the screen.

'*Men in the Sun* is the name of perhaps the most well-known Palestinian novel of all time. It's a story about the harshness of exile. The protagonists are desperate to earn their livelihood in Kuwait. They pay a smuggler to take them across the desert inside an empty water tank. By the time their transport crosses the border, the men in the tank are dead – defeated by petty bureaucracy and a lack of human compassion.'

Rachel passed back the phone.

'That's not a happy story.'

Khattak stared out the window, thinking.

'Mohsin used to say that the story of Palestinian exile was the most tragic one of our times – dispossession, statelessness, the denial of the right to return. An endless cycle of suffering and violence, the diary of a Palestinian wound, the diary of a Nakba.'

The way Khattak said it reminded Rachel of their work on the Drayton investigation. He was quoting Mohsin Dar, but he sounded as if his sympathies were engaged.

She wondered if she would ever understand the complex nature of Esa Khattak's identity.

She didn't have the nerve to raise the issue in his car.

'So this ties in to the Nakba plot?' she asked instead. 'Mohsin and his group want revenge for Palestinian suffering? Then how is this message for you?'

Khattak pondered the search result on his phone.

'I think he wrote the message in such a way that it could be read as his commitment to the Nakba plot. But he knew it would have a different meaning for me.' His voice was somber. 'When we were at university together, Mohsin and I participated in a theater production. We mounted *Men in the Sun* as a play.'

The idea of a young Esa Khattak playing a part on stage fascinated Rachel.

But she drew a different conclusion from the message than he did.

We will show you the proof of it.

What if Mohsin had fallen for the plot?

'Where do the photos fit in? Why did Mohsin leave them for you?'

Khattak reached over to remove a bit of chocolate from Rachel's hair. Flustered, she fumbled in her pockets for a napkin.

'Sorry, sir. I eat like I breathe – like it's my last chance.'

If she was hoping to make him smile, it didn't work.

'People suffer, people die,' he answered. 'I think Mohsin wanted me to understand how personally Ashkouri was affected by the destruction of Baghdad. He may have gotten these photos from Ashkouri – Ashkouri might have been using them for recruitment purposes. They're powerful, because they tell his story in a way that anyone would sympathize with. But Mohsin would have seen something else. The pictures tell us about Ashkouri's pain, and perhaps they tell us how determined he is to inflict that pain on someone else.'

'What do you mean?' Rachel asked.

'"We are men in the sun",' Khattak quoted. '"We will show you the proof in time."'

9

RACHEL DROVE DOWN THE CHARMING Main Street of the village of Unionville, a part of the greater Toronto area she rarely visited. Founded in 1794, with quaint signposts at regular intervals, the village had been settled well before Confederation, and was older than the nation of Canada itself. It reminded her of the township of Waverley, where she and Khattak had worked their first case, the murder of a young woman named Miraj Siddiqui. Old Unionville had the same small-town charm, with the sense of having receded from winter.

The little shops huddled together in the cold, a cascade of snow gilding the flanks of the pretty town gazebo. As Rachel's car bumped over the railway tracks near the planing mill, she stopped before the Old Firehall Confectionery. With her instinctive habit of observation, she noticed that people were carrying their steaming-hot cups of coffee into the confectionery from the coffee shop next door to it, rather than the other way around.

Ice cream instead of coffee, she mused. That wouldn't sell in December. Gourmet fudge and tartlets might, however. Everyone who came out of the red-brick building was carrying a small cardboard box tied with a gold ribbon. Rachel's stomach began to protest in response. A quick stop wouldn't hurt, but it would mean she'd miss the afternoon prayer, and her chance to observe and blend in without drawing too much attention to herself. She'd have to satisfy her cravings another time.

She drove past the Frederick Horsman Varley Art Gallery, with its single narrow steeple, and made the turnoff to Toogood Pond. The pond was frozen over. Young skaters raced one another over its rutted surface, small bits of color against the white glass, a perfect mirror of winter snowfall.

Rachel sighed with pleasure. It was going to be a wonderful season.

And there at the far end of the pond was a large two-story house in daffodil yellow with freshly painted gables in blue. She parked on the road and trudged through the snow to the front door. A discreet notice above the door identified the building as the Masjid un-Nur. Otherwise, it looked much the same as the other houses gathered around the pond.

When she tried the door, she found it unlocked. She entered into an overheated space, and immediately her breath began to steam. She divested herself of coat, scarf, and gloves and dumped her boots on a nearby rack.

The foyer had been transformed into a reception area, with a desk, shoe caddies, coatracks, and several portable bulletin boards. The room was empty save for a woman of indeterminate age seated behind the desk. Her smooth round face was settled in folds of fat. Her striking blue eyes were sunk beneath a pair of heavy eyebrows that if left to themselves would have met in the middle. An expression of permanent dissatisfaction marred what would otherwise have been a pleasant face. The woman was dressed in a long beige gown that matched the headscarf wound tightly about her skull, sealing off her cheeks and forehead.

Rachel toyed with the headscarf in her hands. Her uncertain manner was only partly a projection of the role she had come here to play. She felt uncertain, and more than a little anxious that no action she undertook at the Nur mosque should undermine the INSET operation. She recognized the woman seated at the desk from the photographs Khattak had shown her. The woman's name was Paula Kyriakou. She was one of the two women who had attended the winter camp with Mohsin Dar. From her surly expression, she did not appear to be grieving.

'Did I miss the prayer?' Rachel asked, checking her watch.

'Prayer should never be rushed,' the other woman said repressively. 'Head to the landing upstairs.' And then as if Rachel had offered a criticism, she said, 'We don't need a bigger space for the sisters. Hardly anyone comes midweek. If there's a crowd, of course we share the downstairs space.'

Rachel was quick to appease her. 'I wouldn't know anything about that.' She tried a smile. 'I'm new and I'm kind of – just figuring things out. I'm a bit lost, so don't mind if I get a few things wrong.'

So much for *dawah*. Paula eyed her with an expression that Rachel found decidedly unwelcoming.

'New to the mosque, or new to Islam?' she demanded.

'Both.'

Rachel held up the headscarf. 'I'm not even sure how to wear this.'

Paula came around the desk and seized the scarf from Rachel. Without asking permission, she tied it deftly around Rachel's face, tight enough that it bit into Rachel's chin and forehead. It was stifling.

'Next time, make sure you are wearing it before you enter the mosque.' And then she recognized the pattern on Rachel's scarf as the blue-and-white logo of the Maple Leafs, Rachel's favorite hockey team. 'When you pray to God, you should not be distracted by the presence of worldly idols.'

'I'm sorry,' Rachel said. 'I didn't know that.'

She wondered at Paula's attitude. Had she genuinely been a newcomer to Islam, she would have found the restrictive rules and the receptionist's hostile approach enough to make her turn around and walk back out the door.

Then again, religion had no place in Rachel's life. And it would definitely have no place if it meant she had to give up her hockey team. There was nothing she prayed for more than for the star-crossed Leafs to make it to the playoffs. The Stanley Cup was just a pipe dream at this point. The playoffs would be ecstasy enough.

A smirk on her lips, she followed Paula up the stairs to the second-story landing. She couldn't help but notice that despite the fact that Paula was a sturdy woman, several inches shorter than Rachel, her movements were nimble and quick. The thick material of her all-encompassing gown did not disguise the fact that her body was curved and well proportioned.

She looked strong.

But then how strong did one have to be to shoot an unarmed man in the woods at close range?

The landing faced over a large salon attached to a kitchen half its size. There was no furniture in the salon. Five or six long, slender carpets were laid out in rows on the floor.

Rachel could hear the shrieks from the pond. The windows of the salon overlooked Toogood Pond. If the blinds had been left open, the prayer hall would have been swamped with light. Instead, the windows were shuttered, leaving the main floor cool and empty.

Men began to gather in the hall. On the upper landing, there was only one other person, an undernourished girl dressed in ripped black leggings, with an oversized jersey thrown over them. The logo of a music group was slashed against the front of the jersey in bold red letters: 'BAD RELIGION'.

From the girl's scowling face, it wasn't meant to be ironic.

Her headscarf was the merest fiction above her head. Most of her blazing magenta hair was exposed. It fell in short, choppy waves to her shoulders. The girl's throat was tattooed with a symbol so menacing that Rachel took a step back. It was a death head set above a pair of crossed swords, its forehead bound by a black banner. In the center of the banner was a single white star. The skull's bony teeth were bared. Embedded in the teeth was a ring of silver staples.

The girl's watery eyes were heavily lined and shadowed.

Beneath the dark smudges of her eyes, cold bits of metal licked against her skin. Both of her nostrils were pierced with small rings. Her cheeks, chin, and eyebrows were studded with a succession of steel bolts. Only her lips were unpierced. It was as if she had done everything she could think of to ruin a perfect complexion. In the unmarked areas of her face, her skin was as thick and creamy as the petals of a camellia.

Catching Rachel's attention, Paula said, 'That's Gracie. Don't be frightened of her. She's another one who's just figuring things out.'

'Shut up, Paula. And don't call me Gracie.'

If Rachel estimated Paula's age as somewhere in her early thirties, she would guess at Grace's as seventeen or younger. Not that she needed to guess at either. She had expected to meet Paula and Grace at the mosque today. Both had been at the camp with Mohsin Dar. And both had been comprehensively evaluated by INSET.

Looking at Grace, she was appalled at what the girl had done to herself. Political correctness and a general acceptance of youth culture would decree that Grace was an individual whose style of self-expression had to be respected. But Rachel didn't buy it for a second. Whether it was an unfair judgment or not, Rachel was a police officer who had spent years searching for a lost boy on the streets. What she had learned was that that kind of mutilation on the outside often reflected much greater damage within. And even if her own gut instinct hadn't told her as much, the INSET file on Grace Kaspernak revealed that she'd spent her life in foster care, until she'd dropped out of school and run away from home.

Grace had been living on the streets until she'd become a congregant at Masjid un-Nur, drawn to its ranks by her classmate, Dinaase Abdi. Dinaase Abdi was under surveillance as another attendee of the camp at Algonquin.

Rachel had made note of the fact that Grace Kaspernak had dropped out of school only after Abdi had done so. It appeared she had followed her friend and classmate to Masjid un-Nur.

'I'm Rachel,' she said to the others. 'Rachel Ellison.'

'Ellison' was her mother's maiden name, which was as far as she had gone in establishing her cover. Rachel possessed little previous undercover experience. She was meant to dig around without talking about herself except when it was essential to do so.

Paula shrugged, paying no attention.

Grace said, 'So what?'

The call to prayer sounded in the hall, a muffled recording that barely reached the upstairs landing. The men below them assembled in two lines behind the imam.

Paula and Grace took their places at the front of the landing, looking down upon the hall. As soon as a lanky black boy shuffled his way into the hall, Grace appeared to relax. The hands that were clenched at her sides smoothed out to knock against her scrawny legs.

Paula was still tense, her eyes casting about this way and that. Whoever she was looking for, she didn't find. She turned on her heel and vanished back down the landing. Rachel took a tentative step toward Grace. She had counted on following Paula's lead when it came to the congregational prayer. Now she'd have to rely upon Grace instead.

'Um – I don't really know how to do this.'

Grace kept her eyes on the boy in the hall.

'Why is that my problem?'

Rachel cleared her throat. Grace's rancor unnerved her a little.

'It's not, I guess. I'd just heard that Nur was – a less threatening place for newcomers. Like it wouldn't be as hard to fit in here.'

Grace Kaspernak spared Rachel a glance. Either her pale eyes were colorless, or it was the effect of the makeup she wore, over-powering her physical characteristics. Grace fingered the staples in her neck.

'Maybe,' she said.

The prayer had begun.

'Just do what I do, and if I screw up like I usually do, just copy whatever they're doing.'

From Grace's expression, Rachel was hardly worth a moment's consideration. Yet something about Rachel's comment on fitting in must have struck her because she unbent a little more. 'Do you speak Arabic at all? If you don't, you'll be even less welcome here.'

She fell into the movements of the prayer and Rachel copied her, standing at Grace's shoulder. She stood tall, bent over her knees, and genuflected as Grace did. Up and down several times, until the motions became familiar. As Rachel touched her forehead to the floor and breathed in the dusty carpet, she stifled the impulse to cough. When it was finished, she mimicked Grace's gesture of raising her cupped hands in the air.

Grace's technique was sloppy compared with that of the boy Rachel was watching in the hall below: Dinaase Abdi, whose parents had come to Canada from Somalia as immigrants, blue-collar workers whose lives consisted of family and community. Nur was not their mosque. Nor was there evidence of neglect inside the family home. Both parents worked several jobs to support the family, but their absence from the home couldn't have been equated with neglect.

It was survival, the kind that attested to love. The chance to pave the way so the next generation could aspire to something better. Dinaase's parents were based in Etobicoke, close to the Dejinta Beesha, the multiservice center that served a large Somali community. Nur was as far from that center as Dinaase could have chosen. He was the eldest of five siblings, and had been in Canada since his earliest childhood.

Why he would choose Nur, and its smaller, more fractured religious community, Rachel couldn't guess. Unlike Grace Kaspernak, he was at ease in his surroundings. The motions of his prayer were fluid and natural – he sat back upon his heels with ease, turned his head side to side in an effortless rhythm.

And then stretched his long limbs out at the end of it, bouncing to his feet, clapping the other men on their backs, smiling throughout.

He didn't glance up at the women's prayer section. Several of the other men did, frowning when they saw that Grace was leaning over the balcony for a better view.

'Why don't you just go downstairs?' Rachel asked her. 'Is that your boyfriend?'

'No.' Grace's denial came out like a snarl. And carried an undercurrent of surprise. This was a girl who wasn't used to thinking of herself as attractive or capable of drawing a young man's interest. She yanked her headscarf down from her head, revealing that the magenta waves of her hair didn't extend to the back of her skull, which was shaved bald and studded with another set of bolts. They descended down the back of her skull like the links of a railway track. The areas around several of the bolts were red and inflamed.

Rachel bit back the oath that would have expressed her alarm, thankful that the back of the girl's skull wasn't as demonically tattooed as her neck.

'What?' Grace said, widening the black smudges of her eyes. 'You don't like it?' Her tone was nasty, dismissive.

Rachel unfastened her headscarf with more care than Grace had shown, grateful that she could breathe again. She looked over the railing at the boy Grace hadn't taken her eyes from.

'It's not that,' Rachel said. 'I mean – live and let live, right? It's just – does he like it? The boy who's not your boyfriend?'

And as she said it, she reflected upon Dinaase Abdi's age. According to the INSET file, Dinaase would turn eighteen in January. He was a confirmed member of Hassan Ashkouri's cell. If the INSET operation went as planned over the next two weeks, the boy would not be charged as an adult. Assuming he was arrested. If the tactical operation were delayed for any reason, Dinaase Abdi's unmarred future would change for good.

'I don't dress to impress any man,' Grace said. 'Neither do you, right?'

A sarcastic comment on the baggy pants and baggier tunic Rachel had hoped would resemble mosque-attending attire. But she hadn't dressed that differently than she usually did, despite the athletic figure beneath the ill-fitting clothes. For reasons different from Grace's, Rachel hadn't made much effort with her appearance. The condo was her first step in a new direction. Maybe later she'd have time to think of herself as a woman, and not just a police officer.

Grace pushed past her, giving Rachel a clear view of the back of her jersey.

The words 'ANGRY FEMINIST' were stamped on the black shirt, this time in white letters that appeared to bleed down her back.

'Hurry up,' she threw over her shoulder. 'They serve refreshments down in the kitchen. If you're lucky, you might get to meet Hassan on your first day.'

Somewhat friendly overtures from a girl who didn't appear friendly at all.

Rachel followed at a slower pace, wondering what had become of Paula.

In the main salon, twenty or so men were milling about chatting, while a handful of older women were busy setting up snacks in the small, updated kitchen. Paula was at the sink, filling a kettle with water.

She glared at Rachel's bare head.

'You're meant to keep that on in the mosque at all times,' she said, just as Grace muttered under her breath, 'Ignore her.'

Halfheartedly, Rachel pulled the Maple Leafs scarf back up. Grace moved to the stove, stirring a small saucepan that contained a vivid, aromatic mixture spiced with cinnamon and cardamom seeds. When the liquid had thickened, she poured it into a crystal tea glass rimmed with gold and placed it in a saucer. Her eyes scanned the group of men in the prayer hall.

Paula wasn't done. The kettle dispensed with, she turned her full attention to Rachel.

'If you're really here to learn about Islam, Gracie isn't the best example to follow.' Her blue eyes made a scorching assessment of the younger girl's appearance that Grace Kaspernak ignored. Maybe because she was used to it.

Paula's indictment didn't bother Rachel. What was worrisome was her use of the phrase *If you're really here to learn about Islam.* Why had she said such a thing? Had Rachel's behavior aroused her suspicions already?

Another voice spoke from behind Rachel's head.

'My dear sister Paula, if anyone knows how to make newcomers welcome at Nur, surely it has to be you.'

The voice was beautiful. It carried the faintest trace of an Arabic accent.

Paula was suddenly beaming, her face seized by a joy so rapturous that she became almost pretty. Her blue eyes shone. For a moment she couldn't speak.

Rachel turned around to meet the owner of the voice.

He was shaking hands with everyone who crossed his path. Even Grace paused to give him a grimace of a greeting. The man's own smile was generous in turn. He touched the crystal tea glass, then lightly tapped Grace's nose.

'It smells divine.' He winked at Grace as he said it. 'I can't believe Dinaase hasn't come running to you.'

Paula's smile began to fade.

'Have it, if you want.' The words were ungrudging, but the man took a step to the side, as Dinaase Abdi approached.

'Take the qahwe you make with your own hands for Dinaase? I'm not such a terrible interloper as that. Din, come on. It's hot and ready.' He made the name sound like 'Dean'. And then he focused on Rachel.

'Assalam u alaikum, sister,' he said. 'Welcome to Masjid un-Nur.'

He was the handsomest man Rachel had ever seen, possessed of every known physical grace. A lean and supple physique. Slim, elegant hands. Midnight-dark eyes tilted in a symmetrical face, the broad, smooth forehead balanced by the line of his jaw. Thick, curly hair in abundance. Eyebrows winged accents against an olive skin.

There was warmth and laughter and compassion in that face, just as the eyes seemed to glow with a secret awareness.

It was the enigmatic face of a poet anchored by something richer and deeper – a thorough and certain knowledge of himself.

No wonder Paula was starstruck.

Rachel cleared her throat. 'Wa alaikum salam,' she said, trying the words out. She had practiced with Khattak. From the warm smiles all around, her pronunciation seemed to hold up.

She waited to see if the man would offer his hand, because she knew that handshakes between the sexes could be political. They pegged you to a specific place on the spectrum of conservatism. A man who refused to shake a woman's hand would have strict views about gender segregation and the place of women in the mosque.

Ashkouri shook her hand, his handshake cool and firm.

'Hassan Ashkouri,' he said. 'Am I right in thinking I haven't seen you here before?'

'It's my first time,' she said, then introduced herself. He was still holding her hand. She was appalled to feel herself blushing a little. She looked down at the floor, thinking that this might be some approximation of how a modest Muslim woman would behave under these circumstances.

Paula Kyriakou stepped right between Rachel and Hassan, edging close into his space, latching on to his arm.

Wrong again, Rachel thought. Modesty wasn't what it used to be.

'You missed prayer, Hassan.'

There was a possessiveness about Paula's manner that she didn't trouble to disguise. If her grip was painful, Hassan Ashkouri gave no sign of it. His face was even more beautiful when he smiled.

'You remembered me in your *duas*, I hope.'

'You know that I never forget you.' She went on to list the precise nature of the supplications she had made on Ashkouri's behalf.

As tiresome as Rachel may have found Paula's recital, there was a genuine warmth in the way that Ashkouri attended to it. His eyes flicked to Rachel.

'I hope you remembered Mohsin as well.'

Someone in the group of people drifting through the kitchen went still.

An eerie, listening stillness.

Rachel tried to pinpoint the source without giving away her reaction.

It was Rachel whom Ashkouri had meant to test.

But someone else had fallen into the trap.

Rachel contrived an expression of mild puzzlement, waiting for someone to speak. Paula hurried to fill the silence, bustling about to make Ashkouri a cup of tea. A tall man in his sixties with a full beard and a woven kufi came to stand on the other side of the island. He snapped his fingers at Paula, who passed him the first cup of tea.

'I prayed for Mohsin. Imam Zikri made the supplication, and I recited the prayer of Yasin afterward.'

When? Rachel wondered. Paula had missed the prayer altogether. She now suspected that what had drawn Paula away was Ashkouri's absence. Paula must have gone to search for him.

With that face, small wonder.

But would the woman dare to tell such a bald-faced lie in the mosque? When either Rachel or Grace could expose the lie for what it was?

Rachel caught Grace's eye. Grace had splayed her hands at the bottom of her shirt, her fingers pointing upward.

Bad religion, Rachel read again. She almost laughed out loud.

'You are always dutiful, Paula. No one could fault you. But Grace here –' Ashkouri bestowed his bone-melting smile on the girl, who still held the glass in its saucer. 'When there's a woman to make qahwe for me, the way Gracie does for Din, I'll know that Allah has answered my prayers.'

Grace didn't protest at Ashkouri's use of her nickname, as she had done with Paula. She gave the glass to Dinaase Abdi, who took it without thanking her. Like two of the other young men on Rachel's list of members of the training camp, his attention was on Ashkouri.

Rachel would have found the whole thing cultlike were it not for Ashkouri's remarkable face. The INSET photographs had not done him justice.

And then another thought occurred to her.

If Ashkouri was the leader of a terror cell whose base was the Nur mosque – why was he clean-shaven? Was his vanity a greater calling than religion? Or was she generalizing her idea of what a Muslim male should look like? Khattak was clean-shaven too, for that matter. But Khattak wasn't a violent extremist masterminding a lethal attack on New Year's Day.

Rachel helped herself to a small piece of baklava from one of the snack plates. She could feel Ashkouri's eyes on her back. She ignored the man who had snapped his fingers at Paula. The man's name was Jamshed Ali. He was another of Ashkouri's proven confederates. Instead, she asked one of the older women if she could help herself to a cup of tea.

Ashkouri interrupted her.

'What brings you to the mosque, sister?'

Paula answered for her, unexpectedly helpful. 'She's like Gracie, Hassan. She's trying to find herself.'

Ashkouri pinned Rachel with his boundless, dark eyes.

'The Masjid un-Nur is a difficult place to locate, even for those who know what they are searching for. How did you stumble upon it?'

Rachel felt that stillness seize the room again. And again she failed to identify its source. She kept her eyes from Jamshed Ali and Dinaase Abdi with an effort. Standing behind them were Zakaria Aboud and Sami Dardas, also on the list. This was her moment to convince Ashkouri of her status as a hapless outsider – or to blow the operation sky-high.

She took another bite of the baklava.

'One of the sisters at Middlefield mentioned this place, said it was much quieter for someone who was new. She said you conduct proper study sessions here. I don't live far, so I thought I'd give it a try.' She pushed her hair under her scarf, the movement clumsy. 'If it's not – is it open to the public? Did I just barge my way in?'

When no one answered her, she set her plate down on the counter and brushed her hands against her trousers. 'Shoot, I'm sorry.' She swept crumbs from her scarf. 'When you're new, you don't get anything right. I'd better go.'

She shouldered her way past Grace and Paula, feeling the tension in the hall dissipate a little. From the corner of her eye, she saw Ashkouri's quick glance at Jamshed.

Ashkouri placed a graceful hand on Rachel's arm, halting her progress.

'Sister Rachel,' he said. 'In God's house, everyone is welcome. There are no gatekeepers to keep you from whatever it is you seek to learn here.' Paula's hand was still fastened onto his arm. 'Isn't that so, Paula?'

Paula struggled to disguise her displeasure at his unwanted invitation.

'As you wish, Hassan. Whatever you wish.'

Rachel caught Ashkouri's discreet nod at Jamshed.

'If you'd like, you may join our halaqa tonight. You won't find it as didactic as in other mosques, perhaps.' Ashkouri said this with a mildly tempered smile. 'We speak of poetry as much as of anything else, but what is poetry if not another path to God? Don't you think so, Rachel Ellison?'

Rachel's answering smile was hesitant.

'If you're sure I won't be in the way.'

Ashkouri shook his head, disarranging his dark curls.

'Just as you seek to learn about us, there is much we'd like to learn about you. About any new member who crosses our threshold.'

Rachel's smile faltered on her lips. She glanced quickly at the four men who had been at the training camp with Mohsin.

Unlike the group of worshippers basking in the glow of Hassan Ashkouri's mystique, she knew he meant the words as a threat.

10

KHATTAK TURNED HIS KEY IN the lock and let himself in. The family home was in Forest Hill, not far from the boys' college where he had spent his youth with Nathan Clare. The girls' school his sisters had attended was also within walking distance, hallmarks of a privileged childhood. His mother spent the winters in Peshawar. His sisters lived in the family home, a space he shared when his mother was away, a fact that Ruksh sometimes quarreled with. Misbah, on the other hand, would look at him with compassion, and whisper to Ruksh that Esa was lonely.

It was late afternoon, and the house was cold.

He could hear his sisters' voices in one of the upstairs bedrooms. He took the stairs two at a time, not pausing to reflect upon how to approach Rukshanda, the older of his two sisters, the one guaranteed to disagree with any suggestion he offered.

Ciprian Coale's words still rankled, as did the easy superiority behind them suggesting that Coale knew Khattak's family better than Esa did. Coale had wanted to get under his skin – Esa would be a fool to let him. But the questions remained: had Esa been so immersed in the Drayton scandal that he hadn't noticed his sister was wearing an engagement ring? Would Ruksh have taken such a step without consulting him?

He knew it couldn't be coincidence. If Ashkouri had found a way to ensnare Esa's sister, knowing who Esa was, it would be part of his design, somehow connected to the Nakba plot.

He knocked on the door of their mother's room. His sisters didn't notice him at first. Ruksh and Misbah were bent over the king-size

84

bed, removing colorful fabrics from their plastic sheeting. On one side of the bed, books and magazines were stacked in a haphazard pile. A dozen of these were wedding magazines: *Modern Bride*, *The Knot*, *Kismet*, *Asiana*. And one peeking out of the stack that Khattak had never heard of: *Lavish Dulhan*.

He took a breath. Ruksh's ring finger was bare. He wasn't the world's most absentminded detective after all. But if Coale had been exaggerating, it wasn't by much. The clothes on the bed were wedding silks – in red, Persian green, and royal blue.

In that moment, he felt the keenness of his sister's peril.

What was Ashkouri's real interest in Ruksh? How was he planning to use her?

Misbah glanced up and saw him, her smile bright and welcoming. But Ruksh was startled, a guilty thing surprised.

Khattak was never home at this time of day. And both of his sisters should have been out, Ruksh at her residency in epidemiology, Misbah at university, studying for her final exams. Instead, they were ensconced in their mother's room, cheerfully picking out wedding clothes.

Whose wedding? When was it to take place? And most of all, who was Ruksh thinking of marrying?

Khattak's habitual warmth with his sisters was beyond him at this moment.

'Would you leave us please, Misbah?'

An apprehensive glance passed between the sisters.

And in that moment Khattak saw that they were not as dissimilar as he had always supposed. Ruksh was younger than him by a decade, Misbah by an additional five years. Ruksh resembled Khattak in physical appearance, if not in temperament – dark-haired, green-eyed, pale-skinned, her striking features made more dramatic by her volatile personality. Misbah was quiet like Khattak, reserved in judgment and pronouncement, less obviously Pathan in coloring, small, dark, and slight, with an ever-present warmth that brought Khattak's mother to mind.

When Misbah was around, he missed his mother less.

Now, in the glance that passed between his sisters, Khattak found a surprising familiarity between them. In the normal course of things, Ruksh had little time for Misbah. Her true sisterly attachment was to Nathan's younger sister, Audrey Clare. Audrey and Ruksh were the same age, they had attended the Bishop Strachan girls' school together, and they still passed most free weekends in each other's company.

Misbah was the afterthought, the late addition to the family, amiable and innocent, indulged and then forgotten by both her older siblings. Left to her own devices, Misbah had chosen to pursue a career in international development studies. Ruksh was the only one of the three siblings to follow the well-traveled family footsteps into medicine. She was bright and impatient, possessed of an overweening ambition.

'Don't dismiss Misbah like a child. She can think for herself.'

As was so often the case, Esa saw that his interaction with Ruksh was destined to be fractious. He nodded at Misbah, knowing which of her siblings Misbah would choose to obey.

She shut the door to their mother's room, unaccustomed to making demands of them.

Khattak moved to the bed, capturing the slippery red silk between his fingers.

'What is this, Ruksh?'

'Why ask if you know the answer?' She was already angry, and Khattak had been in the room less than five minutes.

'Because I'd like to know it from you.'

'I'm not one of your suspects, Esa. You don't get to trick me into a confession.'

Khattak pushed the fabrics aside, making a space for himself on the bed.

Weighing his words, he asked her, 'Do you have anything you need to confess?'

A slight smile touched the corner of his mouth. With her arms crossed in front of her, and her hair pulled back in a ponytail, his sister reminded him of the much younger Ruksh who would follow him and Nate around, getting into scrapes that required his intercession without damaging her pride. A wave of tenderness washed over him.

'These look like wedding fabrics,' he said, wishing he could let Ruksh tell him in her own time. 'Have you met someone? Are you thinking of getting married?'

'Have you been spying on me?' she asked at once.

And how could he answer that?

I haven't been, but you're caught up in an antiterrorism investigation. Do you know anything about that?

Coale had warned him that Ruksh was under surveillance. Whether that meant electronic surveillance of the Khattak home, or of Ruksh's phone calls and daily routine, he couldn't be certain. And Coale would take a specific perverse pleasure in denying him access to that information on national security grounds.

He wasn't spying on his sister. He had never thought to spy on her. It was Ashkouri he needed to watch, Ashkouri whose motives could only be sinister.

But Ruksh would have no idea of this. Her reluctance to confide in Esa was based on her first failed engagement.

'I'm not spying on you, Ruksh. But if you're thinking of getting married, that's obviously of interest to me.'

'No.' She shook her head. 'You're not acting like my brother, you're using your detective voice. And I don't need Inspector Esa Khattak in this room.'

She pushed a bolt of lavender silk away from her. It slid from the bed to the floor. When Khattak moved to recapture it, she blocked his attempt to help. He reached for his sister's hand and held it, turning it palm up.

'What is it, Ruksh? Why are you so angry? Shouldn't this be a time of happiness for you?'

She jerked her hand away.

'As if you don't know. As if you don't remember what you did.'

Khattak stood up. He rubbed a hand across his brow in a gesture that Ruksh imitated without realizing she was doing so.

'Would you have preferred to remain in ignorance? Wouldn't you have blamed me more if I had let you marry a man in love with someone else?'

Ruksh had been twenty-two the first time she had decided, on impulse, to marry a man she had met at school.

He'd shared the same background, faith, and culture. He'd also been dating an Irish-American student in an ongoing cross-border affair.

At twenty-two, Ruksh hadn't wanted to know.

Khattak had hoped that time would mature his sister, lessening the pain of that early betrayal. He hadn't expected that she would still blame him so many years later.

She rushed in to defend herself.

'It's not what he did, or the fact that I was young and stupid. It's what you did, investigating him. I never asked you to do that.'

To this day, Ruksh didn't believe that Esa had simply stumbled upon her fiancé with his other girlfriend. Esa had accepted the anger and the blame, knowing that Ruksh needed an outlet that wouldn't hurt quite as much.

Her brother was a safe target because Esa would always love her.

Though sometimes, he found it hard.

'Samina would have hated your chauvinist attitude.'

Khattak blanched at the mention of his wife.

'Staying at the house when Mum leaves the country, checking up on us. Samina never let you treat her that way – the all-knowing Inspector Khattak. She led you around by the nose.'

'You don't know anything about Samina,' Esa said quietly. 'What she thought of me, how she saw me. She would have expected me to be involved in your life. That's what family does.

If you're planning to be married, I would like to know. I would like to meet him.'

Ruksh had the grace to look ashamed. She sank down on the bed, sending the magazines to the floor in a slithery heap. A book of poetry appeared at the top of the pile.

Rooms Are Never Finished.

A collection of poems by the great son of Kashmir, the poet Agha Shahid Ali.

Khattak studied his sister.

'He wants to meet you, too,' she said at last. 'We haven't decided anything. We're still – just talking.' She shuffled one of the silks with her foot. 'I'm probably getting ahead of myself.'

'How did you meet?'

'At a halaqa.' Her eyes lit with excitement. 'Esa, his poetry is beautiful, transformative. You won't believe it.'

She rummaged through the pile of books until she found a loose sheet of paper. She passed it to Khattak, who read it through. The last few lines of the poem made him pause.

Reclaim me in promise
Of victory sweet.
O homeland,
O heartache,
When shall we meet?

Did Ruksh see what he saw? The poem followed a well-established tradition of Arabic poetry, conflating the personal with the political.

In this case, the markedly political.

Did the poet mean Jerusalem, the eternal homeland, the longest exile of contemporary history?

Where shall we fly when all else is lost?

Or did he mean Iraq?

A land that promised us wheat and stars.

And if it were the latter, he could no longer deny to himself that his sister was speaking of Hassan Ashkouri.

He gathered his thoughts, returned the poem to her.

'The halaqa was on poetry?'

Ruksh frowned at him. 'Not exactly. I mean, it was a proper halaqa – on theology, and historicity. It wasn't lacking in any way, if that's what you're getting at.'

It wasn't. He was intrigued by his sister's use of the word 'historicity'. In Khattak's experience, most amateur scholars of the Qur'an chose to treat it as an ahistorical text, or as a fixed articulation of principle, disconnected to seventh-century social conditions. Any attempt to make use of context to modify meaning or to extract an ethical reading of scripture from the prevailing conditions of the day was generally met with condemnation. Innovation in matters of religion was considered unlawful and destined to lead to misguidance, regardless of the poison that spilled forth in the name of purity, disguised as fidelity to the past.

Khattak had never heard of a halaqa where anything other than primary or secondary religious texts were studied – poetry was far afield. In most mosques, any mention of literature or poetry in this context would have been roundly condemned, reading beauty out of the Qur'an – an extraordinary irony for a civilization whose crossroads met at poetry, and where the Book itself was the greatest poetical expression of the language.

As much as Khattak despised the *idée fixe* of men like Ashkouri, he was also intrigued. How had Ashkouri found recruits to his cause, if he was ready to stray from the most adamantine orthodoxy? What path would he have chosen as a scholar of Islam?

'Is he Pathan?' Esa asked his sister.

She was angry at once.

'Does it matter? Are you really hung up on tribal affiliations just because you married a girl from Swat Valley?'

A girl from Swat Valley.

Samina. Gone these seven years, the loss still fresh in moments like this. Her photograph faced him on his mother's dresser. He turned his head away, trying not to think of what the last decade had brought to the people of Swat, and to himself. The Taliban ascendancy, the Pakistan army's counteroffensive, and the innocent whose bodies were littered between them. Samina's parents had refused to allow their daughter to return to visit Swat, though they had taken heart from Malala Yousafzai's courageous stand against the Taliban.

Malala's defiance had consisted of her insistence on going to school.

'Not at all. I'm just curious.'

'He's Iraqi, Esa. And someone who's more at peace with himself, I've yet to meet.'

If that were truly the case, which Khattak knew it couldn't be, he would have hoped that some of that tranquillity would have rubbed off on Rukshanda. Her words were aimed at shattering his composure. At engaging him in long-forgotten battles.

She was a strong, self-reliant woman. Yet she still felt the need to prove herself to her brother, the brother who had struck out on his own path at every opportunity. And had suffered the consequences of doing so.

Khattak quickly refocused.

'What is your poet's name?'

Ruksh looked defiant. 'Hassan Ashkouri. You don't know him.'

Would to God that he didn't. If Ruksh hadn't forgiven him over a short-lived infatuation, what would she do when he was done with Ashkouri?

He didn't know what to say to his sister. Everything he did from this point onward, she could only view as betrayal.

He couldn't tell her about the operation. And even if he disobeyed orders and told her what he knew, Ruksh was too stubborn to believe him. And much too sure of her own judgment to be swayed in the slightest by his.

He looked at the wedding clothes that had slipped from the bed to the floor, a liquid ripple of jewel tones.

'It looks as though you know what you want. How long have you known each other?'

'Quite as long as you knew Samina.'

Less than six months. Long enough for Khattak to know that he had been granted God's most generous gift. And he had been younger than Ruksh was now.

He remembered a line of Nizar Qabbani's ravishing poetry.

God gave me the rose, and them the thorn.

He felt powerless. Trapped in a web woven by Ciprian Coale. The only bit of light in it, the words Ruksh had tossed out at the beginning of the conversation.

He wants to meet you, too.

'I'd like to meet him whenever you think best.' He paused. 'Does he know about me? What I do?' Khattak's profession had kept many of his sisters' suitors at bay, but he knew that Ashkouri would have chosen Ruksh because of it.

For a moment, Ruksh's expression softened.

'Yes. Don't worry. He hasn't run screaming in the opposite direction. You're quite famous, you know.'

Khattak's smile was wry. 'I think they call that "notorious."'

Both inside the Muslim community and without.

A gifted, promising student who'd chosen the police as a career, instead of taking over his father's medical practice – followed by the promotion to head of CPS, which most members of Esa's community viewed as another surveillance tool, and a kind of betrayal.

These were no longer debates Khattak had with himself.

If he'd been in doubt, his role in the investigation of Miraj Siddiqui's death had convinced him of the value of his work. Miraj had spent her young life in pursuit of the truth, the years ahead of her rich in potential and promise. Her death had been ascribed to an honor killing – a cursory characterization that had set a small community ablaze. He had spoken for Miraj, spoken for her community – and with the help of Rachel's perseverance and insight, spoken for justice as well.

He would do no less for Mohsin Dar.

Ruksh began to scoop the clothes from the floor. She still hadn't asked Esa which of the colors he liked best. Nor would he venture an opinion.

Not for Hassan Ashkouri.

As if reading his mind, she asked him, 'Did you hear about Mohsin?'

This was the opening he'd been waiting for. He nodded.

'I've been asked to consult on the case. I'll be making an announcement at the mosque where he spent most of his time. In case anyone has information that could lead to an arrest.'

Ruksh bit her lip.

'There's something you should know, then. The halaqa where I met Hassan? It's at the same mosque. I've been spending a lot of time there. In fact, I was supposed to go to Algonquin that weekend.'

Khattak kept his face impassive. He bent to help his sister collect the fabrics.

'Were you?' he said. 'He was killed at the camp. We're trying to narrow down the pool of suspects.'

'You don't think it was a stranger? Some hunter who made a mistake and fled?'

'Not with that caliber of weapon.' His voice was bleak. 'I wouldn't have expected Mohsin to meet his end this way – to die at the hands of someone he knew.'

Ruksh dropped the fabrics back on the bed with enough force to send them to the floor again, alongside the book of poetry.

Rooms Are Never Finished.

Love is never finished, Khattak thought, glancing at the picture of Samina.

'It wasn't someone he knew,' Ruksh said with some urgency. 'And it won't be a good start to whatever relationship you're hoping to have with my fiancé if you start off by interrogating him. Hassan had nothing to do with Mo's death. No one at the camp did.'

Khattak reached for the book of poetry, avoiding his sister's gaze.

'I'll have to determine that for myself, Ruksh.'

She snatched the book from his hand, flinging it onto the bed.

'Hassan gave that to me. Mohsin is dead, Esa. What can you do about that? Why can't you leave things alone?'

'You knew him, Ruksh. He has a wife, a father. People who deserve justice. And the crime itself that must be answered for.'

'He's gone. There's nothing you can do for him. If you start digging around the mosque, making people uncomfortable, you're going to ruin everything. Not least our family name.'

And Esa found it sad that even in the midst of discussing Mohsin Dar's tragedy, Ruksh was only able to worry about herself.

He found Misbah in the kitchen, her books spread before her at the breakfast bar. Before he could say anything to her, she asked him, 'Are you upset about the engagement?'

Unlike Ruksh, she didn't focus on her own role in events, or her personal feelings. It was possible that Esa was angry at her over the secret she'd kept. Her first thought was still for him.

He slid onto the stool beside Misbah, helping himself to a handful of grapes from the crystal bowl on the counter.

'Is it an engagement? I've seen the clothes, but Ruksh said she wasn't there yet.'

Misbah quirked an eyebrow at him.

'It's not official, and you haven't answered my question.'

If he answered it, he would be lying to both of his sisters.

'I don't know that I have any right to be upset. It's not how I would have preferred to do things. If something is right, it doesn't need to be hidden. And what of our traditions? What about our mother? Does this seem like the right thing to you?'

He studied the giant portrait that hung to one side of the breakfast bar.

Each morning at his mother's house, he was greeted by the sight of his beautiful bride, gorgeously arrayed in a red-and-gold *lahenga*, while he stood at her side in a lustrous *sherwani*, a *sehra* of jasmine and roses descending from his forehead to shelter his face.

Had his face been uncovered, it would have disclosed his undiluted joy.

'You'll get the blame either way. For interfering. Or for not interfering enough.'

'Have you been attending these halaqas too? Have you met this Hassan Ashkouri?'

Misbah checked a line in her textbook before answering him. It wasn't a delaying tactic. She was preoccupied by her upcoming exams.

'No, Ruksh has never invited me. And Unionville is so far from here. Plus, when I'm at school, I never leave the campus.' She grinned at her brother. 'Just the way you like it.'

'Am I so overprotective, then?'

Misbah squeezed his hand. 'Don't worry about it. One of my friends has four older brothers, so I count myself lucky.'

Perhaps not lucky enough. For Misbah's sake, he needed to make his position clear. There was a reasonable chance that unlike Ruksh, Misbah would listen to him.

'If you haven't been to the mosque, and you haven't met Hassan yet, will you hold off for the next little while? You must have heard about Mohsin Dar. I've been asked to investigate his death. Until I can get a handle on what happened to him at Algonquin, it would be better if you stayed away. Safer for you in general – and best if you're not associated with me.'

But Misbah was looking over his shoulder. She squeezed his hand again, but it was too late. Ruksh had followed him to the kitchen. And heard every last word.

'So you've already decided that Hassan is a murderer. That should make for a wonderful introduction. Just stay out of it, Esa. And stay out of my life.'

Khattak found himself out of patience.

'Don't talk nonsense, Ruksh. I can't stay out of it – it's my job. Someone who was at that camp with Mohsin killed him. And whoever that person is, I don't want Misbah in his sights. End of discussion.'

Ruksh brushed past him into the kitchen.

'Your roots are showing,' she said coldly. 'Your chauvinist blood is up. If I choose to introduce Misbah to the man I'm planning to marry, that's no concern of yours.'

She was pushing him. And Esa didn't know why.

He stood up, pushed his stool aside with slow, deliberate gestures.

And came to stand within an inch of Ruksh, his green eyes locked on hers.

'This isn't a game, Ruksh, and I don't have time for a power play. Until I know who killed Mohsin Dar – who shot him in the dark, and left him to bleed to death in the woods – I don't want Misbah anywhere near your boyfriend. Or near anyone else at that mosque. Is that clear?'

He took a step back, glad to see that the details of Mohsin's death had shaken Ruksh out of her complacency.

Misbah tugged at his elbow, her face ashen.

'I won't, *bhaiya*, don't worry. I promise you that I won't.'

Ruksh blinked back tears.

'You don't scare me, Esa. No matter what you say.'

He'd had enough. He stooped to kiss Misbah on the forehead.

To Ruksh he said only, 'When I'm trying to scare you, you'll know.'

11

Rachel slipped in to the small sunroom that led off the mosque's kitchen, another space where the windows were screened instead of open to a commentary of stars and blue sky.

She was beginning to discover that she liked old Unionville. She'd eaten a late lunch at one of the restaurants that crowded Main Street, and found her way to the Old Firehall for a mousse tart. As a gesture of reciprocity, she had brought a box of assorted desserts to the halaqa.

The idea was to make herself as unobtrusive as possible, while discovering any clues that opportunity might present. Despite these silent precautions, she couldn't stop herself from suggesting that the blinds in the sunroom be raised.

Hassan Ashkouri glanced in Rachel's direction. Then he nodded at the older man with the melancholy face and portentous brow – Jamshed Ali, a combination of caretaker and father figure, according to the INSET file.

Eight or nine young men were part of the group, including Dinaase Abdi, Zakaria Aboud, and Sami Dardas. Rachel had been appalled when Khattak had told her that the name 'Zakaria' was the Arabic equivalent of Zachary. Her brother had been a lost boy once, just as she imagined these young men to be – lost boys with Jamshed Ali standing in as a father.

They had arranged themselves in a circle on a threadbare Persian carpet, its blue-and-white motifs reminding Rachel of nothing so much as a cabin in winter at Algonquin Park, a silence heavy with starlight and snow.

A wintry light saturated the room, the moon hanging like an earring upon the sky. Hassan Ashkouri seated himself in the center of the moonlight, its cool paleness gilding his features, lending him an aura of mystery.

He followed Rachel's gaze.

'The moon is my beloved.'

And when Rachel looked surprised, he added, 'The vanishing moon, the crescent moon, the sheltered moon – the enduring symbol of our poets. A ripple across the twilight.'

Rachel ducked her head. 'I don't know a lot about poetry,' she mumbled.

It was a lie. She'd done her undergraduate degree in English literature, and was unfashionably taken up with Tennyson, rather than Ginsberg or Sylvia Plath.

Tennyson had written the line that spoke more to Rachel of her own life than any other.

The tender grace of a day that is dead will never come back to me.

And like the waves of the sea in Tennyson's poem, Rachel had broken against the oncoming tide of grief, believing Zachary lost forever.

But it was true that she knew nothing about Arabic poetry, hadn't read so much as a verse. She didn't think she'd ever seen a translation in a library or bookstore.

Ashkouri held up a brown leather book, its cover tooled in gold.

'Who can tell me what the moon represents?'

Paula, seated beside Rachel on the floor, reached out her arm, bringing it as close to Hassan Ashkouri as possible. Grace shifted away from Paula, a sneer on her face. The movement brought her closer to Dinaase Abdi, who looked away.

Ashkouri placed the book in the center of the circle.

Fazail-e-Amaal, Rachel read. And the subtitle, *On the Worthiness of Righteous Deeds.*

Which sounded nothing like poetry to her.

The vanished moon, the ripple of twilight.

The book was more in the vein of a Sunday school lesson.

Ashkouri tapped the book with his fingers.

'The crescent moon – the red crescent, the green crescent – of course, that's a shorthand any of us would recognize from places as distinct as Somalia or Turkey. But do we understand it as a metaphor for our Prophet and the purity of his message?'

Rachel examined the faces of the others. 'Purity' wasn't a word she enjoyed. It was a short stretch from there to 'puritanical', which might have described the glow she saw in Paula Kyriakou's eyes.

How had Paula ended up here? Was she drawn by the message or the man?

Paula had pulsated at the mention of Turkey. But why? According to her INSET file, Paula was a Greek Cypriot; Rachel could hear traces of her accent when she spoke. And if she remembered her geography, the Turkish and Greek peoples of Cyprus were on uneasy terms at best, burdened by the dismal escalations of history.

She must have missed something in Paula's file.

She tried to pay attention, but the halaqa had fallen into more muted channels, the leather book passed around to anyone who was willing to read aloud one of its passages, simple pieties that no one could fault on principle. Rachel wondered if there wasn't almost a socialist element to them – the emphasis on the poor, the notions of individual responsibility.

Rachel listened with her head down, attuned to every nuance of the group: Grace's outright boredom. Paula's hunger for attention. Dinaase Abdi not quite at ease, whispering to Zakaria and Sami. And Hassan and Jamshed, watchful over them all.

What was Ashkouri getting out of this? Why was Grace here? Could Din's unease be attributed to Grace? Paula's infatuation with Ashkouri explained her presence, but Din wasn't singled out by Ashkouri any more than any of the other young men in the group.

And what were they communicating beyond these modest pieties?

When she raised her head again, Ashkouri was staring straight at her.

'You don't find this interesting, Rachel? You're not engaged?'

He was wondering why she had come. A glance at the moon gave her a passable answer.

'I like what you said about the moon as a metaphor. Even if I don't quite understand.' She patted Paula's shoulder. 'I guess I'm not that different from Paula or Grace.'

Paula glared at her, shrugging off Rachel's touch. 'I'm hardly a novice. And I didn't think the halaqa was open to newcomers.'

Ashkouri ignored her. He pointed at the brown leather book.

'You found that difficult to follow? You must have some schooling in the basics – from Middlefield, if nowhere else.'

When Rachel didn't answer, he adopted a more grandiloquent style.

'Do you know what it is you came here to seek?'

She made a point of looking away. Let him think his bottomless eyes were the source of her discomfiture.

'Friends. Peace. But I thought more – one-on-one, like with the imam.'

'Peace has to come from within,' Ashkouri said.

'Isn't everyone here looking for peace? Especially – you know. You said someone at the mosque had died, one of your friends. I thought we were here to give each other comfort. Isn't that the point of community?'

It was a risk, but something in Rachel's bones told her it was the right risk to take. It was something someone stumbling toward faith might say. She was startled by his reply.

'Do you come from mud and crime, Rachel?'

It was a strange thing for Ashkouri to say. And it made no

sense to her. Did it mean anything to the others? She began to wonder if he might be a little unhinged.

Then again, wouldn't he have to be, to be plotting such a catastrophic event?

'One of the great poets to break with the inherited poetical traditions of the past was a man named Adonis. His poetry runs like fire through the veins of the Arab people, a fire that cannot be quenched. When he speaks of mud and crime, he is speaking of our origins. Do we come from mud and crime? Or have mud and crime been inflicted upon us?'

She mentioned Mohsin Dar, he spoke of mud and crime.

'Think of what we have come to as a community, as a nation – this low tide, this farthest point from the sun. And ask yourself, should we not find our way back to the center? Ask what a righteous person would do watching the pain of his people? Ask yourself if you have ever felt the fire of a poet like Adonis.'

He examined his circle of listeners, reading each one of their faces.

'When we try to crawl out from their mud and their crimes, we find ourselves called terrorists.' Hassan shook his head, his dark eyes doleful. 'But isn't the murder of Rohingya in Burma terrorism? The Indian army's atrocities in Kashmir – isn't that terrorism? The destruction of Chechnya, the obliteration of Baghdad, the bombardment of Gaza, the murder of children at play on a beach – are these things not terrorism?'

His voice fell into a rhythm, an enchantment in it to beguile the unschooled and the susceptible. Rachel was neither, but there was still something about Ashkouri she found compelling.

'What of the torture and degradation of Muslims in Egypt, Palestine, and Syria? Everywhere, prisons are filled with our captives, our chaste women are raped, while a war is waged against their modesty in France and Belgium and Holland. But that is not terrorism. The mockery of our Prophet, the cursing of our religion, the defaming of our Holy Book – these things are not terrorism.

When we rise up in Tunis or Libya or Egypt, when we rose up in Iraq to defend ourselves from their wars, we were the terrorists. How strange are their notions of freedom and democracy.'

He spared a smile for Paula.

'As the citizen of a devastated nation, I can tell you I have felt terrorized. Bombs destroyed my family, my house, my neighborhood, and my city. Bombs from so far away that we couldn't see the enemy, we couldn't imagine his reasons to hate us – we couldn't imagine anything that would justify so much destruction.'

He looked out at the moon.

'The tyrants, the dictators, the allies of the West – aren't these men terrorists? Those of us who aren't taken away to be tortured or killed are refugees in our own countries. Is it wrong to ask who keeps these tyrants in power? Whose governments buy their oil when they cease invading our lands? Whose weapons they use against us? Whose drone strikes kill our children as they make their way to school?' Ashkouri drew a shuddering breath. 'Ask yourself these questions. Ask if you would feel terrorized in turn. Then ask if you came from mud and crime, or if mud and crime were inflicted upon you.'

He took a moment to take stock of the impact of his words on his listeners. And then he added a little more, dropping the words into the strained silence.

'The worldly life is temporary, the Hereafter exists for eternity. So ask if you should seek death where you expect to find it.'

With a creeping sense of horror, Rachel realized that she recognized the words. They had been part of the dossier from INSET. A frequent tag on jihadist websites: *seek death where you expect to find it.* An exhortation from a speech delivered by Abu Bakr Al-Baghdadi, spiritual leader of ISIS, the Islamic State of Iraq and Syria, delivered during the month of Ramadan.

'Well? Do you agree or disagree? Do you have anything to share?'

Rachel was surprised when Grace Kaspernak spoke up.

'It was not a crime to love you,' she said, 'though they will hang me for it.'

Her heavily painted eyes sought out Dinaase's dark face. He was hunched over his knees, avoiding a connection with Grace. Zakaria looked over at Sami and snickered.

Grace unearthed a crumpled piece of paper from the back pocket of her leggings. She smoothed it out with nervous fingers. Rachel craned her neck to read the words over Grace's shoulder. The poetry described a romance that ended in tragedy. It was signed, 'The Rose of Damascus'.

Realization was swift and a little sad.

Was it possible that Grace herself was 'The Rose of Damascus'? Or had she stumbled across words that spoke to her longing for Dinaase, as desperate in its way as Paula's hopeless enthrallment with Ashkouri?

Because it *was* hopeless. Khattak had been frank with Rachel, though she could see that it cost him to speak of matters within his family. If Hassan Ashkouri was engaged to Khattak's sister, Paula's fate was sealed; Ashkouri was out of her grasp. And Rachel didn't think Paula had joined the Masjid un-Nur for the sake of religious enlightenment.

She had to wonder, who in these difficult days would choose to enter the fold of Islam? It was hardly a popular choice when outrages connected to political Islam were becoming routine and mundane. Unless the message struck deep to the soul.

Or maybe its extremist practitioners attracted a particular kind of personality: deranged, friendless, suffering from alienation or a kind of spiritual want. Or all of the above. Angry at the injustices of the world, as Ashkouri had described them, in search of an outlet for that rage.

The poetry Grace offered spoke of rebellion, a hope of genuine grace in a tyrannical climate. Was this something the Nakba group would support?

It was not a crime to love you, though they will hang me for it.

It also suggested that the reason Grace had joined the Masjid un-Nur was because of Dinaase Abdi. Rachel studied Dinaase, to see if the poem had affected him at all. His face was fine-boned, narrow, triangular, his teeth large and white, his forehead high and smooth. No beard, no stubble, just a loose accumulation of curls that bounced back from his skull, giving him an inch or two of added height. Tall and nearly as skinny as Grace.

It was clear that Dinaase recognized the poem. And wished to dissociate himself from it.

Why? Because the other young men were mocking him? Or for Hassan Ashkouri's sake?

Rachel didn't know if despite her careful training she was trading in stereotypes, or if it was a valid judgment that the feminine rebellion expressed by the poem would not be in line with a terror cell's patriarchal orthodoxy, misogyny and murder walking hand in hand.

Beneath the heavy makeup and the agonizing assortment of piercings, Grace's plump, red lips were unmarked. Except for the damage she was doing by picking at them.

'Mohsin liked these poems – you remember, Din?' Grace asked him.

Dinaase Abdi shrugged. He looked over at her, and something in the forlorn expression of her eyes caught at him. Ignoring the others, he gave her the ghost of a smile.

'I know, Gracie. Mo loved poetry. He was always drumming up a line from somewhere.'

Dinaase spoke like any other Canadian kid, with a touch of hip-hop swagger.

Grace's eyes were wet. 'He looked scary, but you could always talk to him, you know? Like he made time for you.' She glared at the other young men in the circle. 'Especially when no one else made you feel welcome.' Her glare encompassed Paula. 'You took up a lot of Mo's time. Too much.'

'I didn't ask to,' Paula fired back. 'Mohsin was a nuisance. He was the one who followed me around, as if he wasn't married. As if he never thought of Alia at all.'

Embroiled though she was with Ashkouri, there was a deep satisfaction in Paula's voice. It gratified Paula's sense of herself to be pursued. It made her desirable, something she wanted Ashkouri to recognize.

Rachel began to wonder at the goings-on at this mosque.

'Sitara,' Grace whispered. 'He called his wife "Sitara"; he said he loved her very much. And he told me "Sitara" meant "star."'

Dinaase nodded.

A sign of support for Grace. And a confirmation of her words.

The preaching continued, Hassan's voice a golden thread of continuity, swelling and dipping with the poetry he espoused, the fables he used as parables, returning to a single theme time and again: the quality of justice.

By the time it was done, Rachel found the quality of justice very strained indeed. She was first to join the line for tea and dessert.

She slurped at her tea, her hand reaching out to a lemon tart.

She needed to clear her head. She felt as though Ashkouri's words had shrouded her mind in fog. And no mention of Mohsin Dar: no mournful lamentation, no indication of the Islamic rituals of grief and remembrance. Why not?

Jamshed Ali faced her across the island, his face grim. And mistrustful.

If Ashkouri was swept away by the spell of his own rhetoric – none of it overtly jihadist – Jamshed was pragmatic, sober, keenly assessing, keeping the three young men in the cell in view at all times.

Rachel swallowed a mouthful of mousse.

Grace and Dinaase were both at her elbow, their limbs knocking against each other in a rhythm that spoke of a long familiarity.

Din's hand skimmed the back of Grace's skull. Jamshed watched him with an unwarranted intensity.

'You need to get these checked out, Gracie. I keep telling you I don't like them.'

Grace brewed another glass of qahwe for Dinaase.

'Where's yours?' he demanded.

From Grace's quick smile as she dipped her head, Rachel guessed that it had been some time since Din had exhibited this much concern for her. The smile, with lips as red as a cherry tree, was enchanting. Grace raised her glass. Din knocked his against it.

They grinned at each other like old conspirators.

'Please,' Din said. 'My Gracie, my own. You get them out, eh? You dye your hair any color you like, but this you don't do. For me.'

Given how pointedly he'd been ignoring her, Grace would have been well within her rights to tell the boy that her appearance was no concern of his. But like the Rose of Damascus in the poem that spoke of a hazardous yearning, she seemed to be in thrall.

Rachel studied them. They were polar opposites – Grace a mix of alt-punk and Goth, Dinaase a kid with a penchant for his faith, and more than a smattering of carefree charm.

Something had brought Grace and Din together. And someone now wanted them apart.

Rachel saw Jamshed's face, the menace in it.

Grace wasn't wanted at Masjid un-Nur. Jamshed Ali didn't want her there.

'That was interesting tonight,' she said to Grace. 'Not what I expected.'

'Sometimes there's more poetry, less politics. Not tonight for some reason.'

Another of Ashkouri's tests. Waiting to see how Rachel would respond.

'This is Dinaase. Din – Rachel's new.' Grace made a little room between herself and Din, shoving him at Rachel.

Dinaase didn't shake Rachel's hand. He curled two fingers at his forehead and waggled them at her. He might have meant it to be rakish. It came off as childlike and sweet.

Grace must have thought so too. She knocked Din's hand away, the gesture unconstrained and easy, a rebuttal to Paula's anxious clamor for Hassan Ashkouri's notice.

'Loser,' Grace said. 'I keep telling you that's not in. You just don't listen.'

'You take out the studs from your head, I give up the signature Abdi salute.'

'You first.'

'You don't trust me?'

'Of course I trust you. It's your grasp of popular culture I don't trust.' She shook her head.

Dinaase lightly touched his fingers to the front of Grace's neck.

'I'll go first. If you take out the staples too, my Gracie.'

Grace didn't object to the nickname. Maybe her objection was to anyone else's usurping Dinaase's pet name for her. People who hadn't earned the right through genuine closeness.

For a girl in the foster care system, closeness was never a guarantee. Rachel could understand why it was precious to Grace.

Din shared the warmth of his crooked smile with Rachel. 'Welcome to the house of Islam. Always room for one more.'

Rachel was quick to demur.

'Oh, I'm not a convert. I'm just – exploring.' She made her next remark sound like an afterthought. 'I'm sorry about your friend. This probably wasn't the best time for me to intrude.'

Paula bustled into their midst carrying a tray.

'We don't say "convert,"' she said, her face cross. 'We say "revert". Each one of us was born in a state of submission. Some of us are lucky enough to find our way back to it.'

When Jamshed Ali turned away to talk to the young men,

Rachel jumped in. 'Was your friend one of them? The one you were talking about?'

Paula's look was incredulous.

'Mohsin? Mohsin talked the talk. He didn't walk the walk.'

So here was one person who did not grieve Mohsin Dar's death.

'My friends.' Din's voice sounded anything but friendly. 'Mohsin was born into his faith. He didn't need anyone to teach him his religion.' Here he smiled at Rachel. 'Sometimes newcomers get carried away, like they have something to prove to the rest of us.'

Another point of tension, and one that hadn't occurred to Rachel before. A clash between those who had inherited their faith, at ease in their skin, and those who had sought it out, bewildered and hopeful. Grasping at the light, like she was supposed to be.

'Mohsin may have been born a Muslim, but he lacked decorum.'

Paula had the final word on the subject, slamming the tray she carried onto the counter.

And Rachel wondered, had Mohsin Dar truly been in pursuit of this woman?

'Will you have a memorial for him?' she asked Dinaase, noting that Jamshed was muttering something to Zakaria and Sami. She would have to check them out later.

A look flashed between Grace and Din.

'We should,' Grace said, biting her lip.

'Don't do that,' Din told her. 'Your mouth is the only bit of poetry left on your face.'

And then Rachel saw it. What connected this girl to this boy, so different from her in everything else, was a fierce, immutable love. With more than a hint of eroticism.

Grace didn't blush. She took Din's hand and folded it between her own. And in that gesture, there was more intimacy than Rachel had known in most of her adult relationships.

'Din writes his own poetry,' Grace said. 'Except – not like Hassan and what he shares.'

'You didn't like the halaqa today?' Rachel asked.

Grace shook her head, impatient. 'Hassan is obsessed with politics. The grandeur of the past, the glory of a dead civilization. The poetry he likes – it's old-fashioned. Old battles, out of step. Always angry, always looking for something.'

'And Din?'

'Din does spoken word. Sometimes he raps. He's won a lot of slams.'

Rachel had heard of poetry slams that pitted talented young artists against one another. She wouldn't have expected this of Dinaase Abdi, who looked like he'd be most at home at the helm of a boat, at the edge of viewless winds, a fine blue mist haloing his curls.

She made the uninspired leap to Somali pirates. Unfair or not, there was a skull and a pair of crossed swords tattooed on Grace's neck. Was that for Dinaase?

'I'd like to hear that sometime.'

As she said the words, Rachel reminded herself that she was a detective. She was supposed to guard against prejudgment. Din was a Somali kid, the son of immigrants, so he couldn't express himself through poetry? Grace was tattooed, pierced, and dressed like a mother's worst nightmare, so she couldn't be in the throes of a genuine, adult love?

It was much too soon for Rachel to arrive at conclusions. Except for one.

Every time she brought up the subject of Mohsin Dar, someone changed it.

Before she could try again, there was a soft knock on the door. Rachel looked up in time to see the flash of wretchedness that crossed Paula's face.

The newcomer was a woman. Slim, elegant, tall. With a face to inspire more of Dinaase's poetry. Pale-eyed, fair-skinned, delicate. She wore her scarf with an artless grace, concealing waves of night-dark hair.

Rachel knew the face. She moved behind the island, pretending to retrieve something she had dropped on the floor. She couldn't afford to be recognized.

The beautiful woman was Esa Khattak's sister.

12

FRIDAY AFTERNOON. THE HEAVIEST SNOWFALL of the year thus far. Record-setting for December.

The highway traffic a random assortment of metal boxes bolted to the asphalt. Everything covered by a carapace of muddy white. Snowplows proceeding at an incremental pace, six of them side by side, the time-sensitive concerns of commuters held hostage behind them.

Khattak used the shoulder and his siren.

The road through Unionville was worse, the side streets the last to be plowed. There were accidents up and down the 401, the 404 was closed north of Newmarket, and as with every heavy snowfall, the city lurched toward a slumberous slowdown.

Too much volume, too few traffic solutions.

But in Unionville, the streets were quiet. Half of the business owners had opted to stay home. Most of the shops on Main Street were closed. Kids chased each other across the pond.

And along both sides of the park, a familiar sight: couples trekking through new-fallen snow in their snowshoes, enjoying the winter tramp.

As a reflex, Khattak checked the warning signs at the pond. Frozen solid. And destined to remain that way, if the forecast was correct. Which meant that Rachel's heart's desire had been achieved – her all-star game would take place at an outdoor rink.

He parked his car on the street across from Masjid un-Nur. In spite of the weather, the mosque's small parking lot was full.

And to Khattak that meant that either the Friday sermon at

this mosque was so noteworthy that no one wished to miss it, or that word had spread that the head of Community Policing had asked to speak to the congregation about the death of Mohsin Dar. Given his past experience of Friday sermons, he thought the latter possibility more likely.

He joined the prayer in good time, keeping to the back, matching the men in the prayer rows to photographs in the INSET files. Several of them turned to look at him, then began to whisper to each other. Khattak was ready for this. Especially since his resemblance to his sister was unmistakable.

Rachel had called to let him know that her phone had been off during the halaqa. She had received his text warning her about Ruksh's presence at the halaqa, just a little too late.

I met your sister after I got your text, but I didn't need to do damage control. I don't think she gave me away.

And Rachel had told him something else. She had told him of Ashkouri's unusual question, along with her conclusion. She suspected that Ashkouri might be suffering from a form of mental illness.

Khattak wasn't as sure. Whoever was behind the planning of the Nakba attacks needed a cool and rational mind, in addition to the ability to map out the various stages of the attack, and the nerve and discipline to see it through. He would also need to be able to maintain control over a disparate group of followers, several of whom were gathered at the prayer – Jamshed, Din, Zakaria, Sami. They were all on INSET's radar, though the files were focused primarily on the trio of Ashkouri, Jamshed, and Din.

Rachel had speculated that Dar's murder, right before the attacks were scheduled to take place, might have unhinged Ashkouri, providing an additional source of worry to add to all the things that could go wrong with his New Year's plan.

But Khattak knew something that Rachel didn't. He understood Ashkouri's question in a completely different context than Rachel would have had access to. And it assured him, if there had been any doubt, that Ashkouri was committed to his plot.

Do you come from mud and crime?

It was the reworking of a line from a poem that had galvanized the Arab world. A cataclysmic poem that well predated Huntington's thesis on the clash of civilizations, the thesis that read Islam as a monolithic force hostile to the West, due to an ingrained inferiority and a permanent sense of inadequacy. The thesis paid scant attention to historical encounters with deeply damaging, long-term consequences, reinforced by new incursions into the Islamic world.

But in Adonis's famous poem, the East spoke back to the West, in a voice that was bold and unafraid. A voice that rejected the judgment of the West, demanding accountability instead.

The poem was called *A Grave for New York.*

And the question Ashkouri had asked of Rachel was taken from the poem's blazing indictment of New York as a symbol of imperial power, an icon of decay. To come from New York was to come from mud and crime, and to be destined to return there.

Without difficulty, Khattak could see how Ashkouri would graft his particular ideology onto the poem's surface, ignoring the work's riches and subtleties, along with its critique of the dearth of creativity within the Arab world.

The poem looked in both directions at once: at the decadence of imperial power, and at the societies whose internal corruption had permitted the imperial expansion. Who even now suffered from postcolonial identity crises.

But that was not how Ashkouri had read the poem. Khattak had told Rachel to keep her guard up, because Ashkouri was using the poem to threaten her.

And Khattak was more concerned about the other ways the poem might speak to a man like Ashkouri.

New York + New York = The Grave and anything that comes from the Grave. New York − New York = The Sun.

At the end of the prayer, the imam invited Khattak to make his announcement to the congregation of some twenty men and five women.

The call to prayer had been a recording. Khattak wondered if that was out of respect for Mohsin, who had always given the call to prayer at Nur. Many of the men gathered in the room would have been able to recite the *adhaan*. Khattak could have done so himself. But that would have been an intrusion, an assertion of a secular police power over a private, religious space. And it would have placed Khattak on the footing of an equal among friends, instead of what he was: a detective investigating a murder; a man who suspected one of his coreligionists of terrible crimes, Mohsin's murder a footnote to a much grimmer agenda.

And there would be several among the congregation who knew that. Not least, Ashkouri.

Attempts to convince them otherwise would be fruitless.

And Khattak realized how much his work as a police officer had become a part of his identity. Because it wasn't the duplicity that troubled him. It was its inadequacy as a tool to further his investigation. He stood behind the lectern, taking careful note of who was in the audience, who hadn't trumped up an excuse to leave without engaging with him.

Ashkouri was there. He nodded at Khattak, an informal introduction. And Jamshed Ali. And Dinaase and two of his friends, Zakaria and Sami. In the back row, he spied Rachel, alongside Paula Kyriakou and Grace Kaspernak. Rachel had described Grace with disturbing specificity. Even so, Khattak was taken aback. The young girl had mutilated herself.

To what end? What anguish did she seek to soothe? That she was a girl on the margins was all the INSET files could tell him. Discarded, ignored, not worried over by anyone. Except for the boy who had left his community to come to Nur. Dinaase Abdi,

Ashkouri's disciple. A boy whose future seemed equally bleak, caught as he was in Ashkouri's web.

And there was one more person Esa Khattak recognized. A woman he hadn't expected to travel to Nur in the snowstorm. Alia Dar. He wondered if it was possible that INSET had overlooked a personal connection she may have had to the mosque.

She was sitting by herself, lost in thought, her knees curled up to her chest, her eyes damp. Out of the ambit of Andy Dar, beyond the reach of ordinary comfort. He hoped that the imam's sermon had provided some solace. And that solace was all she needed, and not some form of expiation. If she had been on uneasy terms with Mohsin, she would need to be questioned again.

'If you can be of help to the police, of course you must try,' the imam said.

Khattak took that as his cue.

'This is my first time at your mosque, and I appreciate the opportunity to meet with you. Naturally, I realize I come at a difficult time, but I hope you'll accept that I'm here to do two things. First, to investigate Mohsin Dar's murder. Second, to make sure that your concerns and priorities are fully represented during my investigation. Should you have questions, I'll do my best to answer them. In terms of my questions, I'm certain that every person who attends this mosque, or who knew Mohsin Dar, would wish for us to achieve justice on his behalf. If that is indeed what you wish, I'm confident you will cooperate fully with my investigation.'

He examined the small group of worshippers, taking the time to make eye contact with each person in the front row. He saw faces that were frightened, others that were confused, some that were skeptical. And Hassan Ashkouri, unaccountably relaxed, accepting that others would follow his lead.

'Why are you here alone?' one man asked. 'Where are the real police? Do they think they can foist a substitute upon us?'

Khattak made careful note of the questioner. Not one of

Ashkouri's inner circle. Someone with a chip on his shoulder, who believed that justice was in short supply for members of his community. From personal experience? Khattak couldn't say.

He recounted his personal credentials as a member of Toronto's homicide squad. And he explained his new mandate in some detail, thinking of CPS's governing legislation. And remembering the difficulties that waited for him at Justice.

You're an investigator, not an advocate.

No way to tell ahead of time where that line should be drawn, the law conveniently silent on the question. Whatever worked best for public relations at any given time.

The man who had questioned Khattak shrugged, only half-convinced.

Khattak read the names on his list. His interviews with the women would be perfunctory. But every person on his list would have to account for his time and his activities at the camp. And to explain what they had done when not one but two gunshots had resounded through the woods.

The INSET transcript was muddy, indistinct. Khattak's interviews might set that in balance. He asked to speak to Jamshed first, phrasing the request so that it sounded like an act of deference to an elder.

They adjourned to the sunroom Rachel had described. Zakaria and Sami set up chairs for their convenience. Tea was offered, but Khattak declined – the mosque was cold, but it was best to establish the boundaries at once.

Khattak studied the older man's face. He was a widower in his late sixties, a retired accountant who wanted to be of use to his community. He undertook small janitorial tasks at the mosque, and was responsible for opening and closing the house each day. He lived above the mosque, in the five-bedroom house. Some of the other rooms were made available to travelers or important guests of the mosque.

Khattak began simply. 'Are you fond of winter camping?'

'Why do you ask?'

The other man was at his ease. His voice was deep, low-pitched, accented, with no obvious signs of strain. He wore loose-fitting *shalwar kameez*, covered by a thick cardigan and a Pashtun shawl. His hands bore the mark of years of physical labor, unexpected for an accountant.

'It's been a cold winter. Unusually cold for December, heavier than average snowfall. Even young people might balk at the thought of spending a week at Algonquin at this time.'

'We were in cabins, not in tents. We were well-equipped for the cold.'

'Whose idea was the camping trip?'

'It was Mohsin's idea. He thought it would make for a good vacation. Have you been to Algonquin in winter, Inspector? The scenery is quite spectacular.'

Jamshed's first lie. Mohsin had been instructed not to take the lead in any part of the Nakba plot, but rather to fall in with the ringleader's suggestions.

'He must regret that decision now,' Khattak observed.

'It is a sad loss.'

But the other man's face was like stone, the cold eyes expressionless.

'Who shared Mohsin's cabin?'

'I did.'

'Did he seem upset to you for any reason? Did you observe anything out of the ordinary in his behavior?'

'Nothing. He was excited to have the chance to show off his outdoor skills. Things he was good at.'

Khattak heard the grudging acceptance behind the words.

'Such as?'

'Lighting fires. Marking out a trail. Snowshoeing. Cooking over the campfire.'

It was on the tip of Khattak's tongue to ask what other outdoor skills Mohsin might have possessed, such as marksmanship or survivalist training. He stopped himself. It was veering too close to the INSET operation.

'Do you know if Mohsin had made any personal enemies? If anyone resented something Mohsin had done, or had a particular grievance?'

'I know nothing of the kind. Mohsin was an important member of this community. He was very well liked. There is no one I can think of who would have reason to harm him.' Jamshed shifted forward in his chair, resting his elbows upon his thighs. 'What of the *janazah*, Inspector Khattak? You know what an affront this is. Why has the funeral prayer been delayed?'

Khattak had to be careful about this. It was the same complaint he heard whenever a homicide victim turned out to be Muslim. Swift, unimpeded burial was both the custom and the religious mandate. Delay was troubling to members of the faith. The soul was not at rest. The process of grieving could not begin until it was.

And there were other traditions. That the body not be seen to decompose in front of the loved ones of the deceased, to minimize the spirit of wailing and lamentation.

'The autopsy has been conducted with utmost respect for the dead. But burial will not be possible until the investigation is concluded.' Which gave him another line to pursue. 'Do you know how Mohsin was killed?'

Jamshed knotted his hands together. And now Khattak saw a kind of heaviness settle upon the man.

'Yes. We all do, those of us who were there. We heard the gunshots, two of them.'

'Were they close together?'

'Yes. One after the other. Terrible and loud.'

Sound would carry for miles in Algonquin's pristine wilderness.

'And what did you do when you heard the shots, Mr Ali? Where were you at the time?'

'It was late at night, nearly midnight. I was in my cabin, preparing to rest. We had eaten, I had prayed. I was tired.'

'You were alone?'

'Yes.'

'If it was so late, as you say, didn't you wonder where Mohsin was?'

Jamshed cracked his knuckles, the noise loud and sudden.

'Mohsin liked to take a walk at night by himself. To think about poetry, he said. To look at the stars, to feel the presence of Allah in the trees. This was the sixth night we were there. It didn't surprise me.'

A lump rose in Khattak's throat. The words awakened an unexpected memory. He remembered this of Mohsin from their youth, even if he didn't remember Mohsin's interest in poetry. Hassan Ashkouri's influence, perhaps.

Then Mohsin's words came back to him.

He's out there, man. He's out there in the beauty of the land. Just open your eyes and look for Him. Open your heart and feel Him there.

Perhaps Mohsin's idea of poetry.

'Did everyone know this? That Mohsin liked to walk alone at night?'

For the first time, Jamshed hesitated. Then he said, 'Yes. I think so.'

'And when you heard the shots?'

'Haven't you read the reports? I rushed outside. We all did. We looked at each other, counting heads, seeing who was there, who wasn't.'

'And were you all there? All at the same time? Apart from Mohsin?'

Jamshed shook his head. 'I can't remember now. I think we were all there. Or maybe Dinaase and Grace met us in the woods.' His mouth tightened at the thought. 'That girl serves no purpose except as a temptation to Din. She's leading him from the straight path. The rest of us, yes. We just came out of our cabins. Hassan and Din shared one, Zakaria and Sami another. And the women were together.'

'Who found Mohsin's body?'

'It took a long time. The woods were thick. No one knew which trail Mohsin would have chosen for his walk. We called out, again and again. No one answered. So we decided to split up – each of us taking a separate path. And then, I found him. It took me half an hour.'

'Was he still alive? Did he say anything?'

Jamshed shot Khattak a look of deep dislike.

'Didn't you read the report for yourself?' he asked again. 'He was dead when I got there. He had dragged himself to a tree. He was sitting up, his back against it. His eyes were open, but he couldn't see. The snow was soaked with his blood. It was terrible. The whole thing was terrible. Thank God the young people didn't find him.'

Khattak believed him. It was the first thing Jamshed had said that didn't reek of calculation. The personal encounter with death, however arrived at, was something that had shaken the man.

'You say Mohsin dragged himself to the tree. How do you know this?'

Jamshed Ali stood up. 'There was a trail of blood in the snow. Perhaps as much as five feet long. Are we finished? I don't want to have to go over that night again.'

'Not quite, Mr Ali, please. Just a few more questions.'

'What else then?' He sat down again, his hooded eyes brooding.

'You noticed the blood trail. Did you notice anything else in the snow? Any signs of disturbance, footprints, the weapon that was used?'

'The only thing I noticed was Mohsin. Everything else was wiped from my mind.'

It might have been the truth. Khattak didn't think so.

'Do you know what type of gun was used?'

Jamshed looked at him sharply.

'Why would I? I assumed he'd been killed by a hunter. Some damn fool chasing partridges in the night.'

Another lie. A shotgun blast would have left Mohsin's body in shreds.

'The wounds from a shotgun are unmistakable,' Khattak said, choosing his words with care. 'Didn't you see –'

Jamshed cut him off. 'We were wearing winter clothing,' Inspector. All I could see was that Mohsin's parka was saturated with blood. I'm no hunter. I couldn't tell the difference.'

'Have you ever used a firearm, Mr. Ali?'

'No.'

That wasn't the truth, Khattak thought. Laine had told him about the practice run with the bolt-action hunting rifles. But the forensics team had tested the hands of each member of the camp for gunshot residue. They had been wearing gloves. There was no conclusive evidence found on anyone's clothes, no traces of spent ammunition, apart from the slugs from the Herstal.

But someone could have worn a different pair of gloves and hidden them away somewhere at the campsite. Khattak needed to see the scene. The parameters of the INSET operation stifled him at every turn.

'What happened next?'

'They heard me calling I had found him. They found me quickly after that. And someone called 911.'

'Who?'

'Hassan Ashkouri. When it was obvious we couldn't save Mohsin, he told us not to touch anything. We backed away.'

Another lie. Mohsin's cell phone was missing. Someone at the winter camp had taken it.

But by whatever mysterious intimation that warns us when danger is at hand, Mohsin had left the phone he used to communicate with INSET at his house before heading up to

Algonquin. Members of the INSET team had already collected it.

So unless Mohsin was killed because someone in the Nakba group had tagged him as an agent, Dar's cover should still be intact. Which would make the killing personal.

If Khattak could trust that Ciprian Coale was telling him the truth, instead of working to sabotage his homicide investigation. But he didn't trust Coale at all. Jamshed Ali and Hassan Ashkouri were dangerous men possessed of a deadly intent. If Mohsin had gotten in their way, they would have taken steps to deal with him. Like two gunshots in the woods.

Esa had one more question for Jamshed Ali.

'I'm curious about something. If this was a vacation as you say, why didn't Alia Dar join you at the camp? Why didn't she come with Mohsin?'

A world-weary expression crossed Jamshed's face, along with a tinge of distaste.

'Mohsin was getting very close to Paula. Alia would just have been in the way.'

Dinaase Abdi slunk into the sunroom like a child who'd been called into the principal's office, his expression managing to convey both rebellion and a reluctant deference.

Esa wondered if Din had had run-ins with the police, stopped to ask where he and his friends were headed, identification demanded on the flimsiest of pretexts, or without any pretext at all. He thought of Desmond Cole's essay on the practice of carding Toronto's black population, and its exertive impact on the city's policing methods. Khattak's community-specific mandate couldn't erase the differences between his experiences and Din's, something he needed to remember.

Without forgetting Din's role in the Nakba plot.

Jamshed Ali might have ice water running through his veins, and Hassan Ashkouri had been so calculating as to entangle himself with a high-ranking police officer's sister, but Dinaase Abdi was a seventeen-year-old boy. If there was to be a crack in the Nakba plot, or in Mohsin Dar's murder, it would start with Dinaase.

The boy was nervous, slinging his hands in and out of his pockets, playing with the long chain he had snapped to the back of his baggy jeans. He wore the Palestinian scarf, the kaffiyeh, wrapped around his neck several times. He burrowed into it like it was a form of protection.

He spoke before Khattak could begin.

'Gracie was at the camp. You gonna call Gracie in?'

'Yes, why?'

'Gracie had nothing to do with it. She didn't even want to go to Algonquin. She was only there because of me. Gracie never paid any attention to Mo. She didn't care about him, one way or the other. And he didn't care about her. So tell me, why would she shoot him?'

'When you put it like that, it's clear that she wouldn't.'

Din stopped his nervous fidgeting.

'Then you feel me, right? You'll leave Gracie out of this. Anyway, she was with me the whole time that night. Except for the time she spent with Paula.'

Khattak heard the uncertainty in his voice, decided he could use it.

'Let's go back to the beginning, shall we?' He looked down at the notes he had taken during his interview with Jamshed. 'Where were you when you heard the gunshots? And before you answer that, let me warn you that Mr. Ali has already said that you weren't in your cabin.'

Din didn't answer in the manner Khattak had expected. Instead, his voice rising, he challenged the inspector.

'Why do you need to warn me? You think I did this? I didn't. I loved Mo. I freaking *loved* Mo. He was my big brother. That he's dead wrecks me, do you get that? It wrecks me.'

There was real emotion in Din's voice, but Khattak had long since learned that emotion was no guarantor of truth. It could just as easily serve as the cover for other feelings – feelings that, in this case, would betray Din. And Rachel had told Khattak of the gentle flirtation between Din and Grace in the kitchen the night before. Carefree and candid, untainted by grief.

'Did you do this?' Khattak asked.

Din muttered under his breath. *Here to represent us? No fucking way.* To Khattak he said, 'I didn't. No way you'll believe me, but I didn't.'

'If it proves to be true that you had nothing to do with Mohsin's death, I'd have no reason to disbelieve you. So help me prove it. Where were you when you heard the gunshots?'

'Out. In the woods.'

'By yourself?'

Din slumped down in his chair. He slid his fingers between the loops of his chain, manacling his knuckles.

'I already told you,' he said, sulking. 'I was with Gracie.'

Which wasn't exactly what the boy had said, but Khattak left it.

'What were the two of you doing out in the woods so late?'

Now Dinaase grinned.

'What do you think? Just how old are you, man? We didn't need a chaperone. We didn't need Paula Policewoman watching our every move.'

'How did Grace know where to meet you?'

'I whispered it to her at the campfire. Over dinner.'

'Did you see Mohsin in the woods? Either of you?'

'We didn't.' The boy's smile widened. 'We weren't looking for anybody, you know?' A thought occurred to him. His mood shifted in its wake. 'Grace is a good girl, you understand? That stuff on the outside, that doesn't mean anything. She's a good girl.'

'And what does it mean to be a good girl?' Khattak asked,

keeping his tone circumspect and civil. 'Why would I think she isn't a good girl?'

The boy's eyes met his.

'You know, right? You're one of us, you said.'

Khattak hadn't said that, but he knew what the boy was getting at.

'So you're saying that your – adventures in the woods didn't go beyond a certain point.'

The big-toothed smile was back.

'It was freezing out there, man. You think we're crazy? And besides, with those piercings? It's like being stabbed by icicles.'

Khattak fought back a grin. There was something genuinely candid and funny about Din Abdi's style of expression.

He covered the same ground he'd gone over with Jamshed. Din's whereabouts and Grace's, at the time the gunshots were heard. Their reaction, their movements. It matched Jamshed's account of events down to the last detail. Which in itself was suspicious.

'Tell me something, Dinaase. Do you have any idea what might have happened to Mohsin's cell phone?'

The boy looked confused. 'No. Why?'

This time Khattak believed him.

'And the gun? Do you know anything about the gun that was used to kill Mohsin Dar?'

The boy's eyes flickered. 'No,' he said again. 'Nothing, man.'

Khattak couldn't tell if that was the truth. But it gave him the idea for a new line of inquiry. He nodded at Dinaase, indicating the boy could go.

'Would you ask Mr. Ashkouri if he'll join me now?'

Din shuffled to the door, the kaffiyeh trailing down his back.

'Didn't you know?' he asked. 'He already left.'

13

RACHEL PRETENDED NOT TO NOTICE Khattak as he made his announcement. It wasn't all that difficult. She was genuinely fascinated by Paula Kyriakou's actions. Like Rachel, Paula paid scant attention to Khattak. Her entire attention – in fact her whole body and spirit – seemed attuned not to the graces of an almighty deity, but rather to the prosaic consideration of a distinctly earthbound male.

Before the prayer, other things had kept Paula busy. Rachel had tied her own headscarf this afternoon, choosing a pattern of red and pink stripes – a bit showy, but all that had come to hand in the midst of her unpacking. Paula's eyes had made the pilgrimage to the top of Rachel's skull. Unable to find fault, she had turned away without speaking. Secretly, Rachel was pleased. Paula was thoroughly unencumbered by the need to put others at ease.

She witnessed as much again as the women's prayer row formed.

Women of all ages shuffled together, laughing a little and talking, complaining about the weather or commenting on the brevity of the *khutbah* and the opportunity it afforded to avoid the rush hour. They were grateful to the imam for being a practical, sensible man.

The atmosphere was easy and good-humored. Rachel found herself enjoying it, nodding at a few young women her own age. They smiled in turn.

And then Paula came around and paced the length of the line, disapproval sketched in every inch of her stout figure. She shoved some of the women forward, pulled others a step or two back, her fierce scowl framed by the constriction of her headscarf.

'Keep the line straight,' she growled. 'Don't forget the etiquette of prayer in the useless drama of the earthly life. *Duniya* versus piety. It shouldn't be a contest.'

When some of the women glared at Paula in turn, she pointed out, 'Your quarrel is not with me. It's with your Creator.'

Rachel raised her eyebrows, which were quite as heavy as Paula's.

'You're new,' Paula struck out at her. 'When you enter a house of prayer, you must leave your other preoccupations behind. Otherwise, why bother to come?'

'Not for the sense of community,' said one of the others. The women near her laughed.

Paula fired back. '*Shaitan* laughs the loudest, sisters. Don't forget where you are.'

'Give it a rest, would you, Paula?'

Rachel turned at the sound of the voice. It belonged to Rukshanda Khattak. She'd slipped in late, and was at the opposite end of the prayer row from Rachel. She wore a long emerald sweater over a thick wool skirt, with an artful headscarf that draped over her clothing. The scarf was secured by two jewel-green pins tilted against her lovely face. Unlike Paula, Ruksh's scarf was a fashion accessory, worn with a casual flair that Paula could never hope to emulate.

And maybe there was a cruelty in that.

Or maybe, Rachel thought, Ruksh had dressed as she had for Hassan Ashkouri.

Ruksh chose a spot beside Paula, who stood with a military stiffness. She laid a warm hand on the receptionist's shoulder.

'Relax,' Ruksh said. 'The Friday gathering is about community. It's meant to be joyful.'

Paula shrugged off her hand, her face tight with anger.

'You think you know everything,' she told Ruksh.

Ruksh's answer was mild. 'I know there's no prize awarded for perfection of the rituals. You don't have anything to prove, Paula. When you've been with us a little longer, you'll see there's no one way.'

Humiliated, Paula replied, 'It's people like you who cause *fitna*. Just ask Hassan.'

Ruksh said nothing else. Her face was eloquent on the subject of the pity she felt for Paula. Rachel looked away. The entire encounter made her uncomfortable. Ruksh might not be as sharp-edged as Rachel had first assumed, but there was a troubling element of condescension in the way she had spoken to Paula.

Khattak had been thoughtful when he'd explained the loaded meaning of the term *fitna*. Rachel wondered which context applied here: temptation, trial, civil strife, or disunity? It was a heavy charge to toss around.

She watched Hassan Ashkouri join the men. His lambent eyes sought out Ruksh, instead of the other way around. And such a look. So might an angel of the pit cast his spell.

When Khattak read out his list of names at the conclusion of the prayer, it was Ruksh who stiffened with displeasure.

She didn't want her brother here, didn't want to acknowledge him as her brother. But she still hadn't singled out Rachel for her attention. Or guessed aloud at Rachel's identity.

'Come with me,' Paula urged her.

Rachel followed Paula up to the upstairs landing. Here she found the unassembled pieces of a series of cubicle boards.

'What's this for?' she asked.

'Brother Jamshed isn't happy with Grace. He doesn't like the way she hangs over the balcony. He thinks she comes here to flirt with Dinaase. He thinks her interest isn't sincere.'

Paula said this with a certain primness that Rachel found comical. For hadn't Paula also pushed her way to the balcony, in hopes of glimpsing Ashkouri?

'You won't be able to see the imam. You can barely hear the call to prayer as it is.'

Paula busied herself with sliding the first flank of the partition into its allotted place. The cubicle board was heavy. After watching her struggle for a moment, Rachel stepped in to help.

'Don't worry about that,' Paula said. 'We've only been using the tape recorder out of respect for Mohsin. He always gave the *adhaan* here. In a few days, they'll find someone else.'

Rachel smiled at the idea. A tape recorder was such an antiquated device. Everyone used cell phones now. It reminded Rachel of the Royal Canadian Legion dinners her father had taken her and Zachary to when she was small. The scratchy sound system had refused to deliver the sense of the Legion brothers' speeches. She and Zach had plugged their ears with their knuckles at its screechy whistle, making faces at each other.

'What did you think of him?' Paula asked.

Rachel knew she meant Khattak, but she needed to dig at Paula's composure a little.

'You mean Hassan Ashkouri? His halaqa was fascinating. He's a deep thinker, isn't he?'

Paula slotted another piece of the partition into place. She used so much force that the board slammed against Rachel's hand. Rachel dropped her side of the board, snatching her hand away. It was her good hand. The hand that maneuvered her hockey stick.

'Good God, that hurts!'

She shook the hand back and forth, hoping to outpace the pain.

True to form, Paula offered neither apology nor empathy. She clucked her tongue.

'You shouldn't take the Lord's name in vain. Not over something so minor.'

Rachel grimaced. She'd have to ice the hand when she got home. For now she wondered if Paula had done it on purpose. To change the subject from Hassan Ashkouri.

But then Paula met her question head-on, her tone contemplative.

'He *is* a deep thinker; it's good that you caught that. Most people don't. You were lucky to be invited. It's usually a very select group of people that are allowed to attend the halaqa.'

Rachel blew on her hand, trying to keep her mind off the pain.

'I noticed it was just you and Grace, from the women. Aren't the other women allowed to attend? I mean, how does Hassan choose? How did I get so lucky?' Rachel pretended modesty. 'I know I didn't do anything to earn the invitation. I just stumbled onto this place.'

Paula's sniff was disdainful.

'Hassan likes converts.' She forgot to use the word 'revert' this time, caught up in the story she wanted to tell. And the fact that she had an attentive audience. 'I think he appreciates the depth of our commitment. Most people are lucky enough to have faith handed to them on a platter. We're not. We have to struggle our way toward it. That makes it more meaningful to us.'

She tugged at her scarf, looking for someone on the other side of the balcony.

'Not like Ruksh, who just takes what she's been given for granted.'

Rachel understood Paula's bitterness. Paula longed for the attention of a man who probably wouldn't think twice of her. Who would use her as a pawn in his game. What's more, Paula's rival was beautiful, successful, glamorous. Ruksh could meet Hassan on the plain of a common heritage, sharing a natural sympathy of thought. Paula was giving it her best, crying out for Hassan's notice, and Rachel felt sorry for her, a pity that hit a little too close to home. How many times had Rachel been passed over, ignored, dismissed as unappealing? Fascinated by a man whose eyes held no spark for her? Too many to count.

And Paula was doing nothing to help herself – the censorious tone, the all-encompassing gown, the suffocating scarf. She had chosen to focus on her spiritual appeal, rather than the usual bag of feminine tricks – shiny hair, classy makeup, chic outfits.

Held up to the mirror of Rukshanda Khattak, Paula didn't stand a chance.

Which made Paula lucky, so lucky to have escaped the coils of Hassan Ashkouri.

Unless she was involved in the plot.

Something else puzzled Rachel. Paula didn't seem to have been disregarded completely. She had claimed that Mohsin had pestered her, following her around, clamoring for her attention. But why? Dar was a married man; Paula was interested in someone else. Nothing in the INSET file addressed the issue of Mohsin pursuing her, and if he had, why? To take up an extramarital affair in the midst of a razor-edge undercover assignment would have been an appalling risk.

Dar seemed like he had been a risk taker all his life.

But never a foolish one.

Then why?

She and Paula finished assembling the cubicle boards into a stand-alone partition that blocked the view of the hall below and the light that leaked through slats in the blinds. The upper landing was now a closed-off, dismal space. Rachel felt her spirits sag. This was not a place she would come to for encouragement, if she had been one of the faithful.

She wondered what the other women would make of it: Paula asserting herself once again, once too often, the partition an unwelcome intrusion.

But Jamshed Ali had requested that the partition be set up in the women's gallery. And he had arranged for the delivery of the cubicle boards in very short order.

Why? Because Jamshed was suspicious of Rachel? And wanted to curtail her access to the mosque? If that was true, this was a bizarre method of going about it. Rachel could explore the upstairs or downstairs of the house whenever she wanted to, whenever she had a moment alone. The only thing the partition prevented was a full view of the men's prayer space.

And why would Jamshed Ali want that?

14

Esa tried to catch his sister in the parking lot, but she was determined to leave before he could accost her. Her car sped out of the lot, her face turned away, the better to avoid him. He made his way around the pond, headed to the library, where he'd asked Rachel to meet him.

He'd finished with Zakaria and Sami, neither of whom had added anything that differed from Jamshed Ali's account. Both claimed to have been together inside their cabin when the gunshots had sounded through the woods. Both seemed to view his presence at the mosque with a sense of bemusement, like children at play in a make-believe war.

Not for the first time, he cursed Ashkouri for his role in radicalizing the others.

It was time to call Coale, tell him what he'd learned, and see if Coale would share anything in exchange. A charming street sign denoted Library Lane. He passed under the library's sloping green roof to the reading room at the back, where a series of windows looked out over the pond. His call to Coale went through just as a hand caught at his sleeve. He muted the sound, turning to find Alia Dar at his elbow.

She looked ill, her eyes sunken in her face, her cheeks pinched. She was shivering under her parka, her hands fidgety in her pockets.

'Did you follow me here?' he asked her.

She seemed lost, aimless, with little to say.

'I wanted to talk to Ruksh, but she left before I could catch her.'

'You didn't need to come to Nur to speak to Ruksh.'

'I wanted to see.'

The words trembled on her lips. Her eyes searched Khattak's face, but whatever answers she was looking for couldn't be found in his unsmiling countenance. He wondered if she had mistaken him as someone who could comfort her.

'See what?' he asked with a frown. 'Or did you come here to meet someone?'

'I wanted to see what they'd have to say about Mohsin. It was nothing.' Tears formed in her eyes. 'They didn't say anything. They don't remember him at all. Nobody misses him.'

'That isn't quite true. Your father-in-law misses him. His friends miss him. Ruksh and I – we miss him.'

Alia stared at him with a flicker of curiosity.

'How?' she asked. 'You hadn't seen him in so long.'

Caught by a theme, Khattak murmured a half-remembered line of poetry at her.

'It's Muharrem again. And I don't see any sign of God.'

The Kashmiri poet Agha Shahid Ali had retreated to poetry to express his sorrow at his mother's death. As the poet did so often, he invoked Muharrem, the month of mourning, to give resonance to his suffering. And Khattak had found it a comfort in his own grief at the passing of his wife.

Alia didn't understand, and he felt foolish having said it.

It didn't matter. She wasn't thinking of him at this moment.

Her thoughts were with Mohsin.

And perhaps with Paula, as well.

Something he needed to keep in mind.

He texted Rachel to meet him instead at the Unionville Arms, a local pub. He doubted other members of the congregation would find their way there after the Friday prayer. He found a seat in the dim interior, buried at the back. He was the only customer. A bored young waiter brought him a cup of black coffee. He ordered hot chocolate for Rachel, and felt he'd made the right choice as he watched his partner make her way to the back of the pub, brushing snow from her shoulders. Her complexion was glowing. It was no secret that Rachel loved winter, the heavier the snowfall the better.

'Can't believe anyone showed up today,' she said in greeting. She took a quick gulp of the chocolate, scalding her throat. 'Good call, sir. Hits the right spot.'

They ordered a late lunch of hot, hearty food, catching up as they ate.

'Your sister's not going to give me away, right? Otherwise, I just blew the whole thing.'

Khattak apologized at once. 'I didn't know she would be there today.'

The hot chocolate bubbled in Rachel's mouth. She snorted. 'You sound surprised. No one in my family ever tells me what they're doing or where they're going to be.'

And was pleased she'd said it, when Khattak shot her a look of gratitude.

'Despite what she says to my face, I don't think Ruksh will sabotage our work.'

'But it's dangerous, right, sir? Your sister doesn't have any experience in this. Suppose Ashkouri asks her about me, flat out? She may not know how to lie. And if Ashkouri figures out what she knows –' Rachel stabbed at the air with a French fry. 'You need to get her out of this.'

'I'm trying, Rachel.' He looked rueful. 'The women of my family don't spend a great deal of time listening to my advice.'

'What's she like, your sister?'

Khattak took a long, slow sip of his coffee.

'Smart, funny, kind, impatient. And "headstrong" doesn't begin to cover it. She has a sense that she's invincible.'

'Maybe life hasn't taught her otherwise,' Rachel said.

'Yet.'

Rachel nodded. She knew what invincibility felt like, at least when it came to her work. She had confidence in herself when it came to two things: her skills as a detective, and her force-of-nature presence on the ice. Her personal life was another matter – a mess of chaotic events that she was seldom prepared for, including the ups and downs of her interactions with her brother. So if anything would teach Ruksh caution, it would be the outcome of this case. When Ashkouri and his associates were arrested on terrorism charges and sent to prison for life.

She thought of Paula and Grace, sadness sinking into her bones.

'What about the women, sir? You think they're part of this?'

Khattak called for the bill.

'You tell me,' he said, studying Rachel. The winter weather had served her well. Her eyes were bright and clear, her skin radiant with good health. The hair she usually wore in a ponytail had fallen around her face, providing a little cover for her ears, a look that suited her.

Rachel paused over her plate of quesadillas and French fries. Her healthy appetite was something else Khattak liked about her.

'I'd like to think not, but I don't see how it could be otherwise. INSET says they were at Algonquin to train, right? For the Nakba attack. So if that's true, how would the others hide that from the women? Especially if weapons were involved. *Were* weapons involved?'

'I'm afraid so. Laine told me they were practicing their skills with hunting rifles. But testing at the scene indicates no gunpowder residue on the hands of any members of the training camp. Maybe they wore gloves and disposed of them later. Along with the murder weapon.' He grimaced. 'We have to believe that if there was forensic evidence relevant to the murder investigation, it would have been shared with us.'

'Do you believe that, sir?'

'I hope to. Once I've acquired a little more information.'

Rachel hated being kept in the dark. It was a fruitless means of conducting an inquiry.

'So what did you ask them? Jamshed and Dinaase and the others?' She pushed her plate away, disgruntled by the thought of wasted life, wasted youth. 'Grace and Din, sir. They're just a couple of stupid kids. This goes through, they're going away for life.'

'The lamps of youth have been extinguished,' Khattak quoted, his voice soft. And then cleared his throat, embarrassed. 'With regard to weapons, I asked what they knew about the gun that was used to kill Mohsin Dar. They denied any knowledge of it. I don't know that I believe them. Beyond that, I corroborated the statements they'd given at the scene. Who they were with, what they were doing when they heard the shots, how long it took them to find Mohsin.'

Rachel thought about Khattak's friend. Waiting for death in the woods, wondering if anyone would come. A terrible way to die, regardless of the beauty of Algonquin in winter.

And Alia Dar the only one to mourn his death.

'Something doesn't strike me as right, sir. Paula thought Mohsin was into her. She said he wouldn't leave her alone. Kind of a stupid thing to do when he was working undercover.'

'What are you thinking?'

'Maybe he was doing that for a reason.'

'Perhaps it's not that strange,' Khattak said. 'Din Abdi told me that he loved Mohsin. That he and Mohsin were inseparable. Maybe Mohsin was trying to connect with each member of the cell. Trying to figure out what role each one of them was to play in the attack. Or which one of them was responsible for communication with the other cell. And how that communication was taking place.'

'Not the other boys, or Grace,' Rachel countered. 'No one's said he was hanging about them. Although at the halaqa, Grace did say he was one of the few people who made her feel welcome.'

But why focus on Paula and not Grace? Despite the piercings and the terrifying tattoo, Grace was the one whose company Rachel preferred. At least the girl had a sense of humor.

Or was she construing the situation the wrong way around? Maybe it was Grace who hadn't had much use for Mohsin. If he was taking up Din's time and attention. If he had driven a wedge between the young people.

Then she remembered Jamshed Ali's heavy-lidded gaze. He was the one who found Grace objectionable, and who wanted her gone from the mosque.

'Sir, I don't mean to be offensive with this, but can I just ask – is it possible that Mohsin Dar was thinking of Paula as a second wife? That his interest in her had nothing to do with the Nakba? She's a bit overzealous, but otherwise I haven't seen any indication of the nihilistic worldview it would take to perpetrate this attack.'

Khattak laughed out loud.

It was a very attractive laugh. It made Rachel smile.

'One, there are the bigamy laws in this country. And two, there are Mohsin's own views on the subject. He used to joke that he couldn't handle one woman, let alone two.'

Rachel was just glad that her boss had such a thick skin.

'So then why? She's not dangerous, she's not a femme fatale. What did he want with her? What does his wife think?'

Straightaway, Khattak became serious.

'Alia's hurt. She's wondering. She thinks he was pushing her away.'

'You haven't set her straight?'

'How can I? I can't reveal Mohsin's role as a police agent. And I don't know the truth of his interest in Paula. But here's something. He told Alia the only way she could come to Algonquin was if she began to wear the niqab.'

'The face veil? Why would he do that?'

Khattak settled the bill. They both shrugged back into their winter jackets. Rachel stuffed her headscarf into one of her many pockets.

'I can only think of one reason. The same reason I don't want Ruksh anywhere near Ashkouri. He wanted to keep his wife safe. So he imposed the condition he knew was most calculated to keep Alia far away.'

But there was another possibility as well, Rachel reflected. Perhaps his relationship with Alia was more troubled than Alia had described. Perhaps Mohsin had had reason to fear his wife.

It was a puzzle, and Rachel excelled at puzzles. She stayed behind to give Khattak enough time to leave without being spotted in her company. And so she'd have another opportunity to visit the Old Firehall Confectionery.

There was something to this.

Something that Khattak had mentioned – the significance of which she hadn't understood until this moment. As she cast her mind back over their discussion, the answers to her questions resolved themselves into certainty.

It was too late to call Khattak back.

And she wondered why her boss hadn't seen it himself.

The answer to Dar's death lay not with the Nakba plot, but in Mohsin Dar's own problematic actions.

She began to understand just how complex a task Dar had set for himself by infiltrating the Nakba group.

And she was astonished at the RCMP.

They had trained Mohsin Dar and placed him in the field, but how poorly they had understood the double game their agent had been playing.

A game that had led Mohsin Dar to his death.

15

'I WANT YOU HERE FIRST thing in the morning, Khattak.'

Ciprian Coale made the demand with an edge to his voice, and a lack of civility that was becoming familiar.

Khattak rubbed his fingers between his eyebrows, pressing down hard. He muttered his acceptance, set his phone aside on the counter, and lifted his head to study his face. And witnessed the worry in his eyes, the secret fear.

Because he was looking into a mirror that could never fully capture his duality, a duality he had never chosen to articulate.

He knew what he was, what his community was. So different from what he saw on the news nightly – the lone wolves, the well-armed gunmen, the rabid mobs, the blistering flags, the overturned tanks, the rocket launchers, the blood-doomed faces, the cries in the street, the slogans of death chanted by those with nothing to lose. The cities to fall, under the guise of liberation, the angry clerics cheering their forces onward.

There was the damage they did to themselves, lost in the fog of an all-pervasive ignorance. Of history – their own history, their scripture, their traditions, their prophetic example – taken, twisted, besmirched, betrayed. The kinder and wiser voices silenced. The still, small voice unheard.

And then there was the state apparatus.

The fruit seller's self-immolation – cracked by the Tunisian republic, the boot on his neck, the whip at his throat. And Neda bleeding to death in the streets of Tehran.

A green death on a brutal pavement, unleashing the freshly reaped carnage of spring.

And Khaled Saeed of Alexandria – learning that death could find you in the most ordinary places, shattered against a wall, a door, setting in a bright field a judgment of stone.

An act that brought a government down.

The Arab Spring, the Green Revolution, the Freedom Charter of Syria. The daily discourse of the hollow and war-ravaged. Afghanistan, Pakistan, Iraq, Syria, Nigeria, Myanmar, the Central African Republic, now – but then it had been the democracy movement in Iran, and the toppling of the parliamentarian Mossadegh, it had been Stalin's mass deportation and purge of the Chechen people, it had been the Soviet invasion of Afghanistan, it had been the independence movements that stretched from Africa to the Levant, when tyrants had come to power and stayed and stayed, until the people had risen up, to be crushed.

Struggles for self-determination had been snuffed out like little candles, the lights of the global south going dark.

The war of independence from France had left more than a million Algerians dead. The tally was still being taken. On the new wars of Iraq and Afghanistan, silence.

This was the missing context for the spreading scourge of enmity and hate, the broken and sprawling politics of the Middle East.

The generations mislaid by decades of war, by centuries of struggle.

The splintered past, the crippled future, nothing to gain, less to give.

A bruised carnation planted in a cup.

A rose exchanged for a rifle.

And the round of bread traded for both, in a fleeting moment of innocence.

Crimson coffee is the morning cup.

These Lebanese children are wreaths on bits of firebomb debris.

A lexicon learned each day by every member of Esa's faith.

A hope of belonging that vanished into itself, diminished by every new act of violence.

A knotting of sinews and bone because you were never disconnected from what the *ummah* suffered, any more than you could understand the madmen who claimed to speak or kill or die in their name.

On the one side.

On the other, there was more.

The manufactured anger that fed the machine. Terror plots, jihadist cells, the enemy within, the national threat, the Patriot Act, Guantánamo Bay, the no-fly list, the torture report, the secret rooms, the shadow prisons, the burning Qur'an, the vandalized mosques, the permits denied, the headscarves torn from girls in the street, the venomous ads on the sides of the bus. The cartoon contests, the Muslim students murdered at school.

The rallies in Germany, the rise of Le Pen, the minarets of Switzerland, the discriminatory laws, the Charter of Values, the hallowed ground. The divulgation of Maher Arar.

And the never-quite-innocent unindicted co-conspirators.

A phrase that had amassed the heft of judgment.

The condemnations and dissociations were variations on a theme.

To prove oneself, remove one's self, make amends for untenable, globalized crimes.

Conceiving of history not as a sliding scale or a recurring interchange, but as a denunciatory finger pointing in one direction.

How unreal it all seemed compared with the lives they actually led. Work, family, love, kindness, charity, yes – and faith. Soccer games. Music lessons. Birthday parties. Small altercations. Dinner with friends. Sailboats on the lake. The ferry to the island. The fields of white snow. The blue fog. The tender mist. The green land. The Friday sermon. The evening prayers of Ramadan.

Bayram, Norouz, the festival days. The rites of Muharrem. The sacrificed lamb.

The green thread tied at the gates of the shrine, the kiss at the wrist, the whirling dance.

The wheel of time. The gift of love.

And at the bottom of it all, a faith that touched every corner of their lives – not in Delphic gestures or monolithic laws, but in humble moments – giving courage and comfort, resolution, hope. And of all the virtues, of the things most asked of the faithful – the patience to suffer adversity.

Seek help.

Help shall be given.

Not in the manner and at the time sought, but in ways that crept into the human heart and plugged up the empty places where blood and light and solace leaked away.

Esa needed help now, needed shoring up. He needed peace from the ferment of his thoughts, from Ciprian Coale, from Laine Stoicheva, even from Rachel.

He began the steady process of his ablutions.

Hands washed, face wetted, hair brushed, feet cleansed. The cleansing an internal thing, the discipline personal.

Then he rolled out the prayer rug, his father's prayer rug, the well-worn red and gold. A gift Esa would have shared with his sisters had they ever asked that of him. They seemed to know it as something rare and tangible that linked father to son through loss, and a long-borne loneliness.

He had lost his father and his wife in the same year.

Seek help.

Help shall be given.

He took his place upon the *ja-namaz*. His hands, his lips, his body observed the ritual of centuries. His forehead touched the floor. Once. Twice. And then again in the second and third *rak'ahs*. He found the pattern. He whispered to an unseen presence. He placed his right hand on his right thigh, and raised his forefinger.

I bear witness.

The dusk prayer that broke his heart anew each night.

The first prayer he had learned to pray with his father, the last also, his father's green eyes glancing back over his shoulder, the gentle, confiding smile, the warm words of reassurance, the hands that had held him so tenderly, all these years.

Each time he raised his head from the *ja-namaz*, he expected to see the kindly face looking back at him, offering encouragement, assaying love.

And after ending each *dua*, the first thing his father said was the same.

'How light we both feel! Can you feel the peace of it, Esa?'

Without his father, he couldn't feel the peace.

Seek help.

Help shall be given.

Bless my father, he thought. *Give him the peace that being Your witness has always denied to me.*

Coale had called a team-wide meeting. He'd given Khattak the option to bring Rachel. Esa had chosen not to do so because he knew what was in store. For an amateur, Rachel was doing excellent work. There was no reason to subject her to Coale's particular brand of humiliation.

He already knew there was nothing that he and Rachel could do that would win Coale's approval. He didn't care. About Coale or the men like Coale, whose sense of their authority derived from the satisfaction of pushing others down, like schoolyard bullies.

But for Coale to have come out into the open, Khattak must have done something to increase his feeling of superiority. And security.

The INSET team was gathered in the center of the room. Khattak joined the others as they listened to Coale give the rundown. Laine Stoicheva stepped forward, in her new incarnation of ice-cold goddess, to provide the current operational status. They still hadn't discovered the means of communication between the two splinter cells. But they were getting closer. Something had happened.

Clusters formed around Laine. A website was projected onto a massive screen that blocked the view of the blizzard outside. The lights were dimmed.

Khattak read the banner that framed the interactive site. His heart sank.

THE ROSE OF DARKNESS.
FIGHTING THE NEW CRUSADES.

There was a drop-down menu to the right of the screen with a list of buttons. The questions were staggered on the buttons, one after the other, each with a link to a video.

Are you one of us?
Are you ready to fight?
Do you have the tools?
Do you know your enemy?
Will you do your part in the global jihad?

The questions and links were superimposed upon a colorful background – a repeating Graphics Interchange Format, or GIF, of a drone attack. The GIF was spliced in two: the first image was that of the explosion over the largest house in a village. The second image captured the devastation of the survivors.

The chorus of a popular song played in the background of the video.

If I had a rocket launcher.

Links on the right-hand side of the screen led to a second series of videos, each with a single word between them, each the image of a violent bombing attack or its consequences.

Gaza. Beirut. Qana. Hamdani. Haditha. Fallujah. Baghdad.

The song was linked to images of Fallujah.

Under this list was an invitation to see more on successive pages.

One of the links was an invitation to visit a chat room. Laine Stoicheva clicked on the link. A group of photographs sprang from the screen. Each was the image of the outcome of an attack, this time perpetrated by jihadists. Visitors to the chat room were asked to rate the images on a scale of 1 to 10. The more graphic the image – American soldiers dragged through the streets of Somalia, the beheadings of journalists and aid workers, Muammar Qaddafi beaten to death – the higher the rating.

At the bottom of the site, a crawl crept across the screen, typed over a ribbon of green.

Hummers are hard to assemble and easy to disassemble at the hands of the mujahideen.

An Afghan warrior with a Kalashnikov poised on his shoulder stared back at the viewer from the corner of the screen. He was standing on top of a burnt-out Humvee.

If I had a rocket launcher.

'As you know, this is the website used by Hassan Ashkouri's group to solicit new recruits. You won't be surprised to learn that many jihadist websites are hosted by internet service providers in the West, who often are unaware of the content on the sites. Yahoo, Google, Microsoft – they've all done it. Many of these jihadist sites are shared before they're taken down, allowing them to be folded and restarted. And we know that jihadist groups are continually refining the techniques they use to keep messages and information hidden online.'

Several of the team members nodded.

'The home page for this website is in Arabic. There's an encryption code that allows those who can pass a preliminary examination onto the English-language pages. It's aimed at a very exclusive group of young people who are targeted by specific messages – you know the purpose of narrowcasting, but for Inspector Khattak's sake I'll clarify.'

All eyes in the room turned to Esa Khattak.

He kept his attention on the screen.

The clarification was unnecessary. He'd spent nearly ten years with INSET. It was a tactic of Laine's, designed to unsettle him. To an end that would play itself out in time.

'Narrowcasting is an internet technique used to attract identifiable segments of a population. In the case of the Rose of Darkness, it encourages the idea that new recruits – specifically young people born, raised, or educated in the West – are critically important to the success of the jihadist mission. Those in the West are in the optimal position to strike – to take revenge for what the Rose of Darkness calls the "new Crusades", the wars waged by imperial powers on the Islamic world. Think of the invasion of Iraq. Or the current occupation of Afghanistan. Or Israel's attacks on Lebanon and Gaza.'

When some of the team members bristled, Laine went on, 'The website uses this language to attract young people to the cause of jihad. And to persuade them to participate in revenge attacks on the West.'

Laine drew a breath.

'Most of you have known about the Rose of Darkness since the start of this operation. There's been a new development.'

She began to scroll through a conversation in the chat room. The time code identified it as having taken place the night before.

HAWIYEGANGSTA:	**What about Mo?**
RDSB:	Not here.
HAWIYEGANGSTA:	**It's gotta be here. It's driving me batshit.**
	You gotta tell me. Now.
RDSB:	Hold it together. Not long now.

HAWIYEGANGSTA: **Can't hold it together. What. Happened.**

RDSB: Pull it together, mujahid. It's all in your hands
now.

HAWIYEGANGSTA: **You threatening me? Is this some kind of joke?**

RDSB: No threat. Have patience, sabr. Nine days left. Stay on target.

HAWIYEGANGSTA: **I'm not doing a fucking thing until I know. Fuck the whole thing.**

RDSB: Offline. Now.

HAWIYEGANGSTA: **You wanna see me skywrite? I'll skywrite. Tell me did you kill him?**

HAWIYEGANGSTA: **Did you kill him, I said? DID YOU KILL HIM?**

HAWIYEGANGSTA: **I loved him, man. I really loved him. You hurt him, I'm done.**

RDSB: Don't know what happened or why.

HAWIYEGANGSTA: **How'd you not know? How'm I gonna believe you?**

RDSB: Wallahi. God's own truth. Will find out after it's done.

HAWIYEGANGSTA: **You swear? On your life?**

RDSB: Wallahi. No reason to lie.

RDSB: You on track?

RDSB: You still with us?

RDSB: Hawiye?

RDSB: Hawiye?

RDSB: Do it for your friend. He called you his best mujahid.

RDSB: Don't let him down.

RDSB: Hawiye?

HAWIYEGANGSTA: **Yeah, ok.**

Laine signaled for the lights to be turned up again. Several of the team members blinked, rubbing at their eyes.

If I had a rocket launcher –

Laine muted the sound on the website.

'So. Thoughts? Conclusions?'

Coale watched his team, his fox face intent and alert.

A young man put up his hand.

'"Hawiye" is a common Somali tribe name. That has to be Dinaase Abdi.'

Laine nodded. 'Good. Yes, we've traced the connection to Abdi's phone. What else?'

'They're talking about the Nakba attack. For the first time. Online. They've hardly bothered to encrypt it.'

Nine days from now was New Year's Day.

It fit with everything Khattak knew of the case.

Coale's eyes flicked to him, and then away.

But Khattak caught the look. That look. And felt the subtle distancing of some of the other officers, though not from his former teammates.

'Do we know who RDSB is?' someone asked. 'Or what the acronym stands for?'

'The connection was made at the public terminal at Nur. But we don't know by whom. It could have been anyone who was at the mosque last night. Jamshed Ali. Ashkouri himself, which would suggest a desperation about shutting Din Abdi down before he could say anything else. We're still going through the surveillance footage. And then we'll know if this is a communication between the different groups, or within the same one.'

Khattak shook his head. Laine responded at once.

'Do you have something to add, Inspector?'

Khattak looked around the room. Seeing many friends. And a few nominal adversaries. Men and women Coale had handpicked for his team.

'It's Ashkouri. Or someone he instructed.'

'How do you know this?' Coale demanded.

Khattak spoke to Laine.

'The name of the website. Do you recognize it?'

Laine made a quick scan of the screen. Her gaze returned to Esa's face.

'No. We ran it through all known databases. It doesn't suggest anything, except a taste for the theatrical. And that's common to these sites. Color, drama, danger, intrigue. It pulls young people in.'

Coale stalked closer.

'No known jihadist groups, no cross-references on the watch list. Spit it out, Khattak. What are you getting at?'

'It's something Ashkouri said to my partner at the halaqa yesterday.'

'No, it isn't.' Coale contradicted Khattak without compunction.

Khattak's eyes narrowed. The team gathered in the room knew this for what it was: a showdown between the old guard and the new. And only one man would emerge as the victor.

'Not in those exact words. If you were able to listen to Ashkouri, you must have heard him use the phrase "mud and crime."'

'So?'

'The words are from a poem. The poem is called *A Grave for New York*.'

Silence enveloped the room, the murmurings hushed.

'That isn't the name of the website, Khattak.' Coale spoke with a fine condescension.

Her face pale, Laine interrupted Coale.

'A Grave for New York? Is that a reference to September 11?'

It wasn't. Step by careful step, Khattak provided a summary of the poem, describing its context. The poem predated the 9/11 attacks by three decades. The richness of its themes, the scope of its imagination, the remarkable expressiveness of its language – none of these could be captured by a jihadist website, let alone in some essentialized form.

Khattak had the attention of every member of the team. He told the story of *A Grave for New York*, its drama and darkness, its prosody to the Arabs, its unrelenting indictment of Western materialism, in as plain and simple a language as he could.

The words shocked his audience, and he understood why. The poem was a declamatory work that built to a thunderous crescendo.

New York + New York = The grave and anything that comes from the grave.

New York – New York = The Sun.

And then Khattak quoted the closing lines of the poem. The quiet denouement.

The words hung suspended on the air, a stillness upon an immensity of snow.

But,

Peace be to the rose of darkness and sands,

Peace be to Beirut.

Ciprian Coale was speechless.

Esa Khattak pointed to the moniker on the screen.

'RDSB. The rose of darkness and sands. The "B" stands for Beirut.'

Khattak took the opportunity to stride to Killiam's office, and to close the door behind him.

Coale wanted an audience for his temper.

Khattak refused to provide it. Let Coale stew over the fact that Esa had just contributed something to the investigation that no other member of the team could have found, the manifest reason he'd been appointed to head CPS and asked by Killiam to consult on Mohsin's murder.

For the prodigal understanding of someone inside the fold.

Something that stuck in Coale's craw now.

He'd been looking for a way to humiliate Khattak.

His manipulations had backfired.

'Well?' Khattak asked.

He walked to the window in Killiam's office, studying road conditions that insisted everyone should have been sent home hours ago. The Nakba group were just as constrained by the weather as they were.

From Unionville to INSET headquarters, Khattak had driven through whiteout conditions. Coale lived near Port Credit. He wondered how the man was planning to get home. At Esa's repeated insistence, Ruksh had texted him the words 'at home'. Misbah had replied with more concern for Esa's situation. She'd told him to book a room somewhere and stay overnight.

And the glimmer of an idea had come to Khattak.

He wanted to check on Rachel as well, but feared that his inquiry might smack of sexism.

If he'd understood his partner a little better, he would have known that Rachel would value the thought that he worried over her safety, regardless of her status as a gun-toting policewoman.

Because what use was a gun against the Canadian winter?

Following Esa, Coale managed to keep his temper in check. He barked at Laine over the intercom.

'You should have caught that, Stoicheva. Now get in here, and then maybe Khattak can explain to both of us what the hell he thinks he's playing at.'

Khattak turned from the window. When Laine entered the room, he nodded.

'You'll have to be more specific. I've no idea what you mean,' Khattak said.

Coale's unstudied elegance was at the mercy of his displeasure. An angry hand had yanked at his five-hundred-dollar tie. In his slate-blue ensemble, he should have appeared as cool as the decorous snowfall beyond the window. Instead, a vein throbbed at the base of Coale's neck. One hand was clenched around his Bulgari pen. He threw it across the desk.

It skidded to a halt in front of Laine Stoicheva, who pocketed it without a word.

'You've no idea, have you? Because you were preoccupied with upstaging me out there.' Coale jerked his head at the meeting room they had just left. 'Tell him, won't you, Laine?'

'Andy Dar spoke to the media today.'

The news didn't shock Khattak as much as Coale had hoped. Keeping Dar quiet had always been chancy. He was the person Khattak least expected cooperation from.

'You had one job, Khattak. One job. Keep Dar quiet, and get out of our way.'

Khattak suppressed the urge to tell Coale he couldn't count.

He glanced at Laine, wondering what her contribution to events was meant to be. Audience? Sycophant? A form of Dutch courage, taken straight up?

'He called a press conference in front of police headquarters. Apparently, he sent out a press release in advance, accusing the powers that be of racist dissimulation.'

She recited the words by rote, her face inscrutable, siding neither with Khattak nor Coale.

Khattak glanced at the snowfall outside.

'And people came?'

'It's everywhere. Online, television, radio.'

'Can I see it?'

Laine gave Khattak her phone. He scrolled through the press release, less than half his attention on it. He was thinking ahead to a task that Rachel could undertake.

It was the same kind of material Dar published on his blog. Bombastic, polemical – opinions without hard evidence, indiscriminate generalizations that had made Dar popular with a certain segment of the hard right.

His blog ran under the phrase 'The Trouble with Islam Is Islam.'

This was more of the same, with the spleen directed at a new target – Esa Khattak.

But there was nothing substantive to Dar's accusations. Dar wanted to know why Khattak wasn't investigating the scene in Algonquin; he demanded his son's body back for immediate burial. Beyond that, there were shadowy insinuations about the life of a Muslim homicide victim being considered less valuable than that of a white Canadian. He called Khattak's assignment to the investigation a pacifier. And he accused Khattak of attempting to buy his silence. But Dar was a man who wouldn't be silenced, not when he had truth on his side. He didn't want Khattak investigating his son's death. He wanted no one less than the police commissioner on the job.

But he'd left the Masjid un-Nur alone. Coincidence? Providence? Neither seemed to apply. More likely that Dar was keeping something in reserve, something to stir up media interest down the line.

The blizzard would be the lead news item tonight. And Dar wouldn't want the spotlight to fade quite so soon. Which meant there had to be something in reserve.

'The headline's unfair, Esa,' Laine said.

Khattak hadn't read it. And he suspected Laine's attempt at commiseration.

He scrolled back to the top of the press release.

'*The Trouble with Islam Is Inspector Esa Khattak of Community Policing, Says Well-known Broadcast Journalist Andy Dar.*'

'We're not here to hold each other's hands,' Coale barked.

Khattak handed the phone back to Laine.

'I spoke to Dar. He gave me assurances that he would wait forty-eight hours to go public.' Khattak held up a hand before Coale could interrupt. 'I didn't take that as a guarantee, but you'll see that he hasn't mentioned the Nur mosque. This could work to our advantage.'

'And how do you figure that?'

'It takes the pressure off Ashkouri. If I'm under attack, and my murder investigation is hobbled, he'll be emboldened. It may help if he sees me as weak.'

'Did you speak to him?'

'Not yet.'

'What are you waiting for, man? You think the solution is going to be handed to you?' Coale mimicked an effeminate voice. '"Please, Inspector Esa, may I confess to you?"'

'No.' Khattak held on to his patience. Coale was goading him for a reason. 'As I remember it, you asked me to proceed without causing undue alarm at the mosque. I've interviewed four of the five people who were at the winter camp with Dar, and my partner has spoken to both women. Ashkouri dodged the questioning today.'

'I should take you off this right now,' Coale threatened. 'You've failed from start to finish. On top of that, you're hopelessly compromised.'

This time Khattak took the bait.

'Meaning?'

'Your sister, Khattak. She's engaged to Ashkouri. They're as thick as thieves.'

Khattak's reply was icy. 'Have you any evidence to support that claim? Among your thousands of intercepts?'

He wanted proof of what he'd found in Gavin Chan's office. Rukshanda Khattak: Cell 1.

Coale didn't answer. He thrust his hand into his collar. If he'd had anything against Ruksh, he would have played his hand by now.

'Then I want my sister out of this.'

'Oh no, no.' Coale took a special pleasure in denying the request. 'Just because we haven't found anything doesn't mean there isn't anything. And if you remove your sister from the equation, that's as good as sounding Ashkouri a warning bell. No, nothing changes except you. We don't need you anymore, and I'm not sure you can be trusted with an operation of this magnitude. It requires careful police work, Khattak. The kind they don't expect from CPS – which let's face it, is just political correctness run amok.'

And there it was, beneath the words. The slow-burning resentment that Khattak had been the one to leap ahead, leaving Coale behind, until Coale's own promotion had come through much later.

It explained a great deal, not least Coale's simmering antagonism.

'That's not your call to make. And if you have nothing but this press release, I suggest that neither of us wastes any further time. I have leads I need to pursue.'

A young officer knocked at the door to Killiam's office. 'We have something, sir,' he said to Coale. 'We're moving on the fertilizer delivery.'

Ciprian Coale brushed by Khattak, a dismissal. And then he turned at the door, with an actor's instinctive grasp of how to make an exit.

'You set another foot wrong, and you're finished, Khattak. You're going to find that you've used up all your rope.'

Laine and Khattak looked at each other.

'Why am I really here?' Esa asked her. 'Has something happened?'

She didn't answer this.

'You know we hear everything that happens at the mosque. But we wouldn't have understood about the poem. That was an incredible step forward for us.'

'And?' Then realization cut deep, as he sorted through her words. 'Is Rachel in danger? Does Ashkouri suspect her?'

Laine moved as though she wanted to reach for Khattak's arm. She checked herself before the gesture could be completed. Familiarity was no longer possible between them.

'It's not about your partner. It's Ruksh. You can't get her out –

she won't listen to you. But maybe I can. I could talk to her, Esa; she knows me.'

But Ruksh had no reason to trust Laine Stoicheva, and both of them knew it. Ruksh had been a front-row witness to the claim Laine had brought against Esa. And to the two-year silence between Esa and Nathan Clare, his closest friend – Laine the issue of contention between them.

'And risk the operation?' Khattak examined Laine's flawless face. He read nothing save the solemn desire to help. Which was how Laine lured otherwise sharp-witted officers into her ambush. 'Why would you do that? Why would you want to do that? We're not friends. There's nothing between us.'

A hand inside his jacket pocket switched on the recording function on his cell phone.

Laine shrugged her slim shoulders. A lock of dark hair fell across her face, giving her the appearance of a downcast angel.

'We don't need complications. This is a complication I could remove.'

And what if she said that Khattak had warned Ruksh off, in defiance of explicit orders? He wouldn't put it past Laine. Her behavior was unpredictable, even at her best.

'I don't think so. I don't need your help, Laine. I can manage my own family.'

'I'm not your enemy, Esa. I don't know why you still see me that way. We used to work well together.'

Khattak raised both eyebrows.

'Is that a serious question, Laine? After everything you did? After what you did to my friend?' He precluded her attempt at an answer. 'Let's not dig up the past. Whatever you're doing now, whatever this attempt at reconciliation is – it's not working. Leave it alone.'

Laine studied Khattak's shuttered face in turn. Whatever she saw in it convinced her that this wasn't the time to press the subject. She moved to the door, one hand clasped on the knob.

She spoke over one shoulder, in an unconscious imitation of Coale's departing gesture.

'Maybe something good came of your presence at Nur today. When Ashkouri left without talking to you, I mean. You've distracted his attention from the fertilizer delivery.'

But she didn't tell him anything further, and Khattak chose not to ask.

16

Rachel had pulled over to a side street to wait out the storm when Khattak called her.

'Where are you?'

'Not far from where you left me. Blizzard's out of control. It's supposed to ease up later tonight.'

'Could you go back?'

Rachel decided not to ignore the note of strain in Khattak's voice.

'To the mosque? No problem. What's going on?'

'Throw yourself on their mercy. Tell them you need a place to stay. And make sure they know you've told several people where you are. I want you to nose around a little. Maybe you'll find something that tells us how the two cells are communicating. Or something that connects to the murder.'

Rachel could almost hear Khattak second-guessing himself.

'I'll be fine, sir, don't worry. You're thinking they're on to us? The wiretaps caught something?'

'Not that exactly. Someone at the camp has already killed once. Whatever their reasons, the murder was cold and rational. If they knew about Mohsin, it's possible they suspect you. I don't like to think of sending you into a pit of vipers by yourself. Someone still has that gun.'

'Well, they won't all be staying over at the mosque, will they? And I'll have the chance to search for the gun. You don't need to worry about me. You know that I can handle myself.'

The words came out sounding more personal than professional.

Rachel hurried over them before Khattak could notice.

'What happened with INSET?'

'Several unpleasant things.' Khattak filled her in on the Rose of Darkness website, and its connection to Ashkouri. He went over the chat log in some detail.

Rachel scratched at her ear, thinking.

'So if Hawiye is Din Abdi, doesn't that put him in the clear? If he's demanding answers about Mohsin Dar's death? And doesn't it sound like he expects that if anyone did this, it was Ashkouri himself?'

She heard Khattak sigh. And wondered how he planned to get home. The road closures had multiplied. Cakes of snow were wedged inside her windshield wipers.

'Yes to the first. I don't think it is Din. He doesn't possess that kind of coolheadedness. If he'd been the one to murder Mohsin Dar, he'd have fallen apart by now. You get a sense of it in the transcript as well. He's unraveling. As to Ashkouri – it sounds like it, but RDSB used the public terminal at the mosque.'

Rachel pondered this. 'So it could have been someone else. Listen,' she said. 'I had a thought about Mohsin Dar. And what he might have been doing at Nur.'

She spoke for several more minutes without interruption. When she had finished, Khattak confirmed her suspicions.

'I've been thinking the same thing. And wondering about the RCMP role in all this.'

'Too laid-back?' Rachel offered. 'Too wrongheaded? Wearing blinders? Fatally misunderstanding their man?'

'All of the above.'

Rachel started her car. The wipers moved back and forth across the windshield, bumping slightly over the hardened snow. She turned on the defrost.

'What else, sir? There's something more, isn't there?'

She had a feeling she knew what it was. And she wondered if Khattak would choose to tell her. After a moment, he did.

'I don't like working with Laine. Ciprian's a known quantity, I know what his agenda is, what he wants, why his feelings are bruised. I can't say the same for Laine.'

Despite the falling temperature, warmth bubbled inside Rachel. The words were a sign of trust, a sign that her partnership with Khattak was expanding, deepening. She caught herself in the rear-view mirror with a ridiculous grin pasted on her face. She wiped it off with a frown.

'She's trying to obstruct you? Get in your way somehow?'

'The opposite. Twice now she's offered me her exclusive help. And access to inside knowledge. It doesn't add up. Not with what I know of her.'

Rachel chewed on this. 'She's up to something. She's just not ready to play her hand.'

'I think I should go and see her. Somewhere away from headquarters.'

Rachel sat up straight in her seat. Switching over to Bluetooth, she eased her car off the shoulder and back onto the road. A passing driver in a pickup truck made an obscene gesture as she cut him off. She turned on the lights of her siren. The driver sped away.

'I think that's the last thing you should do. You'd be playing right into her hands.'

'The INSET operation is too finely balanced as it is. It won't survive whatever form of sabotage Laine has in mind. Shouldn't I get in front of this?'

Rachel hesitated. Khattak's awareness of his magnetism could be subliminal at times.

'Her interest might be more personal than you're imagining, sir.'

She heard the sharp intake of Khattak's breath over the noise of the traffic.

'Then what do you recommend?'

'Stay away,' Rachel advised. 'No matter what. I can talk to her if the need arises.'

'Laine offered to get Ruksh out of this.'

'That's a trap, sir. If you need help with Ruksh, maybe you should talk to your friend. He's close with your sister, right?'

Nathan Clare. The friend Laine Stoicheva had used without a qualm.

When Khattak didn't answer, Rachel continued. 'Or maybe you should just sit tight, let things play out. It's what we've been ordered to do anyway.'

She swore as she narrowly missed a collision with a winter-challenged driver.

'Sorry about that, sir. I'm two minutes from Nur.'

'Be careful, Rachel.'

'You, as well.'

It wasn't dark yet. It was that twilight time when the sun had dipped down from the sky for the day, and blues and grays skirted the soft outline of its rays. The yellow house was folded between white rimples of snow. A small light burned beside the door. And beyond, the streets fell away from gently banked hills.

A Catalina blue drifted across the landscape.

To Rachel, it felt like a burden, reminding her of so many evenings without Zach, wondering where her brother was, whether he was safe or loved or ever coming home.

And then one day he had.

She tried the door. It gave way at her touch.

There was no one at Paula's desk in the reception area. And no one in the prayer hall, though she could hear the tender sound of music. Textured voices layered over each other. A calling and sounding back of multitonal rhythms, the sound of devotion. It was a recording of religious hymns known as *nasheeds*.

Rachel stowed her boots in one of the caddies. She hung up her winter coat. Then she padded up the stairs on stealthy feet. Paula and Grace were not on the landing, nor was anyone else. The

162

space was deserted, the partition a dull reminder of exclusion. Rachel peered around it.

The kitchen was as deserted as the rest of the main floor. Rachel waited several minutes. No one came. The hymns continued to play. Under her breath, Rachel hummed along.

Khattak had said to undertake a search. Where should she start? She glanced up the stairs to the second floor. She could explain her presence on the main floor of the house more easily than she could if she were caught searching the bedrooms upstairs. Khattak had told her the bedrooms were used for guests of the mosque who were visiting from out of town. Best to be quick then. Not giving herself time to think, she scurried up the stairs.

Five doors led off the hall, two on each side, one at the very end. The door at the end was closed. The two on the right were open. Both led into bedrooms, one with an attached en suite. Rachel began with one of those, a slow, methodical search. The room was decorated with a lemon-yellow counterpane, folded back on a French country bed. The pillowcases that matched it were frilly, the lamps rustic. A chest of drawers was tucked away into a corner.

Rachel searched the drawers. She found numerous sheet sets and more pillowcases. Successive drawers were occupied by gleaming prayer rugs woven of heavy silk. She checked under the mattress. Then she checked out the second bedroom, which was equally uninhabited.

The two doors on the left were closed. She nudged one open. A third bedroom, this one showing signs of occupancy. A battered backpack was flung over a small wooden table that served as a desk. The backpack was covered in heavy lapel pins and buttons. Death heads, crossbones, political slogans, a white star in a blue circle, the Palestinian flag. A dozen buttons in a row with the word 'Misfits' stamped above a grinning black skull.

A stack of cassette tapes with handwritten labels divulged

a list of punk rock bands. Bad Religion. The Casualties. Social Distortion. The Suicide Machines. Black Flag. Rancid. The Damned. An unappetizing selection of names. And one that was out of place: An-Nahda Hip Hop. Rachel pocketed the tape. *An-Nahda* meant 'the awakening.' And was possibly connected to Ennahda, Tunisia's long-suppressed Islamist political party.

The drawers contained a meager selection of underwear and socks, and a few additional T-shirts in a style Rachel thought she could safely ascribe to Grace. The Jack and Jill bathroom took her to the fourth room, which was set up as an office.

Here was the public terminal. Computer, printer, and a set of loudspeakers. A gaming system. And a not-inexpensive digital turntable with an accompanying mixer. Thousands of dollars' worth of equipment.

Rachel switched on the desktop computer. It booted up with a groan of protest and she shut the door. She turned her attention to the desk drawers. They were stuffed with notebooks and CDs – too many for her to sort through when she could be discovered at any minute.

She used her cell phone camera to take a rapid series of pictures. She photographed the computer setup, the electronic equipment, the contents of the drawers. Then she moved to the notebooks. One was a sketchbook. Rendered by an amateur architect, it contained a selection of crudely drawn structures and floor plans. None represented the Nakba targets. One was simply the drawing of a skating rink, two crescent moons that faced each other hanging over it.

Rachel glanced out the window to the pond below.

A figure detached itself from the trees that circled the pond.

She drew away from the window quickly.

The light from the computer would give her silhouette away. Up until now she had used the light from her cell phone.

The computer was still cycling, running through updates.

She chose another notebook at random.

Notes for the Friday sermon.

Most of the writing was contained within the notebook's borders, but someone had scrawled down the side of one page, *'Marginal notes on the book of defeat.'* Rachel photographed the page, along with consecutive pages of the sermon.

'Do not delay your prayers. Do not perform good deeds only to be seen. Remember the care of the downcast, the lonely, the orphans, the forsaken, the hungry and the poor. And do not refuse the gift of small kindnesses.'

She scanned the rest of it and could see nothing that served a jihadist interpretation. And Nur's imam wasn't on INSET's list.

She returned her attention to the computer. First, she checked the documents folder. It was empty. Then the recycling bin. Empty as well. Nothing on the desktop itself. No recently saved documents.

In the search window, she typed the words 'rose of darkness'.

No matching results were found.

Now she connected to the internet. And checked the bookmarks bar. The list was some forty or fifty sites long. Her eyes ran over them quickly. YouTube videos of Mecca during the Hajj. *Nasheed* sites. A link to Muhammad Asad's translation of the Qur'an. Several punk music videos. Numerous sites on the history of Somalia. A long selection of news articles on the 2003 invasion of Iraq. Some on ISIS. Some on Syria and the tyranny of Bashar al-Assad.

And one item that caught her attention. Someone had bookmarked websites where bolt-action hunting rifles could legally be purchased. Mausers, Winchesters, Sakos, Brownings, and several other models. Someone had been comparing the accuracy and durability of the rifles.

But there was nothing else. No blueprints, no schematics, no instructions on the construction of a fertilizer bomb, not a single map of the city of Toronto.

Rachel photographed the bookmarks bar, planning to check the search history next.

A footfall on the carpet outside the bedroom door gave her a two-second warning.

She dropped her phone into her pocket, shoved the notebook back into the drawer.

Into the Google search bar, she typed the single word 'GO' and hit 'Enter'.

The door opened behind her.

Casually, she turned around.

She was face-to-face with Jamshed Ali.

He closed the door behind him.

Rachel remembered her unabashed grin from the car, the grin she would have been mortified for Esa Khattak to witness, and tried it on Jamshed now.

'What are you doing here?'

He moved a step closer.

Rachel sank down into the office chair, affecting an attitude of unruffled friendliness.

'The blizzard has made a mess of traffic; I was checking timetables for public transit. Paula mentioned there was a computer for public use upstairs.' She tried for a tone of injured innocence. 'It wasn't password-protected.'

Paula had mentioned nothing of the kind. Rachel prayed the woman had gone home. It would give her time to regroup before her lie could be exposed.

And then she remembered that part of her cover at the Nur mosque was that she lived locally. She hoped Jamshed Ali hadn't heard this.

His rancorous eyes moved to the screen behind her shoulder.

The green-and-white symbol of the GO Transit system flashed up against the screen. A list of train and bus timetables ran down one side of the screen.

'And where are you going, Miss Ellison? I understood that you lived in this neighborhood.'

Sweat broke out on the back of Rachel's neck. His commonplace words were laden with foreboding.

'That's right, I do. But I'm supposed to meet my girlfriends in the city. I just called them. They're meeting me at Union Station.'

She swiveled the chair. Her eyes darted to the screen.

'I was just checking the time of the next train from Unionville.'

Jamshed Ali leaned down. He braced one hand on Rachel's chair. She could smell the qahwe on his breath. Cardamom and cinnamon, and the scent of smoke. He was reading the screen in front of her.

'The GO trains do not run after rush hour, Miss Ellison. If you were to take the bus, you would encounter the same difficulties on the road as if you had driven yourself. The snowfall makes no exceptions.'

Rachel pretended to dither.

'I didn't realize that, but I guess you're right. What should I do? Maybe ask my friends to come and get me?' Wondering if she was overdoing it, she pinched her temples. 'No, that doesn't make sense. They'd have as much trouble as I'm having. Is it possible – that is, Paula said you often let guests stay overnight. Do you think I could crash here until the snow lets up?'

Jamshed's gaze probed Rachel's face. She stared back with the same oblivious grin, her palms and her underarms damp. She wondered if he could smell the metallic tang of her fear.

'I wouldn't mind sharing with Paula,' she offered as an add-on.

She flinched as Jamshed reached past her. He turned off the computer and moved away.

'The computer is not for public use,' he told her. 'Neither is the house. In any event, the rooms are all taken. We do not have space for anyone else.'

He opened the door to the room, indicating that Rachel should go ahead.

She wondered if he planned to push her down the stairs.

The moment she reached the landing, she was swamped by an enormous feeling of relief. As she approached the main floor, she could hear voices. Jamshed left her and joined the small group of young men gathered in the prayer hall, none of whom Rachel recognized from the INSET list.

Grace was in the kitchen. Instead of brewing qahwe for Dinaase, she was keeping watch over a saucepan of boiling milk. Her headscarf was tied around her waist over a long-sleeved shirt with the band logo 'Rancid' stenciled across the front. There were several holes near the bottom of both legs of her black leggings. Based on what she had seen in the room she took to be Grace's, Rachel didn't think the holes were a fashion statement. Grace Kaspernak was one of the city's invisible poor.

Rachel drifted over to the saucepan.

'That smells good,' she said.

'Thanks. You want some? I thought you left.'

'Roads are a mess. I can't get home tonight.'

Rachel found two mugs in a cupboard and set them upon the counter beside Grace. The mugs were imprinted with one of the sayings of the mystic poet Rumi.

I looked in temples, churches and mosques, but I found the Divine within my heart.

Rachel snorted.

'What?' Grace asked. 'What's funny?'

Rachel nodded at the mugs. Grace poured the hot chocolate mixture into them.

'You believe that?'

'Don't you?'

'If I had any answers inside myself, I wouldn't be coming here.'

Grace had opened the blinds in the kitchen. The snowfall outside was a white wall of noiseless fury, the symmetry of the stars eclipsed by a cataract of quiet.

'How are you getting home, then?'

Rachel sipped at her hot chocolate. It tasted as good as the aroma of the qahwe.

'I was hoping to crash here. But Mr. Ali said the bedrooms are all taken.'

The pan slipped in Grace's hand.

In spite of the heavy makeup, Grace was no good with a poker face. Rachel decided she'd never have a better opportunity to find out about the camp. Jamshed Ali was busy with the group of young men, leading some kind of Arabic recitation effort.

'I'll figure something out,' Rachel said. 'No matter how bad it gets on the roads, I still love winter. I'm even a winter camper. But I'm guessing you're not much of an enthusiast. You're shivering inside the mosque, and it's really not that cold.'

Grace took up her mug. She wandered over to the windows, to the point farthest from the circle of young men. Rachel followed behind.

'It looks so pretty,' Grace said of the snowfall. 'But the truth is, it's cruel and brutal.'

Rachel dropped her voice. 'You're thinking of your friend? Up north in the woods?' And when Grace turned to look at her with those puffed-up, swollen eyes, Rachel went on, 'The news is everywhere. Everyone was talking about it after that police officer left.' When Grace still said nothing, she added, 'What did you think of him?'

Grace pressed hard against the staples in her neck. She muttered her answer.

'He should have come a long time ago.'

The words stunned Rachel. But she had a much better poker face than Grace.

'Why? Did you know your friend was in danger?'

'No. I didn't mean that. Look, forget it. Forget what I said. I don't know how you can like this weather. I hate it. It never seems to end. It's hard on people, you know?'

Winter would be grueling for a teenage girl who was homeless.

Sleeping on the heating vents of unforgiving pavements, passed over by a thousand strangers who refused to meet your eyes.

'I guess so. I mean, the roads aren't great, but it's nice when you get out into the wilderness and just see the stars and the fields full of snow. You can snowshoe, or toboggan, or if there's a creek nearby, you can go skating. I love to skate, don't you?'

'I don't think the wilderness is all that it's cracked up to be.' Grace flattened her voice. 'That's where Mo died. And they still want to go back. Pretty heartless, if you ask me.'

She finished her hot chocolate and dumped her mug in the sink.

'Go back?' Rachel asked. 'To the same place?'

'Yeah. They said it would be a personal memorial. Something they couldn't do at the mosque. Din is all for it. He's like you – loves the snow, loves the cold. Even though neither of us can skate. But I wish he wouldn't go. I asked him not to.'

'What did he say?'

Grace's watery eyes met Rachel's. 'I don't know why I'm telling you this. It's not like we're friends or anything.'

Rachel shrugged. 'We're both bored. And we're trapped here for a bit.' She waved a hand at the study group. 'Unless you want to join them. It's up to you. If you want to talk, I mean. I'm usually a good listener.'

She continued to sip at her chocolate, keeping her attention on the blanked-out pond. The monotonous sound of the memorization swelled to fill the room.

'Yeah, whatever.' A piercing in Grace's left eyebrow appeared to be bothering her. As she spoke her hand fiddled with it, massaging the skin above and below. 'When Din's with these guys, it's like I don't exist. Like he can't hear anything I say. It was the same with Mo. Mo was *always* with him – big-brother stuff, I guess. Like they'd be talking their private bullshit, and whenever I'd want to join in, they'd drop the subject and go their separate ways.'

'But you said Mo was the one who made you feel welcome.'

'Yeah, I guess. One-on-one. He was friendly and fun. But he just kind of – got in between me and Din. Like when he was around, I was the afterthought. Not like how it used to be. And then sometimes I thought, maybe Mo didn't want me here either. He kept asking if I was sure I wanted to stay at the mosque. He said there were a lot of other places that would take me.'

Grace made a despairing gesture at her attire.

'I mean, look at me. Look at this.' She pressed a hand to the tattoo at her throat. 'Who do you think wants to hang around this?'

'What's that for?' Rachel asked gently. 'Does it stand for something?'

'Yeah.' Grace's pale skin flamed. 'It's an in-joke between me and Din. He calls me his personal grace, I call him my pirate. The star is for the Somali flag, 'cos Din is really proud of his identity.'

'Sounds like you're really close to each other.'

Grace dropped her hand. 'We used to be. We've been at school together since we were little kids. Two misfits. The only place we ever fit in was with each other. Until Din found this place. And now I don't know.'

'But you're staying at the mosque,' Rachel reminded her.

'Yeah. It's not a big deal, but Din told them he'd have to head back to the West End unless they found a place here for both of us. Jamshed doesn't like it, but who gives a shit?'

The expletive sounded staged on her lips.

'Then he's not as far gone as you think. If he made sure you have a place to stay.'

Though she didn't smile, Grace's eyes brightened.

'If you can't get home, you can crash on the floor in my room,' she offered.

It touched Rachel deeply that a girl with so little to give would give this. But she was conscious of the tape she had stolen, a hidden bulk in her pocket.

'That's really kind of you, Grace. Thank you. But I'm going to give it another shot, if I can dig out my car. Tell you what, though – I'd love to teach you and Din to skate, if you're ever interested. I have a couple of extra pairs of skates.'

Now the smile broke through on Grace's lips. It was every bit as lovely as Rachel remembered.

'Yeah, maybe. Maybe it would be something we could do up at the camp. Once I get these studs out. It was freaking cold last time.'

Grace ran her hand over the back of her skull.

Rachel needed to know about the camp – the timing, the details. She had no way of knowing what the INSET team knew about the plan to return to Algonquin.

She was just on the brink of a much closer confidence.

'I've got an extra Maple Leafs toque. I know it's not Bad Religion, but it might be of more use. And you wouldn't have to switch allegiances.'

Grace actually laughed, a quick choked-off sound.

'Maybe you should come with us, since you love to camp.' And then, in case Rachel thought there was too much undiluted welcome on offer, she added with a trace of sullenness, 'It would be great to get Paula off my back. She can attach herself to you instead.'

Rachel didn't ask any questions about the destination or the specific makeup of the group that would be heading to the camp. She didn't want to scare Grace off. Suppressing her excitement, she said, 'I'd love to come. It would be the perfect time to teach you both to skate. If you're still interested. Do you want to ask Din?' She scanned the room. 'I don't see him.'

'He went to the convenience store. Hassan needed supplies for the trip. And I asked Din to get me some tapes – Hassan keeps borrowing mine. Punk sounds better on a cassette deck. I like to record my own stuff. And the spoken word that Din does.'

Which reminded Rachel that this was something she wanted

to hear for herself. Maybe it was a connection to the tape that was buried in her pocket. Al-Nahda Hip Hop.

'When do we leave?' she asked Grace.

Grace took Rachel's empty mug from her and stacked it beside her own in the sink.

'The Monday after the halaqa.'

'Won't Mr. Ali mind if I just show up?'

'Who gives a shit?' Grace demanded. 'He doesn't own me. And he doesn't own Din. If I say you're coming, Din will back me up.' All the same, she spoke in a whisper. 'Just show up here ready to go, first thing Monday morning. We'll sort it out from there.'

17

WHEN KHATTAK RETURNED FROM MEETING a friend Sunday night, the family home was lit by Christmas lights that swung in loops of crimson, yellow, and green. A second set of lights festooned the doors of the carriage house a little distance back from the garden.

The roads had been cleared, the blizzard had passed. Khattak had been with his friend, a professor of modern Arabic poetry, for just over two hours. In that brief time, the character of his parents' house had changed. The Khattak family had never hung Christmas lights before. They borrowed the tradition, much like the Chinese New Year, and illumined the house on the festival days of Eid. Now the house shimmered in the dark like its neighbors.

The lights weren't meant for Christmas.

The streamers of lights were a signal sent to him by his sister.

In the tradition of the Indian subcontinent, the house had been lit for a wedding.

There were two other cars parked in the driveway of the Khattak home; Khattak recognized the plates from the INSET file. Jamshed Ali's. And Hassan Ashkouri's. He was engulfed by a feeling of despair, as he understood what his sister had done.

She'd moved Ashkouri's halaqa to their home.

Coale would have known. And he'd said nothing, waiting for Khattak to fall into the trap.

Khattak was not given to self-pity or melodrama; to acknowledge

174

his duality was also to accept it. Yet inexorably, he felt the tightening of the noose. He parked his car to block Hassan Ashkouri's. His cell phone rang. It was Laine, calling to warn him.

'It's too late, I've just found out. Why didn't Coale tell me about this?'

Laine paused. Khattak let the silence build.

'I don't know,' she admitted. 'I'm just the Outreach Coordinator. I'm not privy to everything he knows. I would have told you if I'd known sooner.'

Khattak gripped the phone. He wasn't impervious to Laine's blandishments. He was about to cross a line with her.

'What's Ashkouri doing at my house? What's his game? The last thing he should want is my undivided attention. Or for me to have any reason to focus on his group.'

Laine answered carefully. 'He's engaged to your sister, Esa. Perhaps he realizes that it's more than time that the two of you were introduced.' She gave Esa time to absorb that, before continuing, 'But personally, I think it's something else.'

Esa waited for more.

'I think he's gotten cocky. He thinks he's untouchable, and that we haven't the faintest idea about Nakba. It's his *coup de grâce*. Seducing your sister under your nose, dragging her into his mess. He's showing you that you're vulnerable. He's using Ruksh as leverage.'

Khattak exhaled, the sound harsh in the confines of his car.

They were both silent for a moment. Then Laine said, 'I offered to talk to Ruksh.'

'I know you did.' It was hard for him to get the words out. 'And I'm grateful.'

He caught Laine's small gasp. And took it for the encouragement to proceed.

'Will you tell me something, Laine? Something I've no right to ask. Is my house under surveillance? Has Coale been watching me?'

There was a longer pause this time before Laine answered. At last she said, 'Yes. From the day that Ruksh first met Ashkouri.' The sound of her voice was muffled. 'You know I can't tell you anything else.'

But she did give him one piece of information essential to his investigation.

Esa thanked her, his voice gruff. He was now desperate enough to take the step that Rachel had urged. He called Nate. There was a click on the line before the call connected him to his friend. His summary was brusque, conveying as little as possible. When Nate consented to speak to Ruksh, Esa found his determination renewed.

He walked through scaffolds of snow to his house.

The living room in the Khattak home was a gracious space, well-proportioned, lit with porcelain lamps. It was painted a pale shade of blue above the white wainscoting that ran the length of the room. Hyacinth drapes in heavy damask shaded Palladian windows. The pattern was edged with silver thread that shone in the room's lamplight.

Khattak was grateful that no family portraits or photographs had been placed in this room. There was a white recessed bookshelf that echoed his parents' taste in art and literature, and a selection of mother-of-pearl curios that his mother had collected from Lahore. Persian ceramics in turquoise and white gleamed from alcoves in the corners of the room. Tables of white glass fronted Venetian sofas in duchess blue.

Hassan Ashkouri was seated in the Egyptian chair that had been a favorite of Esa's father. Khattak took it as a personal affront. And he thought he had never understood his sister less. Why had she held the halaqa in their home, when he had done what he could to warn her?

She was stubborn, obstinate – all those things. But she had never been blindly belligerent.

Or had he spent too little time with her after their father's death? Drifting away, shutting everyone out. For a while, that had included Nate. Khattak hadn't realized he had also rejected Ruksh.

Rachel watched from a seat in the corner. She was crammed into a love seat, not designed for either of their proportions, with Paula Kyriakou. She shook her head, a silent apology for not warning him about the halaqa's change of venue.

Khattak took a chair across from Ashkouri. He nodded at the other man, introducing himself. At first glance, Ashkouri seemed pleasant enough, polite without being presumptuous. He was dressed in a navy suit, with a crisp shirt and matching tie – dressed to make an impression, with an elegance that enhanced his preternatural good looks. Dressed to win the favor of a prospective brother-in-law.

But what Ashkouri said to Khattak was, 'Ah. The thin bureaucrat himself.'

Beneath the words, the insult was obscured. Rukshanda didn't catch it.

Ashkouri had just paraphrased the opening line of Agha Shahid Ali's elegiac poem 'Muharram in Srinagar, 1992'. The 'thin bureaucrat' to fly in from the plains was Death.

On the table was a copy of the slim volume of poetry, *The Country Without a Post Office*. It was a book that belonged to Khattak's father, an ardent admirer of the Kashmiri poet, who was also the author of *Rooms Are Never Finished* – the book Ashkouri had given to Ruksh, a book Ruksh had failed to discover on the shelf in her father's library.

Since meeting Ruksh, Ashkouri must have acquainted himself with Agha Shahid Ali's works. But something else intrigued Khattak about Ashkouri's reference to 'Muharram in Srinagar'. The poem's principal metaphor for the violence enacted against the people of Kashmir was the historic Battle of Karbala, a paradigmatic moment on the calendar of Islam, dividing forever the houses of Shia and Sunni.

Khattak knew the subtext as well as he knew the poem itself.

Ashkouri viewed himself as a martyr to his cause.

But Khattak didn't think that Ashkouri's own death was a part of his calculations, or his idea of martyrdom. However the Nakba plot was meant to be carried out, there was no evidence that Ashkouri had sought a place on the front lines.

Once introductions to the circle had been made, Khattak gestured for Ashkouri to continue. Like Rachel had before him, he found the style of the halaqa strange and disjointed, while also unable to deny that it possessed a certain hypnotic appeal. The themes were as Rachel had described: Justice for the victims of tyranny. Solidarity with the oppressed. Vengeance upon the unrighteous. And then, out of nowhere, love poetry. And when he quoted it, Ashkouri's black gaze would dwell on Ruksh's face. Whether the feeling was real or simply the means to an end was impossible for Khattak to discern.

Ashkouri selected Din this time from his group of listeners, a test of some kind. Din's face fell. Grace reached for his hand and squeezed it.

'If you subtract the night from the day, the new moon will blossom over the square.'

'Very good.'

Ashkouri continued his own recitation, but the sense of what he said was just out of Khattak's grasp. The poet who would have been most on point for Ashkouri's peroration was Ali Ahmed Said, Adonis himself, but Ashkouri was careful to make no reference to the poet with the most transparent connection to the Rose of Darkness website.

The website was clearly a jihadist construction, promising retribution against the West, fluent in a litany of grievances – some legitimate and nuanced, others the blind outpouring of a blunt, premeditated rage, founded on three central beliefs: Muslims were ubiquitously under attack. Jihadists were the sole defenders of the *ummah*. And those who refused to support the jihadists had taken sides with the oppressors of their community. These oppressors were identified reductively and collectively as the 'new Crusaders'.

The third principle allowed for a clear demarcation of 'us' and 'them'. Under this demarcation of those who belonged and those who had to be excluded and were therefore vulnerable to jihadist retaliation, Khattak was clearly one of 'them'.

Esa Khattak and Hassan Ashkouri, members of the same faith, were standing on opposite sides of a door. Each man's understanding of divine justice was antithetical to the other's.

They were enemies.

Seek death in the places you expect to find it.

But for Khattak, it was life that was the most precious of all gifts, all callings.

And looking at Ashkouri, he thought of a different line of poetry.

The criminal law, like the criminals, has not evolved.

18

'I WONDER IF WE SHOULD discuss my intention of marrying your sister.'

They were standing in the kitchen near the pitcher of rosewater-scented milk prepared for their guests by Ruksh. Ashkouri savored a glass, examining the portrait of Esa and his bride that hung beside the breakfast bar. The cold smile that edged Hassan's lips raised the hair on the back of Esa's neck. Khattak's wife had gone beyond Ashkouri's power to harm, but Ruksh was still at risk.

'I think you'll see that it's best that we not proceed further on the subject of my sister until the investigation into the death of Mohsin Dar has been concluded.'

'And why would that be, Inspector?'

'It's clearly a conflict of interest, given your relationship with Ruksh. I shouldn't be part of this investigation as it is.'

'Then why are you?'

'I'm here at Andy Dar's request.'

Ashkouri's fingers traced the rim of his glass. He spared a smile for Ruksh, who made no secret of listening as she joined them.

'From what I understand, Mohsin's father singled you out for his rather... extreme displeasure.'

'He was speaking from the emotion of the moment. He thinks there's been a lack of justice for his son. I'm sure that's something you can understand.'

Ashkouri's eyes narrowed.

'Why? Because I am from Baghdad, a city so continuously

180

under threat? Our liberators are coming.' He downed the rest of his drink, while inwardly Khattak shuddered. Could Ashkouri possibly mean the besieging forces of ISIS? What kind of liberation did he imagine lay in store for the people of his city?

'Those with power think their power is unassailable,' Ashkouri continued. 'Let them douse the moon, if they can. Then I might come to believe in their power.'

Khattak had no difficulty interpreting Ashkouri's referential manner of speaking.

To douse the moon, to snuff out the crescent – Ashkouri had taken a metaphor used by the poet Faiz Ahmad Faiz and twisted it. Ashkouri's subtext was jihadist – the point being that the new Crusaders could not subdue the defenders of Islam. And the insult was doubled by using a poet of Khattak's ancestral homeland.

Did Ashkouri not know – or did he simply not care – that in this instance the poet's dire critique had been of his own society?

It was like very bad theater, poorly scripted and just as poorly received.

Except that the Nakba plot was real.

Of all the men his sister could have chosen, why had God placed her with Ashkouri?

This time Khattak took his father's chair, motioning Ashkouri to a different seat. Esa wasted no time. He asked for an account of Ashkouri's actions on the night of Mohsin Dar's murder. It tallied in every respect except one with the statement Jamshed Ali had given. Ashkouri had shared a cabin with Din Abdi. He'd been alone, asleep. He'd heard the gunshots and rushed outside. The others were all there, including Din and Grace.

Which was not how Jamshed had remembered things. And not what Din himself had confided. Khattak went over that part of Ashkouri's statement again.

But Ashkouri would only repeat that when he had gone outside, Din and Grace had joined the others in the circle. Whether they had taken some time to appear, he couldn't say. And whether Din had left sometime earlier for a private rendezvous with Grace, he didn't know. He knew nothing about the gun. He wasn't a marksman. He had no personal experience with small arms. He didn't have a permit. And he wasn't a hunter.

Khattak looked down at his notebook.

The line was there. Esa wanted to cross it. But his position was perilous enough as it was. He'd been told to leave questioning that related to the training aspect of the camp alone, and that included the bolt-action rifles. He was meant to say nothing that would alert Ashkouri to INSET's knowledge of the Nakba plot.

And yet Esa wondered. Ashkouri's unnatural calm, his baiting of Khattak, his willingness to appear in Khattak's own home – his entanglement with Khattak's sister. It didn't add up.

Did Ashkouri truly believe himself invincible? Or was his composure due to the fact that he was a step or two ahead of the INSET team at all times? Had he known Mohsin was feeding them information? Did he know about the plan to switch out the ammonium nitrate with inert material?

There was something about the evening that festered under the surface, something that had been said at the halaqa. Esa concentrated, trying to remember. And then he had it. It was the singling out of Din Abdi.

What had Din said?

If you subtract the night from the day, the new moon will blossom over the square.

But what did it mean? Tahrir Square in Cairo? The movement that had launched the Arab Spring?

It reminded him of the article Mohsin Dar had written for the student paper when Esa and Mohsin had been young men.

When the Russians rolled into Afghanistan, they imagined it would be as effortless as their conquest of Czechoslovakia. And now their empire lies buried in Afghan lands. By rocket launchers and Stingers.

If I had a rocket launcher.

The song on the Rose of Darkness website.

But Czechoslovakia? The Prague Spring? Was there a connection to the Arab Spring? A connection he had missed? Because he couldn't shake the feeling that Ashkouri's cryptic halaqas were delivered in some kind of code.

And Esa asked himself a necessary question. Did Ashkouri lay the blame for the deaths of his family at the doorstep of the country that had taken him in? He doubted Ashkouri would separate Iraq's sectarian violence from the invasion that had preceded it, the invasion that many blamed for the destabilization of Iraq, despite the horrors of Saddam Hussein's rule.

Officially, Canada had refused to join the U.S.-led coalition without the proper United Nations sanction. Unofficially, the waters were murky.

'Can you think of anyone who would have reason to murder Mohsin Dar?'

'No one at all. He is one of the few people I know who can claim to have been beloved by everyone he met.'

'Was Mohsin alive when you found him?'

'His eyes were open, but his body was cold.'

'Did you notice anything unusual at the scene?'

Ashkouri shook his head. 'The only thing I noticed was my friend dead alone in the woods.'

'Mr Ali said there was a blood trail. That Mohsin must have dragged his body to rest against the tree.'

'Perhaps. I do not recall. Why does it matter?'

'I don't know that it does,' Khattak said slowly. 'But I thought perhaps you might have noticed something else. Footprints in the snow. Or blood on someone's shoes.'

'I noticed nothing of the kind. You think that one of us did this to our friend, but isn't the more likely explanation that a hunter escaped your grasp? That the provincial police forces weren't quick enough to cast their net and seek this man out? Mohsin had a beard, wore a kufi. Perhaps his murder was an act of prejudice as his father says.'

Khattak noted the gleam in the other man's eyes. He was pushing Khattak's buttons, much as Coale had done at the INSET meeting.

And just as Coale had learned, Khattak couldn't be rattled so easily. He pushed back. 'So you don't feel responsible for not finding Mohsin sooner? If you had, he might still be alive.'

'What can the wound do when the knife is already drawn, Inspector? You ask me to predict the unpredictable. To assume my knowledge and capability are greater than His.' He pointed a finger upward. 'God has His plan for all things and all beings. So it was with Mohsin.'

A spasm of anger shook Khattak.

To blame God for a man-made death. To invoke what was good as a cover for evil – the bile rose in Khattak's throat.

He didn't know if Ashkouri was a murderer, or if he'd somehow determined that Mohsin was in the employ of the RCMP. What he did know was that Ashkouri intended murder on a devastating scale, something that a team of dozens of police officers was working to prevent.

He answered in as offhand a manner as he could. 'If God has any plan at all, surely it favors life rather than death.'

Hassan Ashkouri leaned forward. 'Sometimes we must destroy in order to rebuild. Do you not know your scripture, Inspector Khattak? The iniquitous must be destroyed to make way for the righteous. Isn't that what they say happened to my country?'

Ashkouri was describing the Iraq wars. But there were other truths he wasn't prepared to accept. Iraq's hundred thousand civilian dead had been caught in the crossfire of a sectarian slaughter, the violence prefaced by those who claimed a divine right to power and the equally divine monopoly of a shared, multifarious faith.

Bombs in one neighborhood, then the next, in a cycle of endless reprisals, until blood and devastation were all that remained of the birthplace of a civilization, in a disastrous mirroring of the Mongol sack of the city in 1258.

Their eyes met and held. And in those fathomless dark eyes, Khattak recognized a priest of the culture of death. Ashkouri had just made his first mistake.

'Are you saying that Mohsin Dar was unrighteous? That he deserved to die? Why would that be?'

Ashkouri recovered swiftly.

'I don't believe I said that, Inspector. I would appreciate it if you wouldn't put words in my mouth. Mohsin was my friend. I grieve his loss as much as anyone else.'

'Yet you've held no memorial at the mosque that I'm aware of.'

'That decision must be taken by the imam. Or by Mohsin's father. It seems precipitate when Mohsin's body has yet to be released. But I understand the police are at a loss.' He gave Khattak a cold smile. 'And that the secular law must precede the demands of the congregation.'

'Even if Mohsin's funeral prayer is delayed, there's no reason not to observe a ceremony for the man you claim is your friend.'

Ashkouri stood up. He brushed his hands against his narrow trousers.

'An interesting choice of words. I'm not certain why it is that you would doubt my claim, but I hope to be on more cordial terms with you when I am a member of your family. Separating Rukshanda from her family wouldn't be an act of my choosing.'

Khattak rose as well. He could see the shadows pressing against the door to the room, hear the raised voices in the kitchen.

'As I said to you before, Mr. Ashkouri, it will be appropriate to speak of such matters only when the investigation into Mohsin's murder has been concluded. Until then, and for my sister's sake, I would appreciate it if you would hold off on your plans.'

Stay the hell away from my sister, in other words.

Ashkouri inclined his head in a brief nod, but Khattak knew this hadn't been a victory.

He was beginning to perceive the extent of Hassan Ashkouri's plot.

19

RACHEL POURED ALIA DAR A glass of *rooh afza*. Tense and wound up, Alia didn't drink it, just held it with a death grip, her haunted eyes focused on Paula. Alia had shown up at Khattak's house wearing blue jeans and a sweater and a matching pale blue scarf.

The others had left with Jamshed. Ashkouri waited for Paula in the entrance hall, speaking quietly to Ruksh. They held each other's hands. Esa watched them, thinking of his mother, and what she would say to him.

Khattak heard Alia's tearful voice and joined her in the kitchen, quietly signaling Rachel.

Alia wheeled to face him. 'You tell me, then. Because this woman won't tell me anything. What was she doing with Mohsin? Did she love him? Did he love her? I know she was desperate to seduce him.'

With each new sentence, Alia's voice rose higher, thinning out at the top of her register to a shriek that must have been painful for her throat.

Paula scowled at her.

'How dare you accuse me of such a thing! I wasn't the least bit interested in him. He hounded me, not the other way around.' She importuned Khattak. 'Tell her it's the truth.'

Rachel intervened.

'Maybe she'll believe you if you tell her what Mohsin wanted. If you weren't having an affair, why did he hang around you?'

Paula shrugged. And Khattak could well believe that despite

Alia Dar's naked grief, the answer didn't impinge on Paula's conscience at all.

'I don't know,' she said impatiently. 'He just thought – the mosque was suffocating me. He said I should spread my wings, share my talents. Get out and meet other people. He kept talking about the value of my contribution.'

Alia's whole body seemed to shrink beneath the revelation.

'Why?' she whispered. 'Why you and not me? I made a contribution, too. I did my best to serve the community. He knew that.'

Paula stared pointedly at Alia's listless scarf.

'Maybe because of that. Maybe because you never observed the proper etiquette of hijab. And maybe because you refused your husband when he asked you to wear the niqab. Maybe that's why he preferred the company of a woman like me.'

Alia's breath rattled in her chest. She stared at Paula for a moment, unblinking.

Then she raised her glass of milk and tossed it in Paula's face.

Khattak led Alia to a seat in the foyer. Rachel had dealt with Paula's hysterics, and Ruksh had helped dry her face. She had left with Hassan Ashkouri, but Khattak knew she was only temporarily contained. From what Rachel had told him, Paula's convictions were etched in stone, and like stone, they were mute in the face of nuance or difference. It was possible that Paula would find her way in time, when the rituals proved empty without a richer commitment to sustain them. Or she would leave the house of Islam, a failure on their part. One that would have eased Alia's many worries.

He thought of the information Laine had shared with him.

Something we've just learned. Alia Dar collected a speeding ticket outside of Huntsville, twenty minutes from Algonquin Park, on the night Mohsin was killed.

As a friend, Esa knew this wasn't the time to ask, not when

Alia was so overwrought with emotion. As an investigator, he knew he'd have no better opportunity.

'Alia,' he said. 'Tell me where you were the night that Mohsin died.'

Alia perched on the small Chinese bench that was placed beside an antique porcelain cabinet. Her eyes dwelt aimlessly on the curios within.

Instead of answering his question, she asked one of her own.

'Do you think Mohsin was having an affair? With Paula, of all people?'

Esa drew up one of the Versailles chairs that framed the marble balustrade.

'It doesn't sound like the Mohsin I knew. But it's been a long time since I knew him.'

Alia brushed at her eyes, tears escaping in a thin, monotonous stream.

'Then what he was doing doesn't make sense to me. So much concern for someone who wasn't his own, so little interest in someone who was. Did you know he called me Sitara?'

But Khattak understood too well, the questions that had been puzzling him resolved by Paula's heedless admission. Rachel had been right in her guess about Mohsin's motivations.

'Alia,' he said again. 'Where were you on the night Mohsin died?'

'I don't know,' she said. 'At home. With Baba.'

'You weren't on the road to Algonquin?' Her shocked eyes met his. 'We have a record of the speeding ticket you received. It was nearly midnight. There's no mystery about Mohsin's time of death. He was killed just after midnight. What were you doing at the camp?'

Alia shook her head side to side, the movement of her neck stiff.

'You know everything,' she said. 'You might as well know this.'

It was several more minutes before she continued. Esa

watched her in silence. She was a woman undone by too many unanswered questions. He knew he possessed answers that would have granted her comfort, but they weren't in his power to give her.

'I couldn't take it anymore. I thought it was time I confronted him. Before that, I never wanted to say the words aloud. I thought they might be the catalyst for Mohsin to act. Maybe he'd taken his time because he didn't want to hurt me, and now if I challenged him, he would make a decision, he'd leave. He would choose Paula.' Her breath caught on a sob. 'I didn't know even as I was driving exactly what I would say. Maybe that I would start wearing the niqab. Maybe that he could have his freedom. Maybe that I would beg him never to leave me, to remind him how much I loved him. All of those things. Any of those things.'

'What did you decide in the end? What did Mohsin say?'

Alia looked surprised. 'I didn't meet him. After I got the speeding ticket, it was like I had come out of a fog. I couldn't do it. I decided to give him a little more time. Maybe I was imagining things. Maybe my words would hurt him. I can't prove I drove home, but I did.'

And yet if she had shot her husband, why would she tell Esa any different?

She wasn't done. She tucked her hair back under her scarf, some remnant of Paula's words still in her mind, Esa guessed.

'I keep thinking about that. If I had gone to see him. If I had found him there. Maybe he would have heard me tell him how much I love him.' She rose from the bench, her shoulders slumped under the weight of her decision. 'Or maybe the last thing I would have heard him say is that he didn't love me anymore.'

Rachel collected the dirty dishes in the kitchen and passed them to Ruksh at the sink. Khattak's sister examined Rachel's unassuming face.

'So you're Rachel,' she said. 'My brother's partner.'

Rachel nodded, well aware that despite the fact that Ruksh had yet to give her away, there was a patent lack of cordiality in Ruksh's voice.

'And here you are in my house, not on your own explicitly stated terms, but undercover, sneaking around. Spying on us.'

Rachel fingered her collar. She was wearing a denim shirt over her fitted cords. She could feel herself begin to sweat. She looked at the door, hopeful that Khattak would appear.

'Not on you,' she said. 'I'm just doing my job.' Rachel tried a halfhearted smile. 'This wasn't how I'd hoped to meet the boss's family, but sometimes needs must.' And then, because she was anxious on this point, she blurted out, 'You haven't said anything?'

Ruksh braced her elbows on the counter, the dishes forgotten. She looked sophisticated and cool in the pink cashmere sweater that topped a pair of white wool trousers. A marquise diamond glittered on her finger. She wore gold bangles on her wrists that played a subtle music as she gestured and spoke.

Rachel felt out of her depth. Ruksh's smile did nothing to put her at ease.

'Not yet,' Ruksh said coolly. 'Although I don't appreciate the position the two of you have placed me in. Conspiring against my own fiancé.'

Rachel cleared her throat. 'I'm sorry,' she said. 'This should be over soon.'

Ruksh's insinuating gaze appraised Rachel's face and figure.

'Esa's quite fond of you. Much more so than any of his previous partners. He says you do excellent work.' Her tone needled Rachel. 'What kind of work are you doing by infiltrating the mosque, hanging about our halaqas? No one invited you, yet here you are.'

Rachel might not have possessed the other woman's casual flair or her air of arrogance, but that didn't mean she was about to let anyone condescend to her. Even if that person was Esa

Khattak's sister. She found she didn't like Ruksh very much. And she pitied Khattak his dilemma. To try and impede such a woman in anything she wanted would be a difficult task.

'I can't comment on that, Ms. Khattak. And given the sensitive job your brother's been asked to do, I'm surprised that you would ask. It should be sufficient for you to know that he's trying to bring a murderer to justice – more than that, trying to secure justice for a friend. Whatever I'm doing, invited or otherwise, is intended to support him to that end.'

Ruksh quirked an eyebrow at Rachel.

'You really do admire him, don't you? Must be nice for Esa to have someone loyal as a partner for once. Someone who doesn't try to set fire to his whole life. Still,' she said, raising a hand to her mouth and yawning prettily, 'I don't see what there is for you to learn among such a harmless circle of people. Look at Zaki and Sami – they're just boys. No member of this halaqa would ever hurt Mohsin. He was the darling of the group, the class clown. And no one could have loved him more than Hassan and Din.'

Rachel's response was as wooden as she could make it.

'Perhaps it's best that experienced police officers make those determinations, Ms. Khattak. We're trained not to take people at face value.'

A genuine smile broke across Ruksh's face.

'I'm being awful, aren't I? Of course you know your job much better than I do.' She ran the tap in the sink, looking down. 'I know Esa thinks he's acting in my best interests. But I wish he would learn to trust me. Hassan is a good man. I wouldn't be marrying him if he wasn't.'

Rachel's inexhaustible supply of compassion welled up once again.

Could Ruksh really have no idea of Ashkouri's ulterior agenda?

'Your brother is under a lot of pressure. If it were possible for him to accept your word, I'm sure that he would.'

When Khattak found Rachel alone in the kitchen, he told her about his conversation with Alia.

'Do you think she could have made it to the camp and back in enough time that no one would notice her absence?'

'It's possible,' Rachel said. 'We'll need to check the alibi with her father-in-law.'

'Who won't be inclined to be helpful.'

'Who'll do everything he can to screw us,' Rachel paraphrased. 'It would be tight, even if he confirms it. What were the roads like? Can we search her GPS?'

'Clear. No accidents, either. And she doesn't use a GPS.'

'So if she was speeding – maybe she'd already seen him.'

'No,' Khattak argued. 'Mohsin didn't take his walk until after midnight. Alia got the speeding ticket just before. She wasn't that far away from the park. It's possible, Rachel.'

'Then if she killed her husband – say in a jealous rage – she would have been driving like the wind to get home. Not much of an alibi at all.'

'Especially if she believed her husband was having an affair.'

Rachel snagged a slice of pineapple from a fruit platter on the counter.

'He wasn't interested in an affair with Paula; Paula made that clear. He was doing the same thing with her that he was doing with Din. It's just surprising the RCMP missed it.'

'Mohsin could be very persuasive. He wouldn't have lasted in Ashkouri's group for very long if he hadn't been.'

Rachel munched on her pineapple, putting the pieces together. 'Mo *was* working as their agent, keeping tabs on the camp, trying to figure out the method of communication between Ashkouri's cell and the strike team. But he was also doing something they didn't know about – something there's no way in hell they would have wanted him to do.'

Khattak listened patiently.

'Mo never had any intention of turning all the members of

the halaqa over to his handlers at the RCMP.' She blew out her breath in a whistle. 'No wonder he ended up dead. He was trying to get Din and Paula out. Grace too, because she and Din were a package deal.'

A mixture of sorrow and guilt settled in Khattak's stomach.

'Yes. That was the Mohsin I knew.'

Rachel remembered the second clue she had been waiting for information on.

'Sir. What about the cassette tape? What was on it?'

'Believe it or not, some kind of hip-hop fusion. Local. Speaking in English and Arabic. And I know the voice that raps over the music. It belongs to Din Abdi. Didn't you tell me that he does spoken-word poetry?'

'Yes. That's what Grace told me. That Din competes at poetry slams. What's he been rapping about?'

'There's music, too. He speaks over it. He calls it a Somali back-beat, and most of what he recites is about Somali pride. Nostalgia for a place he's never seen. He calls himself a pirate.'

Rachel tapped her neck. 'The tattoo on Grace's throat refers to the same thing.'

'Grace's voice is on the tape as well.'

'What does she say?'

'"I came between a man and his thoughts/like a breeze thrown over the face of the moon."'

'The moon again. What does it mean?'

Khattak had been wondering the same thing. His friend, the professor of poetry, had been able to offer no additional illumination on the subject of the moon as a symbol in Arabic poetry.

'I don't know if it means anything. It could be a symbol, a code of some kind. But why would Ashkouri need a code to communicate with members of his own cell? Or could it be his way of obscuring what he's actually up to? Whether he knows he's under surveillance, or whether he's just taking precautions – the poetry might be a diversion, unrelated to the Nakba plot.'

Rachel had done a little reading of her own.

'Sir, that first section of poetry that you found in your sister's book. Do you remember that poem? Do you have the rest of it?'

'She put it back in his book. It's in the other room.'

Rachel waited as Khattak retrieved it from the coffee table. She had an idea that she wanted to test against Khattak.

Esa produced the small book and leafed through its pages. The poem was still there, this time in its entirety. It appeared like a flame on the page, unattributed to any poet by name. But Ruksh had told Esa that this was Ashkouri's own work.

O homeland
If I fly on the wings
Of a nightingale's song
To alight in your heart
With a will to belong
Will you light up my sky
With your rapturous flame
Unfettered, unfold me
Dismantle my name
Reclaim me in promise
Of victory sweet?
O homeland,
O heartache,
When shall
we meet?

They read the poem in silence. It was not quite a sonnet. Nor could it compare with the musicality and nuance of the verse Ashkouri had recited throughout his halaqa. It did, however, recapture a theme of modern poetry. In the aftermath of the Six-Day War, no poet was credible unless he or she addressed the themes of dignity and freedom for the Arab peoples.

'What's this poem about, sir? Identity? Belonging? Exile?'

Khattak nodded. 'All those things.' But he could see what Rachel was driving at, wondered why he hadn't spotted it for himself. 'It's about homeland.' He thought of what the professor had discussed with him after listening to the cassette, a lesson Khattak had known for himself. 'To Palestinians, homeland is everything.'

They were back at the beginning. At Martine Killiam's insistence that he work with INSET on the murder of Mohsin Dar. At her revelations about Hassan Ashkouri's plot.

'Ashkouri wrote this poem. It's a poem about the Nakba.'

Catastrophe. Cataclysmic catastrophe.

And extrapolated to Ashkouri's homeland, it was also a poem about what had happened to Iraq. What was still happening.

Catastrophe.

Devastation.

A Nakba. And one that was tied to the Nakba plot.

'You need to get closer to them,' Khattak advised Rachel. 'But not at the camp. They still have those rifles.'

'I have to go,' Rachel said. 'Maybe I'll find something at the scene that INSET missed. And isn't it crazy they would ask us to investigate without letting us anywhere near the park?'

'They weren't all that concerned with finding Mohsin's killer,' Esa said with some bitterness. 'Their focus was on the success of the takedown. It still is.'

'Which is why it makes sense for me to go. My priority is the murder. The rest is gravy.' In case that sounded dismissive, Rachel added, 'It never made any sense, this CPS consultation. Mohsin's murder and his work as a police agent are bound up together in such a way that one determines everything about the other. Mohsin was running his own game. A game that was a flat-out contradiction to the operation. And it cost him his life.'

Khattak remembered what Laine had told him about the surveillance of his house. He didn't know if that meant wiretaps or cameras or both.

'Let me walk you to your car.'

It was a ten-minute walk in the cold through a tracery of shadows. A necrotic light had infiltrated the sky, and under its reflection, Rachel's face was a faint round disk.

'You have a beautiful home, sir. Nice Christmas lights by the way.'

The expression on Khattak's face tore at Rachel. It was a fleeting glimpse of an inconsolable wound.

'They're not for Christmas, Rachel. My sister is planning her wedding.'

At the car, he made himself put Ruksh out of his thoughts. He could speak to Rachel freely now. But she was ahead of him, as usual.

'I'm betting INSET wishes they'd date-stamped that gas receipt differently. It would place Alia at the scene, it would mean she lied, it would destroy her credibility. And she has motive.' And at Khattak's grave look, 'What? Did I say something wrong?'

'It's not a wretched institution, Rachel. It's a necessary one. The people who commit these kinds of crimes, they've made it necessary.'

'You mean National Security?' she asked. 'INSET? I forget you used to work with them. But you weren't seconded, were you?'

Khattak leaned against Rachel's car, gazing up at the waterfall of stars, the cold wind welcome as a means of honing his thoughts.

'I was core personnel.' He glanced over at Rachel. 'I had language skills, background. A certain need to prove myself.' A feeling he knew Rachel would understand.

She fumbled with her response. 'But didn't you feel...'

'What, Rachel?'

He turned to look at her. His partner. His friend.

'I don't know. Set apart? A bit alienated? A stranger in a strange land?'

Rachel's scarf had slipped down her shoulder. Khattak reknotted it at her neck with steady hands. Trust Rachel to have the courage to ask such a question. To know him well enough to know that it needed to be asked.

'It's the price you pay for doing what is necessary.' His voice was firm and dark. 'For what you think is right.'

His gaze encompassed the sleepy streets of Forest Hill, a glossy theater of silence.

'And for knowing where you belong.'

He should have known that wouldn't put an end to Rachel's questions. She was gearing up to ask him something else. He didn't like the thought that she had to prepare herself to be direct with him. He wanted her to know that nothing was off limits.

'Spit it out, Rachel. What else is on your mind?'

She looked over her shoulder at the house they had left behind, a silhouette against the night, dressed in garments of snow.

'Ashkouri was rude to you in your own home. I guess I was just wondering why you still live with your family.'

Khattak considered the question. His reply was grave, but not off-putting.

'I'm the eldest. My sisters are my responsibility.'

Rachel's voice squeaked in her throat. 'If you don't mind me saying, sir, they sound like fully competent women to me. It doesn't seem like they need a minder.'

Esa could tell that Rachel was wondering if she had blundered again by making assumptions about his culture or faith. He wanted to reassure her.

'You sound like Ruksh. Though Ruksh doesn't hesitate when she calls me a chauvinist.' His smile negated Rachel's quick apology. 'My sisters know they can reach me whenever they need me should they ever have a problem of any kind. I stay at my parents' house when my mother is out of the country, for the sake of her peace of mind.' He tipped his head back, wondering if that was enough of an explanation. Or even one he believed himself. 'You don't have to agree with it – I'm not sure that I do – it's just that at this stage of my mother's life, I want to ensure that she's free of any worry.' A speculative look came into his eyes. 'Didn't you feel something similar about your parents, Rachel? Isn't that why you lived with them for so long?'

A hollow silence fell between them. A car passed by, its snow tires crunching against the ice on the road.

'Something like that, sir. My Da was pretty tough, though. I wouldn't say he needed me at home.'

'And your mother?'

Rachel turned away. The shared confidences had gone too far. But with her sense of fairness, she offered something in exchange anyway.

'It was the happiest day of her life when I left.'

20

RACHEL AND KHATTAK HAD DECIDED between them that it was best to take the day off from Masjid un-Nur, to avoid making Ashkouri or any other members of the cell suspicious. Khattak had made an appointment to see an old friend, and he'd asked Rachel to come with him. He'd also suggested an alternate method for Rachel getting closer to the group. Din and Grace were going to an underground club for an open-mic night. He wanted Rachel to meet up with them.

They hadn't yet reached a decision on Rachel's attending the winter camp.

But Rachel had every intention of going, a decision she would bring up with Khattak later. She found it more than a little strange that Ashkouri would plan a second trip up north so close to the activation of the Nakba plot. It was less than a week from New Year's Day. Was this Ashkouri's attempt at providing the members of his cell with an alibi in connection with the plot? Or was he planning to leave the group at Algonquin and double back?

He had to be watched. And the INSET team would be focused on the tactical operation. Ashkouri's retreat would be dismissed as a distraction. Rachel knew that for a mistake.

She glanced across at Khattak, who was dressed so formally that he would not have been out of place at a wedding. Or a funeral. Rachel had dressed for the underground club, not the appointment with Khattak's friend, the Crown prosecutor Sehr Ghilzai. Rachel's blue jeans were faded and tighter-fitting than usual. She'd found the H&M version of a kaffiyeh in gray and blue and had wound it around her neck. Under the scarf she wore a band jersey that had seen better days, though her taste in music ran more to The Police than alt-punk rock, a choice that was entirely without irony. The words 'Regatta de Blanc' trailed down one arm. The other arm read 'The Bed's Too Big Without You'. She saw Khattak read the words before he glanced away.

'Sting fan?' he asked her.

Rachel snorted. 'With that Elizabethan lute?' She didn't want to admit how deep her obsession with the front man of the band ran, so she added, 'Stewart Copeland's more my style, sir. He was always a bit crazy behind those drums. I found that endearing.'

Khattak grinned in response.

They discussed the case as Khattak's BMW wove through the traffic. Union Station was still under construction for the Pan Am Games. Front Street was a gnarl of stops and starts, as frozen pedestrians attempted to reach safety through a maze of improvised crosswalks. Christmas stars glittered at the intersections.

He suggested a new line of questioning to pursue with Grace and Din, whose alibis for Mohsin's murder he wanted to pin down. He didn't trust Ashkouri's rendition of events. He wasn't sure that he trusted Din's either.

Rachel asked a few questions about Paula. Her obsession with Ashkouri was well documented by now. And Rachel had witnessed her animosity toward Ruksh firsthand. What if there had been a similar animosity directed at Mohsin, whom Ashkouri had taken into his confidence?

They talked companionably as they drove past the assorted buildings of the University of Toronto and rounded Queen's Park. The prosecutor had said she would meet them at a café behind the observatory. Not at the Department of Justice, Rachel noted. Which was sensible, considering what they hoped to discuss with her. None of them needed to be seen in one another's company.

'How do you know Ms. Ghilzai, sir?'

Khattak slid the BMW into a nearby parking spot and switched off the ignition.

'You asked me if I felt set apart at INSET.'

Rachel perked up. Because it sounded like Khattak was on the verge of a personal confession.

'I did ask you that, yes.'

His green eyes were candid upon her face.

'I am set apart, Rachel. I've always been. Because of who I am and because that's been conflated with what I do. On both sides. But Sehr belongs to the same network of friends as I do, doing the same kind of work, facing the same unspoken challenges. We can be honest with each other, without worrying about keeping up our guard. If Sehr can tell us something useful, I know that she will.'

Rachel noted the pronunciation of the other woman's name with care. It was two syllables, not one, with the emphasis on the first syllable. *Se-her.* She asked Khattak what it meant.

'Awakening. The dawn.'

They met in the sunroom of the Café des Artistes. It was located inside a large Victorian house that had been built as a private residence in 1875. The new owner had refurbished it with a slate stone roof and the copper eaves and downspouts that had enhanced its original character. The stairs that led to the café were carved of cut stone. The café seating dwelt in the light of a dozen soft windows, under a rounded cupola. Khattak and Rachel swept past a massive oak staircase to enter the picturesque room.

Seated at a round wood table under the unsparing light was a well-dressed woman whose russet-gold hair fell around her shoulders in a style of simple elegance. She wore a fitted dress in a deep shade of caramel, a matching leather briefcase set on the floor beside her. Her light brown eyes were wide-set in a thin, intelligent face. Her jewelry was muted: braided gold earrings, a bangle on her wrist, an understated watch. She wore no rings on her fingers. Unmarried, then, and not as young as Rachel had expected. Probably in her mid-thirties, with surface lines deepening the character of her eyes and mouth.

The woman hadn't seen them yet. Her head was tipped to one side, light from the windows striking sparks off her hair. She was listening to the music that played in the background as she jotted something in her notebook. Rachel recognized the music from her mother's recordings. *Liebestraum #3 – Dream of Love –* composed by Franz Liszt, a piano work of enduring popularity. It was like a painting of solitude. And something in the music and the sight of the woman writing in her notebook, the wood table captured in a shaft of light, caught at Rachel. And at Khattak, too. He looked sad.

Sehr Ghilzai rose to greet him. Rachel noticed that he didn't embrace Sehr, nor did she move to embrace him. They clasped hands briefly, and then Khattak introduced Rachel.

He held Rachel's chair, choosing a seat for himself with his back to the window.

'Still?' Sehr asked Esa, a question that Rachel didn't understand.

'For now,' he answered, deepening the mystery.

They ordered coffee and sandwiches, the room redolent of the scent of apple pie.

'What's happening at Justice is ridiculous,' Sehr told them, her warm gaze encompassing them both. 'It's nothing more than sound and fury. I hope you haven't been worried.'

Rachel grimaced. 'It's a lot of sound – at least. It doesn't seem like CPS can come out of this unscathed.'

She didn't add what she really thought – that thanks to Khattak's insistence on keeping Rachel in the background, he alone was taking the brunt of the nasty allegations of corruption and incompetence. Rachel's career would survive. She wasn't so sure about her boss's.

Sehr Ghilzai seemed to know as much without being told.

Was this what Khattak had meant by not being on guard?

Rachel hadn't realized that her boss felt that way about his professional environment, and she supposed it was because he not only seemed at ease wherever he found himself, but because he made others feel at ease as well. Including herself.

'We've other things to worry us at present.'

'You mean the operation.'

Rachel was startled that Sehr knew about this. Khattak hadn't briefed her in the car, even though there'd been time.

'You've been tapped on the case,' Khattak confirmed. 'You've been working with INSET for months. I've just come on board.'

Their drinks and sandwiches were served, and Rachel took the opportunity to eat, trying to remain in the background. She was hungry, but she ate with restraint; no need for a Crown prosecutor to think of her as a barbarian. But as was always the case with her boss, the restraint would have been a lot easier if he'd remembered that Rachel was an athlete whose body required a regular supply of fuel. Or that she was a normal human being.

On most occasions she drank her coffee black. But tempted by a neighboring table's order, she'd succumbed to the craving for a French vanilla latte. Its taste was as sublime as its aroma. She eased back in her chair, better able to focus.

'I'm not lead prosecutor, by any means,' Sehr was saying. 'But even in my role as senior counsel, I can't advise you on matters related to the case we've been building. I can't even discuss the case. You know that, Esa.'

Her tone was chiding rather than critical.

'Both of our security clearances are current.'

Rachel couldn't decide how Khattak regarded the woman. Was Sehr a friend, or merely a colleague? His language was formal, but there was an undercurrent of warmth.

'I've been made aware of that,' Sehr said with care. 'Just as I've been made aware that the INSET operation is off limits to you both. Your purview is the murder investigation. There's not meant to be any overlap.'

'How can that be, Sehr?' The name sounded beautiful in Khattak's rich voice. 'When one must have determined the other. You must have gone over Mohsin's testimony. You must have some idea of how his death is related to the role he played for the RCMP. Don't you want justice for him?'

Sehr's hands tightened around her coffee cup. She didn't seem to notice that it was scalding hot. Until Esa reached around and unlaced her hands from it.

Startled, she glanced up at him, the light from the windows rendering her eyes the same shade of gold as her dress. She gathered her thoughts and answered him.

'Of course I want justice for Mohsin. But I'm not involved in the murder investigation, and I'm not likely to be. My role has been to advise on the legality of the surveillance and to establish the elements of the offense. My job is to make sure the terrorism charges stick. The lead prosecutor was responsible for preparing Mohsin to testify. I was nowhere near Mohsin.'

'For this moment, I need you to be. I need you to tell me anything you might have known about Mohsin's interaction with the members of Hassan Ashkouri's cell.'

'I cannot comment on an ongoing investigation, not even to you. Either of you. Isn't that what you tell the public when the hounds are at your door?'

Khattak sighed. He had yet to touch his coffee, searching for a way to get through to Sehr. An army of clouds had massed outside the café's windows, leaving behind striations of sky, turning the mood in the café somber. It was unfair what Khattak was asking of Sehr. Rachel hoped he knew that.

'Could you do this much, then? Don't say anything. Rachel and I will fill in some of the details. Things we can't yet prove, but hope to. If we're on the right track, say nothing. If we're off base, tell Rachel to order the apple pie. She hasn't been here before.'

Sehr wanted to help; Rachel could see it in her face. But the woman still had her doubts.

'I'm guessing the lead prosecutor had a difficult time preparing Mo as a witness. What the RCMP had groomed Mo to do once he infiltrated Ashkouri's Nakba cell was not necessarily what Mo intended to carry out.'

Sehr's eyes widened. She stirred the spoon in her coffee cup without speaking.

'You were expecting Mohsin to deliver Ashkouri, Jamshed Ali, Dinaase Abdi, Zaki Aboud, and Sami Dardas, and possibly the two women who were at the training camp as well.' Khattak watched Sehr closely. 'But Mo would only confirm the activities of Ashkouri and Jamshed. He left you hanging when it came to the others. Do you know why?'

Against her better judgment, Sehr admitted that she didn't.

'Rachel and I think it's because he didn't intend to deliver them to you. He was trying to get them out before they could be implicated in the plot. Din and the other boys are underage. Grace was only there because of Din. And Mohsin must have believed that Paula's conversion was sincere, and that she just happened to stumble upon this particular mosque. He probably saw that as a terrible misfortune. And one that Paula shouldn't have had to trade her freedom for. Because Paula would be tried as an adult.'

Rachel could see that Sehr had suspected something of the kind. Mohsin Dar must have been cagey in his dealings with the Crown prosecutors. Yet Sehr was nonetheless shocked to hear her suspicions confirmed.

Sehr took a sip from her cup, buying herself some time.

Then she asked a question that made Rachel appreciate why Sehr Ghilzai had achieved the rank of senior counsel so early in her career.

'Even if what you're saying is true – and I cannot confirm any of it – that doesn't exonerate them from the possibility of murder. They were closely connected to Mohsin. They were with him at the camp. Any one of them could have killed him, isn't that true?'

Khattak listed the alibis each member of the group had provided.

'It would help to know something more about the gun. Whose gun? Where did it come from? It wasn't registered to any of them. It's not a hunting rifle, although we know there were rifles on site.' He made a quick, dismissive gesture. 'Mohsin was killed by a nine-millimeter pistol at close range. And we don't know anything about that gun. Or about the training, for that matter. What was it supposed to consist of?'

He drummed his fingers over the cover of the notebook that Sehr had been writing in when they entered the café. She pushed it to one side, out of Esa's reach. In exchange, she offered one small bit of information.

'They were rank amateurs. I think the idea of weapons training was some kind of fantasy. God knows what they were doing up there. They were supposed to sleep in tents, but they were so poorly prepared for the winter at Algonquin they had to switch over to a site with cabins. Mo was the only one who could get a fire going. And they don't have the rifles anymore. They're in the hands of the second cell.'

Rachel's blood thrummed. But not at the mention of the rifles.

There was something else.

Sehr Ghilzai might not understand, but Rachel knew it was something.

A breakthrough in the case.

A group of amateurs running around in the woods.

No one with survivalist training, except for Mohsin himself.

Ashkouri attempting to enforce a martial discipline by having his team camp out in tents in temperatures well below freezing, then retreating to the cabins instead. A last-minute change.

But had it been a retreat? Or had Ashkouri deliberately led Mohsin to unfamiliar ground? Separating him from the others by using cabins. Placing Mohsin with Jamshed.

Rachel went over the witness statements in her mind.

It wasn't that Ashkouri couldn't alibi Dinaase Abdi at the time the gunshots were heard.

It was that Din Abdi wasn't around to provide an alibi for Ashkouri.

To confirm that Ashkouri had been in his cabin alone, and had wandered into the clearing with the others.

Rachel ventured a question of her own.

'Can you just confirm that neither Ashkouri nor Jamshed Ali had discovered that Mohsin was working for you?'

Sehr signaled the waiter.

'Three pieces of apple pie, please.'

The pie was as good as the coffee had been. Not too sweet, a little salty with its dusting of cinnamon, the apples piled high under a golden-brown crust. And a crème anglaise drizzled to one side, to complement its taste and texture.

Rachel was relieved to see Khattak pick up his fork. He needed to eat. He needed to remember that the outcome of the case wasn't predetermined. Rachel had never believed that she was destined to fail at anything, including the search for her brother. She was given to a hopeful optimism that was at odds with her training and that stood in sharp contradiction to her experience of life. Nothing was hopeless. CPS wasn't doomed to self-destruct. There was a good chance they would find the killer of Mohsin Dar, despite the restrictions imposed by the INSET operation. They just needed to catch a break. And now they had one, she was convinced of it.

Ashkouri had changed the campsite for a reason.

And the reason could only have been to expose a vulnerability in Mohsin Dar.

Either Ashkouri had killed him...

Or he'd had Din Abdi kill him.

Rachel frowned, a moderate amount of pie teetering on her fork.

If Din had killed Mohsin, how did that explain Grace?

Din had claimed to have been preoccupied with Grace in an intimate encounter.

But Rachel knew very well that Grace would provide Din with any alibi that he required. Din was the only solid thing in Grace's life. She wouldn't give him up; she wouldn't turn her back on him. Because then Grace herself would be lost.

'What?' Khattak asked her. 'Rachel, what is it?'

Setting down her fork, Rachel explained her theory.

Khattak took his time before responding, finishing the slice of pie on his plate.

'Maybe,' he said, as both women waited. 'But that's not all. You're missing the bigger picture.'

He described his own suspicions at length. When he was finished, Rachel nodded. He'd reached the same conclusion as she had about Ashkouri's alibi. She grinned at Sehr.

'See what we can do when you help us just a little?'

A quick frown marred the smooth skin of Sehr's forehead.

'I didn't help you.' Her tone was firm. 'You learned nothing from me, although I've learned more than I expected from you.' She looked up into Khattak's eyes. Rachel didn't know how her boss could resist the genuine empathy in Sehr's face. But he held himself aloof and apart, even when Sehr went on to confide, 'Andy Dar is brewing trouble. The press conference was just his first salvo. Don't believe him if he's offered you cooperation.'

'What does he want?' Khattak asked. This, at least, they could talk about.

'You've heard his broadcast, I'm sure. "Tough Talk with Andy Dar". He wants what he's always wanted – an audience for whatever's on his mind. A vindication of whatever he chooses to support or attack on any given day. This week it's CPS.' Her eyes were warm with concern. 'You shouldn't dismiss him as a crank. He's much more influential than you may realize, and among people that matter.'

'CPS has the support of the Minister of Justice. And of the commissioner.'

'True.' Sehr smiled her encouragement. 'There may be a way that I can help you.' And when they both perked up, she clarified, 'Unrelated to the prosecution's case. Andy Dar has an interview at CBC News tonight. They've given him a full half hour to elaborate upon his allegations of bias and incompetence.' Rachel's face fell. 'You didn't know? They didn't offer you the opportunity of rebuttal?'

Khattak answered her.

'They did, but what can we say at this point? The Drayton case may be heading to an inquiry, so we can't speak to those allegations. And the current investigation is so sensitive that any mistake we make could damage the operation on the ground. Putting my face in front of the cameras is not the solution to CPS's public relations problem.'

'It's such a nice face,' Sehr teased.

When Khattak didn't respond, Sehr looked a little lost. She continued in a more serious vein. 'Andy Dar is sensitive about the reputation of his family. Half of his credibility as a right-wing blowhard comes from his ability to project a front of personal infallibility.'

'No one is infallible,' Khattak said.

'Exactly,' Sehr agreed. 'In Andy's case, I think you may have discovered his point of weakness. I would use that if I were you. And look!' She pointed outside. 'The sun's found its way out of that mess of clouds. Let's count that as a good omen.'

Khattak didn't believe in omens. Nor did he turn to look out the window.

Rachel noticed.

'Why'd you sit with your back to the window, sir?'

Khattak hesitated. And then he saw that Rachel wasn't just curious. She was asking out of worry over him.

'Is it something to do with INSET? You think they're tracking you?'

He managed a tired smile.

'I have it on good authority that my house and my sister are under surveillance, but that's not the reason why.' He gestured at the round glass windows of the Café des Artistes. 'This is where I met my wife. She was a close friend of Sehr's. The first time I saw her was through that window.' He shook his head, dissatisfied with himself. 'It's foolish, I know. I can't stand to look out that window knowing she's not there.'

And Sehr knew it. Yet still she continued to push him.

A friend who couldn't understand that he loved Samina still. No matter who else crossed his path in life, Samina would always be part of him.

Nothing had changed, Sehr thought as Esa left.

He was still in mourning for his wife. Seven years had passed since her death, yet he mourned her like it was yesterday. And Sehr wondered what it would feel like to be loved like that. To mean as much to anyone.

If Sehr had met Esa first, met him on her own instead of with Samina by her side, the whole encounter would have played out differently. Perhaps she would have had a chance. Instead, they had never moved beyond this somewhat stilted friendship. And not for lack of trying on her part. Nor for lack of courage.

She closed her eyes, lost in a rootless nostalgia, the excruciating memory that time had not dulled. The reason that Esa couldn't bring himself to look at her.

And that other one – the illumination of Esa's face the first time he had spoken to Samina.

He had never looked at anyone that way but Samina.

And afterward –

Well, nothing had changed.

Sehr had been doodling in her notebook, not engaged in her

work, as she had been pretending when Rachel and Khattak had arrived.

She looked down at the words she had aimlessly scrawled on the page.

He loves me.

He loves me not.

It was putting her job on the line, she knew. And despite the high road she had taken earlier, Sehr found she didn't care. She had listened to Esa's review of the investigation, and discovered the connections that were invisible to the detectives. And understood the implications of those connections as well.

Rachel and Esa had yet to penetrate through to the heart of things. They couldn't move forward in any meaningful way, despite the breakthrough Rachel was convinced of.

Because they still didn't know.

And Sehr didn't understand why Ciprian Coale had withheld the single most critical piece of evidence from them. The evidence that made the identity of Mohsin Dar's murderer plain. The evidence that would put an end to any chance of disrupting the INSET operation by careless intercession. Rachel was so much closer than she realized.

It was Ciprian Coale's personal agenda that kept the truth from the CPS detectives. Did Ciprian's hostility to Esa run so deep that he was prepared to risk the two years of assiduous effort by his team? Was he prepared to risk the lives of innocent people, just to bring his personal enemy down? Couldn't Ciprian see the danger to his own career if the Nakba plot were to succeed? Why was he so wholly focused on Esa?

She pondered the facts for several more minutes. In her briefcase, there was a memo from the Outreach Coordinator, written on Ciprian Coale's behalf.

She searched for the memo, read it again.

Lingered over the signature.

Made the inevitable connection.

And realized why.

Esa needed to know the truth, or he would go astray. Much farther astray than he already was, threatened from every side. Sehr knew what that felt like, remembered the hush in the room when her name had been selected to join the team of prosecutors. The sideways glances and hasty recoveries. The murmurs about her personal background. The silence that fell just as she entered a room. The loneliness of exclusion.

Where did her loyalties lie?

There was nothing save the years of this carefully sustained friendship between Sehr and Esa. He'd given her no reason to hope for more. But she wasn't about to let Ciprian destroy what was left of Esa's career.

Not if it was in her power to help him.

She made the decision and picked up her phone.

21

RACHEL MADE HER WAY TO the Queen Street West venue where Grace and Din were meeting. She wouldn't have thought that the posh bars and hipster clubs that dominated the neighborhood would be a likely venue for upcoming rap artists.

She was right. Between the Hideout Bar and the Good Son, there were rooftop clubs and restaurants, and basement doors that beckoned the unwary. She slouched her way into the one at 885. The stairs below the street level were narrow and dim. The stink of garbage accompanied her descent into the netherworld.

Under the exterior light, a name was scratched over a metal plate, the graffiti artless and casual.

Gori.

Rachel recognized the name from her tenure in the West End, working gangs and drugs in the area known as Dixon City, six high-rise apartment buildings that had seen more than an ordinary share of violence.

And now the name of this hip-hop club.

She squeezed herself between dozens of gyrating young bodies, the throb of the bass ricocheting through her chest. Clubs were not Rachel's scene. The occasional bar, maybe. But never an underground club that was in clear violation of the fire code. A hundred or so people – many of them underage – squeezed into a small space, laughing, talking, barely able to hear the kid behind the microphone, in this case a pimpled youth in his early twenties with two large black buttons extending the lobes of his ears.

She caught sight of Grace in the flickering lights – no disco ball, but a flashing sound and light system generated by someone's laptop. The stage was just over a foot higher than the wood floor where the audience swayed to a single groove.

Grace's magenta hair was brushed straight up, the dark eye shadow traded for two bold smudges of silver. The tips of her eyelashes gleamed with it. She looked surprised to see Rachel, but not unhappy. The corner of her mouth lifted in what could have been a smile or a sneer. One thin arm waved Rachel over.

Din Abdi hovered by the single step that led to the stage, waiting his turn. His lanky body was graceful as it swooped and curved in time to the music. Grace's arms were linked about his waist as she danced with him.

'You come here often?' Din asked. 'Never seen you here before.'

'Never,' Rachel shouted. 'I'm supposed to meet my brother here.'

That Din couldn't hear her was obvious. His lips pulled back from his teeth, but it didn't look like a smile.

'Quite a mix in here,' she said close to Grace's ear.

The kids were black, white, brown, Asian.

Grace shrugged. 'It's Toronto,' she said.

A group of men approached Din – tattooed, pierced, some with kaffiyehs, others without. They spoke to him in a language that didn't sound all that different from Arabic to Rachel's ears.

'Somali,' Grace said, pulling Rachel away.

One of them grabbed hold of Grace's arm.

'Casper the not-so-friendly ghost. Been a long time.'

Grace shrank away, trying to free her arm.

'Chill,' Rachel said, detaching the man's grip with a strategic application of force. He held up both hands, his mouth wreathed in smiles.

Rachel drew Grace away, putting some other bodies between them. Grace's eyes followed Din, surrounded by the circle of newcomers.

'You don't like them?' Rachel asked.

'They're Goonies,' she said. 'Dixon City Bloods. It's never good when they come looking for you. A couple of them used to go to our school. Din was kind of in. And then because of Hassan, he got out.'

Rachel knew from experience that once you were inducted into a gang, fighting your way free was not a simple matter of choice. And if Din had been in the Bloods, if he had been blooded as part of an initiation ritual, it was something else for her to consider. It made Din more of a threat, more grown-up and ready to face the consequences of his actions.

'He wanted out?' she asked Grace, who was no longer moving to the music.

'None of your business,' said Grace. 'You ask a lot of questions about things that don't have anything to do with you.'

Rachel blinked in surprise. If anyone were to cotton on to what she was really doing at the mosque, she wouldn't expect it to be Grace.

'Yeah, I know,' she said, making her tone casual. 'My brother says that about me all the time. But he's a kid, and I try to watch out for him. You looked a bit worried, so I thought maybe I could help.' She jerked her head in Din's direction.

Grace sighed. Maybe in light of Rachel's rescue, she thought her hostility wasn't worth it. 'There's not much future in the Bloods, you know? I didn't want him to end up dead in some back alley. But the Bloods can find you anywhere. Unionville's not far enough to run. They killed a kid at a house party in Scarborough.'

But Hassan Ashkouri was no safer a bet for a young man who found himself alienated and outcast. Who'd been swept up by the Rose of Darkness website's flattering personal attention.

'Hassan did something,' Grace muttered, in answer to Rachel's thoughts. 'Got them off his back for a while. We shouldn't have come here tonight.' She tugged at her spear-shaped bangs. 'It's just – when I'm not with him, he tends to do stupid things, and then I'm the one who has to figure out what to do.' She fixed her clear-water eyes on Rachel. 'It's a big responsibility, looking after him – but it's like the one thing I'm good at.'

Silently, Rachel agreed.

A kid looking to escape a gang should not have returned to a club whose name was *Gori*, the Somali word for 'gun'. The incentive must have been powerful. More than just the chance to preach from a stage where no one could hear your oratory.

'Why did you come, then? It's pretty hard to get here from Unionville, isn't it? I can give you a lift back, if you need one.'

The night was freezing. And Grace was dressed in a leather miniskirt over her leggings, wearing a sweater full of holes over a tank top that didn't reach her ghostly white midriff. Her navel was one of the few things she hadn't pierced.

'No. That's okay.' Grace nodded to someone in the distance. 'Hassan's arranged it.'

Rachel turned to look.

'Hassan Ashkouri comes to these clubs?'

Grace rubbed at her stomach. 'Just this one. He says he likes poetry. He doesn't care what kind.'

The teenager on the stage had finished his jam. It was Din's turn. But the Dixon City Bloods hadn't shifted position. They had cornered Din in their midst. His voice rose. He gestured angrily behind them.

One of them turned to look.

Hassan Ashkouri stood just inside the door of the club. He was dressed in black jeans and a black shirt. A silver *tasbih* was threaded around his wrist. And on the fourth finger of his left hand, there was a raised carnelian mounted in a silver setting.

His otherworldly face was taut with anger.

The Bloods fell back, the tallest one offering a salute. Din hurried to the stage and grabbed the mike. He nodded at the DJ, who thumped out a sluggish backbeat. Din paced the stage with a natural grace, pouring words into the microphone.

Rachel held up her cell phone to record him. And swiftly snapped photographs of each of the members of the gang that had accosted Din. And asked herself why they had backed off. And where Zakaria and Sami were. And the more pressing question of precisely what Hassan had done to arrange things for Din.

Hassan found his way over to them, his eyes taking in Rachel's markedly different attire.

'Sister Rachel,' he greeted her. 'We meet again so soon. Did Grace invite you here?'

'No,' Grace answered for her. 'Rachel's meeting her brother here.'

'Ah. You have a brother, Sister Rachel?'

Rachel could see he didn't believe it for a minute. It was one coincidence too many. Mohsin Dar had kept up his masquerade for two years. Ashkouri had rumbled Rachel in little over a week.

'Yes,' Rachel said, bobbing her head in time to Din's music. 'He told me about this place. Said it was underground, that the people weren't just posers, they were serious artists. Like Din.' She lifted her chin toward the stage. Ashkouri didn't turn. He kept his focus on Rachel, reading the band logo on her shirt.

'There is a song off that album that I like,' he said conversationally.

It was a test. To see how deep Rachel's cover went. But this was something she hadn't invented. The closer she stayed to the truth, the less chance there was of giving herself away.

'Don't say "Message in a Bottle",' she said. 'It's much too obvious. You strike me more as a "Walking on the Moon" fan.'

It was weak and a little obvious, but it diverted Ashkouri.

'Perhaps,' he said with a half-smile. 'Though I don't think you know me well enough to guess.'

How true.

On the stage, Din was rapping vigorously. Rachel struggled to hear the lyrics.

It sounded like the poem – Hassan Ashkouri's poem. Except a little different.

O homeland/O heartache/There is no retreat.
O homeland/This heartache/ends in defeat.

Whose defeat? She didn't think she wanted to know.

'So what song do you like then?' Rachel asked.

'"Bring on the Night."'

It was another quiet threat.

Because wasn't that just what Ashkouri was doing?

Bringing on the night?

And did he realize that the lyrics of that song were about the execution of a man who had murdered two people?

There was a clever self-awareness in those dark eyes. Of course he knew.

Ashkouri looked around the club, at the writhing bodies wrapped together under a blanket of smoke and noise.

'Where is your brother?' he asked Rachel. 'Why don't you bring him to the mosque? Young believers are the backbone of our community.'

Even if Rachel hadn't been taking on the role of an undercover cop, she never would have brought the kid brother she loved within a thousand miles of Hassan Ashkouri's ambit.

Grace blinked several times, the silver eye shadow resembling two flat metal coins. Rachel recognized her panic. Though Rachel had no claim of friendship over her, Grace was trying to warn her.

Don't bring your brother to the mosque. And don't come yourself either.

Or was Rachel imagining it because she was growing fond of the girl?

'Mark goes his own way,' Rachel said. 'He's not too keen on the path I've been exploring.'

Ashkouri bared his teeth.

'It's more than an exploration, I think. You've been with us quite often of late. Wherever I go, there you are.'

O homeland/O heartache/This life's just a cheat.
O homeland/O heartache/In Junnah *we'll meet.*

Rachel tried to look innocent.

'I guess I like poetry, just like you.'

Ashkouri moved close enough to Rachel that she could feel his breath on her neck. He might have mistaken her for another Paula, entranced by his good looks and glibly sibilant tongue. But Rachel had been in the company of attractive men before. Her boss was one such. Nathan Clare was another. Hassan Ashkouri repulsed her. The handsome façade couldn't disguise his true identity, the persona she wasn't meant to see. The man who gauged life and death by some other calculus.

She'd had enough of Ashkouri.

She wanted to be there when INSET arrested him.

And if a murder charge could be brought to bear in addition to the terrorism charges, even better.

Rachel checked her phone.

'Looks like my brother can't make it.' She held up her car keys. 'Grace. You want a ride uptown?'

Grace chewed her lip, her gaze darting between Rachel and Ashkouri. It was clear that there was something she wanted to tell Rachel, that she was starting to open up, but it was also clear that she wouldn't take another step in Rachel's direction as long as Ashkouri was around.

He bowed his head politely.

Din was still rapping from the stage.

You calling this a bum rap/you calling this a heart attack/you don't know what's loaded up and waiting on the tarmac/downfall coming, no jack/new year's rain is night black/do you hear the ice

219

crack/worse than any hijack/speeding down the wrong track/call this one a death hack.

'I'm okay,' Grace said at last. 'I've gotta wait for Din.'

'He's good,' Rachel said. Her phone was still recording. She'd palmed it in her hand. 'Tell him I said so. Oh, and Grace. I brought these for you. I thought you could use them because you said you like to make your own mixtapes.'

Rachel groped inside her bag until she found the cassette tapes. 'I can't believe they still sell these anywhere.' She handed them over with a grin.

Grace shoved them into her backpack with muttered thanks.

And Rachel looked up to face the cold rage in Hassan Ashkouri's eyes.

Why was he angry? And not just angry, but furious?

She shivered as she hustled her way back to the car. What had she done to cause such an overt reaction? Ashkouri couldn't tell that she'd been recording Din on her cell phone. Or that she had been worried by Din's spoken word.

You don't know what's loaded up and waiting on the tarmac.

It was like a dangerous forecasting of future events. But Rachel had thought that the would-be bomb materials were being delivered by truck. Trucks on the tarmac? Had the ammonium nitrate been switched out for the inert material yet? She wished that Coale would put them out of their misery and keep them apprised of developments with the INSET operation.

New year's rain is night black/call this one a death hack.

She swallowed the lump in her throat.

What rained down from the sky in this context wasn't a remotely detonated bomb brought in on a truck.

The lyrics suggested a missile attack.

And surely to God that wasn't possible.

Because that was the first thing Mohsin Dar would have told his RCMP handlers.

Who hadn't understood Mohsin's objectives at all.

But where would the missiles have come from? How could they possibly have entered the country? Did INSET know? Why hadn't they acted to confiscate the missiles? And if they didn't know – because they still didn't know how the two cells were communicating – wasn't there a possibility of not just the plot INSET thought they had neutralized, but of a real Nakba?

Rachel wiped a hand across her perspiring forehead.

There was another connection there – a connection between the insistence on poetry and the use of the public stage. Maybe something to do with the Dixon City Bloods, maybe not. She'd swept the club with her cell phone and sent the video to Khattak. Maybe the open mic night was the method of communication. A coded message in a public gathering picked up by members of the second splinter cell.

But if Ashkouri and Din were under surveillance, surely INSET would have tumbled to that long ago. The poetry wasn't difficult to decode.

In Junnah *we'll meet.*

Junnah was the Arabic word for 'paradise'. The end goal of a suicide bomber, the language plain as day.

Her questions were mounting up.

She needed to tell Khattak. He would tell her if she was on the right track or not, and whether they needed to consult with Ciprian Coale and his team.

Unlocking her car door, she tried Khattak's number. Once. Twice. It took her a third try to remember that Khattak had been heading to the offices of CBC News. If Andy Dar's interview was live, Khattak would have shut off his phone.

Maybe she should drive down there and meet him in person. She'd have to cut across the downtown core, through a tangle of traffic and construction, but this couldn't wait.

She left a message on Khattak's answering machine, keeping it brief.

'I need to talk to you urgently. There's something you need to know.'

She threw her bag onto the passenger seat and tossed the cell phone down beside it.

A firm hand gripped her wrist before she could climb into the driver's seat.

Hassan Ashkouri had followed her to her car. The car she had parked on a dimly lit side street instead of the public parking lot across the street from the club.

His smile was bland.

'I wonder what could be so urgent, Miss Ellison.' He'd dropped the pretense of calling her Sister Rachel. 'And I hope that you'll take a moment to tell me.'

22

KHATTAK STOOD IN THE SHADOW of the CN Tower, catching its reflection in the glass building that housed the Canadian Broadcast Corporation's headquarters. The red gem of the CBC logo leapt out from a field of blue, branded in Khattak's memory as it was in most Canadians', along with the theme music of *Hockey Night in Canada*. Rachel's tirade about the loss of the rights to the beloved classic and the ridiculous contest for a new theme song still rang in Khattak's ears.

Grinning at the memory, Khattak showed his ID to a South Asian girl with a laissez-faire attitude, who handed him a visitor's badge and directed him to the newsroom. He hoped he wasn't too late to deter Andy Dar from his course of action, a course of action he didn't understand.

Yes, it would put Dar in the spotlight again, a spotlight the man craved – but the exposure would come at considerable cost. A cost he had warned Dar about. And he questioned whether Sehr's advice would be useful in this context – would it silence Dar, or even slow him down? The man was an enigma to Khattak. His actions couldn't be written off as a means of ingratiating himself with members of the right.

Dar had to have some personal feeling for his son, some spark of compassion for his daughter-in-law. A diatribe against Community Policing, and law enforcement in general, wouldn't bring about a swift conclusion of the investigation into his son's murder. It would have the opposite effect: hardening the attitude of those investigating Mohsin's death, ensuring a lack of cooperation with the family, slowing the entire law enforcement apparatus down. While at the same time, whoever had murdered Mohsin would be buttressed by a feeling of safety – of the spotlight turning elsewhere, to a secondary sideshow.

Khattak exited the elevator and headed in the direction of the CBC set. A bank of television screens glowed red and blue against a dark backdrop. Two swivel chairs had been placed at either end of the curvilinear desk. The news anchor was on the floor, speaking to his producer through a headset. Andy Dar was nowhere to be seen. A young reporter whose name tag read 'Vicky D'Souza' pointed Khattak to the green room.

'His daughter-in-law is with him,' Vicky said. And then proved how clever she was, by asking, 'You're not planning to say anything to him that would derail our big interview, are you? That would be interfering with freedom of the press. And it wouldn't look good for the police.'

Khattak's response was weary. 'At the moment, my only concern is the continuing freedom of the person or persons who murdered Mr. Dar's son.'

Vicky seized on that with alacrity. '"Persons"? Can I quote you on that, Inspector?'

'It's a general description. And no, you cannot quote me.'

The green room was neither green nor a room. A small space had been eked out behind the rows of cubicles where news was collected and collated. It consisted of a beige love seat, two club chairs, and a coffee station beside a lighted mirror.

Alia Dar was seated in one of the chairs. Andy Dar had taken the other and repositioned it in front of the makeup counter. A white napkin was tucked into his collar as a makeup artist dusted his face with powder. Khattak asked the young man to leave them alone.

Nervous and agitated, Alia Dar jumped to her feet.

'What is it? Do you know something? Did you find out anything? Did you believe me?'

The questions came at Khattak one after the other, a rapid-fire series of words.

Khattak was about to do something he despised himself for. Yet he could see no other way. Andy Dar had to be contained.

'Sit down, Alia,' Esa said. 'I'm here to talk to your father-in-law. Your questions will have to wait.'

Andy Dar snatched the napkin from his throat and dropped it on the makeup counter. He stood toe-to-toe with Khattak.

'You can't intimidate me, Khattak. I intend to say whatever is on my mind, and there's nothing you can say that will influence me otherwise.'

'What happened?' Khattak asked him. 'You were supposed to arrange a memorial for Mohsin at the Nur mosque. You said you would assist with the investigation.'

'What investigation?' Andy Dar roared back. 'What exactly have you accomplished in terms of finding the murderer of my son?'

Reporters at the surrounding stations looked up at the sound of his raised voice.

Khattak examined the fleshy face that must once have been handsome. There was no real rage in it, just a studied calculation. He was hoping to provoke Khattak into some kind of revelation, though Dar had no true idea of what that disclosure might be.

'I promised that you would be able to announce the arrest on your program before anyone else did. I didn't offer you anything else, and surely you don't expect me to discuss the investigation while it's still ongoing. That would be a violation of professional ethics.' Esa's tone was dry. 'And I understand that a lack of professionalism is one of your main criticisms of CPS.'

'You won't get me that way, Khattak. I have a platform and I intend to use it.'

Alia moved closer to both men. She took hold of her father-in-law by the elbow.

Dar shook off her touch. 'Don't. I don't know why this man bewitches you, but there's no place for you in this discussion.'

'That's where you're wrong,' Khattak said. 'There's a lot about Alia's role in this that you don't know. That you should know.'

Shocked, Alia took a step back.

'What is this, Khattak? Some game? What could Alia possibly know? She doesn't do anything. She doesn't go anywhere. She's not capable of thinking an independent thought.'

'Tell him,' Khattak said to her. 'Before he makes a fool of himself on national television. Before he destroys Mohsin's reputation. Tell him what you know. Tell him what you think Mohsin was doing at Nur.'

Andy Dar took a step toward Alia. Khattak immediately pushed him back.

'You're going to listen. And that's all you're going to do. You think your son was killed by radicals at Nur? You think they killed him for some reason of their own? You want to go on CBC and tell the whole country that extremists murdered your son, when you don't have any proof? And that you're the Muslim who'll stand against them all, calling them out for their barbarism? Because that's what you were planning to do, wasn't it? That's why you couldn't be bothered to arrange a memorial for your only child.'

Spittle gathered in the corners of Dar's mouth.

'You expect me to protect those bastards? My son was an idiot to fall for their rubbish. His big beard and phony religious language, his wife with her stupid pieties and homespun headscarf – is that what my son had to look forward to in life? Did you think I would let that pass? They took him, they corrupted him, they killed him. And now they have to pay for it.'

'I'm afraid you have it wrong,' Khattak said softly. He waited until he had Dar's full attention. The older man watched Esa with hatred in his face.

'Tell him, Alia. Mohsin wasn't at the Nur mosque because he'd fallen under the spell of extremists, which is how you refer to all mosque-attending Muslims. He was there because of a woman, a woman Alia knows about.'

Alia's eyes were wide and blank. She crushed the long tail of her headscarf in her hands.

'No,' she whispered. 'That's not true.'

'Isn't that why you drove up north to the park?'

'I didn't.' Her reddened eyes beseeched him. 'You know that I didn't.'

Dar interrupted them. 'What is all this? What the hell are you talking about, Khattak? Alia, tell me at once.'

Vicky D'Souza approached them. A glance from Khattak sent her away again.

'I don't know. I don't know what he means, Baba.'

'What about the fact that Mohsin didn't want you at the mosque? What about the fact that he insisted you wear the niqab? What about the fact that Paula Kyriakou is much stricter than you in her observance of dress code?' The questions landed in Alia's face like small grenades. In the face of her hurt and confusion, Khattak was relentless. 'And what about the fact that you were so jealous of Paula Kyriakou that you were spying on your own husband? You drove to the camp that night to confront him about his affair.'

Alia floundered, the backs of her knees knocking against the club chair. She mouthed at the two of them soundlessly, her breath coming in little gasps. She stumbled to the elevators.

A knot in his chest, Khattak said nothing to stop her. Now he simply waited.

Dar's knees buckled. He collapsed into his chair. Khattak took Alia's seat and turned it to face Dar.

'What are you saying?'

'I'm saying you have it wrong. You were planning to give this interview for one reason only, and it has nothing to do with bringing

227

Mohsin's killer to justice. I've listened to your show. I'm well aware that denunciation is your platform. You're not troubled by the need to provide evidence of your claims – your pseudo-outrage is a law unto itself. But if you do that in this case, you'll find that the tables will be very quickly turned. This has nothing to do with the efficacy of CPS.' Khattak's voice was level, calm. 'It has everything to do with Mohsin and his wife. And it will turn out to be just another ugly domestic squabble, with nothing grand or impressive about it. You'll end up looking like a fool; your enemies will go to town.'

He let Andy Dar think about this for several long moments.

'Mohsin will be a hypocrite who couldn't stay true to his terrorist calling. An Abu Nidal or Mohammed Atta getting drunk at a strip club.'

'My son never touched alcohol.' Dar looked shattered at the thought of it. 'Don't you dare say that about him.'

Khattak shrugged. There was always that line that even the person most distant from his faith was unwilling to cross.

'You didn't know that he was unfaithful to his wife, did you? Who knows what else will come to light when you start spinning your wheels? It won't stop with you. Every journalist in the country will be at the Nur mosque, digging around. Do you know where Mohsin spent his nights? Are you prepared for what they might find?'

'This is some kind of trap.' A flicker of rebellion crossed Dar's face. 'You think you're clever enough to silence me, that I won't choose to sabotage my son's reputation.'

And Khattak wondered at a man who didn't mind painting his son as an extremist, but who drew the line at adultery.

'Don't take my word for it, talk to your daughter-in-law. Why do you think she went running from here? Because she knows it's true.'

'You don't have any proof.'

Khattak withdrew the copy of Alia Dar's speeding ticket from his breast pocket.

'Take a look at where she was when she got that ticket, and the time of night.'

Dar read the ticket in silence. His well-preserved face began to sag.

'The woman's name is Paula Kyriakou. She's a recent convert your son was courting. That's why he was at Nur. And it's why he didn't take Alia to Algonquin. What you do with this information is up to you.'

He reached across and took the ticket from Dar's nerveless hands.

He didn't know if his stratagem had worked. He only knew that it was the worst thing he had ever done in the name of a greater good: betraying a woman who thought of him as a friend, and putting her in Dar's power.

Dar looked up, his eyes empty of emotion.

'Did Alia kill my son?'

'She says not. Have you ever seen her with a firearm?'

'No,' Dar whispered. For a man who gave every indication of despising his daughter-in-law, he seemed gutted by Khattak's revelations. 'I haven't. She loved Mohsin. I would have said she worshipped my son, if the stupid girl didn't find that blasphemous.'

'We haven't concluded our investigation, so I can't answer your question, not yet.' He gestured at the row of television screens. 'You need to give me more time. If it's not Alia, I need a clear field at Nur. I can't have you muddying the ground.'

He checked his watch. The interview was due to begin in five minutes. Just out of earshot, Vicky D'Souza hovered, her young face anxious.

'What have you decided?' he pressed Dar. 'What are you going to do?'

Dar lifted his chin. 'You don't intimidate me. You don't frighten me. And you won't silence me. I'll do exactly what I planned to do.'

Khattak nodded. It was what he had expected from the beginning.

'Then I'll ask your hosts for a chance at rebuttal. And I'll explain the line of inquiry that we've been pursuing.'

'That's blackmail,' Dar hissed. 'You disgust me, Khattak. Look at the depths you're prepared to sink to to protect your manufactured career. And in any case, I think you're bluffing.'

Khattak's eyes were diamond-hard.

'Try me and see,' he said. 'Because I don't think you understand me at all. I've never given a damn about what you have to say about Community Policing. I think your rhetoric is dangerous and deceitful, and that it does a huge disservice to the community you purport to represent, but that's not within my purview, nor is it my primary concern. What I want is justice for Mohsin. And I'll do anything I have to to get it. I'm just surprised you don't share my commitment.'

'Don't you dare say that about me. Don't you ever suggest that I didn't love my son.'

Dar rose from his chair, his movements quiet and dignified.

The anger in his face was replaced by a much more human sorrow.

Khattak looked away.

He had let things go too far. And he understood that whatever Dar thought of him from this point on would be something he deserved.

He watched the interview from Vicky D'Souza's station, the young reporter eyeing him with a mixture of wonder and speculation behind the frames of her glasses.

When Dar had finished, she said, 'You killed it. I don't know how you did it, but somehow you killed the story.' She flicked a hand at the set that Dar had just vacated. 'I don't know what that was, except a lot more of Andy Dar's bluster. He didn't target you like he said he would. He took the story in a totally different direction. Why? What do you have on him?'

'I don't have anything, Ms. D'Souza. That's not how Community Policing works.'

She chewed on the tip of her pen. 'Uh-huh, so you say. You made his daughter-in-law skedaddle from here in tears. And you shut up a man I've never known to keep quiet. He spent the better part of the interview asking the public to do what they could to help. He didn't mention you, he didn't mention the mosque.'

'Maybe there's nothing to mention. Now if you'll excuse me, I'm running late.'

'Uh-huh,' Vicky said again. 'I'm young, not stupid.' She fiddled in one of her desk drawers. 'Hang on, would you? Here, take this.' Khattak looked down at the card she pressed into his hand. 'It's my business card. It's got all my numbers. I don't know what's going on yet, but chances are pretty good that I'll find out.' She stared at him through her owlish glasses. 'And when that happens, you might find yourself in need of a friend.'

Khattak turned the question around on her, leaning down to meet her on her ground. She eased away from him, startled by the proximity.

'I appreciate your tenacity, Ms. D'Souza. But if you get in the way of my investigation, you might be the one who ends up needing a friend.'

She brightened at once, as if they were playing a rather enjoyable game. 'Are you threatening me, Inspector? Because I've never been threatened before.' She made the words sound flirtatious.

Khattak sighed. 'Ms. D'Souza –'

'Vicky,' she interposed, with a wicked little smile.

'Vicky, then. I'm not threatening you, I didn't threaten Mr. Dar. Threatening the public isn't an occupation of mine. Nor is it my main consideration.'

'Oh no? What is, then?'

Khattak's fatigue showed in his face.
'Only that a good man is dead.'

When he'd left the newsroom, Vicky D'Souza scribbled the words in her notebook.

23

RACHEL SHOOK OFF ASHKOURI'S GRIP. It was dark on the side street, the naked branches of the trees silvered by the icy light of the moon. But Rachel was cold from the inside. Her gun was locked in the glove compartment. She was relatively confident that she could take Ashkouri down without it – a step she wouldn't take if there was any chance of salvaging the INSET operation.

She slid out of his grasp, plastering a breezy smile on her face.

'Did I forget something in the club?' she asked, ignoring his question. 'Or did Grace change her mind? I'd be happy to give her a lift – I hate driving at night by myself.'

'You said you live in Unionville. Near the mosque. Where, precisely?'

Rachel had her answer ready.

'Not quite in Unionville. Closer to Middlefield. Not too far from Pacific Mall.' She gabbled on, trying to distract him.

She referred to the dumbfounding reproduction of the Hong Kong shopping district that served as the anchor of the new Chinatown, north of the city. Busloads of passengers came from all around the country, as well as from across the border, to shop and dine at Pacific Mall. Its overcrowded parking lot was a nightmare to negotiate.

'And yet you chose to come all the way down here, in these conditions.'

'We've seen worse, right? Like the blizzard the other day? If no one drove because of bad weather, this city would be a ghost town. Plus, I was meeting my brother.'

'Yes, your brother. You didn't say why he didn't come.'

'He got held up by some friends so he made another plan. I was supposed to grab him from Union Station. Then he said he'd find his way to the club on his own.'

Ashkouri didn't advance upon Rachel. Nor did he free up an avenue of retreat, his body pressed disturbingly close to hers.

'Gori. Your brother recommended it to you? An unusual choice, isn't it?'

'My goodness, no. Mark is an artist. You know the kind of stuff they get up to. He's really into hip-hop, just like Din. That's why I happened to have so many cassettes. He likes to mix his own stuff. Would you like to see a picture of him?'

With the agility that came from her police training, Rachel twisted away from Ashkouri and lunged for her bag. Much though she wanted it, she left her phone where it was. Ashkouri might yank it from her grip. And then he'd see Khattak's name and number.

She rummaged in the bag for a photograph of her brother.

'Here. This is Mark.'

Eagerly, she pressed the photograph into Ashkouri's unresisting hands.

He studied the picture.

Rachel's brother, Zachary, was at the center of a group of friends, rangy and relaxed in their midst. His hair was long and shaggy; his brown eyes were lined with black eyeliner. He was dressed in the hipster uniform of skinny jeans, narrow tie, and fitted shirt under a casual blazer. And there was some indefinable element that made his style uniquely Zach. He looked like a more graceful version of Rachel.

'He's a bit younger than me,' Rachel said, settling into her role of overeager big sister. 'But he's cool if we hang out. Most of the time, anyway. I have to admit, I was disappointed when he didn't show. It wasn't a completely wasted trip, though. It was nice to see Grace; she's such a sweet kid.'

Ashkouri returned the photograph to Rachel.

Her heart skipped a beat when she saw that she had scrawled Zachary's name across the back. Thank God Ashkouri hadn't turned it over. She stuffed it into her purse with clumsy fingers.

Ashkouri still hadn't moved.

'Not many people see that,' he said. 'Given the tattoo and the hair.'

'The tattoo's for Din, right? I get the impression that they're a pair of lovebirds.'

She talked on about this for several more minutes, waiting to see if Ashkouri's suspicion would abate. It didn't. When she was done, he repeated his original question.

'Who were you speaking to on the phone? You said it was urgent.'

They were both aware of the current of nervousness that ran beneath Rachel's lighthearted commentary.

'Aren't you the nosy one?' she chided. She pretended to take his question as a sign of concern. 'I'm not one of the kids at the mosque – you don't need to watch over me. I was leaving a message for my brother. I was going to tell him that I don't think the club is a good hangout spot for him.'

'And why is that?' Ashkouri asked, the handsome face shadowy and dim, the hands tense at his sides, ready to strike.

'Didn't you know?' Rachel asked, all innocence. 'Grace just told me. It's a meeting place for the Dixon City Bloods. Grace said they're a gang. I don't want my brother getting mixed up with a gang. He's young, you know? Artists can be impressionable.' She tried a nervous grin. 'No pun intended.'

Ashkouri considered this. Rachel couldn't tell if he believed her or not. She hurried on.

'I thought Mark might end up coming later on. And I didn't want to stay that late.' She forced a yawn. 'It's exhausting looking after him. I'm sure you feel the same about Din and Grace.' She goggled up at him, her wide eyes credulous. 'Isn't that why you came tonight? A hip-hop club doesn't seem like your natural element.'

She massaged the ache at the back of her neck, something she didn't have to feign. Her muscles were strained and tense.

'Of course,' Ashkouri said smoothly. 'As long as they reside at the mosque, they are my responsibility. You are right about young people. They require a great deal of care.'

Right now Rachel was the one who needed care. She shivered in the cold.

'If you don't mind, I'm freezing out here. I should get going before my car stalls. It was nice to see you again.'

Ashkouri reached out and placed a gloved hand against her car door. Gently. With just a hint of threat.

'One more thing,' he said. 'I understand you're to join us when we head up to Algonquin.'

Terror leaked through the back of Rachel's brain. She blew on her fingers, making rapid calculations. The only way Ashkouri could have known that was by talking to Grace. A fact Rachel needed to acknowledge at once.

'Grace invited me,' she said, sounding awkward. 'I hope that's okay.'

'You don't seem to like the cold all that much,' Ashkouri pointed out, watching her.

'I love to skate,' Rachel managed. 'I promised Grace I'd teach her. And the others too, if they want.'

'That was kind of you. I'm sure that Grace appreciated your offer.'

'It's nothing. Oh wait, I just thought of something.' She hadn't, but she figured it was a good opportunity to push back against Ashkouri's vague threats. 'Is this some kind of memorial for your friend? I wouldn't want to intrude upon a private ceremony.'

Her smile weakened on her face, until it was just the approximation of a smile.

Ashkouri didn't answer at first. He moved away from Rachel's car, preoccupied. He would be considering whether to allow Rachel to come to the park or not, and what excuse to give if he refused. In the end, he deferred to Grace's wishes.

'Of course you may come. We may decide to observe a ceremony for Mohsin at the campsite. Another well-wisher is always welcome.'

He waited until Rachel had started her car.

Rachel gave him a jaunty thumbs-up, relieved beyond measure to be inside her car, though she hadn't dared to lock the doors while Ashkouri stood beside her rolled-down window.

But she did just that as soon as she drove away, keeping sight of him in her rearview mirror.

He'd given her his blessing to come to the winter camp.

Why?

Either he was so arrogant he thought there was nothing she could do to impede his plans – or he'd bought into her gullible-rube routine.

She knew it wasn't the latter.

Ashkouri had been poised to attack throughout the entire conversation; he hadn't once relaxed his guard.

Whether he realized she was a police officer or not, he must have decided that any threat she posed to him would be more easily dealt with in the remote environs of the park.

Which meant there was no way she should be going to Algonquin on her own.

'Rachel, what is it? What's happened?'

The concern in Khattak's voice meant that she hadn't quite managed to conceal her reaction to being cornered by Ashkouri.

Her hands were clammy on the steering wheel.

'I'm sorry, sir?'

'You called me three times. I heard your message. I'm sorry, I was dealing with Dar.'

He listened as Rachel filled him in, careful to gloss over her fear.

'How soon will you be home?'

She told him.

'I'll meet you there. We need to go over this again, if it's not too late.'

The acrid taste of fear was still in Rachel's mouth. After her encounter with Ashkouri, Khattak's company would be welcome. By the time he left, she'd be able to sleep.

Half-haunted by Ashkouri, Rachel tucked her gun into her bag, keeping her cell phone and her keys in her hand. She glanced over her shoulder more than once. She wasn't good at picking up a tail, if there was one.

She pictured Ashkouri on his cell phone, giving orders to Jamshed Ali.

Watch her. She's not who she says she is.

She knew it might have been paranoia on her part.

Were it not for the fact that Mohsin Dar was dead. And he'd been a lot more skilled at undercover work than Rachel was.

When she looked back over her past few meetings with the members of Ashkouri's group, she realized she'd been stupid. She'd been forcing things, pushing them too fast. As a result, she'd shown up in places she wasn't expected to be one too many times.

The story she had peddled to Ashkouri about the club was ludicrous.

First the mosque, then Ruksh Khattak's house, then the club? He wasn't a fool. If he wanted her at Algonquin, it was because he'd decided to act. To protect himself and his plot. Two days before the new year. Two days before the attack.

She pulled a cold can of Cherry Coke from her refrigerator and drank it in several long gulps. She slumped against the fridge. Her clothes had been damp with sweat, and reeking of smoke from the club. She'd changed into yoga pants and a fleece pullover. Though she still needed a shower, she felt better, if only marginally.

At the thought, she remembered another use of the same word. *Marginal notes on the book of defeat.*

Where had she seen that? What did it mean?

She let her thoughts roam over the minutiae of the case, feeling herself slip into a comfortable, trancelike state.

It came to her, the lyrics of Din Abdi's rap.

O homeland/O heartache/There is no retreat.
O homeland/This heartache/ends in defeat.

Wasn't that it? Or was she thinking of something else? Ashkouri again.

She was padding to her sofa on bare feet when the intercom sounded. She buzzed Khattak in, then unlocked her door. She called to him from the plushy depths of her sofa.

'It's open.'

'That's not sensible, Rachel. Especially not after what's just happened.'

He entered carrying a large paper bag.

'You haven't eaten, I hope.'

She held up the half-empty can of Cherry Coke.

'Nutrition comes first,' she joked.

Khattak set the bag down on the coffee table, examined Rachel's face.

She sat up, discomfited.

'What?'

'You're as white as a sheet. What happened with Ashkouri? I knew you hadn't told me everything on the phone.'

Rachel eyed him. He looked rather ragged himself.

'I'm not the only one. What happened with Dar?'

She set about getting plates and glasses and forks, as Khattak summarized his meeting with Dar. And with Vicky D'Souza. From the kitchen, she saw his expression in the mirror. It was a curious mixture of shame and satisfaction.

'What gives?' she asked, helping herself to chapli kebabs and naan.

Khattak passed her a small container of red chutney, the spice level of which she expected to be devilish. The kebabs were spicy enough on their own.

'I'll tell you after.'

They shared a contented silence as they ate, emptying the bag of its contents.

'Dessert?' she asked him, after a time.

'Tea if you have it. I need to stay awake.'

She made it for him, helping herself to a bowl of ice cream.

'In this weather?' he asked, scandalized.

'I need something to douse the flames of those kebabs.'

Khattak sipped his tea, watching Rachel.

She was lost in her thoughts, sucking on her chocolate-coated spoon.

When he thought she was ready, he asked her, 'So what do we have, Rachel?'

She told him about the Dixon City Bloods, and Din's performance on the stage.

'Two things. How did Ashkouri get the Bloods off Din's back? And what in God's name was Din rapping about? Did you check the video?'

'I did. I sent it to Ciprian Coale and Laine. If there's some overlap between the people at the club and the second cell, they'll know. I can only speculate about the first of your questions.'

Rachel savored her mint chocolate chip ice cream. 'Go ahead, then.'

'You say some kind of signal passed between one of the Bloods and Ashkouri. Did you get it on your phone?'

'No. I was afraid Ashkouri would see me.'

'What did the gang member look like?'

'What do you mean?'

'White? Black? Arab?'

'I think he was Somali.'

Khattak took a moment to think this over.

'It's tenuous, especially when INSET still hasn't determined how the two cells communicate, but if the gang member was of Somali background – if he was a Somali Muslim, he might be plugged in to Ashkouri's network. The plot might be something he respects, something he considers bigger than the Bloods. And that's why the gang backed off.'

'Do you think Ashkouri would be so careless?'

'I don't know that he would need to be careless. There's a lot of talk all the time about grievances and justice – nearly all of it bluster. The Bloods wouldn't have to be in on the execution of the plot to support the idea of taking revenge.'

'A bloody kind of revenge,' Rachel observed.

'War is bloody. These people think they're fighting a war.'

And with that sentence, it was clear that he'd resolved his duality. What he believed in was a clear line, glowing and unambiguous.

Rachel missed the significance of it.

'You're right. It's tenuous.' She turned her attention to the second point. 'What about the rap or the spoken word or whatever you want to call it?'

'Play it again.'

They listened to the recording on Rachel's phone.

When it was over, Rachel asked, 'Why is INSET letting this play out so close to launch? What if something goes wrong? What if there's something they haven't seen? "You don't know what's loaded up and waiting on the tarmac." What *is* waiting on the tarmac, sir? Isn't INSET taking a terrible risk? I hope to God they've neutralized the bomb plot.'

She expounded her theory about the meaning of the succeeding lyrics – downfall, New Year's rain. Khattak shook his head.

'No. I think missiles are a stretch. Wishful thinking on their part more than anything else. It would be impossible to get that kind of weaponry into their hands. And Coale wouldn't have missed it.'

'Maybe it was too easy,' Rachel speculated. 'Maybe Ashkouri was playing Mohsin Dar all along. Drawing him away from the real plot. And that's why he ended up dead in the woods.'

'I wish we knew. I wish Coale would let us into the operation, enough to know what we're dealing with here. We could rule a lot of things out.'

'He hasn't said anything about the video?'

'Not yet.'

Rachel mentally crossed her fingers before she asked her next question.

'Did you try Laine?'

Khattak's reply was noncommittal. 'I asked. She didn't answer.'

'So what do we do?'

Khattak took their dishes to the kitchen. He made himself a second cup of Earl Grey tea. He searched in Rachel's well-organized cupboards and found chamomile. He made a cup of this for Rachel and set it down before her on the coffee table, ignoring her token protest that tea and ice cream didn't mix.

'I think I'll have to talk to the superintendent myself, but I want to sleep on it first. It feels like we're missing something.'

'At least you can tell her you handled the Dars. What happened there – you didn't say. I mean with Mohsin's wife.'

Khattak hit the replay button on the video Rachel had recorded. He muted the sound.

'I made Alia believe that Mohsin was having an affair with Paula Kyriakou, in spite of the fact that the opposite is true. I used the same story to threaten Dar into backing off the investigation. All while promising a young reporter that I hadn't made any threats at all. Not my finest hour, Rachel.'

Rachel didn't try to dissuade him. If Alia was innocent of her husband's murder, it had been cruel to mislead her about the affair. But she wondered if what Khattak had done to Andy Dar hadn't been worse somehow – shattering his illusions about his murdered son. At the time, the lie had seemed necessary. Perhaps Alia and Andy Dar would find solace when they learned the truth about Mohsin's work for INSET. And when his murderer was apprehended.

As eventually, he would have to be.

'If we set things right at the end, maybe they'll forgive us.'

An unexpected warmth stretched between Khattak and Rachel. It had been the right thing to say, because he found comfort in it. Just as Rachel had found it comforting that Khattak had made himself at home in her kitchen, not bothering to ask her permission.

The tea was for her nerves. The familiarity was that of a friend.

He looked at her for a moment without saying anything. And then he patted her hand.

'Thank you, Rachel.'

Her gracious response was to slurp at her tea.

Khattak hid a smile.

'It goes without saying that you're not going to Algonquin.'

Rachel grinned. 'Yet you still feel the need to say it.'

'Even if they've handed over the rifles to the second cell, it's too dangerous for you. Look at how Ashkouri accosted you tonight. He's on to you.'

'He was just so angry,' she agreed. 'But why? What did I do beyond what I normally do to irritate people? He didn't hear me on the phone until after he'd made the decision to follow me. It was something before that.'

'Did you comment on Din's performance?'

'Just to say it was good. For all Ashkouri knows, I couldn't even hear the lyrics.' She cast her mind back over the order of events at the club. 'Christ,' she said. 'I don't know how I missed it.

It was the tapes. I handed some cassette tapes to Grace. He must have realized that I'm the one who stole the An-Nahda cassette.'

'There's nothing incriminating on that tape, no code that either I or the Arabic professor could decipher. It doesn't make sense.'

He turned up the volume on Din's rap.

You calling this a bum rap/you calling this a heart attack/you don't know what's loaded up and waiting on the tarmac/downfall coming, no jack/new year's rain is night black/do you hear the ice crack/worse than any hijack/speeding down the wrong track/call this one a death hack.

'And there's no code here that I can think of. It's just a form of braggadocio. And if he's advertising the plot, it's inordinately foolish of him. Do you have any of those cassettes left?'

Rachel checked in her bag. She passed the remaining cassette to Khattak.

'What do people use these for anymore? Why do they need them? You can record anything you want on a cell phone now.'

'It's a different kind of sound,' Rachel mused. 'My mother used to record herself playing piano. She said the background noise on the tape provided an ambiance she wouldn't get otherwise.'

'There has to be a pattern of some kind. Hang on, Rachel. Let's go over the information the superintendent gave me.'

He found his briefcase and divided the contents of the folder between them.

'Look for anything that explains it.'

They read for several minutes, Rachel running her finger down the lines.

'They go to a lot of different places. And they meet with a lot of different people,' she said. 'When they're not at Nur. But none of those people are members of the other cell, according to this.'

'Martine Killiam said the second cell is the strike team. So how do they get their orders? When do they get them? Rachel –' A note of excitement crept into Khattak's voice. 'Is there any place that all three of them go? At different times? Jamshed Ali, Din Abdi, and Ashkouri? Would you check?'

Rachel went over the summary report again.

'There's a gas station,' she said. 'It's also a convenience store. Grace mentioned it once. It says here it's owned by a man named Ashiq Ayub.'

And now she remembered exactly what Grace had said.

Din got me some cassette tapes from there because Hassan keeps borrowing mine.

'Sir –'

But Khattak had it too.

He slapped the folder against the table.

'How did we miss it? How did INSET? It's a drop spot. The wiretaps didn't pick up any communication between the cells because they weren't using landlines or cell phones. They didn't speak about the details of the plot inside the mosque – they could have done that outdoors, or anywhere there was a lot of background noise. They avoided surveillance by using these.'

He held up the single cassette.

'Recording updates and instructions on the tapes, and using the gas station as a drop. It was how they avoided the wiretaps.'

'But then how did INSET know anything about the plot at all?'

Khattak's answer was thoughtful.

'They were tracking the Rose of Darkness website. And all computer communications, including websites visited by members of the group. But Rachel, don't you see? Most of the information INSET used to coordinate their operation came to them through Mohsin Dar.'

'That's why Ashkouri had him killed,' Rachel whispered.

'It has to be why.' He gave the tape back to Rachel. 'And that's why he followed you to your car. He thought you'd uncovered their most important secret. The poetry was a blind. INSET must have spent months attempting to decode it.'

'When all along the answer was so simple. Old-fashioned,

even. But one thing doesn't make sense. If the gas station is a drop, why wouldn't surveillance have connected the dots to members of the second cell? Someone must have picked up the tapes from there.'

'It wouldn't be the only drop, Rachel. They could use the tapes to vary the pickups. How often were members of Ashkouri's group at the gas station?'

Rachel checked against the record.

'Three times in total.'

'Very little over two years, then. And each of them went once?' She nodded. 'What about the other two, Zakaria and Sami?'

'Not that I can see. Whatever their role is, it's low-level.'

'Are there other connections, other places?'

'Not for Ashkouri, Jamshed, and Din.'

'It might have been a fallback option, when other locations couldn't be arranged. The rest of the time they adapted. It makes sense that they wouldn't have used the same drop each time. And even if members of both cells frequented the same places, they didn't do so at the same time. That's how INSET missed it.'

'Sloppy,' Rachel commented.

'It's obvious to us now,' Esa amended. 'But who would think of something so outmoded in this era of modern technology?'

'It's liking sticking a note in a sandwich bag and stuffing it into a knot in a tree. Anyone could have picked up the tapes.'

'I'm guessing they were a bit more sophisticated than that.'

'Is the owner of the gas station in on the plot?'

Khattak consulted his share of the papers.

'He's not. Another reason they missed it. How many places could INSET canvass?'

'Especially if Mohsin didn't know about any of this.'

'Ashkouri didn't completely trust him.'

'That's why he's dead. He did something to tip Ashkouri off.'

'Possibly the fact that he was trying so hard to get Din and Paula out of the group.'

'He risked everything for them. The INSET operation. His marriage. His life, in the end.'

Khattak moved to the window to study the landscape below. The windows of Rachel's living room looked out over a busy neighborhood bounded to the west by a park. Christmas lights bathed the untrammeled snow, a luminous field of gold and green.

The night was dark, but not lonely.

Perhaps that was because of Rachel.

These were discoveries that needed to be shared with Killiam and Coale without delay. Everything turned on them. Perhaps it would accelerate INSET's intervention. His phone showed that Sehr Ghilzai had called him twice, and Alia Dar once. Neither of them had left messages. Reason enough not to call them back. Yet.

Before he could press Coale's number, Rachel asked him another question.

'Why is Ashkouri taking his group to Algonquin tomorrow? Why absent himself from the scene two days before the launch of the attack?'

'It will be New Year's Eve. The roads out of the city will be empty. Maybe it's a strategic retreat.'

It was a plausible explanation, and Rachel seemed to agree with it.

She didn't answer as she could have, that the roads out of the park led nowhere. Not to the border. Not to the frozen seas. Not to a tiny airfield like the Buttonville Airport.

He was missing something. The encounters with Ashkouri, the message of the halaqas, the random bits of poetry, Mohsin Dar's death and the missing gun, the information that had leaked through the sieve of INSET's intelligence operation.

The reason Dar had died.

There was still something just out of reach of his understanding.

You don't know what's loaded up and waiting on the tarmac.

Could Rachel possibly be right?

Missiles raining down on New Year's Day.

Was it conceivable in a city as good-naturedly diverse as Toronto? And why New Year's Day, if the answer was yes? It didn't mark the September 11 anniversary. It didn't mark the anniversary of the actual Palestinian Nakba. Most people would be out of the city, on holiday with their families. The business district would be closed.

Yes, there would be increased travel out of Union Station – but enough to justify the timing of this plot?

Why wouldn't Coale tell him what he knew?

The answer to that was obvious enough.

Your only job is to handhold Andy Dar. Beyond that, we have no further use for you.

The words arrogant, offensive, intended to wound.

Khattak had made his name at INSET. Pushing him out defied logic. He could have worked the CPS mandate, and been of value to INSET.

Coale had screened the operation from Khattak from the outset. Esa had been let in only because Martine Killiam had seen the value of bringing Khattak onto her team.

Coale's agenda was personal, he knew. But was there more to it than that?

How had Mohsin Dar ended up dead in the woods of Algonquin Park when he was the INSET team's most valuable source of information? Why hadn't he had cover from INSET?

It hardened his determination that Rachel not go north with Ashkouri's group. And he came to another decision just as quickly. He needed to confirm that RCMP agents had delivered inert material in lieu of ammonium nitrate to the members of the second cell. And then he had to convince Martine Killiam to activate the strike team without further delay.

There were too many unknown variables.

And he wasn't any closer to solving the mystery of Mohsin's death.

Why kill him? What had tipped Ashkouri off? And where was the gun?

A text came in from Laine Stoicheva.

Be careful. Dar might not be as controlled as you think.

Another source of concern. Why the about-face from Laine? Was her attempt to assist with his objectives sincere, or were there deeper layers to her involvement? He knew from experience that Laine's mind was complex and devious; she was capable of working several tracks at once.

But if she wanted to strike out at Esa, there was no simpler means of doing so than to go along with whatever Ciprian Coale had in mind. So why the extra effort? What did Laine want from him? Redemption? Forgiveness? An expiation of her sins? She owed that more to his friend, Nathan Clare, than she did to him. She had caused Esa professional discomfort. The wound to Nathan had been personal and enduring.

He didn't have time to worry about Laine. She was a distraction he couldn't afford.

He called Martine Killiam for answers.

And explained his rationale at length.

24

THE BROW OF THE MOON was stenciled against the sky. Khattak crossed the park to reach his car, passing under the tangled branches of a stand of Japanese maples. The cold air penetrated the scarf at his throat, waking him from the gates of sleep. In the wind, the fir trees shivered, a quiet susurration through the park. Followed by another sound. A footfall slipping on the ice.

With a half-second's awareness, Khattak turned in its direction, avoiding the blow aimed at the back of his skull, but unable to dodge it altogether. A metal object pounded into his right temple with enough force to send him sprawling back against his car. His eyes watered. He couldn't see. Blows rained against his stomach and his ribs with the same metal object. He couldn't tell what it was.

He used his left arm to block his assailant, trying to keep his balance. He was struck on the temple again, and this time he went down. He felt his ribs crack as heavy boots kicked at his torso. Pain sliced through his head. He fumbled in his pocket for his keys. Swearing at his attacker, he thumbed the car alarm. The noise blared through the empty park. His assailant kicked him once more, then fled.

Khattak felt a stickiness at his temple. Blood leaked into his eye. He lay still for another moment, evaluating his injuries. Even for a police officer, personal violence possessed the power to stun. He breathed through his mouth, getting his bearings. He struggled to sit up against the front tire of his car. His fingers found his phone. He called Rachel, who didn't answer. He left a message telling her to double her guard and to make sure her doors were locked. Then he called Laine, and asked her for a surveillance update on the members of Ashkouri's cell. The man who had attacked him was strong and well built. For a brief moment, he entertained the notion that it might have been Andy Dar. But what he wanted to know was where Jamshed Ali was at this moment.

Laine promised to call him back without questioning his reasons.

Khattak lurched to his feet. After a few minutes, he found that he could open his car door, and swung himself into the driver's seat. He found tissues in the glove compartment and dried off his face. His head was swimming. It wasn't safe to drive, but he had no intention of calling either of his sisters to the scene. He tried Rachel again; no answer. He thought of calling Nathan, but it would take Nate forty minutes to reach the West End.

His thoughts were going dark. He leaned his head against the steering wheel, trying to remember who lived nearby. He hit a button on his phone. A woman's voice answered. He didn't ask her to come. He asked her to keep trying Rachel.

Before he lost consciousness, he left a detailed recording on his phone.

He was woken by the sound of an insistent rapping against his window. It was Sehr Ghilzai, her pale face looming out of the darkness. He unlocked the car door, passed her his phone, closed his eyes again.

The next time he woke he was in a hospital bed in the emergency department. Rachel was seated at the foot of the bed, sipping at a cup of canteen coffee and frowning her way through a crossword puzzle.

When she saw him open his eyes, she put the crossword book away.

She answered his question before he could ask it.

'Two fractured ribs, twenty-four stitches, and a mild concussion. You'll be just fine.' She gave him a crooked grin, and pointed at the round stamp on his forehead. 'Gives you a bit more street cred.'

'Any idea who did it?'

He was surprised to hear that his voice sounded slurred.

'That's the painkillers,' Rachel advised him. 'Nothing yet. Your phone's password-protected so I couldn't dig too deep. How are you feeling?'

The painkillers were effective. He felt drowsy and a bit thick-headed, nothing more. He gave Rachel the password to his phone.

'You should have had it long ago. Did you tell my family?'

Rachel shook her head. 'I knew you wouldn't want them to be worried. And honestly, I didn't know how to handle Ruksh. I was afraid of what she might say or do with the news of your attack. If it had been more serious, I would have called her. Was that okay?'

He nodded. A vision of Sehr's pale face floated into his mind. Had he imagined that she had been there? He asked Rachel.

'She brought you here, don't you remember? I told her to go as soon as I got here. I wasn't sure we could risk the association.'

'Didn't ask her to come,' Khattak managed. 'Asked her to call you.'

'From the state of our Crown prosecutor, I'm guessing she was too panicked to wait for my response. Sorry about that, by the way. I was in the shower; I didn't hear the phone.'

Khattak waved her apology away.

'Have to see Killiam.'

'They're keeping you overnight. I called the superintendent. Your meeting's been moved to later in the morning. I'll stay with you until you're discharged and drop you back to your car.'

Khattak let his head fall back against his pillow. Rachel had done everything he would have done if he'd been able to act for himself.

He thanked her wearily, asked her to go home.

She scoffed at that, and told him to go to sleep.

Which was a much calmer reaction than Rachel had had when Sehr Ghilzai had reached her. Sehr had gone with Khattak in the ambulance, and used Khattak's police ID to push him to the front of the queue. The private room and the first available bed were also due to Sehr's influence.

Sehr's phone call to Rachel had been a garbled mess, something much stronger than friendly concern in her voice.

He's hurt. He's bleeding. He's not waking up. Rachel, what do I do?

Frightened herself, Rachel had kept up an imperturbable front of calm, assuring Sehr that Khattak would be fine, he was a tough nut to crack.

'Don't tell anyone who you are,' Rachel had warned her. This wasn't the same woman Rachel had spoken with earlier, calm and decided in her judgments. When Rachel met Sehr in the emergency room, her pale face was streaked with tears, her eyes fearful and wide.

Sehr left unwillingly, texting Rachel often.

And she'd said something else, something significant, before she left.

'There's something I need to tell Esa about the case. I called earlier; he didn't answer.'

'You can't tell us anything, you know that,' Rachel said.

Sehr disregarded this.

'When he wakes up, ask him to call me. At once. Please, it's important.'

Rachel didn't think that less than a minute of wakefulness counted. The phone call to Sehr Ghilzai could wait.

It was five in the morning when Rachel received the call that galvanized her into action. It was Misbah, Khattak's youngest sister. Rachel had called to let Khattak's family know that he would be working late on a case. The phone call had been intended to allay any worry or suspicion. And she'd offered her own number in exchange, remembering what Khattak had told her.

My sisters know they can reach me whenever they need me.

Rachel still wasn't sure if she had done the right thing by not telling them.

'I can't reach my brother and I don't know what to do,' Misbah said, her voice strained.

'What's the matter? Tell me and I'll do my best to help.'

Misbah drew a deep breath. 'It's Ruksh. She asked me not to tell my brother, but I'm worried.'

She'd found out, Rachel thought. Somehow Ruksh had learned about the attack on Esa.

'I don't understand. What did Ruksh tell you?'

'My brother told me not to have anything to do with the people from the mosque. He wouldn't even let me meet them.'

'All right, yes. I knew that. Has someone come to your house? Is your security system on?'

'It's not that.' The young woman's voice cracked. 'Ruksh was planning this all along.'

Sweet Jesus, Rachel prayed. *Don't let her have eloped with Hassan Ashkouri.*

Her prayer was answered with something much worse.

'She's left for Algonquin with Hassan.'

Conscious of the escalating pressure of time, Rachel considered her options. She still hadn't learned why Ashkouri was heading up to the camp, but it was a moot point now. He was on his way, with Ruksh as his willing hostage.

She glanced over at Khattak, asleep in the hospital bed. His stitches stood out sharply against his green-tinged skin. There were harsh shadows under his eyes and a drawn quality to his expression in the depths of his slumber.

What would he want her to do?

Family was everything to him, more important than the case, more important than Mohsin Dar, but was it more dear than the outcome of the operation?

She called Martine Killiam again, without success. She didn't have Coale's number, but she remembered Khattak's phone. She keyed in his password to unlock the screen, scrolled through his recent calls. She saw the missed calls from Laine Stoicheva and Sehr Ghilzai. And the call to Laine without a reply.

Should she call Laine and ask for her help? Or was that precipitating Khattak into another kind of danger?

Coale's number flashed on the screen. He was her best bet, Rachel decided.

A voice with a sneer in it answered the call.

'What do you want, Khattak? I thought you were in the hospital.'

Rachel disliked him at once.

'He is. Inspector Khattak's under observation. This is his partner, Rachel Getty.' Quickly, she outlined the recent developments in the case to Coale. 'We need backup. You need to send officers to the park.'

Coale's voice was filled with a vicious satisfaction.

'You don't give me orders, Getty; you have no role in this operation. Did you honestly think we'd flush down two years of work because of Khattak's sister? She knows what Ashkouri is. She's made her bed, now she'll have to lie in it. Which I think is what she was after anyway.'

Rachel sucked in her breath.

'With all due respect, sir, have you any proof of that?' Coale was silent. 'I didn't think so. Which means that as far as your operation is concerned, Rukshanda Khattak is an innocent bystander, and a civilian in harm's way. You have to do something to protect her.'

'My tactical team is in position, Getty. The operation is priority one.'

'That's two days away, sir!'

'It could be a month away, my answer wouldn't change. And I'm surprised that Khattak used you to do his dirty work.'

Rachel ground her teeth. She couldn't risk being called out for insubordination.

'Fine,' she said. 'I'll speak to the superintendent directly.'

'I'm afraid you'll find that a little difficult,' Coale said, not troubling to disguise his gratification. 'She's gone to Ottawa to brief the minister.'

'She has a meeting with Inspector Khattak in a few hours.'

Rachel checked her watch.

'I'll be taking that meeting on her behalf. And as of this moment, you're off this case.'

'You can't do that, sir!'

'I'm the ranking officer,' Coale said pleasantly. 'I think you'll find that I can.'

Five in the morning. December 31. New Year's Eve was nineteen hours away. And Grace had told Rachel to get to the mosque by six a.m. if she wanted to come with the group to Algonquin for the spiritual retreat. There was still a chance that Rachel could make it to Unionville, if she left right now and used her siren all the way.

But what to do about Khattak and his meeting, assuming he was recovered enough to be discharged? What if his injuries were worse than they appeared at first blush?

She was reading through Khattak's contacts on his phone without paying close attention. Now one name leapt off the screen.

Someone she could trust. Someone who would understand

the nature of her difficulty without demanding information she couldn't give.

She called Nathan Clare.

From the fuzzy quality of his voice, she knew she'd woken him from sleep.

Groggy at first, he soon picked up on the urgency of her tone. He was at his door before Rachel ended the call.

25

RACHEL KEPT A DUFFEL BAG in the trunk of her car. It contained a change of clothes, a flashlight, and two sets of thick outerwear in case her car broke down in a snowstorm. There were also three or four pairs of skates in her trunk, one of which was intended for figure skating. The thick leather of the skates would be frozen and intractable, but Rachel didn't have time to move her gear into the backseat. She had no contact information for Grace. If she didn't make it to the mosque in time, she'd have no idea which campsite the group was headed to.

Algonquin Park covered a massive amount of territory, some three thousand square miles in all. This was no peaceful advent into the wilderness. She was speeding like a demon through freezing rain, the roads heaving like a slippery current, cursing Ciprian Coale as she drove.

This was what Khattak hadn't told her – the ridicule, the condescension, the lofty superiority. Khattak hadn't shared a word of it, updating her on each of his meetings with INSET in as logical and focused a manner as possible. She had thought that Laine Stoicheva might choose to cause him some difficulty or unpleasantness. Instead, it was Coale who thwarted cooperation, watching catlike from the shadows, waiting for Khattak to fall from his tightrope.

How did Khattak bear it? she wondered, fuming on his behalf. Khattak should have refused the case the moment he knew his sister was involved. He should have thought of something, spirited Ruksh away on a family trip, dreamt up a plausible excuse.

The lights are for my sister's wedding.

He'd looked bleak as he'd said it, and now she understood why. Ruksh was headstrong and foolish, too certain of her own judgment in the face of her brother's long and distinguished experience of police work. Why hadn't Ruksh heeded his warning?

How frustrated Khattak must have felt on all fronts, and how alone – without comfort or support from those who should have understood him best. Powerless to do anything to change the course of events, except by getting to the bottom of Mohsin Dar's murder.

Rachel had to give him credit. He had concentrated all his efforts to that end, and he had done so without speaking of the things that must have weighed upon him so personally.

Successfully? He'd put a stop to the machinations of Andy Dar, but otherwise it was too soon to tell.

Hunger gnawed at Rachel's stomach.

She found a couple of Rice Krispies squares in her glove compartment and munched them down, one hand on the steering wheel. Her car skidded into the slow lane. She wheeled left to recover, cutting her speed by a third. Two more exits to the mosque. But she hadn't thought her plan through.

What she wanted was exact directions to the campground, along with the ability to convince Din and Grace to remain behind.

If the halaqa at Khattak's house the other night was an indication, Ashkouri would drive Paula and Ruksh. She didn't know about the two young men she hadn't spoken to, Zakaria and Sami. Jamshed Ali would bring Grace and Din. Rachel didn't want any of them being alone in a vehicle with Jamshed Ali. Not when Khattak suspected him of being responsible for the assault in the dark.

If her boss had been struck a little harder on the skull – she swallowed back her fear.

She tried to remember where she'd seen that distinctive mark that had appeared on Khattak's forehead, the small circular depression that had been punched against his skull. It wasn't a tire iron. It was something compact and precise.

Not ski poles, because their length would have made them unwieldy. And Khattak had recounted that he'd been struck twice in the same spot with two rapid blows.

She pulled off the highway, rehearsing her approach.

If she made it in time.

The parking lot beside the mosque was black and silky with rain. A green SUV idled in one of the parking spots, Grace and Din standing at its rear amidst a collection of camping gear, backpacks, and two large coolers.

The rain had begun to thicken into a slushy snow. The air felt mossy against Rachel's unprotected cheeks. She parked her car and loped over to the SUV, the extra Maple Leafs toque in her hands.

'You sure you want to go in this weather?' she asked Grace, tossing her the toque.

No sign of Jamshed Ali yet.

And she noticed something else. Grace had removed the studs from the back of her skull. A row of painful red dots trailed from the crown of her head to the nape of her neck. When Grace noticed Rachel looking at them, she stuffed her streaky hair under the toque.

'You came after all. I thought you'd changed your mind.'

'I didn't want to let you down when I'd promised to teach you how to skate. But this doesn't seem like a good idea, does it? The roads are pretty bad.'

'Hassan says they're better once you get out of the city. The weather's clear up north.'

'You want to drive with me?' Rachel nodded at Din. 'Both of you?'

She'd stashed her siren and anything else that could identify her as police.

A glance passed between them – Din stuffed into a duffel coat that enveloped his rangy body, the kaffiyeh wrapped around his head in a new style that suited him as well as the scarf's previous incarnations, Grace with her leggings tucked into a pair of ragged mid-calf boots and an equally threadbare coat in navy blue that skimmed the tops of her thighs.

Grace wasn't dressed for winter camping.

She wouldn't survive the night in a tent.

But there were no tents stowed with the gear that was assembled by the car.

Din began to pack the SUV, leaving Grace to deal with Rachel.

'Din won't let Jamshed drive alone. He'll want to give him company.'

The wind blew a blade of scarlet hair into Grace's eyes. She fished it out with an impatient gesture. It flicked against her mouth instead.

'That's okay,' Rachel said. 'You can keep me company, then. There's plenty of room in my car.'

Grace cast a skeptical glance at Rachel's tiny Neon.

'No offense, but that's not a great vehicle to drive to the park. The roads aren't usually plowed up there.'

'You're back again, Miss Ellison,' a voice said from behind Rachel's shoulder. She couldn't help her instinctive flinch, any more than she could help herself from stealing a glance at Jamshed Ali's boots.

Not steel-toed, but thick-soled and solid.

He had the grubby look of a man who'd been up most of the night, yet his eyes were clear and alert. Did he suspect Rachel of knowing about the early morning attack on Esa Khattak? She couldn't tell.

'I'm back,' she agreed. 'I'm looking forward to teaching these two to skate. What about this weather, though?'

He made the same demurral that Grace had.

'I'll follow behind you, then,' Rachel said. 'You coming, Grace?'

Grace shook her head.

'I'm gonna go with Din. He likes it when I'm around.'

From the heavy scowl that marked Jamshed's forehead, he didn't agree. But nor did he want Grace to accompany Rachel.

'Where's Paula?' Rachel asked. 'Maybe she could come with me.'

She was puzzling over Grace's response.

It wasn't that Grace wanted to go with Din, she thought. It was that Grace didn't want him alone in Jamshed's company, any more than Jamshed wanted Grace to travel with Rachel.

Did Grace know more about the Nakba plot than any of them had suspected? Was she, like Mohsin, trying to get Din out? If so, Rachel didn't want to leave Grace with Jamshed Ali, even with Din there.

'Paula left with Hassan.' Jamshed didn't volunteer anything other than that, which left Rachel wondering where Zakaria and Sami were, and whether she would find them at the camp.

'That's too bad,' Rachel said. 'I enjoy talking to her.'

'Do you?'

Jamshed wasn't fooled, Rachel realized. Perhaps that had been a stupid thing to say, given Paula's abrasive demeanor. On the other hand, Grace was just as abrasive, in her own way.

Din finished packing the car. He pulled down the rear door, stamping his feet in the cold. He was more sensibly dressed for the weather than Grace. And that made Rachel wonder why he didn't see that Grace was shivering beside him in the snowfall? Was he blind to everything except his mission?

'Coming, Gracie?'

'I don't think you need to follow us,' Jamshed spoke to Rachel. 'We can take one more, if you're determined to come, as no one else is coming with us. But perhaps you should reconsider the weather, Miss Ellison.'

Rachel considered her options. Should she go in the SUV with Jamshed and Din Abdi? She'd have no recourse to backup, and no way of getting herself out of the park – or anywhere else, if they decided to strand her on an empty stretch of highway in the dark.

And Rachel's gun was locked away in her glove compartment, with no easy means of removing it privately to stuff it into her duffel bag.

She saw a flicker of hope flit across Grace's face.

And decided.

'If you're sure you don't mind.' She waved a hand at Din. 'Could you open the back again? I'll load my gear.'

'What gear do you have, Miss Ellison?'

'Won't you call me Rachel?' She smiled blandly into Jamshed Ali's face. 'My duffel bag, and the skates.' She moved to her passenger door. 'And I'll just grab my phone charger.'

'You won't have any use for that,' Jamshed told her. 'There's no cell phone reception at our campsite.'

He was watching Rachel, weighing her. And possibly trying to scare her off.

Or just as probable, calculating what to do with her once they were en route to the park.

And like Khattak, she asked herself the same question.

Why was Ashkouri's Nakba cell returning to Algonquin, the day before the attack?

The Lake of Two Rivers Campground was officially closed for the winter. Jamshed drove the SUV off the main road to a twisty, snow-covered dirt track that ran parallel to the tree line.

The vehicle bumped over ruts in the track, jostling its buckled-in passengers. Much to Rachel's surprise, she had slept on the drive north, Grace a sullen presence beside her in the backseat. From time to time, there would be murmurs from the front seat, the low, masculine voices of Dinaase and Jamshed, their conversation muted and private.

Rachel had listened for her name or Khattak's before drifting into an uneasy rest. The long night and the worry over Khattak had taken its toll on her stamina.

When she woke, it was with the refreshed air of a police officer accustomed to grabbing snatches of sleep where and when the opportunity arose.

She found herself gazing out upon a wonderland of snow.

Canyons of snow, caverns of snow, great polished pastures of snow, the imperial majesty of the pines perched high above them on the rise.

The campground wasn't part of the old-growth Algonquin forest, with its increasingly scarce hemlock and birch. The ancient trees were part of an ongoing logging dispute. Logging was legal in sections of the park, under cautiously managed five-year plans. But modern forestry plans were premised on hundred-year rotations, without taking into account the forest's irreplaceable great age. The park was one of the last refuges of sugar maples, yellow birch, and hemlock. Logging in the recreation-utilization zone of Algonquin was a subject that had sorely exercised Rachel's father, police superintendent Don Getty.

Don Getty had spent the summers of his childhood canoeing and camping in Algonquin's pristine wilderness. Rachel's grandfather had been a conservationist who had taught his son early lessons in the destructive nature of the human footprint. Rachel's father had passed the lessons on to Rachel and her brother.

'There are three things that don't belong together,' Don Getty was fond of saying. 'The call of the loon, the tracks of a moose, and the harvesters of loggers. It's our oldest provincial park; if we don't protect it, who will?'

Gazing upon the undiminished hinterland, Rachel understood the lesson better than she had as a child. She recollected Ashkouri's fixation with poetry, and she thought, the park was a genuine, truthful poem. You could measure yourself against its beauty. And you would know what kind of a person you were from the imprint you left behind.

As she stepped from the car to feel the satisfying crunch of the snow beneath her boots, the air held an unforeseen sweetness, soft and kind against her cheeks. She was struck at once by the crisp tang of the jack pines. The campground was deserted, the campsite office closed. Firewood was stacked in neat bundles at its rear. The Lake of Two Rivers, partially frozen over, was to the west, the Old Railway bike trail to the east. There were no tents or cabins at the site.

'We have to go around,' Jamshed explained. 'The river is to the north. There are some abandoned cabins on its banks.'

Which didn't sound right to Rachel.

The park was meticulously managed and maintained. They were trespassing if Two Rivers was closed. Ashkouri must have chosen it for that reason. The Mew Lake Campground was open year-round, and could be counted on to be populated, even in winter.

But the two campgrounds were less than a mile apart, just off the highway, at the heart of a system of lakes with beautiful names like Littledoe, Longspur, Misty Lake, and Burnt Island. The park encompassed some twenty-four hundred lakes altogether, and more than seven hundred miles of lake-fed rivers and streams. The Lake of Two Rivers was its most popular campground.

Jamshed motioned Rachel to the car. He had stopped to collect two bundles of firewood.

Now they traveled deeper into the park's interior, away from the highway, away from the long, deep trough of the lake, past the wide spread of its wings, toward the muffled roar of the Madawaska River. It was snow-crusted, dipping well below its banks. Rachel took note of the river's narrow margin of winter frost. The river was beginning to thaw. It wasn't safe for skating on. And she realized that any evidence that might have connected members of the camp to Mohsin Dar's murder was probably long gone – either buried in the snow or thrown into the river.

Jamshed drove them through the wild backcountry, where the track was now forged by the wheels of the SUV. The blue sky of night was in retreat, the pallor of dawn creeping into its place. A lusterless gold limned the pines and the undressed maples.

Rachel was losing her bearings. She hadn't thought to bring a compass, but the GPS tracker in her phone was active. She cast a surreptitious glance at it. They couldn't have traveled as far into the wilds as she'd thought; her phone was still receiving service.

She texted her last known location to Khattak, and as an afterthought, to Sehr Ghilzai.

And in case she didn't get another chance, she added the words, *Haven't found Ruksh, but think I'm close.*

Their car pounded the snow for another mile until they reached a clearing of jack pine and spruce, mantled beneath slow-forming ice. Just beyond the clearing, Rachel made out the murky outline of a series of cabins. They had lost the river, a cottony thread that wound beyond the trees into the crackling distance. A black SUV was stationed east of the cabins. Jamshed parked his vehicle beside it.

They tumbled out of the car, eager to stretch their legs – and in Rachel's case, more than eager to find Ruksh Khattak, her mind running through various scenarios. She'd have to steal the keys to one of the cars, somehow coerce Ruksh and Grace into it, and get herself to Huntsville, twenty minutes away, to liaise with the local police.

She'd figured out what to tell Ruksh.

She had no idea at all how to convince Grace, or whether she should bother.

Grace was in no immediate danger.

She couldn't say the same for Ruksh.

Ashkouri must have brought Ruksh with him for one reason. If he was identified in connection with the Nakba plot, he must have thought he'd need a hostage to fight his way out.

Not much suicidal inclination there, Rachel thought. Nor any particular desire for an immediate ascension to paradise.

Ashkouri had sacrificed younger men to that end, and in that he followed the pattern of jihadist commanders, who preached the glories of martyrdom without partaking of those glories themselves.

The young were sent to die, their mentors exempt from the same prescribed sacrifice.

Rachel didn't know the identity of the members of the second cell. She reckoned, however, that it would be a bunch of kids not much older than her brother Zach. Stupid, gullible, alienated kids looking for something to hold on to, something to believe in, and ending up in the clutches of Ashkouri and Jamshed. And then rationalizing the violence as if it were a video game with a tally of kills in the right-hand column.

If I had a rocket launcher.

If they had a rocket launcher, she knew what they would do.

It wasn't enough to say that the same faith that had produced Hassan Ashkouri had also produced Esa Khattak, good and evil sketched out in broad strokes

It wasn't easy and two-dimensional like that. It was nuanced, complex, difficult – it required an understanding of history, of the power vacuum that erupted in the aftermath of invasions, of the *longue durée* outcomes of occupations and looted capitals, of bombs that leveled the infrastructure of cities, of drones that did their killing without accuracy or due process, of those who rose to fill the vacuum of the deposed and despised, of the dialogue between civilizations, of the decades-long struggles for rights and democracy, of the stultification of independent thought by those who were steeped in authoritarian traditions.

Like Hassan Ashkouri.

With her limited knowledge, Rachel thought of all those things, and she didn't see Esa Khattak.

And she wouldn't reduce it or him by saying, *He must be one of the good ones.*

What else was Community Policing about, if not seeking a greater understanding of diversity? And respecting those who themselves respected a nation of communities, bound together by the things they held in common. All the things, so many things.

Ashkouri had chosen a different path, a different means of addressing his anger and grievances, his choices vindicated by his reading of history. Something could be beautiful, humane, encompassing. Or it could be made ugly. And maybe that was the lesson. We bring to a tradition what is already within ourselves, however our moral compass is designed, whatever our ethical training is. And then the tradition speaks.

It was on that basis that Ashkouri had set his plan in motion.

The New Year Nakba.

And there was an evil in that that Rachel wasn't sure Esa Khattak recognized.

She couldn't accuse her boss of having been partisan about anything connected to Mohsin Dar's death, setting aside his reasonable concern for his sister. And she hadn't expected that he would be. Khattak was the counterterrorism expert, not Rachel.

Rachel was the one who found herself thinking along the same lines as Mohsin Dar. She didn't want these kids to be swept up in the plot. She wanted to get Paula and Din out; and if not Din – if he was too deeply implicated, if he had killed Mohsin Dar at Ashkouri's command – then at least Grace.

Was it wrong of Rachel to see the innocence in Grace, the injured spirit? Was it wrong to want to rescue her?

Would she always be partial to the young and dispossessed, because of Zach?

Wasn't that the very quality that made her so good at her job?

Wasn't that the one aspect of her approach to policing that Khattak had never asked her to moderate?

She had disobeyed a direct order from Ciprian Coale not just for Ruksh's sake, but also because of Grace. And maybe Paula.

She didn't believe that these women had no agency of their own. They had made foolish choices, each for the same reason – Paula's infatuation with Ashkouri, Ruksh's dubious relationship with the same man, and Grace clinging to Din like he was the only thing that connected her to the world. Because without him, the world was cruel and uncaring.

Rachel didn't know what that felt like.

The most intense love she'd known in her life had been for her brother Zachary.

But she was possessed of a fertile imagination.

And all that poetry at the mosque – passionate, dramatic – had to spring from somewhere, something.

A very real depth of feeling.

And then a thought struck Rachel.

Paula Kyriakou was the only one who hadn't mentioned poetry or recited it.

Paula, the pragmatic one.

Hassan Ashkouri's faithful admirer.

On cue, the woman bustled out of the nearest cabin, trudging her way through the snow to their SUV.

'Give me the firewood, Jamshed. You have no idea how cold it is.'

Paula had changed her comfortably loose robe for a full-length down parka with a furry white hood that framed her round face. Without the scarf pulled tight around her forehead and chin, and with the crispness of winter bathing her cheeks, she looked lively and pretty.

If still of the same sour disposition.

Jamshed unloaded the firewood from the back of the car. He carried it into the clearing.

'Where's Hassan?'

'He's taken Ruksh for a walk.' Paula firmed her lips as she

shared the news. 'They shouldn't be alone together.'

Jamshed broke off an icicle from the branch of a spruce tree. He held it up to Paula.

'What can they get up to in this weather, Paula? They're grown-ups. You don't need to police them.'

His eyes slid to Rachel.

Din smirked at Grace, perhaps in recollection of his last trip to the park. The night that Mohsin Dar had died, when the two of them had been alone in the woods of Algonquin.

And from the slight emphasis that Jamshed had placed on the word 'police', Rachel understood that Jamshed Ali knew exactly who she was.

And if he did, there was no reason that Rachel shouldn't make a bolder move.

'This clearing is so pretty,' she said. 'Hassan said you intend to hold a memorial for your friend. The one who was killed in the park. Is this where he died?'

Paula stared at Rachel with distaste. Grace answered before Jamshed Ali could speak.

'No. He was up beyond the rise, near the river. That's why no one heard him cry out after the gunshots. If he did cry out, that is.'

Her voice began to shake.

'When someone has returned to God, we do not mourn his passing.'

It was an indictment. Delivered by Jamshed with no regard for the fact of a young girl's sense of loss. Rachel had witnessed Islamic funeral rites before. She knew they could be gentle, a comfort to the bereaved, in the hands of a capable preacher.

There was a sternness and rigidity to Jamshed Ali's construal of his faith that was consistent with the nihilism of his worldview. If he wished that for himself, Rachel wouldn't have faulted him. But she suspected the real power and pleasure of his orthodoxy lay in his ability to constrain the happiness of others.

Including Grace, however little she may have been wanted at the mosque, or on this trip.

The tears formed muddy tracks on Grace's face, her eyeliner and mascara streaming down her cheeks in two ragged trails.

'Whatever,' she said, trekking off in the direction of the cabins. She glanced back at Din. 'Coming?'

He caught Jamshed's eye, shook his head.

His refusal made Grace angry. She swore loudly enough for them all to hear, Paula clucking her tongue behind Grace's back. Rachel started after her.

'Leave her,' Paula said to Rachel. 'She liked Mohsin the least of all of us. I don't know why she bothers to pretend. Help me build the fire instead.'

Rachel shuffled over to Paula's side. As they busied themselves over the fire pit, Din and Jamshed retreated under the cover of the trees.

Paula issued a series of instructions that Rachel, who was an excellent camper, chose to ignore. She had the fire roaring at the center of the clearing in short order, casting a professional glance over their stores of firewood.

'That won't be enough,' she warned Paula.

'We can drive back to Two Rivers for more in the evening.'

'When's the memorial?' Rachel asked.

'Tonight. Over the bonfire. Hassan will lead us in a halaqa. He says it won't be like anything we've experienced before. He says we should think of death as a celebration.'

Rachel found a stick in the snow to prod the fire.

'Don't you find that a little creepy?' Rachel asked. 'Or disrespectful?' But she saw that she had taken the wrong tack with Paula by criticizing the man she idolized.

'How did you get into this?' Rachel waved a hand at the campsite. 'Your exploration of Islam. You never said.'

Paula began to unload the rest of the supplies from the car.

'Work,' she said to Rachel. 'Don't talk.'

'Can't I do both? I'm curious to know if your experience has been anything like mine.'

Paula paused by the SUV's rear door, one mittened hand on her hip.

'I didn't run away from home like Grace, if that's what you're thinking.'

Rachel pawed at her toque, pushing it back on her head.

'Neither did I,' she said. 'I was just in pain. From not having answers.'

Rachel found it interesting that Paula didn't question her further. The other woman couldn't seem to summon up an interest in any subject other than Hassan Ashkouri.

Paula carried the heaviest pack to the closest cabin.

'You can share with me,' Paula said. 'I don't want to room with Ruksh.'

Rachel expressed her thanks, though truthfully, she'd hoped to find herself with Grace. She had no desire to spend the night in either Ruksh's or Paula's company. On the other hand, she didn't know how else she was going to get Ruksh away on her own.

She grabbed her gear from the car and stowed it inside the cabin, under the nearest bed, after a momentary dilemma. She needed it close at hand, in case she had to run. But that also meant that anyone who slipped into her cabin would find it at once.

Then again, she'd left her gun back in her car, parked at Masjid un-Nur. Her cell phone – the other object that could have given her away – was on her person.

Paula didn't answer Rachel's question about her past, so she tried another.

'You don't like Ruksh very much, do you?'

Paula spread her sleeping bag over the bed farthest from the door. She sank down on top of it, the bag deflating with a quiet sigh. The cabin was ice cold.

'Hassan brought heaters,' Paula told her. 'He thinks of

everything. He thinks of everyone. That's why he shouldn't be with Ruksh. She thinks only of herself.'

Rachel sat down on her own bed, feeling its chill through the layers of her coat.

'You think he should be with someone like you instead? Someone who shares his vision?'

Paula seemed flattered by the comparison.

'I had a boyfriend once,' she confided. 'He was Turkish, which wasn't an easy choice for me. He expected all kinds of things from me in terms of more conservative behavior – he wanted me to change how I look and behave and speak. I did those things for him – all those things. I mean, look at me. And then he left me to go clubbing with a twenty-year-old in a miniskirt. A girl not that different from Ruksh.'

'But Ruksh is an observant Muslim, isn't she?'

Paula's rejoinder was sad.

'It's not what you eat or don't eat. It's not what you drink or how short you wear your skirts – it's not just being born to something. It's committing yourself – your inner self. Maybe I didn't understand that before, but I do now. I don't think Ruksh is committed to God. I do know that I am.'

Paula's blue eyes were candid.

She was telling the truth.

She had taken a step beyond Hassan Ashkouri.

And Rachel saw a way out.

She leaned across and patted Paula on the knee.

'Maybe I can help you,' she said. 'I've been wanting to talk to Ruksh – you know, about being a newcomer at the mosque, and not fitting in. Maybe if I ask her those questions, she'll realize that she's not committed, as you say. Not in the way that she should be.'

Paula snorted.

'Good luck with that. Hassan doesn't let her out of his sight.'

Another reason for Rachel to worry.

'Maybe you could distract him. Keep him busy with something so I can get Ruksh alone.'

But Paula wasn't convinced.

'Why would you do that?'

Rachel thought about her reasons – what she could share, what she couldn't.

'I think that you and I are a little bit alike. Both of us are on the outside, when maybe we don't deserve to be.'

Paula stood up, brushing her hands down her coat, her eyes not quite meeting Rachel's.

'Most of the women at Nur don't like me.'

And Rachel heard in Paula's voice the same lost note she'd heard when Grace had spoken of Jamshed and Din.

She gave Paula a tentative smile.

'There are deeper things than popularity. They haven't had to learn that, I guess.'

Grace, Ruksh, and Paula. Rachel needed to get the three of them out.

She made her way to the public washrooms, locking herself inside the shed. Close by, she heard the voices of Ruksh and Ashkouri, murmuring in the soft tones of lovers. She peeked her head out of the shed's tiny window, hoping to catch a glimpse of Khattak's sister.

Noon light. Hot bright bursts against the peacock sky.

The temperature was rising. The air inside the shed was frigid. She stood on tiptoe, following the sound of the voices until she found them. They were on the ridge behind the shed, Ashkouri shaking down snow from the surrounding pines onto Ruksh's dark hair as she laughed.

Rachel snapped a picture with her phone, texted it to Khattak.

Along with the message that she didn't have her car or her gun.

When Khattak didn't answer, she forwarded the message to

Sehr Ghilzai. And after a moment's thought, to Martine Killiam as well.

Her cell was half-charged, the service spotty.

Grace knocked on the door.

'It's freezing out here, hurry up.'

It was much colder in the shed than it was outside in the white glare of the sun. Grace was cold because she wasn't dressed for the weather.

Rachel tucked her phone deep inside her parka and traded places with the teenager. She offered the extra fleece and thermal leggings she had packed to Grace, who was shorter than Rachel.

'I'll take the fleece, thanks.'

Rachel returned to her cabin to get it, to find that Ruksh and Ashkouri had circled back to the clearing. Ruksh did a double take.

'Rachel, isn't it? How did you get here?'

So Ruksh was still covering for them.

Ashkouri nodded pleasantly at Rachel.

'When I didn't see you at the mosque, I thought you must have changed your mind.'

She heard the same threat in his voice that she had heard the previous night when he had stopped her by her car.

It shocked Rachel that only a handful of hours had passed.

She felt as though she had run a marathon in that time.

And she thought of Khattak in his hospital bed, the stitches at his temple, how close he had come to fatal injury.

She couldn't muster a smile for Ashkouri.

'I didn't think you'd leave so early,' she said.

'I didn't want to waste the light.'

It was dark when Ashkouri had driven. Unless he meant he'd been waiting for this moment: sunrise over the trees, a glancing plenitude against the snow. He looked beyond Rachel to Jamshed Ali's car.

'You came alone?' he asked.

'I came with the kids. I was going to teach them how to skate,' Rachel said. 'There must be a creek around here. You should come, Ruksh. I have an extra pair of skates with me.'

No way to convey her sense of urgency to Ruksh without also conveying it to Ashkouri.

Rachel challenged Ashkouri with a look. And echoed his provocative manner of speech.

'You can spare the kids for a bit, can't you?'

His nod acknowledged it.

'Grace, yes. Din, no. Grace will show you the way.'

She could loan the skates to Paula instead. If she could just get hold of the keys.

Jamshed had left the SUV unlocked rather than giving the keys to Paula.

And then, by a stroke of luck, Ruksh asked Hassan for his keys so she could grab her bag from his car. Rachel walked to the car beside her, scanning its interior.

It was a stick shift.

Rachel could drive stick like a race car driver; that was no problem.

'The skates?' Ruksh asked with a smile, probably wondering why Rachel was shadowing her so closely.

'They're in Jamshed's car.' Rachel dropped her voice. 'A man was murdered here, Ruksh. Why would you come here when your brother warned you off?'

Ruksh stiffened beside her.

'I can think for myself,' she hissed. 'I know my fiancé better than either of you do.'

This wasn't the moment to convince Ruksh. Rachel hung over the car door as Esa's sister retrieved her bag. Speaking into Ruksh's hair, Rachel said, 'I need you to keep those keys, Ruksh. Whatever you do, don't hand them back to him. Please.'

Ruksh froze, half-crouched over the passenger seat, her hands searching in the glove compartment for something Rachel couldn't see.

'You're not dragging me into this,' she muttered. 'Hassan has nothing to do with Mohsin's death.'

She had one move left, Rachel realized. And Ruksh's reaction to it would be unpredictable.

'Don't react to what I'm about to say. Your brother is in the hospital with a head injury. He was attacked last night by someone from this camp.'

Ruksh's gloved hands clutched at her handbag.

'He's all right,' Rachel whispered. 'But you have to come back with me.'

A knock on the driver's window made Rachel's skin flinch. She controlled her reaction just in time. Ruksh wasn't as lucky. She banged her head against the roof of the car. It was Grace, not Ashkouri.

'Should I show you the creek?' Grace asked.

Rachel made a subtle gesture with her hands at Ruksh.

Keep the keys, she mouthed. *Bring your phone.*

'Absolutely,' she said to Grace. 'Ruksh wants to come too.'

If she could get the two of them alone by the creek, maybe she could convince them of what needed to be done, get into the car and drive off. It wouldn't work if they didn't cooperate; the cars were too close to the clearing, where Ashkouri and Jamshed were now seeing to the fire.

Ruksh dropped her bag at the cabin.

Rachel couldn't tell if Ruksh had done as she'd asked or not.

Each of the women grabbed skates from the back of Jamshed's SUV. Rachel looked around for Paula, stopping at the cabin, which was empty. No sign of her. This couldn't wait.

'Lead the way,' she said to Grace.

They trekked over flat, crunchy snow up the rise, using branches to haul themselves over the slippery portions, trampling pine needles beneath their feet. The roar of the Madawaska became louder as they approached, water rushing against stones and lichen and ice.

Rachel palmed her phone from her pocket.

No cell service. She sent the text to Martine Killiam anyway.

Activate strike team. My cover is blown.

They were climbing higher than she'd expected, nearing the side of a drumlin.

'Isn't this where you said Mohsin's body was found?' she asked Grace.

'On the other side of the rise. The creek is on this side.'

'Can I see it?' Rachel asked. 'Will you take us there first?'

'Why?' Grace scowled. 'Why would you want to see it? Isn't that kind of morbid?'

Ruksh intervened, though why she was trying to help, Rachel didn't understand.

'I'd like to see it too, Grace. Just to pay my respects.'

Grace's steps slowed, sliding on the slippery surface of the forest floor.

'I don't want to go back there.'

'Will you point it out then? Just the tree?'

Grace shrugged. 'And they say I'm the weird one.'

They climbed the drumlin at an angle, moving sideways to minimize the risk of tumbling toward the river. Small stones and pebbles moved under their feet as the covering of snow and ice thinned. They reached a secluded grove of trees, a mix of maples and birch and ash. The largest of these was a sugar maple, its branches cracked like the mast of a ship veering into a storm. Rachel looked down from the summit. The cabins were far away, screened from her view by the quivering trees.

Closer to where she stood, a mixture of rain and snow had washed the blood off the ground. But there was a telltale reddish bruising around the trunk of the maple.

Grace stalked away. 'I'll wait for you by the creek. I want to try on my skates.'

A moment later, they heard a whoosh as Grace slid down the side of the drumlin.

Ruksh asked about Esa the moment the two women were alone.

'He was attacked near his car, leaving from my place. He has a couple of fractured ribs and a headache he won't soon forget.'

'But why do you say someone from the camp must have done it?'

'It's where the investigation has led us. You know I can't tell you more than that.'

Rachel trudged through the small clearing, her eyes searching for overlooked clues, for things the INSET team wouldn't have found important at the time. The ground was well trodden, the maple tree wordless.

She turned and surprised Ruksh in the act of murmuring a prayer for Mohsin, her eyes closed, her hands clasped. When Ruksh was finished, Rachel held out her hand.

'The keys, please. We have to get out of here now.'

Ruksh took a step back. 'Not until you tell me why. Because I know that Hassan didn't kill Mohsin.'

'Do you also know that he didn't attack your brother? Where was he this morning at two a.m.? Was he with you?'

'No, of course not. He was at Nur. Jamshed will tell you.'

'I'm afraid I can't rely on Mr. Ali, any more than I can rely on Mr. Ashkouri. You have to trust me. You have to know that I'm acting as your brother would have wished.'

'Why don't you just tell Hassan who you are? Have it out with him? Tell him whatever it is you suspect him of?'

Rachel's face paled.

'That would be the worst thing I could do. Please listen to me, Ruksh. I think he already knows, but you cannot confirm it, do you understand? Just come with me in the car, and I'll explain to both of you on the way.'

Ruksh ignored her. She pointed to the tree at Rachel's back. 'Rachel, do you see that?'

Rachel moved closer to the maple and squatted down upon her haunches.

At the bottom of the reddish bruise, and filtering off to the side of the tree, three letters had been carved.

FAF.

They might have been there forever. They might have been carved by a dying man. Rachel tried to remember if a pocketknife had been found on Mohsin Dar's body.

'I don't know what that means,' she muttered to Ruksh, quickly snapping a photograph. She texted it to Khattak. Once she made it back to the outdoor shed, the photograph would transmit. Along with her text to Killiam.

'FAF,' Ruksh said. 'It's the name of a poet. Faiz Ahmad Faiz. Mohsin must have carved it into the tree. To send someone a message.'

Rachel saw the realization creep into the other woman's face.

'Poetry,' Ruksh whispered. 'The main theme of the halaqas.'

'We have to leave now.' Rachel tried to cover her panic by being firm. 'Without delay.'

They heard the sound of loose gravel and crunching snow. Both women moved to look over the edge of the snow-ridged drumlin.

Grace looked up at them, her skates tied together around her neck, her cheeks red with exertion.

'The creek's frozen through,' Grace said. 'I tested it to make sure, just like Jamshed showed us the last time we were here.'

She held up a small metal object in one hand, ten inches long with a crank handle at the top and a rounded strike node at the bottom.

It was a ninety-millimeter-thick Omega Pacific ice screw.

It was normally used for belaying, or testing the thickness of ice for mountain climbing. It could also be used on a lake or creek surface, provided the lake wasn't deep. When depressed into the ice, it left behind a circular indentation. Like the one in Esa's forehead.

'Where did you get that?' Rachel breathed.

Grace gave them a quizzical look.

'It belongs to Jamshed,' Grace said. 'I grabbed it from his car.'

26

KHATTAK MET CIPRIAN COALE ON his own ground, at the downtown offices of Community Policing. CPS occupied half of the fourth floor of the imaginatively designed police headquarters on College Street, where blue glass met pale pink stone in a flurry of right angles and triangles.

The offices commanded an impressive view of the downtown core, the deep mauves of the skyline edging toward night.

Khattak's hospital discharge had taken the better part of a day.

He'd woken from his sleep to find Nate in his room, and listened to a concise recital of the steps Rachel had been forced to take in his absence. As he read Rachel's texts, he fought back panic at the thought of his sister's being ensnared by Hassan Ashkouri, in the remote spot where Ashkouri had deliberately placed her.

There was no answer from Rachel when he called her. Or from Ruksh. Or from Killiam.

Coale, the next best thing, had deigned to meet Esa downtown, likely because Coale was liaising with officers at headquarters. On the phone, Khattak had demanded that backup be sent to Algonquin, or that local police from Huntsville be sent to locate Rachel and Ruksh.

His sister was in danger. And Khattak had been attacked beside his car for a reason.

'You take your orders from me,' Coale had said. 'Not the other way around.'

There were messages on Khattak's desk from the Department

of Justice, and some from his personal contacts as well. Coale had taken Esa's chair, the gesture symbolic, premeditated. A reckoning of what he thought had always been his due.

Laine hovered behind him at the window, her face watchful and serious.

What now? Esa thought.

A dozen members of the INSET team were assembled in the outer offices, outside Khattak's door.

'Did you send agents to the park?' he asked Coale, without preamble.

'My team had other priorities today.'

Khattak raised his head. He understood why Coale had agreed to meet him downtown.

'You've acted? You intercepted the delivery? Your takedown was successful?'

Coale nodded. 'We've arrested sixteen people, including Zakaria Aboud and Sami Dardas. Team members are going through their homes and offices now.'

'So you listened to Rachel. You moved your timetable up. Did you get them all – didn't you say that two dozen people were involved? And what about Ashkouri? If this makes the news –'

'Did you miss the microphones on your way up, Khattak? The press conference takes place within the hour. We're waiting on the superintendent.'

Khattak swallowed hard on a ball of fear.

'You told me the takedown would be on New Year's Day.'

Coale rose from Khattak's chair. He paced around the desk until they were standing chest to chest. Coale's narrow gray eyes alighted on the stitches at Khattak's temple.

'I couldn't be sure whose side you were on, Khattak. Given your close association with your sister, I couldn't be sure how far the knowledge would reach. So I played it close to my chest. And I was right to do so. Besides which – did you really think Ashkouri's people would strike on a day that the city is empty?

A few of them have gone to ground, but we're confident we'll get them all in the end.'

The New Year Nakba.

It was all that either Killiam or Coale had told Khattak of the terrorism plot.

And both of them had chosen to lie.

Because they had never fully trusted him. Because they had always thought his loyalties might be torn. Blood thundered in his temples. His face flushed a dark red. But when he spoke, his voice was controlled.

'What the hell do you mean by that?'

Coale signaled Laine with a flick of his wrist. She passed him the folder she was holding, her eyes blank and inscrutable on Esa's face. 'Do you know what this is, Khattak?'

Coale stepped from Khattak's office to the outer environs where his team members were assembled. Laine followed him, her back to Esa. Esa stood in the open door, beside the name and title that were stenciled on the glass.

Esa Khattak, Director of Community Policing.

He felt it slipping beyond his reach.

Yet all he could think of was Rachel and Ruksh, so far from help, at Ashkouri's mercy.

Rachel didn't even have her gun.

'Whatever it is you have to tell me, say it.' Khattak's voice was curt. He needed to be on the road to Algonquin.

As he spoke, his phone buzzed. There was a voicemail from Sehr Ghilzai that he had ignored. And two photographs that Rachel had texted him.

One was of his sister with Ashkouri.

The other was a set of initials carved into a tree. FAF. Above the photograph, Rachel had texted him the message, *Tree where Dar died. Ruksh says it means Faiz Ahmad Faiz.*

An icy chill ran down Khattak's spine.

Mohsin followed your career, Alia had told him. *He was*

proud of you. He called it 'a spectacular ascent.'

Mohsin had understood that he was dying. If he was going to communicate anything, it would have to be in a way that would mean something only to Khattak.

Still woozy, Khattak braced his hand against the glass doors.

Laine saw the color leave his face.

'He needs to sit down,' she said. 'He came straight here from the hospital.'

'Give him a chair then. It doesn't change what I have to say.'

Khattak shook his head. 'I'm fine. Get on with it, Ciprian.'

Coale waved the folder at him.

'These are transcripts of your phone calls, Khattak.'

'So?'

Why Faiz Ahmad Faiz? Esa wondered. When Esa and Mohsin had been undergraduates at the University of Toronto, writing for the same newspaper, he'd told Mohsin that Faiz was his favorite poet. He'd explained how Faiz's poetry spoke both to the elites and the masses, using language that was conversational in tone, but formal in its diction – progressing from themes of idle love and beauty to the more pressing concerns of social justice and the interconnectedness of the human experience.

The letters FAF had been carved into the frozen bark of the maple tree for Khattak to find. And to decipher.

But what did it mean? Ashkouri had addressed the poetry of Faiz referentially, not as the main subject of his halaqas. He had spoken of the moon, Faiz wrote of the moon, every poet of the East that Khattak knew of had written about the moon.

Chandni was a common Urdu nickname for girls. It meant 'moonlight'.

The calendar of Islam was based on the lunar calendar. The full moon, the half-moon, the crescent moon, the new moon.

The beginning of the month of fasting depended on the sighting of the new moon, as did its end.

The festival days of Eid-ul-Adha and Eid-ul-Fitr were

predicated on the changeover of the lunar month.

But Faiz had written of the moon as one of many poetic symbols, not as a cornerstone of his work.

Not as the poet Nazik al-Malaika had – where the moon was Muhammad, the messenger who delivered the message of Islam.

Why then? What had Mohsin wanted to tell him?

'It's all here.' Khattak looked at the folder that Coale aimed at him, without seeing it. He'd scarcely listened to Ciprian. Until he heard him mention Sehr Ghilzai.

Coale gestured at Khattak's name on the glass doors.

'I told you it wouldn't amount to anything, just as I told the commissioner and the superintendent that your unit was a mistake. It was like setting a fox to watch the henhouse.'

Abruptly, Khattak understood what Coale was driving at. And why he had named Sehr.

'Are you accusing me of wrongdoing? Of misusing my authority somehow? Or of being in collusion?'

When Khattak didn't take the folder, Coale dropped it on a nearby desk.

It was Rachel's desk, a fact that infuriated Khattak. Another emotion he couldn't reveal. Not with so many eyes upon him, the audience to Coale's spiteful sense of theater.

'You were asked to keep our operation under wraps. To discuss it with no one, to give no one the slightest indication of it, least of all your sister.'

'You've placed my sister in grave danger,' Khattak said evenly. 'She's still facing that danger, because of your lack of action. Even so, I haven't contravened your request.'

'Ashkouri was at your house, man! Do you expect me to believe that was a coincidence?'

Khattak didn't have time for this.

'You've had my house, my sister, and from what I now understand from you, my cell phone under surveillance. If you have any evidence that it wasn't a coincidence, I suggest that you produce it.'

'Maybe I can't prove that you warned Ashkouri off, Khattak. But do you know what I can prove? I can prove that you compromised my operation. That you went outside official channels. You met with Sehr Ghilzai, one of the prosecutors.'

A sense of uneasiness surfaced in Khattak. Why had Sehr called him so many times? Why had she come to the hospital?

'She's a friend. She didn't disclose anything she wasn't authorized to disclose.'

'Didn't she?' Coale said with relish. 'She told you about the gun.'

'What gun? What are you talking about?'

'The gun that killed Mohsin Dar. You see, we knew about the gun – we knew where it came from, we knew who had it. It seems that given your stay in hospital, you haven't checked your voicemail.' He reached for Esa's cell phone, keyed in the password, and hit the speakerphone.

Sehr's disembodied voice faltered into the silence. 'I've been trying to reach you, Esa. I know I shouldn't be telling you this, but it's important. You asked if there was anything I knew that could help you with Mohsin's murder. INSET should have told you about the gun. One of the members of Ashkouri's cell brought it across the border. It was meant to be used at the training camp. As far as I know, the gun that was used to kill Mohsin Dar is still in his possession. It was the boy – his name is Dinaase Abdi.'

Khattak stood without moving.

Din Abdi was at the park.

I freaking loved him, man. You killed him, I'm done.

A charade? A masquerade for the benefit of those monitoring the Rose of Darkness website?

Or the truth: Din smuggling the gun across the border, and handing it off to someone else – to Jamshed, or to Ashkouri himself.

Coale silenced Khattak's phone. His manner became no-nonsense.

'So you see, we have you, Khattak. Your security clearance will be voided. Your partner will be disciplined for insubordination, unless you admit you sent her to Algonquin in direct contravention of my orders. And your friend the prosecutor will be suspended, pending an internal investigation.'

'You hindered my investigation at every turn, Ciprian. I was asked to join this team, asked to handle Andy Dar – asked, in fact, to bring Mohsin Dar's killer to justice.'

'Not by me.'

Coale appeared unsettled. He must have thought Khattak would blink and step back, unable to offer a defense to the accusations. The concrete evidence.

'By the superintendent, then. Sehr was right. You should have told me about the gun. You've placed my partner and my sister in a life-threatening situation, and if anything happens to either of them, it's not my career that will be on the line, it's yours. If you intend to go live with your press conference before I can get them out of harm's way, you'll be hung out to dry.' Khattak gripped Coale's shoulder. 'Why haven't you taken Ashkouri? What are you waiting for?'

Coale shrugged off his grip.

'Watch yourself, Khattak.' His hand strayed to his tie. His hard gaze moved around the room, assessing the reaction of his subordinates to Khattak's assertion of authority. 'I've a team in place. You're panicking over nothing.'

Khattak pressed a hand to his aching ribs. His voice was deathly quiet.

'What are you waiting for, Ciprian?'

He glanced around the room. A few of his former colleagues shook their heads, communicating something that Khattak should have known, if he hadn't been misdirected.

What wasn't he seeing?

Why was Ciprian focused on Khattak instead of on the final phase of his operation?

Was it the final phase of the operation?

He took his phone back from Coale, studied it. And then he realized the unpalatable truth.

'You don't have him.' He saw Laine look at him, widen her eyes, blink twice, nod. He tamped down all other emotions. 'That's why my house is under surveillance, why you wouldn't let me pull Ruksh out. You can't tie Ashkouri to any of this. You've been using Ruksh as bait.'

He took the folder and tossed it at Coale's feet.

'Do what you want with this. Just give your team the order to extract.'

He turned on his heel. Two members of the INSET team followed him to the door.

'You won't get there in time,' Coale called after him. But for the first time, there was a hint of doubt in his voice, a sense that he might have taken a step amiss.

'You better pray that I do.'

He couldn't afford his rage, couldn't afford to broadcast it.

Ciprian's allegations were wildly misguided. He'd veered from accusing Khattak of collusion with the Nakba cell to more general threats of corruption. He wanted Khattak to be guilty, to be inseparable from the members of the cell because of who he was.

And that was an anomaly. For reasons particular to Ciprian Coale.

Esa's colleagues had seen through it because they trusted him. Just as he'd never had reason to doubt them. They'd worked with Esa for more than a decade, known that Coale's agenda was personal. He had confidence in his friends, his colleagues, his city, and himself. If they could have told him about the gun, they would have. To do otherwise would have placed them in the same regrettable position that Sehr was now in.

He'd do what he could to rescue Sehr when he'd cleared his head of the threat facing his sister. The voicemail implicated Sehr, clear as day. She would be reprimanded, suspended – he didn't know what other repercussions she would face.

He found himself wishing she'd been more circumspect, even as he didn't regret the fact that she'd passed him vital information. Information Coale should have given him.

Din Abdi had the gun. But INSET hadn't found the gun on-site.

So where was it now?

And who had used it to kill Mohsin Dar?

27

LATE AFTERNOON. THE SUN ON the verge of setting. The roads empty, the highway streaked with traces of the earlier rainfall. And Gavin Chan wasn't driving fast enough.

'Hurry. Please,' Khattak said. 'Rachel's not answering her phone. Neither is my sister.'

'The service in the park is spotty, at best.' Gavin Chan had worked with Khattak for five years at INSET, which was why he'd allowed him access to his cubicle. He'd spoken up for Khattak in each of the team meetings that had taken place without Khattak's knowledge. He'd argued that the murder investigation would assist with INSET's goal by bringing the tactical operation to a head much sooner. Coale had disregarded Chan, then sidelined him.

That was why he was in the car with Khattak, driving north to Algonquin.

And Khattak was grateful.

'But we've traced her GPS transponder to an exact location?'

'And sent it on to the tactical team.' Chan glanced over at Khattak. 'They haven't moved in yet.'

Because Coale wouldn't give the go-ahead. And Khattak couldn't reach Martine Killiam.

It seemed foolhardy beyond reckoning to hold a press conference in the midst of an ongoing operation, when there were so many things that could still go wrong.

Fact. Paula Kyriakou and Grace Kaspernak had never been confirmed as members of Ashkouri's cell.

Fact. Neither had Rukshanda Khattak, sister of a veteran police officer.

Fact. An undercover operative was also at risk, unarmed and without backup.

Although Rachel had been ordered away from the park, she had acted exactly as Khattak would have in a situation that put civilians at risk.

With great bravery, and the hope that luck would break her way.

It was an act of desperation on INSET's part to use the press conference as a means of flushing Ashkouri out. How could Ashkouri learn of the operation, when he was so far removed from things at the park? And if Ashkouri was able to communicate with the Nakba strike team, Khattak should have been able to reach Rachel.

Ashkouri had known enough to leave town on the day of the take-down.

It had to be coincidence.

Unless…

What did Mohsin's final message mean?

FAF.

You love poetry, man. You're old-school. It's like you and Faiz share a language of secrets that shuts the rest of us out.

Mohsin's words. And he'd encouraged Khattak to spend his energy on better things – political commentary, polemical battles, human rights activism.

But Faiz Ahmad Faiz could be polemical, his poetry an indictment of the political status quo. His most famous poem, 'Darling, Don't Ask Me for the Same Love Again', spoke to a loss of innocence, of a man no longer able to turn away from the miseries of the world in the selfish pursuit of love.

It wasn't Faiz per se, Khattak realized. It was poetry, the language of secrets that Mohsin expected Khattak to decipher.

He thought of the strange exchange between Ashkouri and

Rachel – the nature of mud and crime, the Rose of Damascus, the equation of love and submission with death, and of Ashkouri's periodic requests for the participation of others in his halaqas.

Jamshed – a man old enough to recite venerable poets like Ghalib or Muhammad Iqbal from memory – had added nothing. Neither had Paula. Grace had offered lines of poetry in passing, but not as Hassan had requested. Instead, she'd made a point of noting the absence of female poets.

It was Din who had complied with Hassan Ashkouri's request, echoing back the themes of Hassan's halaqa with the clumsy line of poetry that Ashkouri had approved.

If you subtract the night from the day, the moon will blossom over the square.

Khattak frowned. The moon was a signifier to Ashkouri. He had referred to it repeatedly, bringing it up in every conversation, in strange, befuddling contexts.

The moon was the key to Ashkouri's code.

It was how he identified himself, in the grip of a staggering self-regard.

In his mind's eye, Khattak revisited a photograph from Rachel's phone, a photograph she had taken while rummaging through the offices of Masjid un-Nur: a drawing in a sketchbook of a skating rink situated in front of two crescent moons that faced each other.

He hadn't taken note of it at the time. Why a skating rink under two moons in a sketchbook filled with rough drawings of various buildings in the downtown core?

Unless... they weren't crescent moons, as Rachel had supposed.

There was a clangorous noise in his head, as realization struck.

He thought of two buildings that were designed in the shape of a sliced banana, easily mistaken for a pair of crescents.

The two buildings that made up Toronto City Hall.

The skating rink was part of Nathan Phillips Square, the square that fronted City Hall.

On New Year's Eve, Nathan Phillips Square would be packed with sixty thousand revelers.

Subtract the night from the day, the moon will blossom over the square.

The Nakba plot had never been intended for an empty city on New Year's Day.

The strike was intended for New Year's Eve.

The code *was* in the poetry.

How cleverly Ashkouri had misdirected the INSET team, his use of poetry a fog that had occluded his true intentions.

And Mohsin Dar had pointed Khattak to the poetry by scribbling the initials of the poet, Faiz, into the tree, instead of using his last breath to identify his killer.

Mohsin had found a way to communicate the true nature of Ashkouri's plot, and if Khattak had been allowed to visit the scene, he would have made the connection much earlier.

It was less than six hours to New Year's Eve.

He was struck by a pang of genuine fear.

Did you get them all? Khattak had asked Coale.

A few of them have gone to ground.

Khattak turned in his seat.

'Gavin, listen to me. You need to go back.'

'You forgot to return my keys.'

Ruksh's masquerade was falling apart. She was visibly nervous as she handed back the keys to Hassan Ashkouri's car.

They were gathered around the fire, three men, four women, on little stools that Ashkouri had brought with him.

'New moon tonight,' he said.

Rachel glanced at him sharply. He was relaxed, at his ease. He took out his phone and checked the time. Rachel longed to do the same, but Ashkouri had upped the ante. He'd sent Jamshed to call the women back before they could follow Grace to the creek.

'The bonfire's ready,' Jamshed had said. 'What are you doing here?'

Ruksh had answered with a slight stammer, 'I wanted to p-pray for Mohsin.'

He'd grunted. 'Hassan wants you, it's getting dark.'

It was dark, the earlier light blotted out, the sun-swept robes of day gathered up. At the campsite, Ashkouri held out a little sack, and asked for everyone's phones. One by one, he had taken the phones, and switched them off. Rachel slipped her phone into her boot, but not before Ashkouri had seen.

He chided her gently.

'I fear for a city that does not read.'

'Depends on what you read,' Rachel said. 'Some subjects are more worthwhile than others.'

It was not as if Hassan had brought the book *Fazail-e-Amaal* to the campsite.

Her phone vibrated in her hand. Two quick texts, both from Khattak.

Din has the gun that was used to kill Mohsin.

Hassan reached out his hand.

'You see?' he said. 'The outside world complicates things. It complicates your reality.'

Her face ashen, the best Rachel could do was to turn off her phone herself, to prevent Ashkouri from accessing her logs.

She was conscious that she was also turning off the GPS tracker.

Pray God Khattak knew where she was. She hadn't had time to read his second text.

'Come sit beside me, Ruksh,' Ashkouri said.

Rachel found herself on the receiving end of an importunate glance. Ruksh took the stool beside Hassan, wincing as he slung his arm over her shoulders.

Rachel tried to appear calm.

Din had the gun. Had Din also killed Mohsin Dar?

Rachel might not have a gun, but she had confiscated the ice screw from Grace, with the help of a made-up excuse. Her gloved hand was wrapped around it in her pocket.

'It's cold,' Rachel said. 'It's New Year's Eve. I'd feel a lot better celebrating it in the city, like most years.'

Jamshed dropped any pretence of politeness.

'No one asked you to come.'

'There's no need to be rude, Jamshed. I'm sure Rachel has her reasons for being here. And perhaps a time of quiet reflection in the park instead of the company of a boisterous crowd will serve her better. Better than she knows.'

Rachel braved Ashkouri's glance.

'Like I said, I came because I promised the kids I'd teach them how to skate.'

'I'm not a kid,' Grace said, her voice sullen. 'And anyway, Jamshed didn't even let us get to our lesson.'

'The memorial first, Grace.'

Grace found a seat beside Din, linked her arm through his, and snuggled close. After a moment, Din patted her on the back.

'New jacket?' he asked her.

'She was freezing, Din. I gave it to her.'

Rachel meant it as a caution to him – he needed to refocus on Grace, to think of Grace's wellbeing as much as Grace thought of his. He looked away, ignoring Rachel.

Jamshed didn't sit. He took up a position leaning against one of the nearby trees, watching them all.

Paula took the stool on Hassan's other side, leaving Rachel the seat across from Hassan. When Ashkouri raised his head to take Rachel's measure, she saw the deadness in his eyes, the luminous doom.

'We came here because of Mohsin, our friend who died in this park.'

The others held up their hands, palms up and close together.

Hassan recited two prayers in Arabic, the first Sura Fatiha, the second the longer recitation of Sura Yasin.

When he was done, everyone wiped their faces with their palms.

Except for Jamshed, whom Rachel watched from the corners of her eyes.

And then she ventured a statement.

'Your friend didn't just die here, he was killed.'

Ashkouri gazed at her steadily.

'The police seem to think that someone who was here that night did it.' She glanced around the circle of faces. 'Ruksh wasn't here, so it couldn't be Ruksh.'

'It wasn't any of us,' Ashkouri said, as pleasantly as if they were discussing the weather. 'Mohsin was beloved to us. He was one of us, the moon to many stars.'

Rachel looked up at the purpling sky. The first hints of starlight had arrived to prick the darkness. If there was a new moon, she couldn't see it.

'How do you think he died, then? Who do you think killed him?'

Din shifted beside her on his camp stool, freeing his arm from Grace's.

'Why do we have to talk about this? Bad enough the first time, Mo lying there in his blood.'

'You saw him?' Rachel asked.

'It was terrible.' Din briefly closed his eyes. 'To see somebody you love, dead like that.'

But had Din truly loved Mohsin Dar? Or was the chat log on the Rose of Darkness website a blind?

'I don't want to hear this,' Grace muttered. 'I'm going to skate by myself.'

Jamshed shifted away from the tree in her direction. Grace tipped up her head and glared at the older man.

'What? You can't stop me. I've participated in your ceremony and now I just want some fresh air. Come with me, Din.'

Din's head swiveled from Grace to Jamshed. He took a second too long to consider.

'Fine!' she shouted. 'Do whatever you want. These people aren't good for you, this camp isn't good for you, but whatever. I'm the one who watches out for you, but you don't seem to care. I'm done with the whole stupid thing.'

She pushed past Jamshed to disappear into the trees.

Ruksh rose from her stool.

'I should go after her, Hassan. It's dark out there, and she doesn't know how to skate.'

'She didn't take her skates with her,' Ashkouri pointed out.

Rachel jumped to her feet. This was it. Her chance. Her moment to get Grace and Ruksh out of this mess. She didn't have the car keys, she didn't have her cell phone – but she was going to seize the opportunity anyway.

And, undetected by the others, she'd thought she'd heard a sound.

The sound that she had been praying for, though nowhere near close enough. The crunch of a car's tires over the compacted snow.

'I'll go with you. Bring a flashlight, Ruksh.'

And then, with a stroke of inspiration, Ruksh made a decision, chose a side.

'I don't have one. Let me use my phone.'

She grabbed it from the sack before Hassan could object, switched it back on, and flashed its light around the camp.

Paula grabbed hold of Hassan's arm.

'Let them go, Hassan. We can start the preparations for dinner.'

Rachel didn't wait. She maneuvered past Jamshed, dragging Ruksh in her wake.

'Grace,' she called up the rise. 'Grace, wait for us!'

Behind them, she saw Jamshed Ali nod to Din. He disappeared into one of the cabins.

Why? To grab the gun?

Ashkouri watched them without moving, a smile twisting his lips in the flickering light of the bonfire. It was Jamshed who followed in their wake.

'Hurry,' Rachel hissed to Ruksh. 'Call your brother, and keep the connection alive, no matter what.'

But they had gone beyond the reach of the cell tower, losing the signal as they climbed. Ruksh was panting along beside Rachel.

'I don't know what you're doing,' she said to Rachel. 'I don't know why I'm frightened. I *know* Hassan. He couldn't have done it. He's a good man.'

'Then why did you follow me?' Rachel gripped Ruksh's arm from underneath, pulling her up the ridge. 'Where's the creek? I don't see Grace. Grace!' she called out again. 'Grace, where are you?'

They stumbled toward a sheltered copse of pine trees, the tang of the needles a counterpoint to the hazy smoke of the bonfire.

Rachel checked behind them. Jamshed had stopped his pursuit. But he had stopped to wait for Ashkouri and Din to catch up.

She swore loudly and fluently.

Where was Khattak? Where was Grace?

'I'm here,' the girl's voice floated toward them from beyond the stand of pines.

Rachel shoved Ruksh toward the trees.

'Kill the light. Get behind those trees and hide. Go as far as you can, and in the name of sweet Jesus, don't make any noise. I'll get Grace.'

'No!' Ruksh hissed back. 'If there's truly anything to fear, I'm not leaving you alone out there.'

'Ruksh! I'm a police officer, for God's sake! I'll be fine. Besides, it's you that Ashkouri wants, it's you he's always wanted. Now go!'

Rachel broke away, following the hollow sound of Grace's voice.

It seemed to drift away behind the pines. She could hear

something else, too: the almost imperceptible rush of running water. The creek was nearby. She could smell the wet-pavement scent of the tumbled stones in the water.

'Grace, where are you?'

'Here, on the ice.'

Rachel spied her fifty yards away, gliding out on her booted feet to the middle of a creek bed less than thirty feet across.

The running water was from a rivulet that cut across the ridge.

To reach Grace, Rachel would have to leave the cover of the pine grove and break into a run through open country.

She'd lost sight of Ruksh in the thick cover of the pines and the hemlock up ahead, but back the way she had come, she could see the dim rounds of yellow light cast by bobbing flashlights. And beyond them, back at the bonfire, a sight that caused a wave of relief to swell in her chest.

An SUV pulling up beside the fire, its headlights left on.

A figure jumped out from the driver's seat.

She couldn't see who it was, but she guessed.

'Up here!' she shouted from the rise. 'They're tracking us – be careful!'

One of the flashlights broke away, headed in the direction of the drumlin, before its light was shut off.

Rachel skidded across the frozen creek bed, panting as she caught up with Grace.

'Are you okay?' she gasped.

'Why wouldn't I be?'

Grace spun around in a circle, her head tipped back, the staple-studded tattoo gaping out at Rachel like the scythe of the reaper.

'Grace, will you come with me? Away from here? There's more to these people than you understand. Like you said at the campsite, they're not good for Din – and they're not good for you.'

Grace slowly came to a stop. She was looking over Rachel's shoulder. Rachel didn't turn. She couldn't. She didn't have time.

'How would you know? You've only just met them.'

The crunch of footsteps was closing in on them. In a moment, Ashkouri or Jamshed would be slipping across the ice to catch up with them.

'Listen to her, Grace. She's a police officer.'

It was Ruksh. She had broken free of the clearing, risking her own safety to come to Rachel's aid.

Rachel spun around. They were all on the middle of the ice now, Ashkouri and Din at its edge. Jamshed must have been the one to break away.

And now she could see Khattak, climbing the rise at a furious pace. He was alone.

'Get out of here,' she shouted to Ruksh.

'I can't leave you out here on your own. I don't understand, but I won't leave you!'

'You knew what they were planning?' Grace asked Rachel. 'You came here to stop it?'

'Yes.' Rachel reached out for the girl's arm. Grace slid farther away. 'Please, you have to listen to me.' And then she realized. 'You knew about the attack? All this time you knew?'

Her heart plummeted into her stomach.

Grace was a member of the cell.

Ashkouri was moments away, Khattak still too far away to help.

Grace or Ruksh? What should Rachel do?

'Ruksh, run!'

But it was too late. Ashkouri's advance upon the ice was slow and predatory. He came up behind Ruksh, caught her at the waist, held her fast.

'Hassan, what –'

He dropped the flashlight onto the ice. Rachel heard a slight wheeze, the sound ominous. The light bounced back across Ashkouri's face. He didn't have Din's gun. He was holding a knife to Ruksh's throat.

'You didn't tell me, my sweet fiancée. You didn't tell me how well you knew your brother's partner. Didn't you trust me?'

Ruksh couldn't speak under the press of the blade. She was staring up at Hassan in shock.

'Let go of her, Ashkouri,' Khattak shouted from the ridge. The terror in his voice echoed across the ice.

Hassan wheeled around, dragging Ruksh with him.

'I told Jamshed to deal with you. Your sister was a distraction. Until she told me all about her brother, Inspector Esa Khattak. Then I saw how useful she would be. And here you are, exactly as I planned. So back off, unless you want me to use this.'

He pointed the tip of the blade straight up under Ruksh's jaw. She whimpered in response.

Rachel calculated the distance between herself and the flashlight. It was a heavier object than the ice screw. She had good aim. If she could throw it from behind... Ashkouri turned back to her, bringing Ruksh with him. He'd altered the angle of the blade again. It was pressed flat across Ruksh's throat.

'I don't need her alive,' he said. 'So think carefully.'

'Let her go.'

It wasn't Rachel or Khattak who spoke. It was Grace, her voice hard with purpose. Rachel looked back at her. Grace was holding the gun – Din's gun – in steady hands. It was aimed squarely at Ruksh's chest.

'Grace, no!' Rachel cried, bewildered. Why did Grace have the gun?

Hassan shifted Ruksh's body more fully in front of him.

'So you took the gun,' he said. 'I wondered. What did you do with it?'

'You don't want to know,' she answered.

Din approached from behind Ashkouri, inching closer to Grace.

Rachel shook her head at him in despair.

'You haven't done anything yet,' she said. 'You can still get out of this, Din.'

'That's what I thought,' Grace said in a monotone. 'I always thought I could get him out, save him somehow. It didn't work. He left me with no other choice.'

'What are you saying, Grace?' Rachel gasped.

'They drew him into their plot. They turned him into one of them. He wasn't the Din I knew anymore. I tried to get him away, but Mo wouldn't let me near him.' Grace jerked the gun at Hassan's head. 'Mo ran interference for Hassan. He made sure that the members of the cell didn't back out. So I took care of him.'

'It was you? You shot Mohsin Dar?'

Rachel couldn't catch her breath. She slid toward Grace, a little at a time. The gun was still pointed at Hassan and Ruksh. Grace used one hand to smooth her hair under the Maple Leafs toque. Then she gripped the gun tighter, letting it dip toward Rachel.

'I had to. To save Din.' Her voice cracked. 'He used to love me once. He was the only person who did. I couldn't let them take him. I couldn't let them hurt him.'

'Gracie, no!' The heart-wrenching wail was Din's. 'You don't know what you're saying. You couldn't have hurt Mo. You could never hurt anyone.'

'Then why do I have the gun?' Grace blinked away tears. Her voice was a whisper. 'It was for you, Din. I did it for you.'

'I loved him!' Din cried. 'He was my brother.'

'He ruined you,' Grace answered. 'He wanted to see you dead.'

'Don't grieve for Mohsin,' Hassan told Din. 'He's become *shaheed*, a martyr to the cause. He's in paradise now.'

Rage rose in Rachel's throat, choking her. She was poised on the ice between a girl with a gun and the man who held a knife to Ruksh's throat. The man who counted up lives and spent them, like so many worthless pennies.

'You're wrong,' she said to Hassan through gritted teeth. 'He wasn't your martyr, and he didn't want to die. He didn't believe in your cause – he was working with us. That's how we knew about your plot. That's how we were able to stop it.'

Hassan smiled. There was nothing in his manner to suggest that Rachel's news had shaken him. Until his blade drew its first drops of blood from Ruksh's throat.

'*Did* you stop it?' he asked. 'It's not yet midnight.'

'We have you,' she said. 'There's nothing you can do now.'

'We've already done it.' He waved the knife at her. 'Why do you think we came back here? To draw you away from the Nakba.'

Rachel gasped. She didn't know what he meant, and she didn't have time to sort it out. She was focused on the tears of blood leaking from Ruksh's throat. She needed to get the gun away from Grace.

'I'm so sorry, Grace,' she said to her, aghast at what Ashkouri's schemes had cost the girl. 'I'm *so* sorry. Mohsin wasn't who you thought he was. He wasn't trying to hurt Din. He was trying to keep him safe – to get him out. You killed the wrong man.' She drew a deep breath. 'Mohsin Dar was innocent.'

A gunshot whistled past Rachel's ear.

Din threw himself to the ice.

Ashkouri didn't move. The gun was trained on Rachel now.

'You're lying,' Grace said. Her eyes were two hollow smudges.

'I'm not, Grace. That's how I knew to come here to help you. That's why I was trying to get you out. Because Mohsin told us – because that's what Mohsin wanted. Please, Grace. Give me the gun.'

'You give her the gun, Grace, the first thing she does is take down your boyfriend. He's committed now. There's no way out for Din.'

Rachel turned on Ashkouri like a cornered mountain lion.

'The first thing I'll do is take off your head. Let go of Ruksh, now!'

Her eyes beseeched Ruksh. Ruksh had to find a way to help herself.

Ashkouri closed the distance between himself and Rachel, dragging Ruksh with him.

The ice shifted underneath Rachel's feet. She heard the ominous wheeze again. She'd been on the ice all her life. She knew what it meant. There were too many of them gathered at the weakest point on the surface.

'Grace,' she said, holding out her hand for the gun.

From her peripheral vision, she could see that Khattak had reached the creek bed. His gun was drawn, but he didn't have a clear line of sight.

Grace raised the gun. She pointed it at Rachel. The ice shifted again. Grace lost her balance, but recovered quickly, the gun still aimed at Rachel's heart.

'Too many people have lied to me,' she said, her eyes wet. 'Including you.'

There was a terrible sense of shock in her face. Her mouth gaped at Rachel, the tattoo on her neck stretched tight with pain. She didn't want to believe Rachel because of what it would mean. She had killed Mohsin for nothing, for all the wrong reasons.

'Do it,' Ashkouri said. 'Be one of us. Help me.'

Rachel shifted farther away from Ashkouri, drawing the gun with her. She'd opened up a field between herself and Ruksh, giving Khattak the clear line of sight he needed. But he had only a few seconds before Ashkouri clued in to his approach.

And in those seconds, Khattak would need to decide.

His sister or Rachel.

There was no choice, really. Khattak couldn't cover them both.

And she realized she didn't want to be a witness to his painful decision.

She made her words flat and no-nonsense.

'If you wanted to save Din, it was Hassan you should have killed.'

She leapt at Grace, wrestling the girl for Din Abdi's gun.

The gun went off, a crack that shattered the immaculate silence. Then a second shot, followed by a muffled thud on the ice. Stars splintered and wheeled above Rachel's head. Grace butted Rachel's forehead, her piercings stabbing into Rachel's skin.

'Gracie!' Din called, scrambling to his feet.

'Don't come any closer!' Rachel shouted at him.

He didn't listen.

Rachel wrested the gun from Grace's hand. It fired again, this time straight down into the ice. The plates of thinned ice jerked against each other, once, twice, then separated under Grace's feet. She plunged into the depths of the creek, a startled expression on her face. She vanished under the surface in a heartbeat.

'Grace!' Din's voice was petrified.

Rachel threw herself flat on the ice, grabbed the ice screw from her pocket, and drove it into the heaving surface of the creek.

'Get off the ice,' she shouted back to Din. 'Let me get her!'

'No!' he screamed. He slid past Rachel on his belly and threw himself into the hole where Grace had disappeared.

He dived once, twice, three times – the minutes between his ragged attempts at surfacing stretching out longer and longer.

On the third try, Rachel grabbed at his scarf. She staked it down with the ice screw, reaching for his shoulders.

He was shivering wildly.

An inch at a time, Rachel propelled his body from the hole, slinging it along the length of the ice, moving toward the banks of the creek.

'No, no, no,' he kept crying.

Rachel shoved his trembling body away to safety, then swung out again, creeping back toward the hole, using the screw as a safety measure, the same way a mountain climber would use a spike.

'Rachel, no!'

It was Khattak's desperate cry.

She didn't listen. She spared a moment to reassure herself that it was Ashkouri who had fallen, and that Ruksh was safe in her brother's arms. Then she kicked off her boots to dive into the hole.

She was a better swimmer than Din, but the cold bit into her body at once, a shock to her arms and legs. The puffy coat weighed her down. All around her was blackness, and the dragging pull of the water.

She couldn't see Grace. She couldn't see the way up.

She kicked out, searching for Grace's body, scrabbling for a break in the surface of the creek.

Nothing.

Ice-cold pressure squeezed her lungs.

She spun around with difficulty, struggling back in the opposite direction. Something soft brushed against her hands. She grabbed it.

A light bobbed against the blackness above her head. She scissor-kicked her feet, propelling her body toward the light. She was weighted down, heavy with cold and fatigue.

Two strong arms reached down to grab her shoulders, hefting her from the water. Coughing up brackish liquid, she was dragged off the creek to the side.

Her soaking coat was stripped from her body. She was gathered close against Khattak's chest, his hands pounding her back.

'Rachel,' he said. 'Rachel, come on.'

She forced her eyes open, coughing harder.

'I'm fine, I'm all right. What about Grace?'

He shook his head.

She struggled against him. 'I have to find her! There's still time!'

He held her until her struggles subsided, then he said, 'Rachel.'

He closed one hand over hers.

She looked down at it.

Grace's Maple Leafs toque was in her hand.

28

It was Rachel's first time meeting Superintendent Martine Killiam of the Royal Canadian Mounted Police. One look at the other woman's strong, square face and her instinctive habit of command, and Rachel could see how the superintendent had risen to her rank in the RCMP.

Rachel made her handshake as firm as she could, given that her wrist had been fractured in the struggle for Din Abdi's gun. The cold from her dousing in the creek had prevented her from feeling the pain at the time. And since then, she hadn't felt much of anything at all.

She'd skated in her all-star game on New Year's Day because she hadn't felt she could let her team down. Her heart wasn't in it. Her wrist heavily bandaged inside her glove, she'd watched as one of her teammates – a good friend – had won the MVP trophy for scoring five times. Rachel hadn't even managed an assist.

Khattak and Nate had come to cheer Rachel on from the stands. They had met Zach at the game, and there had been nothing in that meeting for Rachel to dread. She was coming to accept that the people who mattered to her could get to know each other, and it wouldn't cause her world to collapse. As she had feared with her father, Don Getty.

Rachel's mother hadn't come to the game.

She also hadn't called to ask Rachel about her injury.

It didn't matter, Rachel thought. She had failed to save a teenage girl from a terrible death, so what did any of it matter?

Martine Killiam was reading from a folder.

'You disobeyed a direct order from the ranking officer, Sergeant Getty.'

Rachel nodded. She had nothing to say to this.

Khattak spoke for her, somber and formally dressed at her side.

'She knew civilians were in danger from Ashkouri and his cell. Sergeant Getty put her own life at risk to save them. Inspector Coale should have listened to her. Just as he should have listened to me. Perhaps then a teenage girl wouldn't be dead.'

The superintendent consulted the file again, before closing it.

'Grace Kaspernak. The girl who murdered Mohsin Dar.'

'Yes.'

'And we have six people who witnessed her confession. One of them is dead. Din is under the protection of a lawyer. Still, the confession will stand. A good day's work. And we took Ashkouri's strike team before they got to Nathan Phillips Square. Thanks to your work, we averted the New Year's plot.'

Khattak had attended the press conference, watched Martine Killiam lay out the operation in clear, concise phrases. She had taken particular care to recognize the role of Community Policing, and to enter a commendation into Rachel's personnel file.

'May I ask, ma'am, what will happen to Dinaase Abdi? What his role was?'

Killiam studied him gravely.

'Inspector Coale should have taken a different approach. He should have let you know about the gun; he should have told you more about the operation. Perhaps then the outcome would have been different. Din Abdi was a courier – he transported the cassettes, and he transported the weapon. He knew every detail of the plot. He's been charged, and he will be tried. And if there's any justice, he'll serve a maximum sentence.'

Rachel flinched at the news. It didn't sound like the RCMP intended to take into account Din's age, any more than their youthfulness would shield Zakaria or Sami. Din was a kid, a stupid kid, snared by Ashkouri's rhetoric, caught up in the make-believe world of the Rose of Darkness website. The world that had just become real for him. He'd lost Mohsin, he'd lost Grace – both of whom had risked everything to save him – and now, he would lose his freedom.

Could anything be worth that? Any dream of paradise?

She couldn't block that night from her mind, Din's lament reverberating through the black branches of the forest.

Gracie, Gracie – she can't be gone. Tell me she's all right. Tell me she'll be okay.

His body had heaved convulsively, until the tactical team had arrived to take him away.

Din hadn't looked back for Ashkouri, cold and dead on the ice, brought down by Khattak's gun.

And Khattak himself, his face after he had pulled Rachel from the water. Pale with terror.

He had saved Ruksh first, and she didn't begrudge him the choice.

He had also saved Rachel, his breathing torn as he'd tried to revive her.

She wouldn't ever forget that.

Recognizing something in Khattak's face, Martine Killiam said, 'It wasn't personal, Esa. It wasn't ever aimed at you.'

Khattak couldn't quite keep the anger out of his reply.

'With all due respect, Superintendent, my phone was tapped, my house was under surveillance, and my sister was dangled before Ashkouri as bait. Even then, Inspector Coale missed the evidence that Mohsin pointed him to.'

'Which is why your perspective was so necessary.' Killiam signaled Rachel. 'Thank you, Sergeant, that will be all.'

Worried, Rachel looked over at Khattak. He nodded at her, rose from his seat to get the door for her.

'Wait for me outside.'

Rachel left him, finding her way to the vending machine down the hall.

What more did Killiam have to say to him? And why couldn't Rachel hear it?

Khattak knew what was coming. No matter Killiam's recognition at the press conference, no matter what he and Rachel had achieved despite being kept in the dark, there was no way around it. He'd been grossly insubordinate. And he knew how the RCMP worked.

'You were under my command,' Killiam said to him.

'Yes.' And then, more than a little angry, he said, 'Yet I couldn't reach you when it was critical to do so.'

'Ciprian was the officer in the field. You were to report to him.'

'We had different objectives. Mine was to understand how your operation affected Mohsin's murder. Coale's was simply to bring me down.'

Martine Killiam sighed.

'He's succeeded in part, I'm afraid. And not just with you. Sehr Ghilzai has been relieved of her responsibilities as senior counsel.'

'That was my doing,' Khattak said quickly. 'Not Sehr's. She wouldn't have advised me about confidential matters if I hadn't pressed her. If Coale wants my head he can have it.' His voice was bitter. 'Though you said yourself, he should have told me about the gun.'

'I can't do anything about that. And it's not just the fact that you met with Sehr, or the message she left for you. It's on the record; it can't be wiped away or made to disappear. Sehr has to face the consequences of her actions. I am sorry about that.'

'What else, then?'

'Your phone was tapped. You asked your friend Nathan Clare to remove your sister from the investigation.'

'I didn't tell him why.'

'It was still a breach, Esa. It endangered the operation.'

'The operation endangered my sister.'

Killiam looked him dead in the eye.

'There was also the call to Laine Stoicheva. You did the same thing with her – asked her to get your sister out.'

'That's what she told you?'

'Actually, she told me she was the one to go beyond the parameters of her security clearance – that she offered you more help and information than you had asked for. But I can't ignore the phone calls, Esa. We have a strict chain of command, and an equally strict protocol. Then there's also the fact that the Drayton inquiry is moving ahead. I did what I could for you in the press conference, whatever I could do for Community Policing, but the fact is that heads will have to roll. I've made my report to the commissioner. And to the Minister of Justice.'

So what he and Rachel had achieved didn't matter. And what Coale had done to him would be set aside. The neatly dug trap, the noose he had felt tightening around his neck. He'd been reckless, careless, blinded by the danger to his sister. And Ciprian Coale had won.

'Is the Minister shutting us down?'

'No. Not yet. You've been placed on administrative leave, pending your post-shooting evaluation. The Minister will reconsider that decision once the Drayton inquiry is closed.'

'I could fight back,' he said, after he had considered. 'Go to the press, file a lawsuit, claim reckless endangerment by the police. Or negligence based on discrimination.'

'Will you?' Martine asked him. 'That sounds more like something Andy Dar would do.'

Khattak thought of his final meeting with the family. Neither Alia nor her father-in-law had been satisfied by his explanations.

Alia Dar had looked at him with her haunted eyes and said, 'You lied to me. You made me believe that Mohsin didn't love me. How could you do that? *Why* would you do that?'

She'd had no forgiveness to offer him.

And he knew her forgiveness was something he didn't deserve, even if he hadn't been able to rule her out as a suspect. The INSET operation had taken priority over every other consideration.

Ruksh's reaction had been little better.

'You should have told me the truth about him. You risked my life for the sake of your career.'

She wouldn't accept Esa's explanation about the constraints he'd been working under, or the impossible choices he'd had to make. And she'd rewritten the history of that night to satisfy her sense of thwarted love.

Ashkouri had stared at Khattak from the ice, his face losing color, his voice still hypnotic.

'You're a traitor, Khattak,' he'd whispered, wiping the blood from his lip, studying the discoloration of his hand. 'But I'm not worried. Others are coming.'

Khattak's response was Qur'anic.

'This cult you're in is destined for ruin.'

Ashkouri's eyes had closed, enigmatic and impenetrable to the end.

And Khattak didn't say to Ruksh as he could have, *Ashkouri would have murdered you without a second thought. He nearly killed my partner.*

He felt again the sickening panic he'd experienced when Rachel's dark head had slipped under the waves. The rising commotion of water that had seemed to pull Esa down with her.

Ruksh needed someone to blame for her ill-advised judgments. As her brother, Esa didn't care if that someone was him. Ruksh was safe. Rachel was safe. Nothing else mattered.

He came to a decision. He reached across the desk to shake Martine Killiam's hand.

'I won't do anything of the kind. And I appreciate the fact that you've kept Rachel out of this. If there's anything at all that you can do for Sehr Ghilzai, I promise I won't forget it.'

In the hall, Rachel offered him a Cherry Coke. He cracked the tab and took a long sip.

'Now I know why you like these, Rachel.'

'What happened in there?'

Khattak summarized the outcome of his discussion with Killiam. A smile flickered across his face at Rachel's outraged response. Her voice trailed off as they let themselves out into the new year quiet that had blossomed over the city.

Rachel stopped him with a hand on his arm.

'Sir,' she said. 'I never thanked you for saving my life.'

Khattak studied his partner's face. In that moment of extremis, Rachel hadn't once considered the value of her own life. She'd flung herself at Grace's gun to protect Ruksh. She'd given him a way to save his sister. And she'd thrown herself under the ice in hopes of saving Grace, the girl she'd always seen as lost and abandoned.

Rachel's heart ran as wide and deep as a continent.

He shook his head.

'I never thanked *you*, Rachel. I just didn't know how.'

He bent his head and kissed Rachel's cheek.

Author's Note

THE TORONTO 18

In the summer of 2006, Canadian law enforcement carried out a major anti-terrorism operation that resulted in the arrest of eighteen suspects on terrorism charges. This group would later become known as the Toronto 18. Radicalized by jihadist websites, and influenced by a charismatic ideologue, members of the group participated in training camps in the woods, and attempted to secure the materials necessary to detonate fertilizer bombs in the city of Toronto. The Toronto 18 plotted to attack Parliament Hill and to behead parliamentarians, as part of a plan to force the recall of Canadian troops from Afghanistan.

Although the participants in the plot were ill-equipped and poorly trained, they attempted to make their plot a reality. They were foiled by an extensive CSIS and RCMP investigation: the group was soon infiltrated by a Muslim police agent posing as a fellow jihadist. Along with tens of thousands of intercepts, information provided by two separate Muslim informants assisted in the take-down of the cell before the plot could be actualized. A sting operation resulted in the switching out of inert material for fertilizer, while tactical units swept across the city to arrest the members of the group.

The arrests in the Toronto 18 case resulted in eleven convictions, including life sentences for two of the ringleaders. Fahim Ahmad, the charismatic ideologue, pleaded guilty to terrorism charges in 2010, and was sentenced to sixteen years in prison. One of the participants in the plot, Ali Mohamed Dirie, served his sentence in Canada, and is reported to have been killed fighting in Syria.

TERRORISM AND ISLAM

There is no inherent connection between Islam and terrorism, despite the rash of events that appear to link the two. Like all religions, Islam is multivocal, and there are different interpretations of Islam available to its practitioners, including those that are justice-based and ethically grounded. These interpretations are embodied in the writings of contemporary scholars such as Khaled Abou el Fadl, Kecia Ali, Reza Aslan, Laleh Bakhtiar, Nurcholish Madjid, Fatima Mernissi, Fazlur Rahman, Abdolkarim Soroush, and Amina Wudud, among others. Perhaps less well known is the fact that a remarkable diversity of opinion on the interpretation of religion can be found among scholars of the classical Islamic tradition, as well.

Radical interpretations of Islam do exist, the most prominent of which is Wahhabism, a puritanical doctrine based on an exclusivist reading of Islam, promulgated throughout the Muslim world by Saudi Arabia. The popularity of radical Wahhabism has been boosted by prevailing social conditions in the Arab and Muslim world. Decades of authoritarian rule followed by war, state breakdown, and state collapse have fostered violent extremism in the name of religion, demonstrating how critical political and historical context is to understanding the rise of extremism. Iraq is a case in point.

The American invasion of 2003 exacerbated Iraq's already dire social and political conditions. Prior to the invasion, Saddam Hussein's dictatorship was characterized by an appalling abuse of human rights, including the extreme persecution of Iraq's Kurdish and Shia populations. The vacuum created by the collapse of the Iraqi state proved to be an ideal breeding ground for extremism, producing cycles of sectarian violence, and ultimately resulting in the emergence of ISIS.

ISIS, the Islamic State of Iraq and Syria, has taken the ideology of Wahhabism to extremes, seeking to impose a new Islamic caliphate that transcends the borders of the Middle East. Primarily, ISIS has been waging a war *within* the house of Islam, marking out for elimination those who do not practice its radical, exclusionary creed. This war is characterized by extreme brutality and horrendous crimes, and has exacerbated existing refugee crises. Its victims include Shias, dissident Sunnis, and members of a vast tapestry of ethnic and religious minorities indigenous to the Middle East. What is even more disturbing in the face of its crimes, is that ISIS's ideology continues to attract recruits from around the world.

With the Paris attacks of November 2015 and other subsequent events in Europe, it is evident that ISIS has expanded its strategy to focus on targets in the West. As such, ISIS will persist in dominating headlines – challenging our notion of what Islam is and rendering Islam a contested ground in global affairs for the foreseeable future.

As I researched the Toronto 18 case, I became aware of how closely jihadist ideology is often linked to other issues: the conflation of Islam with violence, the perception that the actions of an extremist fringe inescapably taint and implicate an entire faith community, and the necessity of moving beyond reductive notions of 'us' and 'them' to achieve a deeper understanding of the present moment in history – one that might suggest a way forward.

Just as the vast majority of the victims of groups such as ISIS and al-Qaeda are and have been Muslims, it's worth remembering the efforts of those who seldom attract similar news coverage: human rights activists, women's groups, student groups, religious leaders, journalists, and builders of civil society – whose courageous and critical work on the frontlines reminds us that Islam is not a monolithic force, and that millions of Muslims aspire to universal values.

All civilizations and religious traditions experience dark moments in their history. The current turmoil in the Middle East reflects a unique set of challenges facing Muslims today: the struggle to reconcile tradition and modernity, to advance democracy and overcome authoritarian rule, and to grapple with the complicated legacy of Western intervention in the region.

For those interested in exploring these questions further, I recommend the following works: the corpus of Khaled Abou el Fadl's writings, particularly *The Great Theft: Wrestling Islam from the Extremists* and *Reasoning with God: Reclaiming Shari'ah in the Modern Age.* For history, context, and commonalities, I suggest Karen Armstrong's *Fields of Blood: Religion and the History of Violence*, Richard Bulliet's *The Case for Islamo-Christian Civilization*, and *The Great War for Civilisation: The Conquest of the Middle East* by Robert Fisk. For an exploration of Islam and democracy, please see Nader Hashemi's *Islam, Secularism and Liberal Democracy.*

And for a better understanding of ISIS, there is Charles R. Lister's *The Islamic State: A Brief Introduction,* Fawaz A. Gerges' *ISIS: A History,* and William McCants' *The ISIS Apocalypse: The History Strategy, and Doomsday Vision of the Islamic State.*

For a comprehensive look at the Toronto 18 case, please see Isabel Teotino's excellent dossier 'Toronto 18', published by *The Toronto Star* in 2010.

Acknowledgments

While there were many people and resources I consulted in writing this book, no one was of more help than my husband, Nader Hashemi, whose expertise on Islam and democracy, and on Islam-West relations and the broken politics of the Middle East, was an invaluable source of guidance. For the many long and demanding conversations about jihadism, for his boundless patience with my questions, and for these fifteen beautiful years, I thank him.

In addition, I would like to thank the two brilliant Crown prosecutors Sarah Shaikh and Moiz Rahman, who spared so much of their valuable time to instruct me about the law as it applies to terrorism charges in Canada, and to speak about their own very challenging work as prosecutors. They answered an endless series of questions with sensitivity, grace, and good humor. Any liberties I took with the story are my own invention.

My gratitude as well to everyone who works so hard and with such enthusiasm on my books, at St. Martin's Press/Minotaur Books and Raincoast Books. To Hector DeJean, for putting up with my correspondence, and providing me with so many opportunities to write. To David Rotstein, who designs my beautiful covers, and who gave me such a fascinating look at his process. To Dan Wagstaff for organizing my events in Toronto, and for many brilliant conversations about books. To Fleur Matthewson for her support and enthusiasm, and to Peter Ganim, for his beautiful rendition of the audiobook for *The Unquiet Dead*.

Many thanks to Ryan Warner at Colorado Public Radio, to the

Tattered Cover Bookstore in Denver, and to Ben McNally of Ben McNally Books in Toronto, for hosting my launch events. And to Lisa Casper for working so hard to spread the word. And to Dylan Scott for such brilliant and generous help in establishing my website. And to the community of writers and readers who responded with such enthusiasm to *The Unquiet Dead*, I'm deeply grateful to you all.

To the amazing women who have seen me through every moment of my journey: Elizabeth Lacks, my champion of an editor, who sees things I don't even know are there, and whose brilliance at understanding the heart of a book is unparalleled. How blessed I was the day my manuscript crossed her desk. And my agent, Danielle Burby, who provides laughter, reassurance, and belief in equal measure, and who has worked so hard on my behalf that I truly don't know how to thank her.

To Reza Aslan, whose eloquent books inspire me, and whose kindness and generosity opened so many doors for me. And to the communities, mosques, student groups, and halaqas that nurtured my understanding of the Islamic tradition – what beautiful lessons you taught me.

My gratitude to my incredible family and friends, whose love and support buoys me up every day. To the Khans, the Hashemis, the Shaikhs, the Ahmads, and the Raos (Shahjehan!), but especially to Hema, Farah, Fereshteh, Uzma, Yasmin, Semina, Haseeba, Red Velvet Irmy, and Nozzie. And to my beloved Summer and Casim, setting out on adventures of their own.

To Ayesha, Irfan, and Kashif – there is just no love like yours in this life, and no secret history as magical as ours. Here's to those years in the Ravenscroft house. And, of course, to Gnu Books.

And to Mum and Dad, for your endless love and sacrifice. Dad, you can't read these books now, but I couldn't have written them without everything you taught me. You will always be my hero and my conscience.

I left for Ramallah with your letter in my hand.